the
dirty
duet

Hot Alphas. Smart Women. Sexy Stories.

the
dirty
duet

NEW YORK TIMES BESTSELLING AUTHOR
LAURELIN PAIGE

paige press

Paige Press, LLC
Leander, Texas

Ebook:
ISBN: 978-1-953520-31-9

Paperback:
ISBN: 978-1-957647-07-4

Hardback:
ISBN: 978-1-953520-25-8

ALSO BY LAURELIN PAIGE

Visit my website for a more detailed reading order.

The Dirty Universe
Dirty Filthy Rich Boys - READ FREE

Dirty Duet (Donovan Kincaid)
Dirty Filthy Rich Men | Dirty Filthy Rich Love

Kincaid (coming 2022)

Dirty Games Duet (Weston King)
Dirty Sexy Player| Dirty Sexy Games

Dirty Sweet Duet (Dylan Locke)
Sweet Liar | Sweet Fate

(Nate Sinclair) Dirty Filthy Fix (a spinoff novella)

Dirty Wild Trilogy (Cade Warren)
Wild Rebel | Wild War | Wild Heart

Man in Charge Duet
Man in Charge

Man in Love

Man for Me (a spinoff novella)

Dating Season

Spring Fling | Summer Rebound | Fall Hard

Winter Bloom | Spring Fever | Summer Lovin

Also written with Kayti McGee under the name Laurelin McGee

Miss Match | Love Struck | MisTaken | Holiday for Hire

Written with Sierra Simone

Porn Star | Hot Cop

DIRTY FILTHY RICH MEN

PART 1

BOYS

If you've already read the novella, Dirty Filthy Rich Boys, skip to Part Two of this book.

ONE

No one on earth could kiss like Weston King.

When his face lowered toward mine, my breath caught in the back of my throat. When his mouth met mine, electricity sparked. When his tongue slipped between my lips, I found heaven. My toes literally curled, just like the trite expression suggested. My heart pounded against my ribcage. Goose bumps stood up along my skin. Butterflies flitted in circles in my belly. Every cell, every *fiber* of my being felt his invasion. His kiss turned a body of flesh and blood and bone into something bigger. Something combustible. Something charged. Something aflame.

At least that's what I imagined his kisses were like.

My only evidence was based on observation, and, of that, I had plenty.

The girl he'd chosen to hook up with tonight definitely looked about to burst into flames with the way she was wriggling and writhing against him. Nichette? Was that her name?

Or Nikita? It had been hard to hear her over the din of the party when she'd introduced herself to him an hour ago, and he'd only said it once or twice since then. It was something unusual and a bit pretentious and it blurred together with all the other unusual pretentious names of his previous hook-ups.

A guy I recognized from my economics class stumbled past, laughing with his buddies, and I pressed tighter to the wall, clutching my red Solo cup so it wouldn't spill. Though I didn't really care for whatever craft beer was on keg this week, it was one of my favorite things about the parties at The Keep. The main attraction was always craft beers and liquor. Most of the other rich Harvard students liked to draw crowds to their soirees with prescription drugs and recipes so experimental the FDA hadn't even had time to disapprove them yet.

The boys at The Keep kept things simple, and—except for a fair amount of underage drinking—legal. *"For those who might not want a blot on their past,"* I'd heard Brett Larrabee, the self-designated house manager, state on more than one occasion, usually when he was trying to convince a guy to suck his dick with his "one day I'm going to be a senator" pick-up routine. I had to give him credit—it usually worked.

My other favorite thing about the parties at The Keep was Weston King. It was actually the only reason I ever went to any of the shindigs. I was absolutely intrigued with him for no good reason other than that he was hot, charming and wealthy. He was my addiction. My obsession. My crush.

Gotta love hormones.

I'd noticed Weston on the first day of Intro to Business Ethics. I'd taken a seat in the front of the classroom (because I was that kind of girl), and he'd walked in late (because he was that kind of guy), smirking at something on his cell phone. The grin was still on his face as he tucked his phone in his back pocket, the glimmer still in his blue eyes. *Ice* blue eyes. The class was in a lecture hall, so it took him several seconds to cross the room, and I couldn't stop staring. I watched him the entire way. Watched him brush his hand through the dark blond hair that swooped over his forehead. Watched him give a wink to the teacher's assistant who was glaring at him for being tardy. This guy was confident. Cocky. Exactly like all the preppy rich kids who made it into Harvard because of significant monetary donations and a family name. He was the kid I wanted to hate, and I'd arrived in Cambridge with my scholarship and my father's lifetime savings wiped out planning to do exactly that.

But then his gaze crossed mine, and I don't even think he actually saw me, but I saw *him* and what I saw was fascinating. It was ease and charm and privilege and it made me buzz. Made me *breathe*. Made me blush with thoughts too dirty for an ethics class. It definitely made me forget every intention I had of hating his kind.

Instead, I wanted to know more.

It wasn't hard to find out about him. His father was Nash King, co-owner of King-Kincaid Financial, one of the world's largest investment firms, and without even having to ask, people talked about him. I soon discovered he was a freshman, like me, and that he lived with a bunch of guys in a four-story brownstone ten minutes off campus that had been passed among a few wealthy families for so long, no one remembered why they called it The Keep. The house was famous for the parties they threw every weekend. And though it was now late October and Weston had never once spoken to me or looked at me directly or even indicated that he knew I was alive, I'd come to every one.

Every time, I spent the evening in a corner watching him pressed up against some girl. Always a different corner. Always a different girl. I'd tried to identify if he had a type, but I hadn't found a pattern. This one was a redhead. Last week was a blonde. The week before, the girl had almost exactly the same shade of brown hair as I did, but she was curvy. This redhead was as rail thin as I was, but she'd obviously purchased a set of breasts. Another time he'd been with a girl even flatter than I was. No pattern. No type. It led me to believe that all I'd have to do was get the courage to talk to him and then maybe...

But then what?

I wasn't delusional. I knew I had nothing special to offer. There was no trap that would set off the minute Weston's cock was inside me. He'd fuck me and be done. And then my obsession with him would be even more pathetic because I wouldn't just be a girl with a crush—I'd be a psycho who couldn't move on.

Still, I dreamt that I'd be different. That one day, he'd notice me and there'd be that spark and it would be the forever kind of spark and when he found out I'd been saving myself for someone just like him he'd want to work to earn me and he would. And it would be sweet and romantic and we'd live happily ever after.

For a business major, I'd always had a wild imagination. I was well aware.

"Hey, sexy!" One of the guys who lived in the house—I truly had no idea how many did—pulled a girl in a thigh-length sweater and printed leggings in for a hug, blocking my view. "Long time since I've seen you. Want to join in the next round?"

I circled around the pool table that the boys kept in place of a dining room table, squinting around people until I caught sight of Weston and his catch of the night. When I spotted them again, it was just in time. They were near the staircase and he was leaning in to whisper something into the redhead's ear. She responded with a giggle and then a nod.

This was it. The Exit. The moment the two of them would slip away to take things to The Next Level. The part that I spent the rest of the week imagining in fine detail—only, in my imagination, *I* was the girl, and very often, I accompanied the daydreaming with my hand beneath my panties.

Seriously, maybe I just needed to get laid.

I took another swallow of my not-so-delightful craft beer and cringed. Usually when Weston took off with his hook-up for the night, I finished up my drink and headed home. He would take her upstairs to his room now. At least, I guessed that's where his room was. The upper level was off-limits, the door to the stairway kept locked, and even if it wasn't, I wouldn't have ever intruded on their private space.

But this time when Weston and his catch went upstairs, he didn't shut the door tightly behind him. From across the room, my eyes focused in on the latch bolt sticking out from the door-frame, and something came over me. Something unexplainable. Because one minute I was standing against the wall like always and the next I was creeping in the shadows up the dark stair-case to the top floor of The Keep.

The stairs were quiet and empty, and at the landing, I paused. The lights were off everywhere on the top floor, and it took a moment for my eyes to focus. There seemed to be a bathroom straight in front of me. To my right was a hallway, to my left was a bedroom with a door slightly ajar. Giggles drifted from the bedroom, and I tiptoed in that direction, cursing at myself every step of the way. What the fuck was I even doing? Was I planning to spy while Weston banged some other girl? Did I want him to suddenly notice me at the door and invite me in instead? Did I want him to invite me to *join*?

Yeah, this was messed up.

I nearly turned around.

I *should* have turned around.

But then Nicorette inhaled sharply and I had to know. Had to see.

I crept closer, peeked inside and nearly jumped when I saw the couple directly in front of me in a lip-locked frenzy. Then I realized that I was actually looking at a reflection in a wall-sized mirror. They were on the other side of the bed and the moon was shining in through the window illuminating the display.

And, oh my god, was it hot.

The redhead had already lost her shirt and her bra, and Weston was bent over her, suckling on one breast, kissing her pointed nipple while squeezing her other breast.

Nikita threw her head back and moaned. Unconsciously, I plumped my own breast over my sweater, and nearly gasped when I found my nipple sensitive and erect. I had to bite my lip to keep from making any noise. Had to cross my ankles to ease the throbbing between my legs.

I watched as Weston peeled off his shirt, the angle giving me a view of his beautiful, muscular back. He was on the rowing team. Of course. So preppy. So rich boy. But those muscles... God bless the rowing team.

And now he was undoing his jeans. And she was drawing out his cock. I could feel my eyes widen, trying to get a better look at his dick. I dared to lean in a little farther. Still, all I could make out was a dark shadow in the grip of the redhead's little palm as she stroked him up and down.

"Yeah, Nicky, just like that." The low rumble in Weston's voice made my knees buckle. I could just hear him over the thump-thump of the bass drifting up from downstairs.

"It's Nichelle," she corrected. Right! That's what it was.

"Yeah, Nichelle." He pulled her head back up so he could devour her mouth. He kissed her for a few minutes, greedily, before pulling away and heading out of the reflection —toward *me*.

I cowered in the corner where the hinge met the frame, certain I was about to be discovered. But all Weston did was shut the door.

I leaned my back against the closed door and let out a deep breath.

Because what the actual fuck?

I could have gotten caught. I could have gotten kicked out of The Keep forever. I could have lost any respect Weston might have ever had for me before even earning it.

And why the hell was I so into this guy anyway? I didn't even *know* him! I needed to get my head in the right place. Needed to remember why my father put in all those years with the furniture store and why my mother's life insurance money was saved and put away. It was so I could go to the school of my dreams. Not so that I could spend all my time daydreaming over a pretty-faced playboy.

But what a pretty face he had.

God, I was in trouble.

"He's never going to go for you," a voice came out of the dark in front of me. "Not while you're a virgin."

I squinted, and when I looked closer, I saw there was

another bedroom at the end of the hall with the door wide open, and though I couldn't quite make out the figure, I could see there was someone sitting in an armchair, smoking a cigarette. Or a cigar maybe.

I took a step forward. Surely he wasn't talking to me, but there didn't seem to be anyone else around. "Excuse me?"

"Weston never goes for virgins. It's one of his rules."

Heat rushed up my neck and flooded my cheeks. "Uh..."

"You're offended."

"Yes. I'm offended." And embarrassed. How long had this guy been watching me? It was pretty safe to assume that he'd seen me spying on Weston. Which was just...mortifying. Thank goodness it was too dark for him to see my face.

"Care to explain?"

I took another step forward. Then several more. Steps I should have taken down the stairs while I was still an anonymous girl in the dark.

But there was something about being watched privately by someone else that made me feel a kinship that I hadn't felt before. All that time I'd spent watching Weston, it was as though I'd been carrying a secret. And the first person to discover it had found it out by secretly watching *me*.

Or maybe that was just an excuse and I was just lonely. Or drunk. Or stupid.

"Well." I paused at the doorway of his room. "A of all, you can't possibly know what your roommate is and isn't into. And B of all, the status of my virginity is not something you can just presume."

He took a puff of his cigar—not a cigarette, it turned out— and the smoke filled the room with a sweet woody scent that reminded me of fireplaces and old libraries. "I beg to disagree. To both."

I huffed audibly. Because what else could I say to something as cocky as that?

Actually, plenty.

I threw my shoulders back, ready to go off when he went on first. "Look. I've known Weston since he was in diapers. I know him better than his mother does, I know him better than that girl who's in there currently sucking his dick, and I certainly know him better than you do."

He *did* know Weston well, I realized. I knew this guy, too. He was the T.A. for my ethics class. I hadn't recognized him at first, but now I did. He was Donovan Kincaid, son of Weston's father's business partner. I hadn't known he lived here. I'd never seen him at any of The Keep's parties before.

My hands started sweating and my pulse picked up a notch.

Donovan was several years older than us and was currently getting his MBA. He was a legend around campus because he was brilliant and ruthless. His business ideas were not only smart but also cutting edge. He was the sort of man who was going to rule the world. Tall, attractive, tough, powerful, strong. Perceptive. He intimidated me in general.

Right now? He scared the shit out of me.

"As for your virginity," he went on, "you wear it like a badge."

"I do not." I really kind of did. Right now, I was at a college party wearing a shapeless sweater and jeans. My hair was pulled into a loose ponytail. My shoes were Doc Martens that my roommate said had gone out of style a decade ago. It wasn't that I *tried* to be dumpy looking. I just liked to be comfortable.

And as the older sister without a mother around, I'd never really had anyone teach me how to be a girl.

"There really is no reason to be offended," Donovan said, taking a sip from a glass. Whiskey, I was guessing. Something told me it wasn't his first glass of the night. "I'm not criticizing. In fact, I'm offering to help."

It took me a second to understand just what he meant. "Oh, please."

"I'm not kidding. Shall we discuss the pros and cons?"

I cocked my head and studied him, as if I could study him in the dark. Was he seriously offering to sleep with me? He obviously had no idea who I was.

"I, uh, don't think so." I tugged on the end of my ponytail, a nervous habit of mine. "I'm sure it's because there's no light in here or because there's so many of us in there, but I'm in your Intro to Business Ethics class. I'm your student."

He stretched to his side and yanked a chain, turning on a lamp next to him. I blinked several times in the newly lit bedroom. He wore a simple black sweater and jeans. His feet were bare. His unruly hair had more red in it in the dim light, his green eyes had more flecks of brown. It made him look more rugged than usual. More intense. His jawline added to the effect. It was lined with scruff, as if he hadn't shaved since class yesterday morning, and, though I'd never had such an impulse before, I found myself wanting to run my hand across the fuzz. Wanted to know exactly what it felt like under my skin. Was it soft? Did it scratch? Who was the last woman to run her hand across his jaw? Did he love her?

"I know who you are, Sabrina Lind." Donovan's declaration shocked me back to the here and now. "Ninety-seven point three average. You're here on a scholarship, so that matters.

Never missed a day of class. Always sit in the front on the right side. Chad Lee cheats off your quizzes, but you don't know that. Your essays are on the detailed side but are creative, and I respect that. I appreciated your response to the unfair firing of Peter Oiler at Winn-Dixie Stores, but your perspective on Ford's decision not to modify the early versions of the Pinto was short-sighted."

My jaw dropped. There was too much to react to. I chose the easiest to respond to first. "Ford's decision killed people."

"It made the company money. It's called utilitarianism." Even as he was heartless, his voice was smooth, like the fine scotch that I imagined lingered on his tongue.

I wondered briefly what it would taste like against my own tongue.

Just as quickly, I forced the thought out of my mind. "And I thought the class was called business *ethics*." The case he referred to had bothered me a lot. In 1970, Ford had discovered a major error with the Pinto that would likely cause several hundred deaths and injuries. Instead of fixing it however, their cost-benefit analysis determined it would be cheaper to settle the presumed lawsuits. So they didn't make the modifications.

"I think I've taught that ethics have to be personally defined." Donovan sat back and crossed one ankle over his knee. He searched my face before taking another puff of his cigar. "The offer still stands."

"What offer?" I blinked once before realizing which offer he meant. "Did you miss the part where you're my teacher?" And why was I still standing here talking to the guy? I should have left by now. But I was glued in place, as fascinated with this discussion as I'd ever been with Weston King.

"I'm not actually your teacher. I'm the teacher's assistant."

This was technically true. Mr. Velasquez officially taught the Monday, Wednesday, Friday class. But he only taught half of the time, and even when he did teach, Donovan still sat at his corner desk and graded papers or read or did whatever it was that he did while the rest of us listened to the lecture.

Apparently one of the things he did was watch us.

Or did he just watch me?

A string of goose bumps popped up along my skin at the thought. I hugged myself and rubbed my hands up and down my arms.

Donovan's lip quirked up, as if he knew exactly the reaction he was having on me. "It's not officially against school policy if I fraternize with students."

I shook off a shiver. "By my own personal definition, it would be unethical."

"And why is that?" His voice wasn't just smooth, it was warm. Coaxing, even with its bitter edge.

"You grade my papers."

"So?" His stare was direct. Intense.

And this conversation was ridiculous. I wasn't considering it. Was I?

I glanced up, just to get my eyes away from him for one minute, and my gaze landed on a framed portrait on top of his fireplace. It was a picture of Donovan with a woman, both laughing as though they were caught candidly. It couldn't have been taken too long ago—Donovan looked nearly the same age as he was now, but his hair was short and clean-cut. And I'd never seen the woman. Maybe she was someone waiting for him back home. Or someone he'd broken up with. Or someone he was cheating on by flirting with me.

I looked back at him and realized he'd caught me looking at

the picture. "If I fooled around with you, my scores might be affected," I said, answering his last question.

"If you *don't* fool around with me, your scores might be affected." His tone seemed hard now. Cold.

I smiled tightly and shifted my balance from the ball of one foot to the ball of the other, trying to decide if he was kidding.

His expression said he wasn't.

I swallowed. "You're an asshole."

"Am I? You're the one who came up here trying to get something from me."

"What do you mean?" The conversation had totally gotten away from me, and wherever it had gone, I was sure I didn't want to be there.

"You're alone with me in my bedroom. What else am I supposed to think you're after?"

A chill ran through me. The hair stood up on the back of my neck. The blood drained from my face.

Donovan set his drink down on the side table and leaned forward so his forearms rested on his thighs.

"Get out of here, Sabrina. This floor is off limits during our parties. Next time you attend one, maybe you'll think about the ethics of obeying house rules."

I turned around and dashed downstairs without hesitating another second.

TWO

I grabbed my coat from the bedroom on the main floor where everyone stacked their jackets and ran outside, tying my belt around my waist while I bounded down the front steps of The Keep. I pulled my phone from my pocket and looked at the time. It was too late to risk walking back to my apartment alone. It wasn't far, but this was campus territory, and I was a better-safe-than-sorry kind of girl. I used my app to arrange for an escort, put my phone away and then rubbed my hands together to keep warm.

It was a cold night. Fall set in right on time in Massachusetts. But like hell was I going back inside. I'd rather freeze.

Which was dumb. I was only punishing myself when I really wanted to punish Donovan. What the fuck was that anyway?

I replayed our entire conversation as I paced the front walk, trying to figure out exactly what had happened between us. All of it had been strange and borderline inappropriate, but there *had* been something else going on. Hadn't there? Something I couldn't quite put my finger on. I should never have engaged, wouldn't have engaged in a hundred other similar situations, yet I'd been drawn to him. He'd drawn me *to* him. That's the thing about Donovan Kincaid, the thing he was famous for—he was a known puppet master. He was a man who pulled the strings, and he'd pulled me to him.

Then why had he turned so icy at the end?

Obviously that was his game the entire time. He was messing with me. He caught me where I shouldn't be, and he made me pay for it. I deserved it. Didn't mean I liked it. And it definitely didn't mean I liked Donovan.

I glanced up at his window and shivered. Was he standing there right now? Watching me through the glass?

I could almost see the flare of his cigar in the dark. Could almost feel his eyes crawling along my skin. Imagining it made me feel both warmer and colder all at once. Like I was less alone and more alone than ever.

The front door of The Keep opened then, startling my attention in that direction. Theo, a guy I'd seen around a few times, ambled onto the porch and sniffed the air. "Fuck! It's cold as balls out here."

Ginger Baldwin followed out behind him with a guy that I guessed she was going home with based on the way they were hanging on each other. "Your balls are cold?" she asked with a giggle. "Is that a normal thing?"

"*My* balls aren't cold," her boyfriend of the night piped in, as if the idea would turn her off. "You've got a problem with your anatomy."

"Har har." Theo adjusted himself. "My anatomy is fine. Shall we whip them out and compare?"

"You're always trying to get me to whip it out. Are you sure you're not trying to tell me something?"

Theo huffed, angrily. "You know what? Fuck off."

I lowered my head and eased into the shadows on the side of the steps. Casual socializing wasn't my forte when all the participants were sober, much less when some were as drunk as these obviously were. I wasn't in the mood for talking to anyone at the moment, anyway.

Unfortunately, the movement must have caught Theo's eye. "Who's that over there?"

I pulled out my phone and pretended to be texting someone, pretended not to be listening to them, but I could feel their eyes on me.

"I know her. She's in my statistics class," Ginger said quietly. Then louder as she came down the stairs, "Hey, Bree. You okay?"

"Yeah." I pocketed my phone. "Just waiting for my escort." Like a loser. With no one to walk her home like the cool kids. I'd managed to drag my roommate to one of the early parties, but it hadn't been her scene. Besides, Sheri and I weren't that close, for no other reason than that our schedules didn't match up and she had a boyfriend who occupied her time.

Ginger smiled a little too widely, and I could imagine her thinking, *thank god, I didn't really want to deal with you, so I'm glad I don't have to,* while she kindly said, "Awesome. Glad you used the app." She followed her boyfriend to his car parked in front of the house.

Her escort, like a gentleman, opened the door for her, then

called out to his friend still standing on the bottom step. "Theo, you coming?"

Theo ran both his hands through his hair and shrugged. "Nah, I'm going to walk." But instead of stepping down to the sidewalk, he strode over to me. "First, I'll look out for Sabrina while she waits. That's cool with you. Right, Bree?"

I didn't know the guy except from having seen him at previous parties. The offer was odd and out of place. "It's really not necessary."

"That's a good idea," Ginger's date said, standing with the door open on the driver's side of the car. "Shouldn't be out here alone. You can never be too careful."

I wasn't alone. There was a whole houseful of people behind me and an escort on the way. But if Theo felt like a good scout to wait with me and if it gave Ginger and her guy an easy way to get rid of their third wheel, so be it. "Right. That's true. Thanks."

If Theo thought I was going to be chatty, though, he had another think coming.

The car had just barely taken off when I realized it wasn't chatting that Theo was interested in.

"Sabrina," he said, inching closer to me. Closer than I liked. "You're a lot prettier than you let on. I'm sure you get told that all the time, don't you?"

"No. I don't. Thank you, but." I pulled on the back of my ponytail and turned my head from him to look at the curb. The problem with the escort service was it was understaffed. Especially on Saturday nights. There was no telling how long it would be before it would get here. Maybe I should have waited inside after all. It wasn't too late to change my mind.

"Why do you hide all that pretty?" Theo reached his hand out and tugged at the belt of my coat, pulling it open.

"Excuse me?" I turned my head sharply toward him and yanked my coat back from him, but he wouldn't let go.

"I bet you have a gorgeous body too."

"Theo, thank you, but I'm uncomfortable with what you're saying. And what you're doing." He was drunk. That was all. He was just being playful.

Except he wasn't just being playful. He stepped closer. "I don't really care if you're comfortable with what I'm saying, Sabrina." His breath smelled faintly of beer, but his words weren't slurred. He was in complete control of himself. He knew what he was doing.

I tried to step around him, but he put a hand up on the wall behind me. I had nowhere else to go. I'd made a mistake when I'd ducked into the shadows earlier because now I was in the corner where the stairs met the house, and Theo was blocking my escape.

"Theo. Please." I swallowed the ball at the back of my throat.

He sniffed, the second time I'd heard him, either from the cold or from snorting, I wasn't sure. "Please what?" he said as if he really didn't have any idea what I was asking.

"Let me go."

He feigned consideration then shook his head as if he was sorry he couldn't comply with my request. "Look." He pulled his thumb along my bottom lip, which quivered under his unwanted touch. "I don't want to draw this out, so here's how this is going to go—I'm going to fuck you. You can either make it easy or you can make it hard. Either way, we both know who has the power here."

I didn't even think. I just opened my mouth and started to scream. "Hel—!"

Theo was ready for me. He clamped his hand over my mouth—cutting me off before I could get any real sound out—and grinned from ear to ear. "I was actually hoping you'd choose the hard way. I like it when girls struggle. It will be better for you too. I'll come a whole lot faster."

"Fuck you," I said, muffled against his claw. And though I hated giving him what he wanted, though he was at least six feet tall and probably two hundred pounds, though I had no chance in hell at getting away from him, I fought back. I pushed against his shoulders with all my strength. I kneed at him. I wriggled. I cried.

Theo only chuckled. "Just like that, baby." He pressed his body in tighter against me, using his thighs to keep my lower body from squirming. With his free hand, he undid his pants and drew out his cock.

I started crying harder. I'd seen a penis before. I was a virgin but not a prude. I'd had a high school boyfriend. I'd given him blowjobs and handjobs and he had done enough to me in return that I wasn't even sure my hymen was still intact.

But looking at Theo's cock made me want to throw up. It had to be the ugliest thing I'd ever seen. Everything about it was disgusting. I didn't want it anywhere near me. Definitely didn't want it inside me.

I had to get out of this.

I brought my hands up to his face and scratched as hard as I could. Scratched until I drew blood.

Theo cursed and let go of his dick so he could wrestle my hands down instead. When he had them pinned tightly under my breasts, he moved his other hand so it covered my nose as well as my mouth.

"I can keep my hand like this, and in a couple minutes you won't have the energy to fight me. Would you prefer that, Sabrina? Is that the way you want to do this?" He locked his eyes right on mine, got right up in my face so he was sure I understood what he was saying. So he was sure that I understood that he was giving me the choice of whether or not he let me breathe.

I shook my head.

"So you'll be good?"

Did I have a choice? My lungs were already aching. My eyes were already seeing spots. My brain was already panicking with the impulse to take a breath.

I nodded.

He didn't move his hand.

I nodded harder. I cried harder. Desperate.

Finally he moved his hand down ever so slightly so that my nostrils were uncovered. I inhaled cold air in long, sputtering draws, taking as much as I could get in through my nose. My chest rose and fell with each gasping breath.

Slowly, Theo let go of my hands, giving me another warning look as he resumed stroking his cock.

I got it. He had the power. I did not. Lesson learned. Lesson fucking learned.

I still struggled. I couldn't help it. It was like a reflex. Like that one time I'd gotten a pedicure and couldn't help kicking the technician because I was so ticklish. I willed myself to cooperate with Theo, and still my body fought him.

"Undo your jeans," he ordered after he'd jacked himself for a minute, his voice tight.

No. Please no, don't make me. I didn't move. I couldn't.

He inched the hand over my mouth slightly toward my nose—threatening—but I was already undoing the snap. Unzipping the zipper.

Tears leaked down my cheeks as Theo shooed my hands away. He licked two of his fingers and said, "Don't want to go in dry," then he stuck them inside my panties, searching for the hole he wanted.

A sob bubbled deep in my chest, and I closed my eyes, wishing I could be someplace else, surrendering to a deluge of mismatched thoughts that went on and on randomly. A panicked stream of consciousness. *I'm not here. I'm somewhere else. I'm on the beach. I'm in the Riviera Maya. I can't tell my father. He'll be so mad. I haven't shaved. Can you get frostbite in October? That redhead had nice breasts. What was her name again? It's just my virginity. It's just sex. Will I tell my sister? This is so embarrassing. I should have waited inside. It's so cold. Who was the blonde in that picture in Donovan's room? That last trip we took with Mom to the Riviera Maya was in October. It will be five years this December. What if he hurts me? What if he really hurts me? I hope no one comes out and sees this. I can't tell my sister. I can't tell anyone. Nichelle. I keep forgetting her name on purpose. I miss my mom. Please, God, let someone come and stop this!*

I was still aware of everything around me. Hyperaware. I knew I'd forever be able to identify the smell of Theo's shampoo. Of his cologne. His watch ticked in the quiet, each second sounding after an eternity while his fingernails scraped along the walls of my insides.

But I must not have been as attentive as I thought I was, because I never heard the door open or the footsteps on the stairs. I didn't see Donovan grab Theo by the back of his jacket and pull him off of me, but I did see him punch Theo squarely in the nose, heard it crack, saw the blood gush.

"What the fuck?" Theo howled, one hand holding his nose while he quickly pulled up his pants with the other. "Jesus, Kincaid!"

My knees nearly buckled in relief. I was free of Theo, free of his sweaty hand and his oppressive body. I scooted away from the corner I'd been trapped in, afraid I might somehow end up imprisoned there again, and fastened my pants as fast as I could. Shock halted my tears, and though I felt steady, I could see my hands were shaking.

Theo, seeming to see that he might be in trouble, took a step away, but Donovan grabbed his arm and yanked him back. "Did I say we were finished?" Theo had Donovan beat on size, yet Donovan didn't seem concerned at all.

I bit my trembling lip and hugged my arms around myself. Donovan might not be scared, but I was. Too scared to leave to get help. Too numb.

"Hey, I don't know what you think happened—" Theo started to say, but Donovan cut him off.

"You don't get to talk." Donovan yanked Theo's arm again. Hard. "It's up to Sabrina whether she presses charges. Sabrina?" Donovan looked at me, his green eyes searing into mine, searching as though he was afraid I was lost.

Maybe I *was* lost.

I blinked. He'd asked me a question. "What was that?" I managed.

"Do you want to press charges against Theo?"

The reality of the situation came crashing back on me full force. I'd been assaulted. That asshole had had his fingers inside me. If Donovan hadn't shown up, he'd have raped me by now.

I choked back bile.

Of course I wanted to press charges. Except...

I thought about it again. Went quickly through the scenario —white rich boy accused of assault by a nobody girl. Alcohol involved. No actual rape. Scholarship at risk. There was no way this would end in my favor, as much as I wanted it to. As much as the world needed brave warriors for violated women, it wasn't what I wanted for myself. It shamed me, but it was my truth.

"It's fine," I mumbled, a tear slipping down my cheek. I just wanted to forget all of this. Go home, take a bath. Pretend none of this ever happened.

"What?" Donovan asked, forcing me to repeat myself.

"I'm not pressing charges," I said louder. "I'm sorry." I didn't even know who I was apologizing to. Myself. Every victim of assault who'd never gotten a chance to face her attacker in cuffs.

"Fine." Donovan let go of Theo's arms, but when Theo turned around to face him Donovan kneed him in the nuts. "You deserve worse, you asshole. Unfortunately, the U.S. legal system probably wouldn't give you much more than that. Penalties at The Keep are more severe though. You're not welcome here. You won't do business with our families. Your investments at King-Kincaid will be canceled. Now get the fuck off my property. You're bleeding all over my Ferragamos."

Theo wiped the blood dripping from his nose with the back of his hand and leaned a shoulder forward as though he were going to challenge Donovan. Then he seemed to think better of it and took a step backward. "All right. All right, Kincaid. Didn't realize you were saving this one for yourself."

"Get the fuck out of here." Donovan never raised his voice, but his tone and his eyes and his posture said it all. Theo took off.

I was still shaking, still crying. I swiped the tears from my eyes and started to turn to thank Donovan when a car pulled up to the curb. I turned my attention there instead. It was my escort. What timing.

When I shifted back to Donovan, he was already climbing back up the stairs toward the front door without a goodbye. Without even an, "Are you all right?"

I cried the entire drive home. Cried for an hour in the shower. It wasn't until hours later when I was curled up in the fetal position in my bed that I realized that Donovan's Ferragamos were boots. And they'd been tied. He'd seen my situation through his bedroom window then taken the time to lace them up before coming downstairs to rescue me.

THREE

I didn't go to classes on Monday.

I said I had the flu and stayed in bed, facing the wall. Sheri brought me microwaveable soup and crackers from the Shell station, and I told her I was only crying because my head hurt.

Tuesday, I managed to pull myself together. Nothing happened, really. Theo hadn't actually raped me. I was the same girl I'd been before. It wasn't like I had to see him again either. I didn't have any classes with him. He was an upper-classman, and we didn't run in the same circles. And no one else knew what had happened—I'd decided not to tell a soul—so all I had to do was smile and pretend nothing had happened. Easy peasy.

If it wasn't exactly easy, it was at least doable. As doable as it had been when my mother had died five years ago and kids at school had pointed and whispered behind my back. I'd put on a happy face and acted as if it meant nothing. As if it didn't hurt.

That experience with tragedy had taught me an important lesson in how to deal with hard things—you smile, you nod, you go on.

That's how I'd planned to handle Intro to Business Ethics too. I knew it would be different because of Donovan, because he knew. But it wasn't like he was going to bring it up in class. We'd never even talked before that night at The Keep. He was my teacher. I looked to him to learn things. He looked at me as another paper to grade. I didn't think it would be a problem.

I walked in to the lecture hall, early as usual, and headed for a seat in the front row. Normally I came in from the door below, but this time I came in from above since I'd stopped for a bottle of water before class and taken a different route to get there. As I walked down the stairs, I glanced down at the teacher's desk, and maybe I was a little nervous about seeing Donovan because I silently hoped it was Velasquez teaching today.

It wasn't.

Donovan sat at his laptop, wearing his grey trousers and a dress shirt and tie under his black pullover, and as though he could sense me, he looked up just then and caught my gaze.

I froze, unable to take another step.

My knees swayed. Sweat beaded on my brow. It was like he was a trigger. My entire pretense fell apart, and I was transported back to that night. I swore I could feel Theo's palm across my mouth. The sound of his nose cracking echoed in my ears. Emotion overwhelmed me.

But it wasn't just terror and humiliation that I felt. There was something even worse underneath it all. Something ugly but undeniable.

As soon as I recognized it, I flushed with panic. Donovan

had to notice because his eyes narrowed and his chin tilted up with curiosity. I wanted to turn around and run out of the classroom, but that would only direct attention to myself. Besides, my legs felt like jelly at the moment, so I slipped into a seat in the row I was already standing in and ducked my head, pretending not to realize that my behavior might be odd or that he was still watching me.

Actually, I wasn't pretending—I didn't *care* if he was watching me. I didn't even care about keeping an eye out for Weston like I usually did. I had to figure out what the ever-living fuck was wrong with me. My heart was pounding, my clothes felt too hot, I felt restless and unsettled.

But it wasn't thoughts of Theo that had me riled up. It was Donovan. From the way he'd taunted me in his bedroom to the way he'd commanded the situation with Theo to the way his jaw set when he studied me with those intense eyes.

God, those eyes...

I snuck a glance at him as he stood up to start the lecture, and another tumultuous, confusing wave rolled through my body. I shifted in my seat, but it didn't help. When he started talking it was even worse. His voice sent shivers down my spine. I drank in every word, yet sentences went by without me comprehending a single phrase.

I was seriously fucked.

Whatever was happening, there had to be a perfectly natural explanation. Like, I was having a psychotic break. My mind was trying to change the terrible thing that happened to me by associating Donovan and pleasant feelings with that night instead of Theo and those awful ones.

Except these feelings weren't exactly pleasant. They were sick and tormenting. They were fierce and turbulent. I had to cross my legs and uncross them at least a hundred times just to make it through his lecture, the whole time hating myself because I couldn't settle down.

It all made me mad. And uncomfortable. And then mad again. For so many reasons. I was mad at Donovan anyway because of everything he knew. Not just about what Theo did, but those other things that he'd said about me in his room. Those things he'd perceived about me so easily. I didn't like him knowing me like that. It felt invasive. Like a violation.

And I was mad about how he'd taken his time in rescuing me.

And how he didn't even seem to really be sure he was glad he saved me at all.

Mostly I was mad about the thoughts I was having about him, even though they weren't really his fault. Yet, if he hadn't been so fucked up with the way he'd gone about dealing with that night, I wouldn't probably be so fucked up with the way I felt about it now. So maybe it was fine to blame him for that too.

Whoever was to blame, it didn't matter. I was the one who had to deal with it. It wasn't like he cared about how I'd come out of the nightmare. I'd figure it out, somehow.

After what felt like the longest hour of my life, the class was finally over. I took off the second we were excused, careful to dodge Donovan by going up the stairs again instead of exiting below. I'd planned to grab lunch with a friend, but I had to run by my apartment first to change my panties before my next class. That's how bad it was.

Once I was out of Donovan's presence, I was sure the whole strange thing would blow over. I thought about Weston to clear my head. He was the guy I'd been into. He was the one that gave me butterflies to think about. Still. Even now.

The rest of the day, however, I found my mind wandering back to Donovan now and then, found myself imagining different endings to the night at The Keep. What if he had asked me back inside after Theo had left? What if I hadn't left his room in the first place?

I was ashamed of myself.

But it's where I got the idea of how to deal with the bad dreams I'd had ever since it had happened. That night when I woke up in a cold sweat with the ghost of Theo's touch on my skin, I slid my hand beneath my panties and erased the memory with thoughts of Donovan.

"Did he hurt you too badly?" he asked, cupping my cheek as Theo hobbled down the street. His hand was warm against my skin, tentative without being gentle.

"Not too badly," I whispered, looking into his hazel eyes. My escort pulled up at the curb and both of us turned toward it, but instead of walking away, Donovan pulled me into his arms.

"Let me take care of you tonight." With a nod, he sent the car away. Then he bent to his knees and pulled down my pants, pulled down my underwear, neither asking permission nor apologizing for his eagerness.

But I wanted him there, so it was different than when Theo had forced me.

The air was cold on my bare legs, but soon all I felt was the heat of his tongue between my folds. He licked up and down my slit aggressively several times, then thickened his tongue to a point and inserted it inside me.

I came almost at once and slept soundly until morning.

Whatever it was that Donovan did to me didn't go away but I got better at dealing with it. I learned not to look him in the eye. I stopped sitting in the front row in class. I did what I always did—I smiled, I nodded, I went on.

And at night, I continued to soothe my dreams with fantasies of him fingering and fucking me, usually in some strange version of my assault. Sometimes it would happen after he'd pulled Theo off me. Sometimes Theo wasn't there at all. Sometimes I asked him to. Sometimes I begged.

And sometimes—a lot of the time—he was as callous and cruel as Theo had been.

FOUR

"Sorry about that."

"No—" I did a double take at the guy who'd bumped into me as he was getting into the seat next to me. Weston King. "—problem," I finished.

I sat up straighter in my own chair and glanced down at what I was wearing. Jeans. Sweater. Ponytail. Boring. Ugh. Well, what did I expect? It was kind of hard to hide from someone like Donovan while still trying to be noticed by someone like Weston. Both were impossibilities, I'd decided in the three weeks since the Theo incident, because it seemed I always saw Donovan and Weston never saw me.

Until today when, miracle of miracles, Weston happened to take a seat next to me.

My heart was pounding a thousand beats a minute, my knee couldn't stop bouncing. Eep! Our elbows were practically touching. Then there was the added glee I had when he pulled out a spiral notebook from his bag. He was a boy who took notes old-school style! Swoon!

This was almost enough of a delight to distract me from the lecture Donovan had been giving before Weston had arrived. Unfortunately, the former still had a pull on me that I couldn't deny. Especially when he was addressing issues that got me worked up such as the one he was tackling today—deregulation in the financial industry.

I'd come a long way on this topic in my short time at Harvard. While I could see the hurdles and obstacles that regulation put on investment firms such as King-Kincaid, I was still a girl who came from the other side. It wasn't the billionaires losing their pensions during the Great Recession. It wasn't the rich having their homes and cars and lives taken away from them. Regulation was how ethics were implemented, as far as I was concerned, and I'd said as much in as many ways as possible in my last paper.

As much as I believed in regulation, I knew that, as always, my annoyance at Donovan had less to do with what he was preaching and more to do with what he did to me in my thoughts on a daily basis in the bedroom. What he was doing even now, as much as I hated to admit it, drawing me to him. Commanding my attention. Demanding my focus.

Damn, I hated him.

"Fuckwaffle," I said under my breath.

Weston shifted in his seat next to me. "What did you say?"

Oh my god. My face went red. "What?"

He leaned in close so I could hear him without disturbing the class. "Did you just call Kincaid a fuckwaffle?"

"I shouldn't have said that." But if that's what it took to have Weston lean in to whisper in my ear then I'd consider saying it again. Maybe. After my embarrassment died down. Like, in the next century.

"Don't take it back!" Weston exclaimed quietly. "That's awesome! I love it."

I spun my head toward him. "Aren't you guys friends, or...?" Man, his eyes were even bluer this close up. And he had freckles—light ones—along his nose.

"More like family, and I love him like a brother. But he's a total fuckwaffle." His brow rose. "And I don't think I've called him that yet. Do you have a pen I could borrow?"

"Uh...yeah." I dug in my bag searching for one.

Weston peered over my shoulder. "That one. That Sharpie would be awesome."

We grabbed it simultaneously, our fingers brushing, and I had to bite my lip not to gasp.

"Thanks," he said, smiling just enough to show that wicked dimple. Jesus, I could fall inside that dimple and never crawl back out. That dimple was going to be the death of me.

I watched as he flipped through his notebook. The pages had single words written across them, all landscape. *Tool, Shitstick, Asshat, Douchebag, Buttmunch, Jizztissue.* He stopped on a blank page and took the top of the black Sharpie off with his mouth. I was seriously going to make out with that Sharpie lid later. Then he started writing: *Fuck—*

"What are you doing?" I asked, suddenly both nervous and excited like I was about to be privy to something that might be a little bit bad but not so bad that words like *expulsion* or *policeman* could be brought up. The kind of bad that always seemed like it might be fun but also might be addictive.

"I always write notes for Donovan when he teaches to let him know how he's doing. *Fuckwaffle* is not a note I've given him before." When he finished writing the word, he held up the notebook as if he was scoring an event.

I was seriously giddy. "And you do this every class?"

"When Velasquez isn't here. Well, sometimes when he is here I try to sneak in a note too." Some other students in the row across the aisle flagged Weston so he'd show them today's note.

How had I missed this before today?

Weston brought the notebook back in front of him and waved it around a few more times for Donovan, who didn't even blink in our direction. If we were sitting farther up in the hall, I'd wonder if he could read it, but we weren't that far from the front and the black Sharpie made it pretty clear.

Genius.

"Does he ever acknowledge you?" I asked, amazed at how stoic Donovan remained.

"Nope." Weston closed the notebook and tucked it back into his bag. "It never gets old either. I must have a nine-year-old's sense of humor or something. It's like when you go to Buckingham Palace and try to get the guards to smile, you know?"

The farthest place I'd ever been from home was here. Even our one family trip to Mexico had been closer. "I've never been to Buckingham Palace."

He looked at me then, really looked at me. Judged me, maybe, for never having been to England—the most basic of rich people places in the world. Did that matter to a guy like him?

A smile eased across his full lips. *Ah, that dimple.* "Then I'll have to take you there." He leaned close again and tugged my ponytail. "I'm Weston."

I almost forgot how to breathe. "I know who you are. I come to your parties." Or I used to. "I'm Sabrina."

Almost simultaneously as I introduced myself, my name rang out across the hall in Donovan's baritone timbre. "Sabrina. Care to share your thoughts on regulation and ethics? I know you have quite a few."

My stomach dropped. I hated talking in front of a class, but more importantly, Donovan never called on students. *Never.* What the hell was his problem? We weren't the first kids to be caught chatting during his lecture, surely.

"Fuckwaffle," Weston whispered next to me, sending me into a fit of nervous giggles.

Thankfully, Donovan noticed the time. "Saved by the figurative bell. It looks like class is over." The resentment in his tone was thick. "Grades for your corporate strategy and ethics awareness assignment will be on the portal by the end of the week. Remember this thesis will count for half your grade." He seemed to be staring at me as he said this, most likely because he was still sore that I'd disrupted his lesson.

I scowled. I hated it when he looked at me like that, but I wondered right then if I'd miss it if he suddenly stopped. I had a feeling I would.

I wondered if he'd miss it if I stopped staring back.

"Do you have another class now?" Weston asked.

I pulled myself away from Donovan's piercing gaze and found Weston holding my bag out for me. "Thank you. And nope. Break until two." I shuffled into the aisle after him. "You?"

"I usually meet up with a friend for lunch."

I nodded. I'd thought for a moment he was going somewhere with his questioning. Guess he was just being polite.

But then he cocked his head in my direction. "Join us?"

THE FRIEND, it turned out, was Brett Larrabee. I'd been aware of Brett from the parties at The Keep, but we'd never officially met, and I was glad for the introduction. An extremely extroverted, politically conservative, openly homosexual African American, Brett was an oxymoron, and I found him absolutely intriguing.

He was also quite a talker. He'd led us to a small Japanese café, that was surprisingly not busy considering how good the food was, and proceeded to monopolize the majority of the conversation while we ate.

I didn't mind. I was happy just to be included on the excursion. Every few minutes I had to remind myself I was awake, that this wasn't a dream. That I was actually sitting at a table making a fool of myself with chopsticks in front of Weston King.

"The DOW is down, the DOW is down, the DOW is down," Brett said with weary distress as he scrolled through his financial app on his phone. Even though he talked a lot, he still managed to eat the fastest. He'd finished and had been playing on his cell for the last five minutes. "The Fed better not raise interest rates. It is not the time."

"Dad says it's coming soon," Weston said, pushing away his plate.

"Oh!" Brett's head popped up with the news of something he'd just remembered. "Did you hear about Theodore Sheridan?"

Theo. I dropped my sticks at the mention of his name.

Fortunately, I'd dropped them so many times, no one noticed. Hopefully no one noticed my hands shaking as I took a sip of my water, my throat suddenly dry.

Weston considered a minute. "Nothing interesting I can think of."

Then you didn't hear the one where he almost raped a girl in front of your own porch? At least it was reassuring to know that Donovan hadn't told all his roomies. Not that I'd thought he was much of the sharing type.

Brett bent over the table and lowered his voice. "He got busted with more than a kilo of coke."

"And you're just mentioning this now?" Weston asked, as if reading my mind. Maybe Theo wasn't a close enough friend for him to consider it headline news, but it was to me.

That wasn't something I cared for anyone to know, though, so I kept my head low, scooting noodles around in my bowl. I'd lost any appetite that remained the minute I'd heard his name.

"Huh," Weston said, running his hand through his hair. "I knew he had a problem with blow, but what the fuck was he doing to draw attention to himself?"

"I don't know, but he was charged with intent to *sell*."

"Theo doesn't need money. He got his entire trust fund at eighteen."

"He's saying it's all cooked up charges or something. Whatever. Daddy Sheridan will get him off, but he's out for the year here."

"Crazy."

While it was a relief to think that Theo wouldn't be around anymore, I didn't get too excited by the thought that he'd face any prison time. Brett was right—his money and his privilege would get him off. Whether it was drugs or rape, he had the get out of jail free card.

Brett, seeming to be done with the Theo scandal, was ready for other gossip. "Did Numbnuts teach today?" he asked, leaning his chair back onto two legs.

"Actually," Weston said, raising a brow in my direction, "it was Fuckwaffle."

"That's a nice one." Brett turned his admiration to me. "You don't like Donovan? I have to hear this."

Did I like Donovan? What a loaded question. My emotions where Donovan was concerned were like paperclips—I couldn't pick up one without several others coming with it. I was grateful to him and resentful. Angry and preoccupied.

It wasn't something I could begin to explain to myself, let alone someone I'd just formally met. Tugging on my ponytail, I tried to think like a typical disgruntled student. "He's just...you know. A pompous, egotistical know-it-all. What about you guys? You live with him."

Weston exchanged a glance with Brett. "That we do. And like I said, I love him like a brother. But sometimes brothers are hard to love. Do you have one?"

It was a smooth change of subject, one I wasn't about to contest. Brett went back to playing with his phone, so I focused my answer just to Weston. "I have a sister. Audrey. But she's easy to love. She's thirteen and awkward and adoring."

Weston sat back in his chair, crossed his arms over his chest, and crossed his legs at his ankles. "She probably puts her eighteen-year-old sister up on a pedestal."

"Seventeen," I corrected.

"Seventeen?"

"I graduated high school early."

"Kudos. That's impressive."

"Thank you." I averted my eyes, embarrassed by the compliment, and sighed. "I'm still not sure I did the right thing deciding to come to school so far away from home."

"Where are you from?" he asked and it almost felt like more than small talk, like he really wanted to know.

"Colorado, but it's not really the distance that's the thing. It's that my mother died when I was twelve, and I feel bad leaving my dad and Audrey alone." I knew he probably didn't get it. He was from a world of nannies and chauffeurs and housekeepers and tutors. There was no such thing as alone. "What about you? Do you have siblings? Not like Donovan, but blood related?"

He'd started nodding before I'd finished the question. "I have a sister. She's ten, and we're in completely different worlds." He puckered his lips as he thought, which was ridiculously unfair, since I was already on hormone overload. "I really grew up closer to Donovan, even though he's four years older than me. We went to the same school, were on the same chess teams. We row together. Our families vacation together. I've always had him to look up to." He sat up straighter, leaning in as if confiding in me. "I guess I idolized him growing up."

"But not now?"

"It's different now."

He let that hang, and I searched for the right words to prod further while, at the same time, trying to understand exactly *why* I wanted to know more—because the answer said something about Weston? Or because it said something about *Donovan?*

I decided not to prod.

But then Brett said, "He's not the same since Amanda died. I'm a sophomore, so I didn't know him very long before that."

"Amanda?" Okay. I was definitely interested.

"Brett—" Weston warned.

Brett glared at him in return. "What? Are we not allowed to talk about it ever? He's not even here."

Weston paused for a beat. "Amanda was Donovan's girl-friend. She died in a car accident a year ago. Around this time of year. Coming back to school after Thanksgiving, actually."

The air left my lungs. "Oh my god! What happened?"

"Another driver didn't check his blind spot. He drove into her lane and pushed her into oncoming traffic. They said she died instantly. She was closer to campus when it happened, so it was Donovan who had to identify her body."

"That's awful. I feel awful." It was the kind of thing I'd say after hearing any sort of tragic tale, but I really meant it right now in a way I usually didn't. In a way I couldn't explain.

"They were the real deal, too," Weston went on. "He wanted the house, the kids, the whole nine yards. He'd planned to ask her to marry him for Christmas. I think he might have even bought her the ring."

She had to be the blonde in the picture on his mantle. He'd seen me looking at it just before he'd turned cold.

"Is that why he's so...?" I searched for the word I was looking for. What was it exactly that Donovan was? Distant? Cut-off? Alone?

Weston seemed to get what I meant. "He wasn't ever what I'd call friendly before that, but he's harder now. Sharper too. In some ways I think he's become a better businessman, if that makes sense."

"I think it does. It's like when you lose one sense and so

your others become more acute." I had my mother's death to draw on as experience, but it was my assault that I was thinking of now. How had I changed since then? Was I harder or sharper or more business savvy?

And what about the thoughts I had at night now, the dirty thoughts with Donovan?

"Yeah. Like that," Weston said as the waiter set down the check.

I reached for my bag, but Weston shook his head. "No, I've got this." He dimpled at me as he handed his card off.

"Thank you. That's really nice." It came off halfhearted, though, because I was still thinking about Donovan. I was pained by his pain, for whatever foolish reason. He certainly hadn't shown any concern for mine. But more interestingly, I was *fascinated* by his pain. I could imagine how he carried it, where he stuffed the details of his misery. Inside this bottle of scotch. Under that heartless remark. Behind this wall of indifference.

He knew the secret I hid behind smiles and nods, and now I knew the agony he hid behind ice and steel.

Maybe we were finally even.

"Well," I said, forcing my attention back to Weston, "you sound like you've been a good friend to him."

"Because I give him notes as he lectures in class?" His tone was sarcastic, but I heard the hint of helplessness underneath. He really didn't know how to help his friend, his brother.

It wasn't like I had the answers, but at least I could reaffirm him. "Exactly because of that."

He looked up from the credit card slip he'd just signed and studied me. "Sabrina, I think you did the right thing coming to

Harvard. I'm sure your dad will do just fine with your sister. He seems to have done a great job with you."

I chuckled dismissively. "You don't even know me."

"Sure I do. I know that you're strong. That you're resilient. That you're smart—probably smarter than both Brett and me. You're obviously beautiful." He reached over to tug my ponytail. "And I know that you're coming to my party on Saturday with me."

The butterflies were back, though they were flying now as though they had pebbles for wings. This was everything I'd wanted, everything I'd hoped for. A date with Weston King. And all the murky, confusing feelings going on inside right now were probably just related to going to The Keep for the first time since Theo.

Yeah, that had to be it.

So. *Smile. Nod.* "I guess you do know me after all."

But how could he when I was only just starting to figure me out for myself?

FIVE

Audrey: Dad won't make stuffing if you aren't here.

Me: Then make the stuffing yourself.

I moved my eyes from the chat box in the corner of my computer screen back to the Excel spreadsheet I was working on for Statistics. It was early Thursday afternoon, two days before Weston's party, one day after he'd invited me to go with him, and I was still vacillating between so many emotions about it that all I felt now was anxious. My sister's efforts to try and get me to buy a last minute flight home for Thanksgiving were not helping.

Another message popped up.

Audrey: But I don't know hoowwww!!!!

Like a true teenager, my sister was as dramatic in her chats as she was in any conversation.

Me: You're 13. Stove Top is cinch.

Audrey: But who's going to put olives on their fingers and make olive monsters with me?

A notification showed up on the top of my laptop saying I had a new item in the Academic Portal.

Me: Put olives on Bambi.

Okay, Bambi was the dog. But seriously. I had homework to do. And homework to follow up on.

I clicked over to the Academic Portal and found that the new addition was to my Intro to Business Ethics folder. My corporate strategy and ethics awareness assignment that Donovan had said would be up this week. I opened up the scores and grades document and waited for it to load.

Audrey: Very funny. Come hommmmmeeee!!!!

Me: Aren't you in class right now or something?

I hit return and then froze. There, on my screen where my **A** should be there was a big fat **F**.

No way.

Not possible.

I'd never gotten an **F** in my life.

I opened up the remarks for details. ***Student's conclusions disregard the corporation's economic responsibilities to its stockholders. Student speaks of moral high ground with poetic sentiment without considering how suggested actions will be funded. The student does not have a firm grasp of the concept of corporate strategy.***

Goddamn, Donovan.

All I could see was red. I understood the concept of corporate strategy. It was Donovan who couldn't understand the concept of an opposing opinion.

And this wasn't just my pride hurt. This counted for more than half the class grade. I wouldn't be able to get higher than a **D** if this wasn't changed and my scholarship required a **B** average.

No. Whatever beef Donovan had with me, he couldn't fuck with my grades.

Within a couple of minutes I'd looked up Velasquez's office hours and found that he should be available for another hour. The weather was great for November—there hadn't been any recent snow. I could make it if I hurried. If he looked over it, I was certain he'd see that my paper deserved to be re-graded and that Donovan was a fucking asshole.

The chat window dinged again.

Audrey: It's study period.

Me: I have to talk to you later, Audrey.

I closed my laptop and headed across campus to fight for my grade.

THIRTY-FIVE MINUTES LATER, I stood outside Velasquez's office. I'd tried to calm myself down on the walk over so that I could present all my points rationally to my teacher, but instead, I'd just gotten more worked up. The paper had been fifteen pages long. I should have gotten a **C** just for turning in the required length. As for my disregard to share-holders—I'd attached a detailed financial plan. If my math had been wrong, that should account for a point or two, but not entire letter grades.

It was obvious this wasn't about my work—this was about Donovan. Why was he doing this to me? Part of me wondered if I should be going to The Keep instead, if it should be *his* door I should be banging on.

No. I wasn't playing games. Velasquez would fix my grade and if Donovan got in trouble for giving me a bad score then he deserved it.

The door was closed, but I could see the light on through

the frosted glass. I knocked and bounced my hip impatiently while I waited for my professor to respond.

"It's open."

I turned the knob and stepped into the office. It was the size of a shoebox, lined with mismatched library-style bookcases, so cramped that the door wouldn't open all the way, and I had to shut it behind me to see Velasquez's desk.

Then, *fuck*, it was Donovan sitting behind it in his place.

Goddammit all to hell.

The son of a bitch didn't even look up from his laptop. "How can I help you, Sabrina?"

My hands were shaking. I stuffed them into my coat pockets. I couldn't talk to Donovan. Not like this. Not when he'd already written me off. "Where's Velasquez?"

"You have to schedule an appointment to see him." His dress shirt was crisp white and his muscles bulged tightly against the fabric.

I'm not looking at him. "I'd like to do that then."

"You can schedule online through the portal."

Jesus. Of course.

I put my hand on the doorknob, ready to leave.

"He's here on Fridays at three," Donovan said to my back.

I did a mental scan of my schedule. "I have class then."

"Then you'll have to skip class. Or you'll have to talk to me." Finally, he looked up at me—caught me, *caged* me with those sharp, piercing eyes. "What can I help you with, Sabrina?"

I didn't want to talk to him. And I didn't want to leave.

"My grade," I said.

He cocked his head, as if he had no idea what I meant, that asshole motherfucker. "What about it?"

Anger gave me courage. I pulled my hands out of my pockets and stepped toward him. "It's not fair, and you know it. I understand that you don't agree with my conclusions, but my reasoning was fair and sound, and I referenced many credible and reliable sources—"

He nodded to the chair facing the desk. "Sit down, Sabrina. You're awfully worked up."

He didn't even ask me to sit. He *told* me. It was patronizing and infuriating. "I'd like to stand." I was getting hot, though. I unbuckled my pea coat and threw it on the chair instead. "My paper was not 'F' work."

He nodded and ticked his jaw a couple times as though considering. After a beat, he said, "I care to differ."

"This is not subjective!" I yelled.

"It is, actually." His tone remained composed, in perfect contrast to mine. "Unfortunately, for you, it's my opinion that matters."

God, the calmer he was the more worked up I got. He was goading me on purpose. I should leave. I knew I should leave.

I started for my coat then stopped. "*Why* are you doing this?"

"It's sad, really." Donovan shut his laptop and pushed it aside. Then he clapped his hands together silently as if praying and pointed them at me. "You showed such promise at the beginning of the term, Sabrina. But this last month you've become a different person. You've arrived late to class. You're disengaged. You're disruptive. The work you're turning in—this paper—is less than acceptable. It's a shame you're letting the events of one night stain the rest of your life."

His last sentence was heavy and weighted with subtext.

"Are you—?" I was incredulous. Was he *really* blaming this

on what happened with Theo? "Oh, and you're a perfect example of how not to let a tragedy stain the rest of your life."

His brows furrowed. "What did you say?"

Besides, I hadn't changed because of *Theo*. I'd changed because of *him*. Not that I was telling him that. "My changes in behavior have not translated into a change in the standard of my work."

"As your teacher, that's for me to decide, and I've decided that it has." His subtext said *case closed*. Especially when he leaned back in his chair and rested his feet on the desk, crossed at the ankles.

Weeks of bottled up emotion rattled through me. Every cell in my body vibrated with rage and want and horror and shame.

"Fuck you," I said in as clear and as controlled a tone as I could manage. I'd leave. I'd talk to Velasquez. I'd report the fuck out of Donovan. I had a solid case. This wasn't even anything to worry about. I'd get it worked out.

I grabbed my coat off the chair and spun once again to leave.

"Don't you mean *fuckwaffle*?"

I'd had the door open, was *this close* to walking out, but I shut it again because I had to know. "Is *that* why you're doing this? Because of Weston?" Was he *jealous*?

For half a second, I thought I'd hit onto something. His expression tightened and a strange prick of heat blossomed in my belly at the idea of Donovan jealous. Because of *me*.

But then he laughed, coldly. "No. I was just teasing you. Can't take being on the other side of the joke?"

Is that what this was to him? A joke?

"This is serious!" I was so mad I dropped my coat and pushed his fucking feet off the desk. "This is my scholarship!"

In an instant he was up and around the desk in front of me. "I told you before how you could fix your grades if you're that concerned about it."

He was referring to his come-on in his room. When he'd suggested he could *help me* with my virginity. It was another way he could trivialize my situation, but it was also a chance to play with my emotions. I hated how it felt like a carrot dangling. How he played that card as if he knew that somewhere deep down I wanted him.

It pissed me off to a new level. I slapped him so hard my palm burned.

Donovan rubbed his cheek, and his eyes sparked. "Is this how you fought off Theo?" he asked, evenly.

"No," I said tentatively.

Something shifted between us.

"Fight me like you fought him."

I could have said no. It was such a strange, twisted request, but I was mad and ready to fight. And after weeks of the thoughts I'd had, weeks of pent-up desire and need, I didn't *want* to say no.

And was it really a strange, twisted request if somewhere on a gut level I understood the impetus behind it?

Without further urging, I shoved both arms against Donovan's chest as forcefully as I could. He pushed my hands away, but it felt good. Both to shove and be shoved. Like being able to pick up a heavy weight and the relief after you put it down.

Donovan nodded, encouraging me to come at him again.

I shoved him once more, but he grabbed my arm and wrapped it around my back. He tried for my other arm. I kneed him in his side then pushed against his face while he was bent over. He was too strong for me, and he captured my wrist easily.

He held me like this for a second as we caught our breath, all the while his eyes glued to mine. "Do you want me to stop?" he asked carefully.

Why wasn't I frightened? I was trapped by a man I didn't have any reason to trust, and I'd been in a similar situation and been violated. I should have been scared out of my mind.

But instead of feeling scared, I felt empowered.

And turned on.

Just like in all those fantasies I'd had.

"No," I said. "Don't stop."

I wriggled against his hold to reinforce my request, using my entire body to fight him. Before I'd been keeping back. Now, I struggled with all I had.

Donovan fought harder too, but only with enough strength to just overcome me. He wrapped his arm around my waist, sliding my shirt up so he touched bare skin. I elbowed him in the ribs. His knee grazed against my inner thigh. Could he tell how wet I was through my leggings?

When he had me captured again, one arm behind me, one across my chest, he suddenly pushed me back until I was pinned against a bookshelf.

I gazed down to where his lower body met mine. Pressed hard at my belly was the firm bulge of his erection.

I'd long forgotten why I'd come here.

When I looked up again, his eyes were waiting. "I could smell you on his fingers."

I barely had time to wish his mouth was on mine before it was.

There was nothing tentative or easy about the way that

Donovan Kincaid kissed. The pressure of his lips was firm and intent. His tongue was thick as it dipped inside, tasting me in long licks. He dropped my arms and with one hand held my face at my chin, sort of cradling it, and it felt sweet, but also like it was meant to hold me in place. So he could kiss me how he wanted. So he could suck my top lip until it was fat. So he could nip along my neck while I wriggled against him.

My knees could barely hold me. I couldn't breathe because I wanted him so much. I threw one arm around his neck, needing to hold on to something. Needing to hold on to *him*. His kiss got deeper as if he liked the way I clutched on to him. Then meaner—pulling roughly at my lip with his teeth while pinching my nipple with his fingers—as if he wished he didn't like it like he did.

His lips never left mine, but I was very aware as his hand slid down my side and under the band of my leggings, under my panties, past the hood of skin to find my clit.

My breath hitched, and he slipped deeper, through the soft curls, burrowing inside me.

"Was this how he did it?" he said, pulling away. I don't know if he wanted to watch the reaction to his question or to what he was doing.

"Yes." It was mechanically the same. Two fingers stroking my sensitive inner walls.

But it was also nothing at all the same. I was so wet. And it felt so good. So fucking good. Like kindling catching on fire, spreading heat, growing hotter. Burning. Blazing. "Donovan," I moaned.

"Say it again," he growled.

"Donovan." I'd said it so many times in the dark, in my head. It felt new to say it out loud in this way but comfortable, like finding a pair of jeans that seemed to have been perfectly tailored.

His lip turned up, the closest thing to a smile that I'd ever seen him give. Damn, his face was really striking. I'd never seen it this close up. Not pretty but captivating. He was only twenty-two and yet he already had lines starting at his eyes. His thick brows and the deep line in his chin gave him a rugged appeal, and the way he studied me while he rubbed and kneaded me below was intense and committed and...god, what he was doing to me...I closed my eyes as the pleasure built toward a climax.

"Did you touch him?" he asked, suddenly withdrawing his hand.

I opened my eyes. "No."

"Touch me." It was the same way he'd told me to sit when I'd first arrived. Then it had pissed me off to be ordered around. Now I was so eager, my hands were shaking.

Donovan caressed my face and kissed along my forehead while I worked to get his black trousers open. When I got his pants and boxer briefs worked down to the top of his muscular thighs, his cock fell out, long and thick and hard. His tip was purple and stretched tight, and all of a sudden I knew that this was going to be *it*. This was going to happen. This was going to be inside me because there was a cyclone of want blustering at the core of me, begging me to have him. But also, it *had* to happen because I had a very real fear that whatever this strange, complicated thing was that was going on with Donovan might never happen again if it didn't happen *now*.

I skimmed my palm across his crown, reverently, then drew my fingers closed around him and pulled down.

He hissed, and my stomach flipped.

Donovan brought his hand to join mine—the one slick with my wetness—and together we stroked up, down. Up. Down.

Up.

He pulled his hand away, but I kept working him, even though I could feel his eyes on me, watching me. *Asking* me.

I didn't look up. Because I didn't want to be asked, and I didn't want this to stop. And that made me an awful person and an awful woman and probably someone who needed to schedule an appointment with a campus psychiatrist as soon as possible, but so be it. *This* was my consent. I was touching him.

He seemed to understand because then he was pulling out his wallet, tearing open a condom, pushing my hand away and rolling it over his erection. Or maybe he was never asking my permission, after all.

I shimmied my leggings and panties down to my knees. Donovan lifted me and they fell to my ankles. I widened my knees, giving him room. He lined his head at my entrance and, without any hesitation, drove inside.

It hurt at first. A lot.

I was too tight and too dry, even as wet as I was. Donovan was persistent, though, pushing and nudging until I opened up for him and he could slide all the way in. Tears fell down my cheeks and my nails dug into his back. Fluid trickled past where we were joined and down my leg. I felt tense and wound up and unbridled.

But then there was Donovan's mouth, kissing me, centering me. He was just as demanding as before. Greedy and impatient like his cock. But as I gave in to his lips, my body relaxed, and soon there was no more pain, just pleasure coiling inside me, tightening and expanding.

He noticed when I gave in. I could feel his attack change.

He hitched me up higher so the angle of his pelvis was better against mine and ground into me repeatedly with deep, merciless jabs. I tried to speak, to say his name, but all that came out was grunts and groans and incoherent syllables.

I was lost to him.

The shelf behind me cut into my lower back and my phone buzzed in my coat pocket on the floor by the desk and I had an **F** on my paper and the door to the office was unlocked and I had a date with Weston, but all I cared about in the world at the moment was the dirty, filthy scenario I was living out. It was everything I'd imagined those nights in my room—a little bit cruel and a little bit hard—plus as erotic as hell. And the man knew how to touch me. Knew how to move inside me.

It was also more. Because I'd never once imagined that, while he did those terrible sexy things, Donovan would look at me the way he looked at me. Studying my face. Watching my eyes. Like he cared about what he'd find there.

I'd never once imagined that I'd *want* that from him.

I came without warning. I'd always been finicky when it came to orgasms—my high school boyfriend had found it hard to make me come with his tongue and fingers. I'd had better luck on my own, depending on my mindset. Maybe I was a girl who needed penetration. Maybe I was a girl who needed Donovan.

He regarded me even closer as I spiraled. I fought to keep my eyes open so I could watch him watching me. He seemed to find this funny because he chuckled, kissed me again, and then plowed into me with renewed fervor.

He came on a long low grunt, and for just a moment at the end, he closed his eyes, and I'd never seen his face so relaxed. We were still catching our breath, he was still inside me, and I brought my hand up to touch his cheek—how young he looked now. How innocent.

He caught my hand against his jaw. His eyes flew open. "I didn't want to notice you," he said so quietly it was almost a whisper. "And now I don't know how not to."

Another cryptic Donovan statement, but this one made my chest feel warm and stretched. "Then notice me," I said.

He considered me a moment longer. Then stepped away, pulling out of me. "I can't."

He motioned for me to stay where I was. Then he removed his condom, tied it off, wrapped it in tissue from the desk and pocketed it before fastening his pants. I had to give him credit— it was probably not a good idea to leave a used condom in Mr. Velasquez's office. Next Donovan brought some tissue and knelt down in front of me so he could clean up the blood and cum that had dripped down my thigh.

Then he left me with my pants still down and went to sit behind his desk.

I dressed myself and watched him, curious as he opened up his laptop and clicked a few keys. "You have an **A** on that paper now, Sabrina," he said, his voice not entirely steady. "I believe that should be acceptable to you." He couldn't look at me.

Dread started gathering in my stomach. "That's not. That's not why I did that." He didn't believe that. He *couldn't*. He felt bad now—as he should—and was fixing his mistake. Surely that was what this was.

"I'm sure it's not why you did that." He was more in control of himself now. He shut the laptop and finally met my eyes. "But now you'll have a chance with Weston King, won't you?"

It was a punch to the stomach. The cruelest thing he could have said.

With tears in my eyes, I grabbed my coat off the floor and started for the door. My hand was on the knob when he added, "Oh, that's right. I forgot to mention, Weston *does* like virgins. My bad."

There were a lot of words I wanted to unleash on him, but even if I tried at the moment, I knew it would come out in nothing but snot and drivel. He'd worn me down. I'd played his game and he'd won.

I opened the door and ran until I was out of the building. Ran until I couldn't run any more because I was sobbing too hard to go on. I stopped at the river to cry and catch my breath and silence my dang phone, which had been going off nonstop in my pocket.

I pulled out my cell and looked at my notifications through bleary eyes—four missed calls and several texts, all from my sister.

Aubrey: *Where are you?*

Aubrey: *Call me ASAP. It's Dad. He's in the hospital.*

Aubrey: *Sabrina! It's a heart attack.*

Aubrey: *He's going to die. Call me. I need you.*

EPILOGUE

TEN YEARS LATER

Ashley tapped her toe, anxious for the server to come by again. "I swear to god, if we don't get out of here in time because of that damn waitress..."

"Calm down, would you? It's really not that big of a deal if I don't see him." I finished the last swallow of my martini and pushed my glass aside.

"Are you kidding me? It's been—what? Ten years since you left Harvard?"

"About that." *Ten years*. It was strange how it hadn't felt like that much time had passed. It still felt like yesterday, and it also felt like it happened in another lifetime, to somebody else.

"You *have* to see him. You never got to explain to him what happened. What if he's been pining for you all this time? And he never knew that your father died. He just figured you ran off and didn't care. Though I still don't understand why you didn't just take Audrey back to Cambridge with you."

"I've been over this already," I sighed.

She threw her hands up in the air, her exasperation with our server translating into exasperation with me. "You had a *full ride*! How could you let that slip through your fingers? I've heard you talk about the jobs you pined for—running big corporations on Wall Street and making the big bucks. You could have had that if you'd stayed!"

"I know! And believe me, I tried. But my scholarship was taken away when I didn't finish out the semester. I couldn't afford Harvard without that." It had crushed me. Almost as much as the death of my father. All my life I'd worked for that scholarship, then to have it yanked away... It was salt on a very deep open wound.

Ashley, ever true to justice, became indignant. "I know, I know. They took it away. You should have appealed it."

I'd explained this part to her before too. Many times. Something she'd probably remember if she hadn't just finished three vodka tonics in less than an hour. "I did appeal it. But the scholarship was privately funded through the MADAR Foundation and since it wasn't sponsored through the university, the donor didn't have to adhere to school policies. Blah blah blah." The memory was bitter in my mouth, months of writing letters only to be rejected time and time again. "If I'd had the right name, the right connections. If I'd had money, I'm sure things would have been different."

"Isn't that everyone's story? Hey, waitress!" she practically yelled across the bar.

"Ashley! Shh!" I didn't know why I was shushing her now. The whole restaurant was already looking at us.

She didn't mind the attention. "We made eye contact. It's cool. She saw me. She's bringing the ticket." She stole the olive from my empty martini glass. "Anyway, you got your masters at

Colorado University and then got swept up by a headhunter for one of the best ad firms in California, moved to L.A., met me and your life really began. You're welcome."

I pretended to roll my eyes, but honestly, Ashley had become a great friend and confidante. Other than my sister, she was the only person I'd ever told about Donovan Kincaid and Weston King. I'd left out details both times I'd shared the story, however. No one needed to know how sick and dirty I'd been back then. With Donovan.

I still thought about him, sometimes. At night. When I couldn't sleep. When I was restless and couldn't figure out what I needed. Sometimes it was just my hand and fantasies of him.

I wasn't admitting that, though. What kind of girl still dreamed about the asshole who'd taken her virginity and thrown her aside like that?

What would have happened if I'd been able to stay?

"Here you go," the waitress said, dropping off our ticket.

She was already off to another table when Ashley caught her by the arm and pulled her back. "And here's my card. Could you hurry please? We have to be somewhere."

"We really don't," I said, but the server was already out of earshot.

"Yes, we do!" Ashley turned the "Advertising in a New Age" program around so it was facing me and pointed at the keynote speaker excitedly. "He probably thinks you stood him up all those years ago. You have to make it right!"

I stared at the program. It was still open to the page that had started this whole conversation and caused us to miss two panels already.

His picture showed he'd aged well.

But I already knew that. I'd seen both of their pictures many times, and they'd both aged well. Weston King and Donovan Kincaid were famous in the ad world. Instead of following Harvard with jobs in their fathers' investment firm, they'd opened up an international advertising agency. Weston ran the office in the States and Donovan ran the branch in Tokyo.

When I'd agreed to go to New York for three days with Ashley for this conference, I'd had no idea he'd be a speaker.

"He probably won't even remember me," I said, staring at his panty-melting dimple.

"Who could forget you? With a face like his, I'd use any card I had to try to get close to him. He's a hottie. Oh, wait, I forgot you're more into brains than looks these days—maybe he'll share all his award-winning inspirations with an old friend."

I shook my head and pulled my hand through my hair—the ponytail was long gone, but the habit was not. I probably should see his speech anyway. And what was the harm in sticking around afterward? Wouldn't it be nice to finally have some closure to those days?

The waitress returned with the bill and Ashley quickly signed.

"All right," Ashley said. "Ready, Bri?"

It was a loaded question. Was anyone ever ready for men like Weston King and Donovan Kincaid?

Pulling out my phone, I used the camera to freshen up my lipstick and took a deep breath. "Let's do this."

PART 2

MEN

SIX

"He won't remember me," I insisted. I had to concentrate in order not to fidget. The martinis I'd had earlier in the night had worn off an hour ago, and I was nervous. How had I gotten talked into this again?

"Would you stop saying that?" Ashley peered around the people in front of us, probably sizing up how long it would be before it was our turn. We were lined up with a dozen or so other women who'd stayed after the keynote at the "Advertising in a New Age" convention to greet the speaker, Weston King. "You're smart. Witty. Put together. Gorgeous. No one can forget you."

The woman she was describing had only existed for the last handful of years. Before that, I'd been awkward and shy. I'd hidden behind plain features and a mess of mousy brown hair that I'd typically worn in a ponytail. "You didn't know me in college. I was definitely forgettable then." And obviously nothing special since I couldn't manage to keep my spot at Harvard for more than one semester.

Ashley inhaled, a sign that she was trying to stay patient. Then she turned to me and gave me her most encouraging smile. "I know you *now*. Even if he doesn't remember you, he'll pretend he does just to keep talking to you."

My lid twitched as I fought not to roll my eyes. "Shut up."

"I can't. I have a perfectly non-lesbian girl-crush on you. You know this. I can't understand anyone who isn't in love with you." She wrapped her arm through mine, and we stepped forward. One more person stood between him and us. Between Weston and me. Between my past and my present. Was I ready for my worlds to collide?

Honestly, I was probably getting psyched up over nothing. Too many years had gone by to make a big deal about the threads that had been dropped back then. A decade, in fact. We'd hardly even known each other back then. I'd had one real conversation with the man—boy, at the time—and the rest of my experience with him had been in watching from a distance.

It wasn't as if I were standing in line to see Donovan Kincaid. Now that would be something to be anxious about. *He* would remember me. He'd have to. What had happened between us had been so small in the scheme of time but so big in the scope of the impact it'd had, at least on my life. Did I have the same effect on him?

I was still thinking about Donovan, about his chiseled jaw and his hazel eyes and the awful way we'd parted when the woman in front of us made her goodbyes and stepped out of line, leaving me standing face to face with Weston King.

Jesus, he was beautiful. He'd always been beautiful, but the last ten years had only made him more so. I'd spent the last ninety minutes staring at him as he'd given his talk in the Javits Center, so I should have been prepared, but close-up, his attractiveness was even more striking. His blue eyes even more shocking. His smile even more stunning.

He had the kind of looks that would make any girl's panties damp. I was convinced of that.

"Hello," he said, smoothly. So smoothly I couldn't tell if it was out of recognition or simply charm.

"Uh, hi." That was all I could manage to get out. I might be coiffed and put together on the outside, but seeing Weston King promptly brought back all the awkwardness of my youth.

Thankfully, Ashley was there to come to the rescue.

She stepped forward, nudging me with her. "Hi, I'm Ashley. This is my friend Sabrina. We work at Now, Inc. in L.A. and we wanted to tell you that we really enjoyed your talk tonight. I particularly liked your insight on the relationship between departments within an agency. I've seen the same competitive struggles between the sales team and the creative in our office."

"Thank you," Weston said. "The war between salesmen versus artists. It's the nature of the beast, I think."

He directed his comment to both of us, but all I could do was nod like an idiot.

Ashley inhaled audibly—that almost silent cue she was frustrated—and put her arm around my shoulder. "Also, she's too shy to say it, but Sabrina went to college with you."

"Ashley!" I warned. This was the problem with having a "no boundaries" type of friend. If I didn't stop her, soon she'd be spouting out that I'd had a massive crush on him back then too. God help me if she brought up Donovan. "I wasn't going to say anything."

"We went to school together?" For the first time since I'd stood in front of him, Weston looked at me—*really* looked at me.

His gaze tickled as he studied my face, and I felt my cheeks flush. "I was only at Harvard for part of our freshman year." Not that that had been my choice. "I'm sure you don't remember me." Jesus, I couldn't even look him in the eye. What was wrong with me? I was twenty-seven, not seventeen.

He cocked his head. "Did we know each other very well? What was your name again?"

Oh god. He really *didn't* remember me. This was utterly humiliating.

"We spoke just once or twice. I'm Sabrina Lind," I said, wishing I could crawl under a rock. "Really, I wouldn't expect you to know me. It was just an interesting little tidbit I could tell my friend to make her think I was cool."

He laughed politely, showing off the dimple I'd been so fond of all those years ago. Come to find out, it still made my knees weak.

"Anyway," I said. There were a few people behind us waiting to meet him. More women eager to melt from thirty seconds of his attention. It was time to get going. "Good to see you. You gave a great speech."

"I appreciate it." Weston continued to survey me, still trying to place me, but then I prodded Ashley to go, and he turned his attention to the women behind us.

"Well, that was embarrassing," I whispered as soon as we were a handful of feet away.

"It was so worth it," she said, fanning herself with her program. "I can't believe you went to school with a wickedly handsome mega billionaire. He's even hotter in person than he was on the cover of *Money* magazine last year. That dimple!"

"Right?" It was nice to have someone else witness the beauty that was Weston King. "You should see him without his shirt on. He was on the rowing—"

From behind me, I heard Weston say a word that caught my attention.

Heart beating, hands sweating, I turned around to see him staring after us. "What did you say?"

"You were in Donovan's class," he repeated, his eyes wide with recollection. *Donovan.* That was the word that I'd heard. "You stood me up."

He *did* remember me.

"Told you so," Ashley whispered at my side.

I pinched her arm and called back to Weston. "I had a really good reason. I promise."

He put a finger up to signal for me to wait as he finished signing the program of the woman in front of him. When he was done, he sauntered toward us. "I'll let you tell me all about it over drinks."

WESTON PINNED his eyes on mine. "Okay, your father died, you went home and raised your sister, finished college, got your MBA. Then what?"

It had been almost an hour and a half since Ashley had so kindly feigned too tired to join us for a nightcap, and Weston had taken me to one of his favorite local nightclubs, The Sky Launch, for a drink, which had now turned into two. The circular booth we sat in overlooked the dance floor below, but because of the way it was set off with glass walls, the music wasn't too loud to talk over. It provided a very unique vibe, one both intimate and alive.

"That's about it, really." I hadn't bothered to tell him about my fight to get back to Harvard or how the MADAR foundation had refused to give me my scholarship back after I'd left without finishing the semester. Though it had happened ten years in the past, it was still a sore spot.

"That can't be it. There's always more," he prodded. "How did you choose advertising?"

"Well. Advertising actually found me," I said, kicking off my shoes and folding one foot underneath my thigh. "I've always been equally left- and right-brained, and I wanted to find a job that involved numbers and metrics but also involved creativity, so I got my emphasis in marketing. After I graduated, I had an interview with a headhunter, and one of the jobs she had available happened to be in a marketing department in an ad agency. Of all the positions she showed me, it was the one I was least interested in. But then when I got the offer and I flew out to Los Angeles to visit the office, I fell in love with the energy there. There was numbers and structure and ideas and art. Where else do you get all of that mixed together?"

Weston had taken off his jacket earlier. Now, he loosened his tie and stretched his arm out across the top of the bench. "Some people think that makes those of us who choose this field crazy."

His choice of words stung at something that hadn't bothered me in a long time. I'd wondered if I'd been crazy back then, when I'd been younger and the thoughts and feelings I'd had were strange and unusual and hard to grapple with. The people and fantasies that had turned me on had been frightening and dark.

But I'd grown up and realized that my time at Harvard had not been the norm. It had been a period of dalliance and in no way defined what I was to be for the rest of my life. My thoughts were normal. My fantasies weren't strange. I wasn't crazy.

Sometimes I worried I had to work a little too hard to convince myself of that.

But I was out with Weston King, and if that was crazy, that was exactly the kind of crazy I wanted to be. The kind of crazy I hoped I was. So I said, "Probably so. But what's wrong with that?"

Our eyes met and held. As the night had passed, we'd moved closer and closer to each other. Now we were tilted in toward one another, our bodies only inches apart. Either this was going somewhere or...

"You're still in the marketing department then?" Weston asked, picking up his manhattan and swirling it around before taking a swallow.

"Started in research, and now I'm the manager of strategy and marketing." I sighed inwardly. Thinking about my job was depressing. While I loved the actual work, the president who'd come on in the last year had been a nightmare to work with.

Besides, what I was interested in was Weston's firm— Reach, Inc. The business was only five years old and yet was already one of the leaders in the industry. It was the kind of career I'd hoped to have if I would've finished school at Harvard. "Your job, though..." I paused, hoping my jealousy sounded more like admiration. "What you've done is incredible."

Weston shrugged dismissively but somehow beamed at the same time. "It's been quite a ride. I can hardly believe it's my life."

This surprised me. He was born with a silver spoon in his mouth—I'd thought he'd expect everything he touched to turn to gold. It was harder to resent his success when he was humble about it. "This is going to sound naïve, but what exactly do *you* do? How do you split everything up?"

"Not naïve at all." He set his glass down, and now we were close enough that my knee touched his. Warmth spread throughout me, gathering in my belly. "I actually have no idea."

I chuckled with unexplained nervousness. "Be serious."

"Well. We're set up in a traditional agency structure with a board of directors that consists of five people." Five men, from what I'd read. Talk about a world of the patriarch. Donovan was the only other one I knew by name. "There's two guys in Tokyo, a guy in London, and Nathan Sinclair and I run the New York office together. Nate oversees creative and account services, and I run everything else."

"Which is a lot."

"Which is a lot," he repeated.

"So operations, marketing, research, finance...that's all you?" I was surprised. Our office had three bosses overseeing all the areas and it was a smaller firm.

Weston shrugged. "Mostly I hide in my office and read Buzzfeed all day, but somehow the checks keep coming in."

"You do more than that."

"We're growing. We'll have to change the structure soon." Abruptly, he altered his tone, dismissing the previous subject and growing serious. "This is boring, though. Let's talk about you."

I lowered my eyes, suddenly shy. "I've already told you everything about me."

"Let's talk about our brief encounter in college."

"It was so brief, it could barely be called an encounter." We'd had a class together, and once we'd shared a lunch. Then he'd asked me out, and I'd said yes, but I'd had to go home because my father died before the party had actually happened.

"I'd never been stood up before you. That hurt." He reached out to adjust my necklace, a simple cross that had belonged to my mother before she'd died. His fingers felt hot on my already too warm skin, like adding fire to fire.

We sparked.

"And yet you didn't even remember who I was when you first saw me." I put my hand on his thigh, lightly, cautiously. His muscle flexed under my touch, and a thrill shot down my spine.

He tugged lightly on a piece of my hair, and I could imagine him pulling it harder. "I didn't recognize you without the ponytail."

"Yeah, that's it."

His face grew somber. "I really was into you, Sabrina."

The soberness of his declaration was hard to believe. "For all of five minutes. Literally five minutes."

"There were a lot of girls at that school. It took me a while to notice you." He put his hand on my bare knee and stroked the skin on the inside of my lower thigh. "Not my fault."

"Uh-huh." It was hard to refute him when my body was swimming in this dizziness. I'd wanted him so much back then. Not just him, but all that he stood for—his school, his money, his future. That want lingered into the want I had for him now.

"If you'd have come to that party…" He trailed off, his voice thick and seductive.

"Then what?" I'd thought about it from time to time over the years. Wondered what could have happened between Weston and me if we'd had the chance.

He leaned in and told me now. "I would have tried to get you into bed."

I inhaled his words, taking them in all the way before responding. "I would have gone."

At least I would have if that other thing hadn't happened. When he'd invited me, I'd hoped for that. After the incident with Donovan, I wasn't sure anymore what I'd wanted.

"You would have?"

I nodded. "You wouldn't have even had to try very hard. I had a major crush on you."

Weston's hand moved higher up my leg, and he leaned in to whisper near my ear. "I'm going to try to get you into bed now."

He was a special kind of catnip. Not only was he someone I'd wanted in the past, but he'd also achieved everything I'd ever desired for myself. There was something unexplainably attractive about that.

But I didn't have to use words to tell him trying wasn't necessary. Weston King had this one in the bag.

SEVEN

I picked up Weston's slacks off the floor, shook them, then dropped them again when nothing fell out. Circling, I scanned the room for the third time. "I can't find my panties," I said with a sigh.

Weston watched me from the bed, his head propped up with his hand. "You don't need them."

"I do. I have to get dressed." I looked again through the skirt, bra, and camisole I was holding, in case I'd missed my underwear clinging to one of them. Not there. I dropped the clothes on the bed and sighed again.

"No, you don't. Stay here," he beckoned. "Stay in bed with me forever."

"I can't. You know I have to get back." After drinks on Friday night, Weston had taken me to his penthouse and fucked me until the sun came up. We'd stayed in bed all day Saturday and most of today, leaving only to eat on occasion. Now it was Sunday afternoon, and I had a red-eye to catch.

"Where did you put them after dinner last night?" he asked, stretching so the sheet fell down his body, exposing his bare torso and the beautiful happy trail that I'd become so familiar with in the last couple of days.

I dragged my thoughts back to the evening before. We'd gone to an Asian fusion restaurant. Weston had fingered me on the cab ride home. "I didn't wear them to dinner last night."

"Oh, yeah." He grinned, his eyes lighting up with hunger.

My belly tightened. "Stop looking at me like that, or I'm never getting out of here."

He reached down to rub the semi that was already taking shape beneath the sheet. "I really don't have a problem with that."

"Weston..." I warned. In support of what she called my much-needed sexcapade, Ashley had taken care of packing my suitcase, but I still had to pick it up from the hotel doorman before heading to the airport. With city traffic, I needed to leave in the next thirty minutes. "I have to go."

He sat up and leaned against the headboard, and based on his new position, I assumed he was preparing to move the conversation in a serious direction. "But why do you have to go?"

Or not so serious.

He knew why I had to leave. "I have a flight," I answered anyway as I unbuttoned the dress shirt that I'd snagged off the floor after my shower earlier.

"Miss it."

"I have to go home." I threw the dress shirt on the bed.

"Why?" He leaned forward and stroked a finger along the curve of my breast.

"I have a job," I said, smacking his hand away.

"Quit your job." He groaned as I put my bra on, covering up the breasts he'd spent so much time fondling over the weekend. He'd been playful, not too rough, and though it wasn't the kind of touch that made me immediately wet, it felt good enough. It was normal and healthy and that's what I always hoped for in a sexual encounter.

"I can't quit my job." I paused as I turned my skirt, finding the back of it. "I need a job. I wasn't born of the means to not have to work like some other people."

"*Other people*," he laughed. "People like me, you mean?"

I smiled demurely and stepped into my skirt. "Maybe."

"I have a job," he said, somewhat defensively.

Suddenly feeling bad, I stepped toward him and hugged him to my chest. "You do," I said, conciliatorily, stroking my fingers through his blond hair. "You do have a job. And I have a job. On the opposite side of the country."

He clutched my ass and pulled me closer. "You could have a job on *this* side of the country," he said into my breasts.

"I could. But I don't."

He kissed along my cleavage. "Come work for me. Quit your job and you're hired. Who even likes L.A.? All that smog and superficiality. Quit and work for me."

He was joking, so I laughed, but also my heart thumped harder. How long had I wanted the life that he was dangling like a toy? "You don't even know if I have any qualifications."

"Oh, I know several of your qualifications." He maneuvered me around and pulled me onto his lap so I could feel his erection pressing into the curve of my back, confirming his lack of seriousness. "Shall we discuss them in detail or shall I let you remind me in other ways?"

"Weston..." I moaned, as his hand found its way up my

skirt. My thighs parted automatically for him, and his thumb slid along my bare pussy until he landed on my clit. "You're making it hard to leave."

"My plan is working then." He circled his thumb slowly, teasing me.

"Mm. That feels good." My body began humming, ready to start climbing the spiral mountain of pleasure. "You have to stop," I pleaded.

"Imagine if you stayed," he whispered at my ear. "We could do this all the time."

Even though I knew he was playing, I let myself think about it for the barest of moments. Weston was exactly the kind of guy who'd be good for me. He was a good guy, and our sex was good, and he made me feel good about myself.

Why didn't *good* feel like *enough*?

It didn't matter anyway. It was a game. He was a playboy. Everything I'd read about him said so, just like he'd been in college. I didn't expect to be the one who could change him. This had just been a good time, a dance with the past. And all this talk was just him being caught up in the moment.

"I can't stay," I said breathlessly, distracted by his thumb still pressing against my clit.

"Give me one good reason," he insisted then licked along my lobe, sending a shudder down my spine.

I smiled. "I like what I do." I really *did* like my job, despite the current environment at my firm and my past aspirations to be involved in something bigger.

Weston brought his other hand up to fondle my breast through my bra. "I'd give you a similar position."

"You can't just boot out your current manager of strategy

and marketing." I fidgeted on his lap, trying to get him to give me more even though I knew I needed to be leaving soon.

"His title is Director of Marketing Strategy, and yes, I could. He has halitosis, and I don't like the way he makes his graphs."

This time I laughed. "You're not serious."

"I'm very serious. He has sushi for lunch every day, and I swear every time he opens his mouth, it smells like dead fish."

I chuckled again and closed my eyes, letting myself enjoy him. He was so charming and funny, exactly like I remembered him. But over all the years when I'd thought about him, when I'd wondered about him, he'd never been the one to make me orgasm in the dark.

I had to go.

I opened my eyes. "Weston."

"Sabrina."

"I need to leave."

A beat passed. "I know."

I tried to stand up, but his grip on me tightened. "You have to let me go first."

"If I must," he sighed and let me go.

I stood and smoothed my skirt. Then I turned back to him as I put on my camisole.

Weston sat forward and draped his arms around his propped up knees. "Seriously, though. Come work for me."

"Seriously, though." I turned around to peek in his dresser mirror and ran my fingers through my hair. "You haven't even seen my resume." He'd take one look and offer me an entry-level position, and then I'd just be another one of those women who'd fucked their way into a job. Not what I was looking for.

"You graduated a year early from high school. You were at Harvard on full scholarship," he said, repeating things I'd told him over the weekend. Then he told me something new. "Donovan said you were by far the person with the most potential in any of his classes."

My hand slowed at the mention of the one person who could always get my attention. Like I was a paper clip buried in the ground, and his name was the most powerful metal detector around. "Donovan talked about me?"

"Once." Weston climbed out of bed while he spoke. "The day you and I had lunch, I think. He gave me shit about hanging out with you because you were the brightest student with the most potential, and you didn't need to be dragged down and distracted by the likes of me."

Donovan had been Weston's friend and roommate, but he was older than us and had also been the teacher's assistant for our business ethics class. And he'd been so much more to me.

But that hadn't given him the right to try to keep Weston and me apart. It was ten years ago, and the mention of it now irked me. It also made me a little bit smug, and that made me even more irked.

"That doesn't seem like something that was any of his concern," I said as Weston reached in front of me to open a dresser drawer and pull out a pair of red boxer briefs. "What did you say to him?"

"That it didn't seem like something that was any of his concern." He stepped into his underwear, tucking his cock into place. "As your teacher, he seemed to think it was. If I remember right, it caused one of our bigger arguments back then. In the end, we agreed to disagree. His mention of it in the first place made me all the more eager to see you. And that made me all the more disappointed when you didn't show up."

Weston began gathering his clothes from around the room, and I sank onto the edge of the bed, taking this in. I'd had lunch with Weston and then he and Donovan had argued about me. After which, Donovan had given me an *F* that I hadn't deserved leading to our own fight, and before I knew it, I'd ended up losing my virginity to a man who'd been both a hero and a demon to me.

It remained the single most erotic moment of my life.

But the whole thing had been fucked up. And, afterward, he'd turned cold. From then on, I stayed away from men like him. Every man I'd dated had been fun and kind and good. Like Weston. Good guys who never worked out. Every relationship felt lacking, and if it was a sign that I needed to have a fucked up sex life to feel truly complete, then I was prepared to never be whole.

Because I didn't think I could get swept into a cyclone like Donovan again and survive.

"I'm sorry I didn't find a way to get a hold of you back then," I said, watching Weston straighten the room. My date with him had been the last thing on my mind after my father's death, but I could have tried harder. I probably could have tried harder with any of the good guys I'd dated.

"I'm just glad you found me now." He winked. "Come work for me."

I let out a huff of exasperation. "You never quit, do you?"

"I'm tenacious. It's one of my best qualities."

What if he really was serious? Not about a relationship, but about a job? Could I come work for him? Entry-level was at least a start. I was years behind, but I could gain some ground, couldn't I? Still end up where I was meant to be, playing hardball in the big league.

It was something to consider...

From where I was seated, I spotted the heel of my shoe poking out from behind the window curtain. "What made you and Donovan decide to go into advertising together?" I asked as I headed over to grab it. "Why didn't you join your father's investment firm?" King-Kincaid was one of the biggest investment firms in the world. Both Weston and Donovan were wealthier than I could ever imagine. Neither of them had to work at all, and they'd started a business in a completely different field.

"There were a lot of reasons. We wanted something that was just ours, you know? Something that we built ourselves. I didn't want to be handed everything. I wanted to know if I could do it on my own. Donovan also had a problem with some of the ethical choices that our fathers' firm has made in order to increase profits."

"Really?" That had been the topic we'd argued about in my class assignment. "The Donovan that I remember had little regard for ethics."

"He changed his mind about a few things since college for whatever reason."

Was it vain of me to wonder if I had contributed to his change of mind?

"As for advertising, that was Donovan's idea. We knew Nate, who was also interested, so he came on board. Then we found Dylan Locke and Cade Warren and we had a team. At first, we planned to all stay in New York, each of us running a different department, but after our first year, we decided to go international. Donovan volunteered to open the Tokyo office with Cade. Dylan went to London, and we've been operating like that for the last four years."

I found my other shoe at the bottom of the bed and slipped it on while I thought about Donovan all the way on the other side of the world. I felt safer, somehow, knowing that that's where he was. Far away. Far from me.

Yet, even from that distance, I could feel his pull. Did he have that same pull on Weston?

Slipping a foot into my shoe, I studied the man who'd given me an incredible weekend. "It must be hard to be so far from Donovan. You thought of him like a brother back in college."

Weston bent to his knees by the side of the bed. "It's not fun. We Skype a lot for work, but I won't lie. I miss our poker games." He lifted the bed skirt and looked underneath. "If I brought you on as an employee, he'd be super impressed. So." He peered up at me. "What do you say?"

I crossed behind him and picked up my earrings from the nightstand. "I can't tell anymore if you're being serious or if you're just trying to get me to give you another blowjob."

"Can't the answer be both?"

I fastened my earrings and wondered again if I should be considering his offer. Because there were things that were tempting about it. There were things that were tempting about *him*.

"Aha!" he exclaimed suddenly. He stood, dangling a pair of black lacy panties from his finger that he'd apparently found under the bed.

"Those aren't mine," I said.

He looked at me, looked at the panties, then back at me. The color drained from his face as he realized what I must have been thinking. "I don't have a girlfriend."

"I know," I said, my voice steady. "You have lots of girl-friends." And that was exactly why I couldn't take his offer seriously. Because he was always going to have another woman and there was always going to be another offer.

He knew I understood without having to say it.

"I'm sorry," he said, because Weston King was nothing if not a gentleman.

It wasn't disappointment I felt—not exactly. But there was something that now felt lost that had almost been found. Like the thread of a thought that can almost be grasped but not quite and then it's gone.

I let out a small sigh. "I didn't think this was anything other than what it was, Weston." That was honest. Too honest, maybe.

Then it was Weston who seemed disappointed. "But what if it's something else?" His tone was disoriented, but hopeful. He didn't know if I was the woman he wanted. He was a man taking a chance.

I didn't want to be a chance. I wanted a man who knew.

"But what if it's exactly what it is?" I reached my hand out and stroked his cheek. "I've had a good time. Can we leave it on that note? And not ruin it?"

He put his hand over mine and brought it to his lips and kissed it. "It's not ruined already?"

"It's not. It's been a special weekend. I needed this. Thank you."

He kissed me goodbye, and I went my way, leaving behind the *what if* that I'd carried around all those years and a mauve pair of panties that I never did find.

And whatever thoughts had been stirred up about Dono-van, I buried under the thoughts I always had about him. The thoughts that I'd had since college. The thoughts I pretended only had life when I was alone with my nightmares in the dark. If I'd thought Weston might have been the one to chase them away, I'd been wrong. If anything, he was the one to bring them into the light.

EIGHT

"And another thing..."

I stirred my coffee and nodded while Ashley continued with her rant about inner office politics. Though I was in full agreement, I didn't need to go over every detail of my indignation.

I raised the back of my hand to my mouth and stifled a yawn. I'd had another one of those nightmare filled nights when I'd woken in a sweat, convinced I'd been pinned down and forced to do things I didn't want to do by a terrible man. As usual, the only way I'd been able to fall sleep again was to imagine that the man forcing me wasn't Theodore Sheridan but instead was Donovan Kincaid.

Those dreams had been recurrent over the years since my near rape by Theo in college. They didn't happen as often as they had in the beginning, but they still happened regularly. It had become so normal that I'd stopped thinking about them in daylight, stopped worrying that the wicked things I fantasized about Donovan had anything to do with the real me. The "awake" me. The me that didn't have dirty thoughts and didn't want filthy men.

But since my weekend with Weston, that had changed. For whatever reason, he'd triggered something. It was as though the past, which I'd done so well to hold down, had resurfaced, and now I couldn't push it back where it belonged. The bad dreams had become more frequent, and barely a day passed when I didn't sit in my office remembering the naughty things I'd thought about Donovan in the dark the night before, having to press my thighs together because the buzz between them was so great.

What was he doing now? Did he ever wonder about me? Was he ever sorry for how we left things? Was he ever sorry that he saved me?

Ashley stopped pacing my office and plopped down in the chair facing my desk, pulling my attention to her. "I'm not shitting you, Bri, Monahan is on a rampage. He is blaming everyone but sales for everything that's gone wrong on every campaign this year. It's a nightmare."

Interesting choice of words. I could tell her a thing or two about nightmares.

But I was frustrated with our boss too. "I know what you mean about Monahan. He asked me to redo the strategy sheet for Dove. Again. This will be the third time. The strategy sheet was good the first time. There was nothing wrong with it."

Monahan, our new president, had turned our friendly office into a war zone. He was keen on showing favoritism to teams he'd worked with before he'd been promoted. Lately, it had been hard to find the motivation to keep giving my all, and a few times I'd even considered looking elsewhere for work.

"You know why he's doing this? Besides the fact that he's just an asshole, I mean." Ashley seemed buoyed to have me join her in her complaints. "It's because he won't get his promotion bonus if he doesn't find another ten percent in revenue this quarter. I don't think it's possible."

"I don't either. I love this job, but if he doesn't calm the fuck down..." I trailed off.

But though I wasn't ready to be that bold, Ashley was. "Time to get our resumes ready."

My phone lit up then. It was the line from my assistant. I pushed the intercom button. "What's up?"

Kent's voice filled the room. "There's a phone call for you from Mr. Weston King on line two. Want to take it?"

My stomach knotted at the mention of Weston's name. I hadn't heard from him since our weekend together in May. It was almost August.

"He's just *now* calling you?" Ashley whispered loudly. "It's been three months!"

"Yeah, Kent," I said, simultaneously glaring at Ashley. "I'll take it. Thanks."

I clicked the intercom button off and stared for a handful of seconds at my friend. "It can't be what you think," I said, finally. Even though I wasn't exactly sure what she was thinking, I could guess it had romantic notions. "We didn't leave things like that. We didn't even *start* things like that."

"It has to be *something* if he's calling you." Her giddiness was making me nervous.

I wiped my sweaty palm across my skirt. "Maybe he's just going to be in town and thought it would be polite to say hello."

"*Or.* Maybe he realizes he can't breathe without you, and he's finally gotten the guts to do something about it. I told you

I've only seen him photographed with, like, one girl in the last several weeks. He's not fooling around like he was. He's *pining.*"

Again, I glared. I actually hadn't put any thought into a future with Weston, but it was nice to be wanted. Did he actually want me? How different would things have been if Donovan had called after we'd been together? Even three months later. Even three years.

"Just answer it!" Ashley squealed impatiently.

I picked up the phone. "This is Sabrina."

"Sabrina. It's Weston." His smile carried over the digital network. I could practically hear his dimple in his tone.

"Hi," I said, unable to stop grinning myself.

"Hi to you. It's good to hear your voice. Really good."

"You too." I swiveled back and forth in my chair, aware that Ashley was watching me like a hawk.

Listening too. Which meant this couldn't turn into phone sex. Not that I wanted this to turn into phone sex. Not that I knew what I wanted at all.

I cleared my throat. "I'm surprised you called. This is out of the blue."

"I know," Weston said, suddenly seeming more official and less flirty. "I'm sorry. I probably should have made an appointment."

"No, no. This is fine. Just. It's unexpected." I wasn't sure how I felt about the more official tone. It wasn't bad. It was different.

"It *is* unexpected. I've had a lot of unexpected things happen in my life lately, actually. And I'm going to shock you again now. Are you ready? Brace yourself."

My muscles tensed automatically like they did when I was

in a car and someone put on the brakes suddenly. "Okay. I'm braced."

"I want to offer you a job."

"HE ISN'T SERIOUS." I'd said it so many times since I'd hung up the phone with Weston that Ashley had to think I'd gone into some state of shock.

I *had* gone into some state of shock. There was no other word for what this feeling was.

"He's serious," Ashley insisted as she stared at my computer screen. "I'm looking at the offer now, Bri. It's on letterhead. This is serious shit." Weston had emailed a formal offer over while we'd spoken, and she hadn't hesitated to swivel my screen toward her so she could examine it in detail.

My eyes had been open too long without blinking. So I blinked. Then did it again. "But why?"

"He obviously followed up, checked out your resume, probably called some references and saw that you do good work. *Because you do.*" She bent to meet my eyes across the desk. "You deserve this, Bri."

I held her gaze for several heavy seconds. I did want the job. That wasn't a question. The pay was phenomenal. The offer even included relocation expenses. The title was exactly the one he'd promised before—turned out his last director of marketing strategy was transferring to London and had been planning to for a while now. Weston had known he might need a replacement when I'd spent the weekend with him. It was essentially the same job that I currently had, but Reach was so much bigger of a firm that it was a huge promotion.

There was absolutely no reason to say no.

Just.

Surely Weston had more qualified employees already on staff, waiting for advancement. If not, there were hundreds of people dying for a job like this. People who already lived in New York. People with much more experience.

"But why *me*?" I asked as I suddenly stood, pushing my desk chair with enough force that it went rolling toward the wall. I looked after it apologetically. I didn't mean to seem angry. I wasn't angry. I was confused. When Weston and I had been wrapped in a haze of lust, the smell of sex still clinging to the air, these kinds of overtures made sense. But now?

"Oh. Ohhhh." Ashley drew the word out, finally understanding what I was really asking. "Because he wants to have a relationship with you. Obviously. Duh."

That's what I had been afraid she'd say. I shook my head. "That can't possibly be true. It's not what either of us wanted." At least, that's what I'd thought. Had I been wrong?

I didn't know anymore.

Ashley wouldn't let that slide. Leaning back in her chair, she crossed her arms over her chest and furrowed her brow. "Why did you even go to bed with him if you didn't want anything out of it?"

"Is that something I have to actually explain?" I turned away from her and busied myself with straightening my computer screen so it was facing the right way again. It was easier to think without her reading into my every expression.

"Well, I know why *I* would go to bed with him," she said to my profile. "He's hot as fuck and has enough money to buy the whole state of New York, but as long as I've known you, you've never been as superficial as I am. You're also not into flings, so yes, you must explain."

With a sigh, I straightened and considered her question. I knew the answer—I just hadn't had to put it into words before. "I went to bed with him because of exactly what you said," I began. "He's charming and attractive and nearly impossible to resist. But, okay, it was also because he was an unclosed door. I had a huge crush on him once upon a time. He stood for everything I once almost had. It was nice to finally be able to see what things could have been like."

Also, secretly there was a part of me that had wondered if a night—or a weekend—with Weston could erase what had happened with Donovan.

Instead it had magnified it.

Ashley's lips curled into a half smile, as if my answer had somehow been a victory for her. "Now that you know, how are you not dying for more?"

"Because it was just a weekend," I said, crossing to retrieve my chair. "He's a playboy. He's moved on."

"Except he *hasn't* moved on. He's still thinking about you three months later. He's thinking about you so much that he called you and offered you a freaking amazing job at a freaking amazing firm. How can you be questioning anything about this?"

It was exactly the kind of thing I'd dreamed about when I'd gone to Harvard. The job. The pay. The boy.

I rolled the chair to my desk and paused, my hands still gripping the seat back. "Do you think a *yes* to the job automatically means a *yes* to a relationship?"

"Do you not want to say *yes* to a relationship?" Ashley's

tone said she didn't understand why anyone wouldn't want a relationship with Weston King, but she was trying to.

The truth was that I was trying to understand myself too.

I sank into the chair and faced Ashley. "I had fun with him. I really did. But that's not enough to build a relationship on. I don't want to get out there and find out that we aren't compatible and then what if it affects our working together? I'd be alone in a new city with no job, no friends and then what?"

"Sabrina, you need to get out of your head and into your life. Seriously." She reached across the desk and put her hands over one of mine. "If the relationship doesn't work out, then fine. You're both grownups. You can still work together; I know it. If I'm wrong, you'll find another job. It's time for you to move on. You're not happy here right now. You said it yourself just today. And every day for a month before this. I don't want to lose you, but you're more important than our friendship, and dammit, this is what you want."

It *was* what I wanted. Not just the job, but Weston. A guy who was charming and sexy and not Donovan.

I shifted my hand out from under Ashley's so that I could squeeze hers. "You're right."

She seemed surprised to have won the battle so easily. "About which part?"

"All of it. Except me being more important than our friendship." I swallowed past the ball that had suddenly lodged in my throat. "You're right about all the rest."

"Damn straight I am." Ashley slammed her hand on the table—a tactic meant to divert me from noticing her eyes brimming with tears, I suspected. "Now pick up that phone, call the guy back and tell him *yes* before I do it for you."

As soon as the decision was made, I knew it was right. It

settled everywhere in my body, wrapped around me comfortably like the favorite blanket I burrowed in on cold nights. I'd spent too long yearning for the life I'd been meant for—it was time to go out and get it.

And maybe Weston would fit into my future as more than just a boss.

But Donovan...

He lived across the world, but it was his company too. His name would be on invoices and letterhead. He'd be present in my life from here on out in some way or another. There'd be no escaping him now.

Still, I picked up the phone, called *the guy,* and when Weston answered, I told him, "Yes."

NINE

"I can't believe you're only two and a half hours away!" my sister exclaimed for the millionth time since I'd first told her about my move to New York. Now, three weeks later, I was finally settled in the city that would be my new home.

I shifted my cell phone to my shoulder so I could dig in my purse for my credit card. I was in a cab, quickly approaching my destination, and I wanted to be ready to pay when we arrived. "I have your bedroom all set up and ready whenever you can get away from school to come visit," I said to Audrey while searching. "Or I could come there. But you don't have an extra bed."

"And you're going to be swamped with the new job. I'll come visit you. When do you start?"

"Officially, tomorrow, but I'm headed into the office now to meet with Weston so he can show me around. He wanted me to meet a few people beforehand so it wouldn't be overwhelming on my first day." *Found it!* I laid my card on my lap and rubbed over the raised letters of my name as we drove through Midtown. I was anxious and fidgety and had been ever since I'd arrived in New York two days before.

I hadn't seen Weston yet. I hadn't even talked to him directly since the offer. It had all been through email, most of which were routed through his assistant, Roxie, who was helping arrange everything. Today was the day I'd know for sure what he expected for our future.

It was almost four—was it too early to drink?

"He's having you come in at the end of day which means he's probably planning to take you out afterward."

"Audrey..." I groaned. "Don't jump to conclusions." Of course I'd thought of that already, but her excitement wasn't helping. I needed her to minimize this—not make it bigger.

"But you have to be prepared," she went on, unaware of the distress she was causing me. "What are you wearing? Is it day to evening convertible?"

"A plum sheath dress. It's professional." It also had a slit that went up to my mid-thigh. "But yes, it would work for evening wear."

"Eeep! I'm so excited for you!"

"That's awesome." I closed my eyes and waited for the most recent wave of nausea to pass. "Because I'm a bundle of freaking nerves. And I can't figure out where I packed my Xanax, and I put my hair up because I've been pulling at it so much I'm sure I'm going to go bald, and now I have nothing to calm myself, and—"

Laughter interrupted my lament. "Oh god, you crack me up."

"I'm glad you think this is funny." The cab turned a corner and immediately pulled over to the curb.

"It's not my fault that you're crazy," Audrey said.

"If I'm crazy, you're crazy," I said hurriedly. "I'm here. Gotta go." I hung up without waiting for her to say goodbye, paid the driver, and climbed out. Then there it was—King-Kincaid Town Center.

I craned my neck upward to scan the length of the skyscraper. Sixty floors rose above me, and while many different businesses leased space in the building owned by King-Kincaid Financial (the corporation Weston's and Donovan's fathers owned together), the top several floors housed Reach, Inc.

Soon I'd be standing up there, taking my place where I belonged.

I could barely even look that high.

There weren't many people inside the lobby of the Town Center, probably because of the time of the day. It made it easy to find the security desk where I was required to check in to get to the sixtieth floor. The guard, an African-American woman named Fran, called up to get my clearance.

"Okay, you're clear," she said, letting me through to the elevators behind her.

"Was that Weston King?" It was possible I was too eager. But I was a stranger in a foreign land, and Weston was the only person I knew here.

"I don't know who it was. Some woman with an accent."

Roxie, I thought. Of course.

Sure enough, it was Roxie, Weston's assistant from Hungary, who met me when I arrived at the top floor.

"Did your ears pop?" she asked after handing my purse and jacket to the secretary at the front desk. "I keep gum in case you need."

I'd talked to Roxie enough on the phone to feel comfortable with her already. Her accent wasn't thick, but occasionally her word choices reflected that English was definitely her second language. "I think I'm okay," I said, working my jaw back and forth. "But, yeah, I wasn't expecting that."

"It's the speed. It shoot past all those floors. Just like going in an airplane. Come this way." She took off briskly down the hall.

"This floor is for executive offices," she said as we walked past several glass-walled suites. Each of them had a waiting space outside, a secretary at a desk, sometimes a couch. The offices themselves were expansive—some half the size of my apartment—all with floor-to-ceiling windows.

"Your office will be here too," Roxie said, and I almost tripped. She chuckled. "Not one of the fancy ones, I tell you that now. But pretty good. Better than mine. I let Weston show you that. He wants to give you the tour."

We passed a bigger office then; this time the walls were mirrored. *Smart windows*, I guessed. The kind that, at the press of a button, the glass changes so that the person inside can look out and no one can look in. It was probably Weston's office.

I battled another wave of nausea at the thought of being so near to him. So near to confronting what kind of relationship we were going to have.

"Meanwhile," Roxie said, "I'm supposed to take you to the upper lounge to wait for him. He's running just a few minutes late."

We'd reached the end of the hall now where four steps led up to two double doors and another area sectioned off with mirrors—or smart windows—for walls. I followed my guide into a large room with modern teal sofas, black lounge chairs, and the most breathtaking view of the city I'd ever seen.

"Is this where you entertain new clients?" I asked, looking around at the liquor cabinet and the coffee cart. There was also a full-size kitchen and a flat-screen TV fastened to one of the glass walls.

"And new employees," Roxie said with a grin. "You will see enough of me over the next few days. I will set you up with Human Resources and get you a security card and a secretary and everything else you need before you start work on projects next week. This afternoon, you enjoy the view. Mr. King be here soon."

I thanked her and promised to have Weston show me where her desk was before I left for the night so I could find her in the morning if she didn't find me first. After she was gone, I walked over to the windows and drank in the scene. The Town Center was high enough that it had an unblocked view of downtown Manhattan, Brooklyn, and beyond.

Giddiness surged through me, starting like a pinprick at my center and moving out through my veins in all directions until even my fingers and toes felt warm.

I was really here.

I made it.

It wasn't the way I thought it would be, but in the end, it still came out of my time at Harvard. I'd always known that connections made the difference in a career, and here I was. Finally. At the top of the world, looking out.

I couldn't stop grinning.

"It's incredible, isn't it?" a male voice came from behind me.

Still smiling, I glanced up and caught his reflection in the window.

And everything disappeared.

The world that had buzzed below, the beautiful scene, the excitement that had unfurled through my body—all of it evaporated and all that existed in its place was a pale, hollow shell of myself and the man in the perfectly tailored suit behind me.

I turned to look at him directly. Our gazes smashed together, and my legs nearly fell out from under me.

"Donovan," I rasped. It was a miracle that I managed to find enough voice to say that much.

And there was so much more that had to be said. So much more that I hadn't prepared for. Which was ridiculous since I'd talked to him so many times in my head over the years, practiced so many conversations, but never did he show up out of the blue looking so dastardly handsome in a dark gray three-piece suit, his face rugged with scruff, his eyes hazel and earnest despite the playful smirk on his lips.

I opened my mouth to say something, but nothing came out. I wasn't even sure how to breathe anymore.

He broke our gaze to nod out the window at the skyline, walking toward me as he said, "I'm sure you found the Empire."

Though his focus was now on the scenery, I didn't take my eyes off him as he approached. He didn't stop until he was right beside me. So close our shoulders would touch if I coughed. Tension ran off him like foam spilling over from a mug of beer. Good tension. Bad tension. I wasn't sure if there was a difference when it came to Donovan.

Which was why I was screwed if he was here.

Why the hell *was* he here?

"I thought you were in Tokyo." I couldn't stop staring at

him. He'd gotten more refined with age, and rougher at the same time. His hair was short and his curls gone, giving him a polished look he lacked before. The lines by his eyes were more defined and his expression seemed harder than I'd remembered. It made him sexier.

As if he was a man who needed to be sexier than the one I knew.

"I came back two months ago," he said offhandedly. "That's it right there." He leaned his face in close to mine as he pointed to the famous structure. "Do you see it?"

Fuck if I cared about the Empire. I was in Donovan Kincaid's orbit. What else was there in the world?

"And that's the One World Trade Center in line behind it." He reached around me to point over my other shoulder, caging me in against the glass without touching me at all.

God, I couldn't just smell his cologne, I could also smell *him*. The musky scent of his maleness, and even after a decade, my body reacted against my will. My nipples budded, and my panties felt slick. Every part of me tuned to him despite how my mind cried to resist him.

"Over there's the Brooklyn Bridge." His breath skated against my neck, hot, but I had to fight not to shiver.

He knew what he was doing. He had to.

"Donovan..." My voice trailed off, drawing out his name when what I really meant to say was *please*.

Please *what*? I didn't even know. I wanted relief. I wanted to cry, and saying his name was as close as I could get.

In the window, I watched as his reflection finally looked away from the goddamn Brooklyn Bridge and stared down at me. His eyes closed momentarily.

"Leave it to Weston to be the one to bring you here," he said quietly.

I inhaled sharply.

But that was all the time I had to process before Weston burst into the room. "You two found each other!" he said excitedly.

Donovan and I turned simultaneously to face our intruder.

"I suppose we did," Donovan said, meeting my eyes once more, punctuating his words.

Had we found each other? What did he mean? What did *any of this* mean?

Then Donovan was gone, our connection broken when he crossed the room toward the liquor cabinet.

Weston hurried toward me, taking his place in my focus. "Sorry, I was running late. Did you find the building okay?"

"Yes. I took a cab." My voice was thin and unsteady, but I forced a smile and hoped he didn't notice.

He put his hand on my arm. It was friendly. *More* than friendly was the way his fingers stroked my elbow. "And Roxie—?"

"Was very welcoming." I looked down at his fingers then up at his face. He was letting me know. About him. About us. That he expected us to be a thing. And I did too. Except—

"Sabrina?" Donovan called, making my heart trip in my chest. "Can I get you something to drink?"

I glanced over at him because I couldn't *not* look at him when he spoke. Couldn't not take notice. He was already mixing something with gin. "Uh. Whatever you're making for yourself. Thank you."

"How was the move?" Weston asked eagerly, tucking a

stray lock of hair behind my ear. "Are you all settled? I've been so anxious for you to be here."

"It was..." I could barely think. Could barely string words into coherent sentences. My attention was halfway across the room on the figure now with his back toward me. Every touch of Weston's felt like a betrayal, which made no sense at all.

Donovan wasn't even supposed to be here.

I shook my head slightly and forced my attention on what Weston had asked. "The moving company was excellent. Thank you for suggesting them. They did great work. I haven't quite figured out where they put everything yet, but I'm definitely settling in."

There. I could do this. Cinch.

"That was Roxie, I think, who arranged the movers. And your apartment?"

The two-bedroom condo in Hell's Kitchen had been the best surprise. Weston had helped find that as well. Or Roxie. The floors were hardwood, recently stained. The kitchen was remodeled. The building was secure and being able to have an extra bedroom for Audrey was the cherry on top. "It's perfect. Even better than the pictures you sent. I can't believe how much time you spent on—"

Suddenly, Donovan was beside us handing out drinks. "Weston—gin and tonic. I presumed." The tumbler he handed me was something different. Golden amber and unmixed. "I made a scotch for myself. Would you prefer a gin and tonic as well?"

His fingers grazed mine as I took the glass, and I nearly dropped it from the electric shock that went through me at his touch.

"No. The scotch is fine." I'd accept a glass of bleach if it meant Donovan would leave me alone. Because that's what I needed more than anything.

Accepting the scotch at least got him to return to the liquor cabinet to retrieve his own drink. I gathered any strength I could find in the absence of his proximity and redirected my attention where it belonged. On Weston.

"Anyway, as I was saying. Thank you, Weston, for all you did to get me moved in. And for finding me such a wonderful place to live." I brought the tumbler up to my mouth to take a sip.

"I can't take credit for the apartment either. Donovan owns the building."

"Oh," I choked, on the burn of the liquor, maybe, but also at this new information. The space I'd slept in, bathed in, undressed in—it belonged to *him*. Why did that make my pussy ache like it did?

Weston patted my back. "Okay?"

"Yeah. I just..." I said when I recovered, looking again toward Donovan. "I didn't know."

Was that why the price had been so affordable? Why would he do that for me?

Donovan crossed to us, his own drink in hand. "Why would you know? I'm glad you've found it acceptable."

Did he know? About Weston and me? He *had* to know. He didn't seem to care.

"More than acceptable. It's." I cut off. Did *Weston* know?

So many questions and not enough answers.

They were both standing in front of me now, staring at me. Weston to my right, Donovan to my left, like a real life game of This or That, and of course the choice was *This*. It was the *only* choice. Practically. For my sanity. The other one wasn't even an actual option.

And yet my body pulled traitorously toward *That*.

I spun away from both of them. "I'm sorry. I'm flustered." I took a seat on one of the couches. Two lovers. One room. Too much. "I guess I'm still in a bit of shock about all of this." I took another sip of scotch. It went down easier this time, warm and comforting.

Until I realized what an idiot I must look like.

"I'm making a bad impression, I'm sure." Here I was, determined to prove I belonged in this world, and I'd fucked it up in the first thirty minutes. Over a guy. Over *two* guys.

"Not at all," Weston said, perching on the arm next to me. "That's why I wanted you to have a chance to come in before you actually started. You're not on show."

That was easy for him to say. He'd never had to justify why he deserved to be president of his own company. He just had to be it.

"I don't know about that," I chuckled. "A true professional is always on show."

"Well..." Weston trailed off.

Donovan unbuttoned his jacket as he sank into an armchair and crossed one leg over the other. "That's what you left Harvard to go learn at that little college of yours? What was it called again?"

The insult burrowed past any armor I'd put on, under my skin, into my very blood. As if he could read my mind, see my innermost fears. As if his only goal was to expose them.

And suddenly, as vividly as my body remembered how it longed for Donovan Kincaid, I remembered how much I also hated him.

Weston caught the dig as well and threw his partner a warning glare. He followed it with a slow scan up my body. "I happen to like what I see," he said, his meaning clear.

Donovan swirled his drink, his expression smug. "Too bad you won't be the one she'll be reporting to."

My throat went dry. Was he implying that I'd be reporting to *him*? Was he *staying*? I had a brief flashback to the class he taught in college, the way he jerked me around. The way he fucked me against the bookshelf in his office.

"Hey," Weston chided. "We haven't decided how that's going to work yet. For now, it stands as it is." There was subtext in his tone that suggested there was more to the situation.

I was feeling dizzy, and I didn't think it was just from the alcohol. "I'm confused. Whom do I report to?"

Weston rested his hand on my collarbone. "It's me. Donovan's just being an ass."

I would have been relieved if the more important question didn't remain lingering. "But Donovan *is* staying? Here? Instead of Tokyo?" I was such a coward that I couldn't even ask him directly. Couldn't even look at him.

"Yes. Thank god. We've gotten too big to run with just two presidents. So he's taking over management and finance. I'm still in charge of marketing."

My gut dropped, but my chest rose, and I felt like I was sinking and soaring all at once. He was staying. He was here, and he was staying, and nothing in my world would ever be the same.

Carefully, I dared to peek in his direction.

He was already looking at me, as if waiting for me to meet his gaze.

"Oh!" he said, his eyes sparkling. "While we're on the topic, Weston...have you told Sabrina about the party on Saturday?"

Then we'd both play this game—talking about one another as if the other weren't present.

"No," Weston said flatly. "I didn't think that her attendance was necessary."

I sat up straighter. Intrigued.

"But that's not fair. I'm sure she'd want to come if she were given the opportunity." Donovan wouldn't stop looking at me. It was bait.

So I took it. "Of course. What's the celebration?"

"Weston's engagement."

TEN

For several uncomfortable seconds, everything stood completely still. All eyes were on me.

"Congratulations," I said finally, breaking the hush. My voice sounded slightly higher than usual, but other than that, I was pretty sure I pulled off calm and reserved.

Inside, however, I was dying. Weston was *engaged*? What the ever-living fuck? Obviously, he was an asshole. And Donovan was even worse, trying to needle me about it, and no way was I letting him get to me.

"Donovan, you shithead," Weston snapped under his breath.

"Oh. She didn't know," Donovan said in a way that made me suspect he knew very well I hadn't known all along. Shithead was right. Add goddamn motherfucker to the list.

"No, I didn't know. But congratulations seem to be in order all the same." With a tight smile, I scooted over casually so that

Weston's hand fell off my shoulder. This was fine. Totally fine. Just had to keep breathing.

Weston looked from me to his friend. "I told you I hadn't told her."

Donovan waved him off. "That was two weeks ago. I assumed you would have told her by *now*. How could you bring her here without fully explaining the circumstances? That doesn't seem very fair to Sabrina now, does it?"

"Hey. I'm right here."

Both men turned toward me at once.

"I should have told you," Weston said at the same time Donovan said, "He should have told you."

"Told me that you were engaged? You're telling me now. I can't wait to hear all about her, Weston." I stood up. "I'm just going to refill my drink."

"It's not how it seems." Weston ran after me, fumbling to help me with the scotch.

"It's really not. Just wait until he explains." Donovan had moved his ankle to his knee, the relaxed position suggesting he was enjoying this far more than he should.

I tried to ignore him—as if that were possible—and trained my focus on Weston, keeping my voice as even as I could. "How is there any way other than what it seems? You didn't even have a girlfriend when..." I trailed off, glancing back at Donovan. Even if he knew that I'd spent a weekend in his partner's bed, it felt somehow wrong to acknowledge it in front of him.

Anyway, I didn't need to. "Was that not true?"

"It was true," Weston insisted. "I *still* don't have a girlfriend."

"No, you have a fiancée," I said.

"A *fake* fiancée," he corrected.

"A *fake* fiancée? Right."

Donovan chuckled behind us. "This just gets better and better."

I shot him a nasty glare, but his smile made things worse. It poked at me like a boy with a stick torturing a trapped animal. Jesus, why did he have to be here?

I took a large swallow of my scotch.

Weston put his hands on my upper arms. "Let me explain."

"Don't." I jerked away, louder than I meant to. Taking a breath, I tried again. "Don't touch me. Please."

He dropped his hands, then, seeming not to know what to do with them, stuck them in his pockets.

Again, I glanced toward Donovan. Was this why he'd come here today? To drop this bomb? To play with me now in the same ways he had in the past? To see me humiliated and disgraced?

Well, I refused to let him see me like that. I lifted my chin. I was resolute. He wouldn't see me down.

He met my stare and held it. Whatever he saw—my determination, maybe—caused his expression to sober.

"I should really let you two work this out on your own," he said, setting his empty glass on the table next to him and standing.

"Thank you," Weston said.

"Though I won't say I'm not tempted to turn on the security feed and listen in."

"Fuck you."

"Kidding." Donovan buttoned his jacket. "Leaving," he called over his shoulder as he brushed past me, shocking me with a jolt of electricity that made me shiver.

I heard him leaving. Heard him open the doors. Dread sank inside me like a lead ball. It was strange and sudden and unexplainable. I couldn't attach it to current circumstances or to anything at all except the fact that the ghost of my darkest thoughts was slipping out of my realm.

I spun around.

"Donovan!" I called out before I could stop myself.

He halted halfway out the door and looked toward me, but I clammed up. I had no idea what else to say to him. I didn't want him to stay necessarily; I just didn't want him to go. Not now. Not so soon. Not when there was still everything left unsaid between us.

Weston watched us curiously, his eyes darting from me to Donovan then back to me.

It was Donovan who filled the silence. "You were right, Weston," he said, his gaze looking nowhere but my face. "She *has* grown up." Then he was gone.

Had I? Grown up? I didn't feel like it. I felt like I was still seventeen—naïve, overwhelmed, and pulled apart by someone I'd escaped years ago. Physically escaped, anyway. But here, in the present, in the flesh, he was still the magnet he'd always been, his tug on me as strong as ever.

And Weston, the man I'd thought could protect me from my sick attractions, was *engaged*?

"Okay," I said, turning back from the doors that Donovan had closed behind him. I folded my arms across my chest and gave Weston the sternest glare I owned. "You better start fucking explaining."

Weston took a deep breath in. "It's going to sound like a story."

"As all stories do."

"But it's not. I'm not making it up. You have to believe me."

With Donovan out of the room, I no longer felt the need to pretend to tolerate the bullshit. "I can't believe you if you don't tell me."

"Right, right." He ran both his hands through his hair, leaving a mess that somehow made him look hotter.

This was the first time I'd looked at him since he'd walked in, actually. *Really* looked at him, anyway. He was wearing a navy blue suit that accentuated his eyes. His face was smooth, even this late, and I wondered if he'd shaved midday. He was devastatingly handsome. So easy to look at.

Funny how I'd forgotten when Donovan was in the room.

But I didn't want to think about *him*. "Well?"

"Do you know who Elizabeth Dyson is?" Weston said, surprising me with his turn of conversation.

I decided to go with it. "The daughter of the media mogul?"

"Dell Dyson. That's right." Weston walked over to the counter and set his mostly finished drink down. "While it's not their main focus, Dyson Media has an advertising subsidiary that is especially large in the European market."

"I didn't realize that."

"They're our biggest competitor overseas."

It was both embarrassing and irritating that I didn't know this. But I belonged here, dammit. I wasn't letting this stupid little fact make me feel out of place.

I racked my brain to try to think of anything else I remembered about Dell Dyson or his company, hoping to prove myself. "Didn't he die recently?"

Weston nodded, slowly returning to me. "Last year. Since his death—before it even—we've been looking to buy out the advertising portion of his company. Dell had shown some interest, but now that he's dead, we have to purchase through Elizabeth."

"Let me guess. She's not interested."

"No, she is."

He was almost to me and yet not any closer to an explanation. "I'm not seeing how this is—"

"I'm getting there." He stopped, two feet away from me, and stuck his hands in his pockets. "The problem is that Elizabeth is twenty-five. Her inheritance doesn't give her full ownership of the company until she turns twenty-nine. Or until she marries."

"Or until she marries," I echoed slowly, everything becoming blindingly clear. "I see." I sank down onto the couch. "How archaic."

"Elizabeth was as desperate to get control of the company as we were to buy her out," he continued. "It was a win-win situation."

"So. You're engaged."

"I'm engaged."

I tested the taste of the words, the sound of them, using them to poke at my emotions. How did I *feel* about this? Definitely disappointed. It was a change in plans, and while I wasn't a rigid person, I'd come to New York under one pretense and this was going to take some adjusting.

Weston seemed to sense this, and he gave me a minute before going on.

"The wedding is in two and a half months," he said eventually. "After we've been married a month or so, we'll get an annulment, we'll buy the advertising subsidiary, and Reach, Inc. will automatically move up a couple ranks in terms of competitive power. We're still a young company. This kind of merger is important for us."

I leaned back into the seat and sighed. It wasn't the kind of business move that I'd necessarily pursue, but I wasn't an aggressive player. Which was why I preferred marketing to sales and operations. It didn't mean I didn't recognize the benefit of a merger such as the one Weston was proposing.

"I get it. I do." I sprung up from my seat. "But why did it have to be *you*? Couldn't it be someone else? Didn't she have a boyfriend or someone else she could marry to get her fortune?" Why did she have to take *my* boyfriend?

Not that Weston *was* my boyfriend. Just.

I was bitter. I couldn't help it.

"No boyfriends. The girl's a real piece of work. I don't think she even has friends. She's kind of..." He rubbed his forehead, seeming to search for the word he was looking for. "A spoiled brat."

Somehow I had a feeling that wasn't what he'd first intended to say. "That sounds fun. Are you sleeping with her?"

His eyes widened only slightly. "No, I'm not."

"I'm sorry." I hung my head, ashamed of the question. "That wasn't any of my business."

"No. It's fair."

Honestly, I wasn't even sure I cared. So what if Weston was sleeping with her? The only reason it bothered me was because it meant he wasn't available to be my armor. I needed a relationship with him so I could stay safe from my thoughts and my feelings. Especially now.

I paced along the window. "If this is all just to get her inheritance, why don't you go to the courthouse? Why an engagement? Why a party?"

"Believe it or not, her inheritance forbids elopement. And Elizabeth has a cousin on the board of Dyson Media who is ready to contest anything to stop her from getting control of the company before her twenty-ninth birthday. So. We have to make it real."

His tone of voice said the situation was making him miserable. I threw him a bone. "That sounds terrible."

"It is. Thank you!"

"But not too terrible." I faced him, sternly. "You still chose this. I'm guessing you weren't forced into this. I don't feel too bad for you, Weston."

"You're right. And I accept my fate."

I wanted to keep scolding him, but it was hard when he was taking his blows so willingly. And he was my boss. My *new* boss. There was probably a line that I didn't want to cross. Somewhere. Hell if I knew where it was at this point.

I pivoted and walked along the window, and the view made me think of Donovan. "What did...everyone else think of this plan?" Why it mattered, I didn't know.

"Who? You mean Donovan and Nate? Those guys?" He waited until I nodded. "It was Donovan's idea. Everyone else thought it was awesome, though I think they're taking bets on how long I can last without getting laid."

I snapped my head toward him. "You're not—? With *anyone*?"

"What did you say about a true professional always being on show?"

Weston King not getting laid was huge news. That man had a voracious sexual appetite. I knew from experience.

And now he looked truly miserable. I almost felt sorry for him. *Almost.*

I leaned my back against the glass. "How many people know about this?"

"Just the guys. Elizabeth, of course. And, now, you." He said *you* preciously, tenderly, and I realized how much trust it took for him to let me in on his secret.

"Well. Thank you for telling me."

"I had to. I couldn't let you think I wasn't interested anymore." He took a few steps, and then he was right in front of me. Carefully, he ran a hand along my upper arm. "I should have told you before you got here, but I was afraid you wouldn't have come."

His touch felt wrong, his fingers cold on my skin, but I didn't pull away. "I didn't take this job because I thought something was going to happen between us, Weston. I did wonder where things would go, but it wasn't a condition of my acceptance."

"Good. I'm glad about that." He used his other hand to tip my chin up to look him in the eyes. "Does that mean in the future, when I'm single again, there might be a chance?"

I did the mental math. He'd said two and a half months until the wedding, another month or so before he was free. "I can't wait for you. Are you asking me to wait for you?"

"No. That's not fair. I'm just saying that if you're still available..."

"Then we'll see what happens, I guess." With my track record, I'd still be single in five months. Then, we'd see. "Meanwhile, you *are* engaged. Whether it's real or not, and I can't be doing...this."

"Doing what?"

I looked down at his hands that were now both on my shoulders. "This. Letting you touch me. You have to stop."

"I know." He dropped his hands to his sides and took a step back. "I'm sorry, Sabrina. About all of this. But I am glad you're here."

It sounded believable enough, but the offer paid so well, and he'd gone to a lot of trouble to bring me to New York. Had it really just been to give me a job?

I cocked my head. "Tell me something—when did you decide to hire me? What was the timeline of all of this?"

He leaned a shoulder against the glass. "I started working on hiring you the minute you left town. I didn't know what might happen between us, but I knew you belonged here. It seemed like fate that we were losing our director of marketing anyway. There was just a delay with his transfer. Then all of this Dyson bullshit delayed things further."

So Weston had already planned to hire me before he decided to marry someone else. At Donovan's suggestion. Had Donovan known Weston wanted to hire me?

It was stupid to wonder if there was a connection between the two, but still I had to know. "When did you tell Donovan you wanted to hire me?"

My skin began to tingle before he even answered.

"I called him the minute you walked out my door."

I was glad I still had some scotch in my glass. I finished it off in one gulp. But the sweet burn couldn't consume the seemingly obvious truth—that even though it had been Weston who got me here, it had been Donovan who had made sure I'd been single when I arrived.

ELEVEN

Roxie grabbed two flutes of champagne off a tray as it passed by and handed me one. "You've had a lot thrown at you this week. It's a shame you have to be here on a weekend night."

Since my initial meeting at Reach on Tuesday, I'd spent the rest of the week coordinating with HR, getting acquainted with the corporation's operations, and setting up my office. I'd barely seen Weston. I hadn't seen Donovan at all.

Now I was dressed to the nines in a long green satin slip dress that clung to every curve of my body, my hair pinned loosely at my nape, hiding in a corner at The Sky Launch so I could attend Weston's engagement party. Not at all how I'd expected to spend my first Saturday in New York.

"It's not that bad," I said, lying through my teeth. The party, Weston had told me, had been pulled together without much notice, yet there still seemed to be four to five hundred people spread across the dance floor of the rented nightclub. I supposed that's what it was like to be part of the rich and elite—popularity was part of the package.

Honestly, there were so many guests my attendance would probably have gone unnoticed. I wasn't sure why I'd come.

Yes, I was.

Because Donovan would notice if I didn't come, and I didn't want him thinking I was avoiding the event. I didn't want him to assume Weston's upcoming wedding meant something to me, that I was hurt or nursing wounds. I wasn't. I was there to prove a point, and I didn't plan on leaving until I did.

Not that Donovan had bothered to show up.

Maybe the whole thing was a waste of time after all.

I took a swallow from my champagne glass and tried not to think about how the green of my dress perfectly matched the green of his eyes.

"Are you ready for Monday?" Roxie asked.

"I think so." I'd been poring over the project files in all my spare time at home so I'd be prepared, barely sleeping. The movers had unpacked most of my belongings, but I hadn't touched any of the personal items that I'd asked them to leave for me. "I've made sure I'm up to date on everything the team is working on."

"Be careful you don't burn out before you even start," Roxie warned in her brusque Eastern European way.

"I won't. *Mom*." I was teasing, but I hoped she could tell I appreciated it. Not only because she was one of the only people I knew in the city, but also because it had been so long since I'd had anyone mother me. It was a nice change after all the years of raising my little sister.

She smiled and glanced over at her husband who was waiting a few feet away. After downing the rest of her drink in three long gulps, she said, "Frank hate these things. I would stay longer if he didn't nag me to go. You be okay?" She seemed genuinely concerned about leaving me alone.

"Yes. I'm fine. I promise." I could see her husband tapping his foot impatiently. "I'm just going to wish the couple well, and then I'm going too."

It took a bit more reassurance, but finally I convinced her I'd be all right by myself.

After she left, I realized that standing in the corner felt more awkward alone. I looked around the nightclub. There was music playing, but it wasn't the kind for dancing. All the guests were standing around in groups talking and munching on fancy appetizers. I didn't recognize anyone. The few people I'd met at the office had already said hello and left. It was getting late, and Donovan still hadn't arrived. There was no point in my sticking around. Either I needed to seek out Weston and give him my well wishes—the thought made me groan inwardly—or else I just needed to go.

I sighed and finished my drink. Then I placed it on a tray as a waiter walked past, and that's when I felt it—felt *him*. Donovan. I didn't turn around, but I could tell he was close behind me. I knew it as sure as I knew anything. His presence was as heavy and thick as molasses, and any intention I had of leaving was immediately thrown out the window. It would be impossible to leave now. I couldn't wade through molasses in these heels.

But where was he? What was he waiting for?

Seconds passed by like hours, and finally he came up next to me, leaving no more than three inches, two maybe, between our shoulders. "The way that dress fits you..." he said, his voice husky. "I see now why Weston hired you."

The grit in his tone felt like the perfect pumice stone, smoothing edges of me that had been rough for as long as I could remember.

But his actual words were a slap in the face.

Another fucking dig at my qualifications. As if the only reason I deserved to be at Reach was because I looked good in an evening gown.

And then there was the other reason his statement was problematic. Because it was *wrong*, and—even though it did things to my insides when he'd said it, made my belly tighten deep and low—I couldn't let it slide by without addressing it. Once upon a time I would have let rich boys get away with shit like that. I had let rich boys get away with much worse. Not anymore.

I spun to face him, to tell him off and felt the wind slammed out of my lungs. He was so damn handsome in his tuxedo with satin lapels, his bow tie sharp and centered, his face still dusted with scruff. I nearly forgot what I was going to say.

I dragged my focus up from the tempting curve of his lips to his eyes, which were more green than brown tonight, and swallowed. "I'm not sure if you meant that as a compliment, but I *am* sure it's sexual harassment."

Donovan's mouth lifted into a slow grin. "Oh, but sexual harassment used to be our thing."

The acknowledgement of the past we'd shared knocked me off-balance. Made me dizzy. I hadn't expected it, and it was a point for him in a game I wasn't even sure how to play.

It was, on the other hand, the opening I needed to say the things—all the things, *any* of the things—if I could just figure out which to lead with. If I could just figure out how to speak at all.

But before I could manage to stop gaping like an idiot, Donovan leaned close and said quietly, "Close your mouth, Sabrina. Though I love imagining ways to fill it, we're about to have company." He straightened. Louder, he said, "Weston, Elizabeth. The stars of the show."

My jaw clamped shut, my cheeks reddening as if I were harboring a flame inside my mouth.

In a daze, I twisted to find Weston with his arm wrapped around a young redhead with bright eyes and a big smile.

"Elizabeth, you know Donovan," he said formally. "And this is Sabrina Lind, our new director of marketing strategy."

"Delightful to meet you." She nodded to me while Weston glanced covertly around us. "It's so fascinating to see how my love—"

Seeming to be satisfied with what he saw, he cut her off. "No one's watching. And Sabrina knows."

"Oh thank god." Elizabeth Dyson dropped Weston's arm. "If I have to gush about him a minute longer I might have to throw up."

Donovan gazed admiringly at the bride-to-be. "Elizabeth, I think you and I might get along better than I once thought."

So it appeared the newly engaged pair weren't getting on so smashingly. Even still ruffled, I found this amusing. *Just desserts.*

Okay, maybe I was a little bitter.

"I told you, Kincaid, this deal was really better suited for you and me. I can't believe you turned down the offer." Elizabeth flirted openly with Donovan, seeming not to notice Weston's exaggerated roll of the eyes.

"You were up for the nomination of groom?" I couldn't meet Donovan's eyes as I asked, and I found myself looking down, which wasn't helpful because I ended up glancing toward his crotch.

Quickly, I looked back at Weston. Then at Elizabeth in case looking at Weston made it seem like I was pining for Weston. Then at my shoes in case it looked like I was trying too hard when I looked at her and because I didn't want anyone to see how I reacted to Donovan's response to my question.

I'd second-guessed myself several times in the last few days about the revelation that he had arranged the whole fake marriage and whether or not it had anything to do with me. It was easier on my nerves to think I was being ridiculous, but if it didn't have anything to do with me, then why hadn't he volunteered to play the part himself?

"No one would ever believe I'd get married," he said dismissively. "Besides, Weston looks much better on Elizabeth's arm."

I looked up to see Weston shoot daggers in Donovan's general direction. Then, with an overly bright smile, he addressed me. "Sabrina, you're absolutely stunning."

"Thank you." I eyed Donovan, indicating how a compliment was supposed to be given and caught him eyeing me with what I guessed was supposed to say *See, what I mean?*

Elizabeth surveyed me from head to toe and nodded approvingly. "She is gorgeous, Kincaid. You make quite an attractive couple."

"We're not a couple," I said quickly at the same time that Weston said, "They're not a couple."

Weston and I exchanged glances. I knew what it looked like —like we were still holding out for each other, and maybe that's why he'd rushed to clarify I wasn't with Donovan, but it hadn't been why *I'd* rushed to clarify.

I'd rushed because there was no way, no how, I could get mixed up with Donovan again. Not now. Not ever.

"You're here alone?" Elizabeth asked Donovan, her eyebrow raised in surprise.

"I'm not."

My muscles tensed in...what? Like hell I was jealous. But I was *something*. It hadn't occurred to me that Donovan would have a date. He might even have a girlfriend. Or a fiancée of his own. And if any of that were the case, why was he playing around with me? But why had he *ever* played around with me?

I was confused. That's what I was. And irritated.

"Sabrina is from Weston's stable," Donovan said next, and then I was also pissed.

"You are a fucking asshole." Weston scowled.

I was too shocked to say anything. He couldn't really mean what I thought he meant. Could he?

"Ah," Elizabeth said, understanding clearly. "Recent?"

"The most recent, I believe. Last significant girl he spent any time with before you, anyway."

He *did* mean what I thought he meant.

Jesus Christ.

Referring to Weston's girlfriends as horses was not only misogynistic and demeaning, it was also just plain shitty.

"Huh." Elizabeth looked from Weston to me. Looked at the way Weston looked *at* me. "I might want in on that pool after all. What were the terms?"

Weston ran a hand through his already rumpled hair. "For fuck's sake, I'm not going to fuck around."

His date—the probable cause for his messed-up style—winked at Donovan. "We'll talk later."

"Fuck off," Weston muttered, doing another scan around the room. "People are watching us. Better play cozy." Without looking at her, he took her hand. "Is it you who wants to fuck around? Is that why you keep bringing up concerns about me?"

She rolled her eyes, but something in her expression had tightened. "It was just a joke. You're so sensitive about everything I say."

"Everything you say is a criticism."

"Everything you do is stupid."

Weston swung his head toward her. "Anyone told you lately you're a bitch?"

"Not since the last time you told me, which was, I think, oh, twenty minutes ago."

"There's the happy couple!" exclaimed an older gentleman from a few feet away.

"Ah, shit," Elizabeth swore as she put on a grin. "Mr. Jennings!"

Weston grabbed Donovan's shoulder and whispered, "Pray for me. I beg of you."

"I'm not religious, man. You're on your own." Donovan clapped him on the back and sent the "couple" on their way. "Maybe we should feel sorry for them," he said, looking after the two. Then, after a moment, "Nah."

No. Definitely no.

So Weston had gotten a handful with his engagement to Elizabeth Dyson. Too bad. I had my own problems, or *problem*, namely Donovan Kincaid.

Alone again, I turned to confront him and found his attention across the room. I followed his gaze to an elegant Asian woman sitting near the bar chatting with a few other people. When Donovan looked at her, she waved.

I glanced back at him. His features had hardened, but he nodded at her.

My gut tightened, and all the definitive things I'd meant to say disappeared from my thoughts once again. "Is she your girlfriend?"

"Sun? No, she's just a girl I like to fuck."

He said the word *fuck*, and suddenly I was there, back in that office all those years ago, pushed against the bookcase with his body pressed into mine. It was one of those images that had stayed hidden during my waking hours for so long, and now it snuck up, crippling me with its potency.

"She's beautiful," I said, and I felt like I wanted to cry because my want was so powerful. Because, in that moment, I wanted to be beautiful like *her*. Wanted to be the beautiful girl he liked to fuck.

"You're thinking about it now, aren't you?" Donovan was a foot away, but I could imagine the feel of his breath along my skin as I craned my neck up for him.

"What?" I was still staring in Sun's direction.

"Me fucking her."

I snapped out of my trance. "No!"

"Your body gives you away."

I wasn't wearing a bra, and I knew exactly which part of my body gave me away. Thank god he couldn't see the way my heart was thumping in my chest or the liquid pooling between my legs.

But what was I going to say? *No, I'm not imagining you fucking her; I'm remembering you fucking me.* It was just as terrible. It was worse, even.

"I'm not offended," he said. "I usually spend events like this thinking about it too. Planning what I'll do to her later on. Wondering what color panties she's wearing." He closed the distance between us, and now I really could feel his breath against my collarbone as he whispered, "Tonight, I'll admit, I find I'm a bit distracted."

I inhaled him, breathed in that familiar smell of cologne and musk and his mouth was so close that all I had to do was turn and lift my chin. Would he kiss me? Did I want him to?

I stepped back, jolted aware by the question. Even asking it made me feel weak, let alone if I tried to answer.

My knees felt soft, like I couldn't remember how to put weight on them, and I wobbled, but I didn't fall. "I'm not sure what you want me to say to you right now."

Donovan studied me carefully. "I'm not entirely sure either," he admitted.

"Are you ready to go?" Sun asked. I hadn't even noticed her approach. She was more alluring up close. Her lips were full, her posture sure. She looked familiar, but it might have been because she had the kind of confidence that made her appear important.

I stared at Donovan, certain desperation was apparent in my expression. He couldn't leave now.

He looked right at me when he answered her. "I am."

Sun linked her arm through his, and he escorted her out. Without an introduction. Without even a goodbye.

TWELVE

I lingered a few minutes after Donovan and his date had gone before leaving the party myself, but apparently not long enough. They were still at the curb waiting for his car when I walked outside into the cool September night.

I hung back so I could watch them without being noticed. She'd dropped his arm, and the two of them didn't even touch. It was as if they barely knew each other, let alone liked each other. Honestly, Elizabeth and Weston seemed friendlier than Donovan and Sun did. Maybe fake dates were a thing around here.

I chuckled to myself at the joke.

Then I stopped laughing.

Had he hired her?

He'd only been at the party for, what? Twenty minutes? Why did he even show up? To make sure I was there? To make sure I saw he had someone when I had no one?

I was reaching, making everything about me. It was

pathetic and I knew it. Donovan had come to show support for his business partner's engagement extravaganza. If Donovan wasn't friendly with Sun, it was because he didn't have to be nice to her to fuck her. And he would fuck her. I was sure of it. Who wouldn't fuck her?

Someone walked up to Sun and seemed to ask her something, then handed her a pen and paper. Asking for her autograph, it seemed.

That's where I'd recognized her. She was a model. I was pretty sure she'd even done some ads with Reach clients. It was probably how Donovan knew her. Of course that was the type of woman he'd date, even casually. A gorgeous, sophisticated model. The kind of woman I could never compare to.

Not that I was trying.

"Need a cab, miss?" The doorman at The Sky Launch asked.

"Oh, yes. Sorry." I still didn't want to be seen, but I figured it was safe now that Donovan's car had pulled up. As the doorman whistled for a taxi, I dallied by the club entrance, watching as Sun slid in the backseat of the Jaguar first, then as Donovan climbed in after. When the car eased into traffic, I stared after them as long as I could and saw Sun close the distance between her and Donovan, practically crawling into his lap.

I didn't care, and I did all at the same time. He could do what he wanted. It made no difference to me. I didn't care who he dated or liked or fucked. But in a different time, in a different place, I *did* care because back then, Donovan had stained all my thoughts, not just the ones I hid away at night.

And now he was pulling me back to that time and place,

making my mind face the past, forcing memories and fantasies to merge together in a nonstop reel of filth.

And he was going to fuck her.

And I couldn't remember a time I'd felt lonelier.

Thankfully, I didn't have to wait long for a taxi. I gave the cabbie my address. As an afterthought, I asked, "Could you take me to a liquor store on the way?"

While New York City was lined with liquor stores on the way from Columbus Circle to my apartment, finding one where a cab could wait outside was nearly impossible. So when we passed one a few blocks away, I paid the driver, and he said he'd drive around and come back for me.

I suspected that was the last I'd see of him, but fine. I'd just catch another.

Inside the store, I passed the vodka and gin. I wasn't a big drinker, but if I were to indulge, it would usually be a martini or a vodka tonic. That wasn't what I had a hankering for tonight.

It took a minute for me to find what I was looking for since I'd never purchased whiskey, but I found it in the back, high up. There was an entire shelf dedicated to scotch—single malts, blended varieties. Each had a price tag to suggest that someone considered it to be quite superior, but hell if I knew which was a good brand.

I ended up choosing a Macallan because it had a name I could pronounce. A pricier bottle because that was more likely what Donovan kept at the office.

Outside, I flagged a taxi and was surprised to find it was the same one I'd been in before.

"Scotch?" the driver asked when he saw the box in my hand. "Figures you were a lady with refined taste."

More like I was a girl with dirty taste—a dirty taste in

thoughts and a dirty taste in my mouth. Hopefully getting loaded on scotch would clean up at least one of the two.

In my apartment, I kicked off my heels and stripped out of my dress so I was just in my panties and then found a tumbler in the kitchen for my scotch.

"Just this once," I said to the empty room, lifting my glass up as if giving a toast. "Just tonight."

I drank the first glass quickly, letting the burn of the alcohol scald away any lingering reservations. By the time I poured the second glass, I was fully on board with my plan. What would it hurt? It was only one night, in the shelter of my own apartment.

Donovan's apartment, I reminded myself, and the thought made my nipples bead, as though he were secretly watching me. As though—because his name was on the building's deed— he might own my privacy as well. It changed the way I moved.

The way I reached up to put away the scotch bottle was for him. The way I bent over to pick up my dress was for him. For his eyes.

Then, when I undressed completely and stepped into the bath, that was for him too.

That was what I imagined, anyway. That was what I was allowing just once, just tonight—this game, this fantasy. While I often used Donovan to calm myself from nightmares and panic attacks brought on from memories of my sexual assault back in college, it had been years since I'd let myself think of him *just because*.

For a while it had become too common. Those obscene thoughts had been my friends in the months after my attack. But then it had gone too far. I'd let Donovan go too far. After that, I'd banished those sick fantasies to the darkness where they belonged.

But tonight, alone and a little bit drunk, I soaked in the hot water and I imagined that he was with me, watching as I pinched my nipples, pulling them until they hurt and made the space between my legs throb.

Fantasy Donovan liked that. Liked how I gasped. Liked how my back arched.

"Touch me," I begged him, my voice echoing against the bathroom tile.

"*No*," Fantasy Donovan said in my head. "*I won't*." Because even though I could ease the ache with my own hand, I knew that there was no way to pretend it was Donovan's—not even in my own mind. "*You do it*."

"But—"

My fantasy protest was interrupted by the buzz of my phone on the ledge of the tub.

It was after ten. People didn't call after ten unless it was an emergency or a wrong number or my sister.

I picked up the phone and looked at the caller ID. It wasn't a number I recognized, but it was local. Curiosity and alcohol got the best of me. "Hello?"

"They were blue," Donovan said, his voice so low and husky in my ear I had to press my legs together.

He had my number. Why did he have my number?

"What were blue?" I asked.

"Her panties."

It took me a beat before I realized he meant *Sun*'s panties. I groaned inwardly. I didn't want to know.

Except, I kind of did want to know. So even though I was too drunk for this, for conversation, I picked up my glass and settled back into the tub. "And you've already left her house?"

"I'm not a guy who stays the night."

"Of course you're not."

I heard a puffing sound. Was he lighting a cigar? I imagined that he was, that he was reclining in a leather chair in his study, maybe, overlooking the city, his tux rumpled but still on.

"Actually, I didn't even get out of the car," he said.

"Then how did you...?" I trailed off.

"We had the car ride."

"But how did you manage—" I cut myself off sharply. He'd fucked her in his car. With his driver in the front seat. "I don't want to know."

"Yes, you do." His smile was apparent in his tone.

"I really don't." I really did. I wanted to know every sick, twisted detail, even as it pained me to hear. Even as it made me hurt with desire.

"I'll tell you because you do." Another pause. Another puff? "She was all over me the minute we got in the backseat. Rubbing against my thigh while sucking on my ear. Which is fine, but not really what I like."

I'd seen her all over him as they drove away. If I thought he might be lying, that one image was enough to back him up. Besides, why would he lie?

I brought my tumbler to my lips but didn't take a swallow yet. "I suppose you're going to tell me what you do like."

He made a sound that indicated he thought it was a funny remark for me to make. "Oh, Sabrina, I think you know."

Teeth, I thought. *Nails*. "I think I don't care."

"Biting. Nipping. Nothing too soft. Something with a bit of pressure."

Vividly I could remember the way he'd reacted to my fingers digging into his back. "I'm not paying attention."

"You will." Another pause, this time with movement,

and now I pictured him cradling the phone while he pulled off his shoes and socks. "Anyway. You saw the dress Sun was wearing. I could easily flip it up. It wasn't tight like yours." He hesitated, letting it settle in that he'd thought about that—that my dress would have been more complicated.

I tipped my glass back and let amber whisky silence the *guh* that formed at the back of my throat.

"I rubbed her there," he continued, "with two fingers, along the crotch of her panties while I bit into the flesh of her shoulder. She wanted more. She kept pushing her cunt against my hand, trying to get me to give her more."

"Did you?" I wanted him to say *no*. Was that terrible? That I cared?

"Not yet. She was too impatient, and she needed to be teased. So I pushed her into the corner of the car. Hard. She yelped. She bumped her head on the window. I suppose it hurt."

Jesus. "Didn't your driver notice?"

"Possibly."

"He wasn't concerned about her welfare?" I sounded angry, and I was, but not at his driver so much as with myself. How could I listen to this? Why did it make me ache with envy? Why did it turn me on so goddamn much?

"I pay my driver to keep his eyes forward. Okay, he probably sneaks a peek in the rearview mirror and goes home and beats off later, but that's a perk of the job. Satisfied?"

No. I was far from.

"So. Where was I? She was in the corner. I pulled off her panties, discovered they were blue, and then pushed up her knees so that her feet were on the seat."

Involuntarily, I raised my legs so my knees were bent and my soles were planted on the bottom of the tub.

"Then I leaned down, put my face between her thighs and licked along her slit," Donovan said leisurely. "Slowly, Sabrina. She loved it."

I closed my eyes and imagined it. Not her, not Sun. But imagined Donovan licking, slowly. Imagined loving it.

"How could you tell?" I asked, hoarse from desire and alcohol.

"She shivered. So I did it again. Then I found her clit. I touched it lightly with my tongue, like a feather, until it was plump and swollen like a tiny little peach. And then I sucked it into my mouth and made her writhe. She came so hard her knees vise-gripped my head."

The envious ache inside had turned into a throb that I couldn't silence, spreading wide and long through my limbs, making every cell cry out in yearning. Did he know that he could do this to me? He had to.

Why did I let him?

Scotch. I blamed it on the scotch.

"All of that in the twelve minutes it took to get to her apartment. Fortunately Sun's not a squirter, so it was easy cleanup."

My eyes shot open. "She didn't return the favor before she left?"

"No."

"What a cunt." I'll admit I said it with a smile.

"Don't be like that, Sabrina. It's sexy to hear you lash out at her, but it's not fair. She did offer." He was patronizing and condescending and it was strangely erotic, but there was something else in his words that caught my attention.

"You weren't interested?" I took another sip of my drink,

prepared for his answer to be flippant or cruel or for him not to answer at all.

"I wasn't hard for her," he said flatly.

My heart skipped a beat. "But you were hard?"

"Yes, Sabrina. I was hard."

Oh, god.

I put my drink down and splashed my hand in the water before running it over my face. "Why did you call me, Donovan?"

"Why did you come here, Sabrina?" He sounded as angry and as desperate as I felt.

"You were in Tokyo."

"And then I had to be in New York."

"*Why* did you have to be here?"

He hesitated before answering, a full beat, the time it would take to puff on a cigar. I pictured him exhaling, a fog gathering around him as he perched on his windowsill looking out over the city.

"You know why I have to be here," he said finally. "Goodnight, Sabrina."

The phone clicked off before I had a chance to make him clarify. Because I *didn't* know why. Not really. Was it because he had to help out the team? Because Reach had gotten too busy to run with just two presidents? That was the story that had been told around the office.

But there was another story. One I told myself once the phone was safely on the ledge of the bathtub and my eyes were closed and my hand was under the water stroking my clit, turning it into a ripe little peach like Donovan had described into my ear. In this story, the reason he'd come home was the same reason he'd come to the party late, which was the same reason he'd left the party early. It was the same reason he'd made Weston marry Elizabeth Dyson instead of volunteering himself.

And it was the reason he'd called.

Because of me.

THIRTEEN

Monday was a chaotic stream of activity. Between team meetings, project deadlines, and staff introductions, I barely had a moment to breathe, let alone think about anything that didn't have to do with A/B testing and calls to action. This job was going to be a test of my abilities, but I was ready for the challenge.

But although I was committed to my new career—or maybe *because* I was committed—I had walked in the building that morning wearing what I considered was my power suit, with the specific intention of speaking to Donovan Kincaid.

Saturday night should never have happened.

Saturday night could never happen again.

I'd had to work harder than those who had graduated from Ivy Leagues, but now that I was where I wanted to be, I was not going to do anything to jeopardize it. Including messing around with the likes of Donovan. Particularly when I knew what he brought out in me.

The only way I could be sure our current trajectory was corrected was by facing it head-on.

The power suit, a gray skirt with a tailored matching jacket, was important not only because it gave me confidence, but also because it was not an outfit that said *sexy*.

It said *mastery*.

It said *domination*.

It said *determination*.

It did not say *girl against a bookcase with her pants down around her ankles*.

So just before my lunch meeting with the head of media—a hard-nosed Princeton graduate who didn't seem to like the idea of taking orders from a woman—I made my way to see Donovan.

Since we worked in completely different departments, Donovan and I hadn't had a reason to interact at all since I'd arrived, and this was the first time I'd sought him out. His office, as it happened, was the one that I'd seen on my first day with the opaque glass walls.

They were still clouded when I arrived today, but his door was open. I peeked in from the hall. It looked like he was preoccupied. He was bent over something on his desk. His jacket was off, so when he brought his hand up to rub the back of his neck, his arm muscles stretched taut against his shirt. He was intense when he worked, and it reminded me of watching him in class as he studied at his laptop at the front of the room. It was something that I knew about Donovan, and while in so many ways he was a stranger, it was oddly satisfactory to find I still knew this.

It also made me wonder what kinds of things he still knew

about me. The thought made me even more nervous. Made me want to turn around and walk back to my office.

It also made me strangely irritated. Because how dare he think he knew things about me. Whatever he thought he knew, he was wrong, and I intended on telling him just that.

I walked up to his secretary's desk. She was an attractive woman with black hair and dark skin, but her ethnicity wasn't immediately recognizable. She looked up from her computer when I got near and gave a welcoming smile, though her expression said she was still lost in whatever project she'd been working on.

"We haven't met yet, but I'm—" I started to say but was cut off.

"You can send Ms. Lind in, Simone," Donovan called from his office. He always noticed me. Even still.

I glanced in at him and found he was leaning back in his chair, waiting, whatever he'd been working on put away.

I turned back to Simone. "...and I guess I'll just go on in."

"Yes, Ms. Lind," Simone said, still smiling, then turned back to her computer.

I hesitated just long enough to take a deep breath. *Ninety-five percent of confidence is looking like you have it when you don't feel like you do,* I told myself. I didn't know if that was true, but it sounded true, and I was going with it.

Now I just had to hope I looked confident.

"Sabrina," Donovan said as the door shut on its own behind me, "to what do I owe this pleasure?"

Great. He had both the walls and the doors on an auto-mated system, probably something he controlled from behind his desk. I bet it made him feel superior to have such power at his fingertips. Likely a useful tool when he was dealing with wayward employees. He could psychologically subdue them without even opening his mouth.

It psychologically subdued me as well. Especially when he took advantage of my hesitation and turned that intense gaze on me.

"Don't tell me you have a grade you need to discuss." His wicked smile said he was remembering in detail the last time we'd been closed in an office together. When I'd given him my virginity.

Bye-bye confidence. There went my dry panties as well.

No, I wouldn't let him get to me. If I didn't go through with this, it was going to be like this forever—him with the upper hand, turning every encounter into another perverted version of our past, never letting me live up to my full potential.

I couldn't live like this. I wouldn't.

"No, I do not have a grade to discuss," I said boldly. "I thought perhaps we could talk."

"Go ahead and have a seat. I'm all ears."

I shook my head. "Not here." Not where he had the obvious power. I'd done that before. I wasn't doing that again. And the conference room wouldn't work. I didn't want other people from the office seeing us and gossiping. "I was thinking we should have dinner."

"Dinner?" he asked, arching a brow. "Or do you mean dessert?"

His devilish grin was distracting. Really distracting.

But I'd been prepared for that type of response, and I kept my spine straight. "Dinner. I think we have things to say. Don't you?"

His smile faded slightly. "I suppose we do."

He tapped his fingers across his desk. Two times. All five fingers in succession.

Then he said, "Eight o'clock work for you?"

"Tonight?" I'd expected we'd pull out our calendars and schedule for something like Thursday or maybe the Wednesday after. Something that wasn't less than twenty-four hours away.

"Unless you have other plans."

I couldn't back down now. It would weaken my position, and I needed to stay strong on this. "No. Tonight is fine."

I looked down at my power suit, which was totally inappropriate for dinner wear. I'd have to try to get out of the office by six, which was going to be tough on my first week, but as long as I left at six thirty, seven at the latest, I'd have time to get home and change.

I turned to go when I realized the other problem with such a short notice appointment. "Do you have any suggestions for a restaurant? I'm still new in town and don't have ideas, though I could ask my assistant."

Donovan leaned forward and picked up his phone. "How about I take care of the arrangements?"

"Are you sure?" I sounded defeated because I was. This was supposed to be *my* dinner on *my* terms to discuss *my* agenda, and somehow he'd already switched the plans to the night and time *he* wanted. Now it was going to be the location he wanted as well.

"I'm sure," he said. Into his receiver, he said, "Simone, send a driver to pick up Sabrina at eight sharp. Her address is in the system. Then call Gaston's and let them know to have a table ready for me around eight fifteen." He paused while she spoke. "Yes. Just the two of us." He hung up.

"The driver will text you when he arrives. I don't want you waiting outside alone." He met my eyes to make sure that I knew he wanted me safe. "Am I clear?"

My chest felt tight.

Of course any man might show that concern for a female coworker's safety. But I knew he meant it as more than that. He meant that he remembered once I'd been outside waiting alone, and I *hadn't* been safe.

And that touched me.

"Yes, you're clear," I said.

And then I stood there.

Had it really been that easy? I'd been ready for a battle. I'd been prepared to have to explain all the reasons why I wanted to take the conversation away from the office and why it couldn't be conducted on a phone call. I'd never expected him to be so amenable.

"Is there something else?" Donovan asked.

"No. I just. Thank you for agreeing." I walked out of his office bolstered. Hopefully tonight's talk would go just as smoothly.

With Donovan, though, I was learning that nothing ever turned out quite like I expected.

I just hoped I could learn not to like that quite so much.

FOURTEEN

I made it home by seven-thirty, which meant all I'd have time for was a change of outfit and no freshening up, but it wasn't like I was trying to impress him. In fact, I was going for the opposite. The dilemma, it turned out, was finding something to wear that fit the bill.

I flipped through my closet for the seventh time. Why did everything I own look good on me?

I chose a red sheath dress. It was short, but the neckline was high, and since we'd be sitting at a table most of the time, my bare legs wouldn't be an issue.

Unless he was in the car with me...

No. I would not think about the things he'd told me about that he'd done to Sun. I was not Sun, and that was exactly why we were doing this—so that he'd know that I was not Sun. That I never would be.

The sheath dress would be fine.

I made it to the lobby at seven fifty-nine, and as Donovan

had promised, the car arrived exactly at eight. It was the same Jaguar that I'd seen him use previously, but when I slid into the back seat, I was alone.

This is good, I told myself.

It was strange how *good* felt so much like disappointment.

"Will we be picking up Donovan next?" I asked the driver as he pulled away from the curb.

"He'll be meeting you there, Ms. Lind," he said, then didn't bother to speak again until we arrived at our destination, a high-rise on Fifty-Eighth.

"Take the elevator," the driver said. "Restaurant's on the top floor."

I shared the elevator with another couple. When we reached the top, the doors opened to the hostess desk for Gaston's. I gestured for the couple to go ahead of me and stepped aside to look out the windows.

The high-rise had an unobstructed view of Central Park. It was magnificent—the long rectangular stretch of garden and life nestled between steel and concrete. Magnificent even now as a purple twilight settled over the city. I could imagine its glory in the daytime, with the trees clothed in yellow and orange and red. I had a feeling it was just as breathtaking covered in snow. Just as awe-inspiring blanketed in green.

I knew everyone loved the view, that it was the draw to places like this, but I felt especially pulled. Maybe it was just because I could never get enough of being this high. It felt so hard-earned to be here, on this side of the world. At the top. I'd never stop believing I should have been here years ago.

The couple before me was seated. I turned to the hostess to check in.

"I'm not sure what name—"

A firm hand rested against my back sending a jolt of electricity shooting up my spine.

"She's with me," Donovan told the woman at the podium.

I looked up at my date, and the world seemed to mute around me. He was wearing the same suit he'd had on earlier, but now he had his jacket on. It was a black three-piece, tailored so perfectly that there wasn't any need to imagine how good he looked underneath his clothes. His scruff had been cleaned up since I'd seen him, and he'd applied aftershave.

He looked and smelled and felt like the kind of guy any girl would die to be with.

And he was here with *me*.

He glanced down at me, his sly smile making me weak in the knees.

"Good evening, Mr. Kincaid. We have your usual table waiting for you."

And that was another reason why I had to remember this *wasn't* a date. Because he was the kind of guy who had a "usual table". Sure, Weston was that kind of guy too, but that wasn't the point. Besides, it didn't bother me so much to think about Weston with other girls. Donovan was different.

But why wasn't something I could articulate, even just for myself, because Donovan kept his hand on my back as he directed me through the restaurant, and the feel of his fingers was hot and charged against my skin, even through the thin material of my sheath dress.

Maybe I'd chosen my outfit poorly after all.

It was a relief when he removed his hand to let me sit, but it was also annoying because now I felt cold. For distraction, I turned my head out the window next to us. The sun had finished setting, and now the view was dotted with twinkling of lights throughout bunches of dark trees below.

"It's beautiful," I said, deciding to open with a compliment. I didn't remark on the view's romantic attributes.

"Is it?" Donovan asked. "I forget to notice."

Asshole. But he was focused on me instead of out the window, and so maybe I had to give him the benefit of the doubt.

I'd meant to dive right into my reasons for meeting with him, but the waiter arrived, and Donovan took it upon himself to order a bottle of wine. Then there was the menu to discuss—I was an adventurous enough eater, but almost everything was unrecognizable to me by name. Donovan had to explain each item, which he did in detail.

I chose the turbot, a Scandinavian flatfish covered in some unpronounceable French sauce.

Then the wine arrived, and Donovan insisted on toasting to my new position at Reach, and then our food came.

"That's quite the service," I said, unsure how the evening had gotten away from me thus far. I was also unsure how we'd managed to make it to the main course of our meal without Donovan having said or done anything extraordinarily Donovan.

"They know whom they're serving," he said, refilling my wineglass, and I noted that I'd already emptied half a glass. It was time to stick to water.

It was also time to get to the point. "Thank you for agreeing to have dinner with me, Donovan."

"The pleasure is mine. Though I should tell you, I think you're under the impression that this outfit you're wearing makes you unattractive. It would take a lot more than a plain dress to hide yourself from me."

I had to grit my teeth. Fuck him. Fuck him for knowing what I'd tried to do. Fuck him for saying something so shitty. Fuck him for the compliment he'd buried underneath.

Double fuck him for what his compliment implied. He couldn't make me feel guilty for hiding. I wasn't his to find.

With a gleam in his eye that said he knew he'd hit his mark, he said, "Anyway. What is it you wanted to talk about?"

I dabbed at my mouth with my napkin. "Well. A of all, I'd like to make it known that misogynistic and sexually inappropriate comments like that one are not appreciated."

He paused with his forkful of madai in midair. "Even when it's just the two of us?"

"Especially when it's just the two of us. Which I'm sure means nothing to you. You'll do as you like and there will be no repercussion because you own the business and that's the world we live in."

"How terribly dour of you." He brought his food to his mouth, the translucent fish sliding between his lips.

His perfect, amazing, kissable lips...

No, not perfect. Not amazing. Definitely not kissable. "I'm a realist," I said, staying on task. "In my experience, reality is dour."

"I'm not going to argue with you there." He lifted his wineglass as though to toast the sentiment.

One item down. One left to go. The major one.

"B of all." I focused on my turbot, unable to meet his eyes. "You and I have a past that needs to be addressed."

God, I was chickenshit. *We've had sex.* I couldn't even say that. How ridiculous was that? It was just sex.

Except it hadn't just been sex. I'd just had sex with Weston and there was no need for a dinner to discuss how things were different now.

But there weren't words for what had happened between Donovan and me, so I had to rely on the vocabulary that I had.

And now that I'd mentioned it, acknowledged it, the weight of the air between us felt twice as heavy.

I looked up from my plate and found his eyes trained on me.

"A past," he repeated now that he had my gaze. "Yes. I was essentially your teacher."

In more ways than one.

He knew that too, knew that I'd been a virgin. His statement was filled with the innuendo.

I took a hurried sip of my wine, hoping that I could use that as the excuse for the blush in my cheeks.

With the wine in my hand, I felt bolder. The door was only open a crack, but I meant to go all the way inside. There were things I never understood about what he'd said and done to me, and I wanted answers.

"You gave me a bad grade," I said, giving him a place to start.

"And then we fixed it." His grin was as wicked as it was distracting.

I scowled. "You were cruel to me."

"Was I?" That twinkle in his eye was another distraction. "Why?"

"Probably the same reason I'm cruel to you now."

His answer made my insides feel sloshy, but I wasn't backing down. "Which is?"

"If you haven't figured it out then hell if I can explain it to you."

I held his stare as I sat back, my arms resting on the sides of the chair. "Was it because of Amanda?"

I was going out on a limb with this one. Everything I'd heard about Amanda had come from Weston when I'd still been at Harvard. She'd been engaged to Donovan and had died in a car accident before I'd arrived at the school. Rumor was that Donovan had taken it pretty hard.

Was that the reason he'd been a dick to me? Because he'd still been mourning his first love? I liked that reason. It was easier than believing some of the alternatives.

"I don't talk about her," Donovan said, in a way that made it clear the subject was closed.

Admittedly, it was probably shitty to bring her up. But so much of what Donovan had done to me had been shitty. Wasn't it fair game?

"Then I'll assume it is because of her," I said. Things would be resolved tonight whether or not he participated in achieving that resolution.

"You know what they say when you assume." He'd lost the playfulness he had earlier, and something about that made me feel like I'd won, but the victory was hollow.

"You're already an ass, so what are you worried about?" I didn't let him answer. "You must have really loved her."

"You didn't ask me to dinner to make assumptions about my dead fiancée."

He was right. I didn't.

I looked out the window, unsure of what I really wanted from him. To say he'd loved the woman he'd been engaged to?

Of course he had. Hearing him say that he had wasn't going to shed light on anything else.

Besides, this wasn't really about what I needed to hear from Donovan. It was what he needed to hear from me.

I turned back to him. "There was more about what happened between us back then, and I think there might be an impression of me that has lingered that is not accurate."

"Oh, really?" He cocked his head. "I'm intrigued."

"It didn't help that I stayed on the phone with you the other night. I should have hung up, but I'd been drinking."

He rolled his eyes dramatically. "You should have hung up on a friend?"

"One who was making sexual comments, trying to get a rise out of me? Yes." I pointed a finger at him. "And don't say that sexual harassment used to be our thing, because that's what I'm talking about. That impression of me, that that's what I want—it's wrong."

"That's *not* what you want?" The way he looked at me—looked into me with those brown-green eyes and that intense gaze—it was hard not to second-guess myself.

But I barreled on, committed to what I knew was true about myself. "It's not. Back then, when I was at Harvard, I developed somewhat of a fixation with you after you rescued me from being raped by Theodore Sheridan."

He dropped his fork on his plate with a clang that made me jump. "A fixation. That's what you're calling it."

He sounded pissed, and even though I couldn't figure out why he'd be angry about *my* issues, it made me even more defensive. "It sounds silly, but it happens. It's even got a name —it's a form of transference. It basically happens when a person falls for someone in an effort to erase or change a past trauma."

"Did you see a therapist to figure out this bullshit?"

"No." I shifted in my chair, uneasy with the conversation. "I've read books and done a lot of online research. Anyway, it was a phase, and it's over. I was complicit in the inappropriate activity that occurred between us, but I'm not that girl anymore."

"Keep telling yourself that, Sabrina," he said sharply.

His condescension stung, but more, he'd missed the point. "I'm telling *you*."

Leaning forward, he practically growled. "Why?"

"Why am I telling you?"

"Yes. Why?"

"So that you'll know."

"You mean so that I'll *stop*. So that I'll stop *saying* things and *doing* things, things that maybe make you feel uncomfortable, but also make you feel alive for probably the first time in years. But you know what the problem with that is? The problem is that the thing you really want to stop isn't me, it's how you *react*. And that's not going to go away with research or alcohol or stern conversations. And no matter how many times you tell this story to me, or yourself, it's still never going to change that it's exactly that—a story."

My eyes felt wet. Not wet enough to cry but wet enough to sting. Yes, I wanted to stop reacting to him. Yes. He knew. He fucking knew even if I couldn't say it clearly. But the thing he didn't realize was that if he stopped then my reactions would stop.

Because he was the one who brought this out in me. No one else.

I finished my wine and set the empty glass on the table.

"We don't have to agree on this." My throat felt dry despite having just drunk.

"No, we don't," he said bitterly as he picked up his fork. "I just have to leave you alone."

We finished the meal in silence. As each terrible, awkward second passed, I reminded myself that this was what I'd wanted. He wouldn't bother me after this. He seemed to hate me now, for some reason I couldn't quite figure out. Honestly, I wasn't trying very hard. I was too busy hating myself.

Was transference just an excuse? A prettier label than the real one underneath?

But if I hadn't been into sick dirty things because Donovan had saved me, then it meant I'd really liked it. All of it. Including the part where he'd been cruel and horrible. Including the parts where he was still cruel and horrible.

I was still in my head by the time we climbed into the elevator together. The tension was wrapped densely around us, and it seemed to thicken in the small confined space. It was solid. Like a wall between us.

We'd only traveled down a couple of floors when the car suddenly jolted to a stop. I glanced toward Donovan—his hand was on the emergency stop button.

My heart began hammering in my chest.

In an instant, he had me caged against the wall.

"Sabrina..." He searched my face, looking for an answer I wasn't sure I could give.

"I'm not frightened of you." I pressed tighter against the wall, but my stomach felt like butterflies had taken over, and *shit, he was right.* I did feel alive.

"No. That was never your problem. The problem was that

you liked that you are." He pushed in closer, so close that I could feel him against the length of me even though he wasn't touching me anywhere. "I still remember every crease on your face when you came."

I looked away, though his nose was inches from mine. "That was ten years ago." But it was as vivid as yesterday in my mind, too.

"The sounds that you made. The way you said my name." There was an ache in his voice, and it pulled my eyes to his.

I could remember the way he smelled. The way the book-case scratched against my back. The way it felt when he pushed inside me—like I was being torn apart and split open, the way it felt like I was only being held together because of him.

And if that were all I remembered then I would beg for him to kiss me, because there was nothing I wanted more in that moment than his hands on me, everywhere on me. Making me feel all those things he'd made me feel back then. All the things he still made me feel when I dared to let him.

But there was more, and I hadn't forgotten it.

"I remember how you dismissed me like a used toy. Sent me to your friend."

Donovan's eyes closed briefly, and he exhaled.

"To Weston." He stepped away, releasing me from my trap. "That's right. That was wise of me."

He backed up until he was on the opposite side of the elevator. "Weston would be good for you. You'd be good for him. After his whole marriage is over, that is."

I let out a harsh laugh. "So I should pursue Weston." Really? He was pushing this again?

"Why not? That's what you came here thinking you'd do,

wasn't it? I think it would be an excellent choice for both of you."

I was almost too stunned for words. Thirty seconds ago he'd been ready to tear off my clothes, and now he was advocating a relationship with his business partner and friend.

Whatever his game was, it hadn't changed since college. But mine had. Back then I'd let this hurt me. Now, I'd play along. "Fine. I'll do that."

He seemed slightly taken aback. "You will?"

"Sure. As soon as his marriage is over. Thanks for the suggestion."

"Glad I could help." He released the emergency button and the elevator started again.

The Jag was waiting on the street, but my worries about sharing a ride turned out to be unnecessary. After holding it open for me so I could get in the back seat, Donovan shut the door and knocked on the hood of the car.

The driver pulled out into traffic, and when I swiveled to look behind us, Donovan was already gone from sight.

FIFTEEN

I pulled my hair nervously as Nate Sinclair studied the bulletin boards in the strategy room. Pinned to them were ideas and inspiration for a campaign we were getting ready to introduce for Phoenix Technology—a multinational tech company that was one of the foremost designers and developers of computer software and hardware. My staff had gathered the pertinent materials into a PowerPoint presentation for the meeting the following day, but the brainstorming boards were still up in case we needed to make any last minute changes. It was much easier to work on a team project in a tactile format, I'd found, so I'd kept this style when I'd joined the firm.

Still, it felt awkward having a superior looking at my work like this. Like it was naked and raw. Like *I* was naked and raw. I was grateful the main lights were off and only the spotlights were on. Maybe the darkness could hide my edginess.

"We'll adjust any of this to fit what Creative comes up

with," I said, in case Nate thought the strategy was lacking. Not that he'd said anything to suggest that he did.

He moved from a magazine article to a graph about the best uses of social media. "I'm not worried about it. This is Weston's department."

Right. Nate didn't care. He was only in here killing time while his own department came up with an ad campaign. They'd come up with several ad ideas, and he'd shot down every one so far.

Weston, on the other hand, had left for the night. He wasn't the type to stay late in general, I'd learned. Especially recently, when he had so much to do to prepare for his upcoming wedding, which was now only six weeks away.

My anxiety was all about me and no one else. I'd been at Reach for a month, and due to the fast pace that the company kept, I'd already seen several of my team's marketing plans put into place. But Phoenix was the first big campaign presentation I'd been a part of. It was important to the entire firm, and nerves were high-strung throughout the staff. I'd just left a handful of my own employees in another work room, quibbling over which color of background looked better in the Power-Point slides like it was a matter of life or death.

I let out a sigh, relaxing my shoulders as I did. "Are you confident your team will come up with something?"

Nate stroked his hand across his closely shaved beard. "A year ago we wouldn't have even had a shot at Phoenix. An opportunity like this doesn't come every day, and I'm going to make sure we make the most of it. That's the best we can do." He turned toward me. "But if we don't get it, we don't get it. It's not because I don't have a good team. Advertising is catching the right wave at the right time. Sometimes you crest high, sometimes you wipe out."

I tilted my head and looked at him in the dim light. "Nathan Sinclair, are you a secret surfer?"

Nate was ten years older than Donovan, who already had five years on me, and except for a vague bio on the company website, I didn't know much about the man. He seemed to like it that way. Every time I'd tried to ask him about himself, he'd evaded my questions. Either he was a serious introvert or a man with a fascinating past.

I was betting on the latter.

Tonight he had his jacket off and the sleeves of his dress shirt were rolled up to his elbows revealing tattoos extending down both of his forearms. I'd seen him riding a Harley once after work. I could totally picture him hanging ten.

But he only laughed. "Just trying to bond with the California girl."

"In the years I lived there, I don't think I ever became a California girl. I maybe went to the beach a handful of times." I wasn't even sure I'd ever gotten a tan.

"Workaholic."

I squinted at the clock. "Says the president still at the office at nine thirty-seven p.m."

"It's only the second time this week I've been here past eight."

"It's Tuesday."

There was a knock on the doorframe since the door was already open. We turned toward the sound. One of the guys from Creative was standing there.

"Hey, Nate, what do you think about the 'American Idea'?

That notion was used a lot in the last election year. Maybe we could try to leverage it as a unifying patriotic—"

Nate cut him off. "Can't use it. The 'American Idea' was trademarked by Donald Trump." He thought for a moment. "But I like the scope. Let's keep thinking along those lines. I'll come brainstorm with you." The two of them left together.

"Send someone to get me when you have something," I called after them. "I'll be here or upstairs in my office." Then I turned again to my boards. If the scope of the campaign were bigger, would we need to adjust our strategy to fit that?

The idea of making changes made me tired—or more tired —but I was determined. I walked backwards, trying to see the entirety of the plan better, until my thighs hit the back of the worktable.

"Fuck it," I muttered to myself, hopping on the table. I was already here late. Might as well get comfortable. I kicked off my shoes while I was at it and brought one nyloned foot up to my knee to massage while I looked over the boards and brain-stormed.

For the next several minutes, I was lost in my head, but not so lost that I didn't notice when the air in the room changed. It felt warmer. Like the heater had just kicked in.

Someone walked in and stood beside the table.

I inhaled slowly. I didn't want to turn my head, didn't want to look in his direction, because I knew exactly who it was, and in this moment, he was next to me, and while I was pretending I didn't know, I didn't have to pretend I didn't care.

But then he held out a Styrofoam cup of coffee in my direc-tion, and I had to look at it.

"You're working late," Donovan said when I acknowledged him.

Beyond seeing him in meetings and passing him in the hall-way, I hadn't really talked to him in the month since the night he'd taken me to Gaston's. We'd left things unsettled, and that gnawed at me when I let it, but when I didn't, our working rela-tionship was fine. He didn't bother me. I didn't bother him. He'd done as I'd asked—he'd left me alone.

That was what I had wanted, I reminded myself often. It was for the best.

And yet I couldn't deny that his nearness now felt like a glimpse of sun after a long winter cold.

I took the coffee, wondering if it was an olive branch of sorts. "I want to make sure the plan we have outlined fits the new creative campaign when it comes through."

After taking a sip of the brew, I set the cup down at my side, trying to ignore the way my stomach flip-flopped when Donovan looked at my work.

It wasn't any better when he looked back at me. "You have a qualified team for that. You don't trust them?"

"I trust them just fine." Honestly, I did. But this was my first big deal. It would have my name all over it. I wanted to make sure every *t* was crossed. Every *i* was dotted.

It wasn't something I wanted to explain to anyone. Espe-cially to him.

"Let me give you some advice," he said, pulling a chair out from the table.

"How about you don't." I was both intrigued and intimi-dated by his actions. It wasn't like him to be on this floor. "Why are you even down here?"

Facing the chair toward me, he sat in it. "To bother you. No other reason." He held his hand out, palm up. "Give me your foot."

I glanced down at the foot in my lap that I was still half-heartedly rubbing. Was he offering to...? "No!"

He side-eyed me. "Come on, Sabrina. You look exhausted. I owe you a foot rub, at least." When I still hesitated, he added, "Completely innocent. I promise. We aren't the only people here. What could I possibly do to you?"

What could he *do to me*? What a loaded question. He could torture me completely in front of a crowd of people, and no one would ever know. He tortured me completely all the time without even being in the same room with me, and *he* didn't know it.

But he'd been right with what he said at Gaston's—asking him to stop hadn't stopped my reactions. In the month that had passed, he'd kept his distance, but I'd still thought about him. And the second he stepped into my presence, I lit up in awareness.

So what did it matter if I let him give me a foot rub? It could be a truce. Make our working relationship better, at least.

Reluctantly, I gave him my foot.

He began rubbing the sole through the black nylon thigh high. He wasn't soft, using his thumb to dig deep into my muscle, but he seemed to know right where to massage and how much pressure I needed to release the tension, not only in my foot, but even in my shoulders and my back.

"You're good at this." I couldn't stop watching him. Couldn't stop watching his face, how serious he was. How focused.

"I know." His fingers moved to my ankle, and my entire leg started to tingle, like I'd been lying on it for too long and it had gone to sleep.

I wanted to pull away. But I couldn't.

He glanced up at me and grinned, as though he could sense my inner struggle and enjoyed it. "Now, my advice."

"I knew there was a catch." I huffed, putting on a show, though mostly it was to cover how shaky my breathing was at the moment.

"Of course there was a catch. Stop fighting this." It was both an order and an appeal, and something about that made me actually pause and listen and wonder if he were talking about more than listening to him spout wisdom.

"Say what you want to say," I said after a beat. It was probably a bad idea to hear him out. I couldn't think of many worse.

He kneaded his fingers up higher into the flesh of my calf. "You already have the job."

"I'm not afraid of losing my job." Okay, I was somewhat afraid of losing my job.

"You feel like you have to prove yourself."

I pursed my lips. "Maybe I wouldn't feel that way if one of my superiors didn't take every opportunity to discredit me."

"I don't know what you're talking about. Nate likes you fine, and we both know Weston is more concerned with what's under your skirt than what's inside your head." But he was smiling. He knew I was talking about him.

"You're an incredible asshole." I smiled back. Begrudgingly.

Donovan let go of my leg. "Now, Weston isn't going to fire you, but if you want something permanent with him, you do have some work to do."

I perked to attention. "What do you mean?"

"Weston will lose interest."

Oh. For a second, I'd thought he'd been talking about my career. I'd forgotten the stupid thing I'd told Donovan about pursuing Weston when his marriage was over.

I started to say something in protest about Weston, but then Donovan reached for my other foot and began to repeat his massage, and my focus was captured once again.

"He's going to stay interested in you longer than usual, I predict," Donovan continued while I swallowed back a groan, "simply because it's forbidden right now. That's intriguing to him."

He found a particularly sensitive spot, and he pressed his thumb in deeper.

I bit my lip.

"But after the wedding ring comes off, he's going to get bored and that's a fact. It's his M.O. So don't bother shedding tears about it. It's nothing to do with you."

Donovan paused massaging and speaking, waiting to make sure I understood.

What I understood was how good his hands felt on me, but hurriedly I mentally replayed everything he'd just said, putting his words into context.

I ran two fingers across my forehead. "Let me see if I get this. 'Go after Weston; you'd be good for him, but don't be bummed when he gets tired of you; that's just his thing.' Correct me if I'm wrong, but that almost sounds like you're reversing your endorsement for our coupling."

If Donovan were actually trying to keep me from being with Weston...well, that would have implications. Implications that I wasn't sure what to do with. Though I liked the way they felt to think about, even as tentative as they were.

"Not at all. I'm doubling down on the endorsement not only by giving you this warning but also by telling you what you should do to make sure he doesn't get tired of you."

"You're going to tell me how to keep Weston interested."

The disappointment in my voice sounded a lot like incredulity. Maybe it was both.

"I am. You have to recognize that the problem lies with Weston. He's a seemingly open book, but the reason he hasn't had a serious relationship with anyone is because he's never let a woman get past the persona he puts up to see his true self." Donovan's hands moved up to my ankle, burning my skin through my stockings.

How was it possible that he could both brand me and give me away all at once? It wasn't the first time. How was I not used to it?

I wrapped my hands along the edge of the table, needing the support.

"If you want to find a place in his heart, you have to get there first."

"Easy enough," I said sarcastically. Maybe Donovan's guidance was meant to be generous, but it tasted sour. It wasn't the advice I wanted.

"I can't tell you how to do it exactly. You're going to have to work that out yourself. But I figure you should know something about hiding, since you do it so well."

I tried to pull my foot away, but his grip tightened.

"You don't know anything about me," I lied.

"Oh, Sabrina," he chided. His conceit irritated me. Why did it arouse me as well?

"While we're on the subject"—his hands moved slowly up my leg—"you aren't going to be true to yourself when you're with him. You know that, already. You'll have to accept it."

I shook my head. He couldn't really be saying what I thought he was saying.

"Don't shake your head at me. You know what I'm talking about. He's not going to be able to fulfill you sexually."

"You know I've slept with him."

"Thank you for the painful reminder. I'm sure you'll tell me he made you come, too. But you and I both know there's more to sexual fulfillment than just having an orgasm, so unless you can tell me that he can make you sleep through the night, then let's not talk about what Weston does for you in the bedroom."

My breathing was so shallow now, my arms covered in goose bumps. How could he know that about me? That I had trouble sleeping? That it was only my dirty fantasies that helped me rest through the night?

He *couldn't* know that, that's how. It was coincidence.

And I was taking all of this too seriously.

I let out a long breath and allowed him a smile. "This is the most fascinatingly bizarre conversation I've ever imagined having with you."

Donovan's caress changed as I relaxed. It was lighter now, long strokes up the length of my calf and to my knee. I shivered.

"Have you imagined many?"

My smile faded. I'd given myself away. Yes. I'd imagined so many conversations with him over the years, but there was no way I could tell him the things we'd talked about in my head.

"I have," he said, his voice thick.

The air suddenly felt heavier, like it was harder to breathe it in, and it didn't matter anymore that he was an asshole or that he was giving me advice about Weston because *he'd imagined us too.*

"What do we say to each other?" I asked tentatively, afraid to break the honesty.

"We say a lot of things." He placed a hand on my opposite calf and stood up, his fingers trailing up my legs as he rose. "Sometimes we say nothing at all."

He was standing in front of me now. My legs nudged open wider, instinctively. Automatically he moved closer, filling the gap and pressing right up against the table.

I hated how much I wanted him to kiss me.

"Why do you do this to me?" I whispered.

His lips hovered above mine. Dancing. Teasing. "Do what?"

"Trap me like this."

"It makes me feel like I have you."

I ached at my core. "I don't want you to feel like you have me."

"Are you sure of that?"

I wasn't, and the joke was we both knew it. Every reason I had for staying away from him was valid, but if he kissed me now, I wouldn't be able to stop. If he kissed me now...

I tilted my chin up.

"Whoops! Sorry to interrupt." One of my team leaders stood at the door, his hands covering his eyes.

Fuck.

Fuck, fuck, fuck!

There wasn't a rule about dating across departments, but this wasn't the reputation I wanted.

I pushed Donovan away and jumped down. "It's fine, Tom. What's up?"

Tom lowered his hand, seemingly relieved that he wasn't in trouble for what he'd walked in on. "They have a campaign. Meeting in the conference room now to see the presentation."

"Excellent. I'm right behind you." I waited until Tom was

gone before turning back to slip on my shoes. "I have to go," I said to Donovan, unable to look him in the eye.

"Right. I'll see you around."

"Yeah." I nodded and hurried to the conference room with my insides twisted up in knots, pretending it didn't mean anything that Donovan had sounded as confused as I felt.

SIXTEEN

"This is the first emergency Friday morning meeting I've called at the executive level, that I can recall," Nate said, looking to Weston for confirmation, "but I'm happy to say it's for a celebratory cause. We have landed the Phoenix account!"

Cheers erupted throughout the conference room. Roxie had already told me the minute I'd walked in the office, but my team and all of Nate's team had yet to hear the news. Whoops and hollers and hugs were shared, even a few tears.

Nate waited for the room to settle before continuing with his speech. "Word came in late last night. You all put in your best work. I'm very proud of what you brought to the table. Party on us tonight at Red Farm. Upper West Side location."

I zoned out as Nate went through the details of the project timelines. Accidentally, I caught Donovan's eye across the table. I'd been avoiding him since Tuesday, or he'd been avoiding me. I wasn't quite sure, but every time we came in contact with each other, we both immediately ducked away in the opposite direction.

Now, I lowered my eyes quickly. My gaze landed on Weston who was typing furiously on his cell next to me.

It's going to seem weird if my fiancée isn't at the celebration, don't you think?

He held his screen so it was visible when Elizabeth's reply came through.

At this short notice, I don't give a fuck. I'm not at your beck and call.

With an audible huff, he stuffed his phone in his suit pocket and sat back in his chair.

Trouble in fake paradise, it seemed. Not that Weston's pairing with Elizabeth had ever been paradise. I sort of felt sorry for him. Though, really, what did he expect when he let Donovan arrange a marriage for him?

I'd been back to wondering about that over the past few days. Why had Donovan suggested they marry after finding out that I'd be coming to work at Reach? And why did he continue to push me into a relationship with Weston while, at the same time, he acted like he was attracted to me? Was that all in my head?

On top of everything else, there was a very real chance there was now a rumor about Donovan and me after having been caught in such an intimate situation. Thoughts of the potential gossip made me groan inwardly. Here I was, finally making strides with my career. I wasn't ready to have it tainted by talk that I'd slept my way to my position.

Not to mention what Weston would say if he found out. If I were going to start a relationship with someone else in the office, then fine, but I needed to be the one to tell Weston. Especially if the relationship were with Donovan.

Which it wasn't because there was no relationship. There was no relationship, nothing had happened, and I'd been tormented about it ever since. I couldn't stop thinking about him. Couldn't stop thinking about what had almost happened, what I'd wanted to happen, what *he* had wanted to happen.

What was he trying to do to me?

I dared another glance in his direction. He was staring right at me this time. He didn't even pretend to look away when I caught him, and then, somehow, I couldn't look away either.

Whatever he was trying to do to me, I was afraid it might already be done.

When the meeting ended, I gathered my things in a hurry, intending to make a quick escape to my office.

"Sabrina," Weston called, detaining me.

So much for my getaway plan.

"Yeah?" I tugged on my hair, noting that Donovan had lingered to talk to someone as well.

Oblivious to my distraction, Weston smiled proudly. "I wanted to let you know that Phoenix was particularly impressed with our marketing objectives. It was one of the main reasons we landed the account."

"I inherited a very qualified and talented team." *Just get through this. Just get through.*

"You did. I know you did." He shifted his weight to his hip. "Tom Burns also let me know a few things."

My attention immediately tuned in on the name Weston had mentioned. Tom Burns had been the guy who'd seen me almost kiss Donovan. "Like what?"

Weston started to say something but then glanced around the room and seemed to realize we weren't alone. "We should talk about it privately. Meet you upstairs in my office in fifteen?"

"Sure." My heart was beating so hard I was surprised it wasn't boring a hole through my chest. "I'll be there in fifteen."

As soon as Weston left the conference room, I dropped my notebooks and my phone on the table and placed my palms down on the wood to brace myself. I took a deep breath. Then another.

Then another.

This wasn't even really that big of a deal because there wasn't anything going on with Donovan. The problem was in all the details—would I tell Weston the rest? That I'd slept with Donovan in college? That I'd been fixated on him then?

That I was fixated on him now?

Sensing I was already struggling, Donovan of course had to come bother me more. Leaning against the table, he said smoothly, "If you're that worried about what a staff member might be saying about you, you're probably engaging in behavior that you shouldn't be engaging in."

I shot him a glare that I hoped held the weight of the angst I was feeling. "This is fun for you, isn't it?"

He shrugged. "It's not the worst day I've had at the office."

His cavalier attitude only added to my misery. I'd been tense and nervous and *wanting* him for three days and when he finally approached me, it was just to make me feel worse?

I couldn't take it. Not right now, anyway.

"Was that your goal all along?" I snapped. "Get employees talking about you and me so that I'd have a harder time with Weston?"

"Are you feeling guilty about you and me?"

"Jesus, you're incredible." I didn't know how I continued to be dumbfounded by the things he said to me, but I did. "You think this is a game. Push me toward Weston, pull me away. Push but then put an obstacle in the way. Push but flirt with me at the same time so I don't know what it is you really want."

"Don't be silly. I want you and Weston to work out more than anyone." He really was a good liar. Better than I was, I realized.

But I wasn't challenging him about this, not in the conference room, not when there were already rumors flying about the two of us, especially not when there wasn't any reason to believe he'd ever be truly honest.

I gathered my things off the table. "I'm sure you do want me with Weston. Because that will be another fun game when you tear us apart."

I spun on my heels, and without looking back, left Donovan behind.

After a brief trip to the restroom to freshen up and calm down, I went back up to the executive floor. I dropped my things off in my office and headed to Weston's.

"He wanted to see me," I said to Roxie as I walked up. Weston's door was open and the glass was clear. I could see he was at his desk, typing something into his phone.

"He's in there. Go on in." I'd just passed her desk when she added, "He's in a mood though. I warn you."

"I heard that," Weston said from his office.

"You were meant to." His assistant was no-nonsense, one of the things I liked best about her.

Which meant if Roxie was warning me about Weston's mood, that was a bad, bad sign.

I walked in, rubbing my mother's cross at my neck for good luck. "Hey, what's up? Is there a problem?"

"Not exactly." He threw down his phone and heaved another sigh like he had when he'd been texting with Elizabeth during the meeting earlier. Then, as if on second thought, he opened a desk drawer and threw his phone inside instead.

"Have a seat," he said, brighter now that his cell was out of sight.

I slunk down in one of the chairs facing him and willed my toe to stop tapping so nervously. "I'm here."

"You're here." He smiled. "Anyway. As I was saying downstairs, Tom Burns spoke to me yesterday, and he had some interesting things to say about you."

"Really? Like what?" I peered back at the office door. Weston hadn't bothered to shut it. I should have closed it when I'd walked in. Now Roxie would hear everything.

It was fine. I'd just lie. About everything I'd ever thought about Donovan. Even though I was a terrible liar.

Weston stood up and circled around so he was standing right in front of me. He leaned back, half sitting on the desk behind him, but he was still looming above me, and I panicked and bolted to a standing position so I could feel like I was on an even playing field.

"Whoa," Weston said. "You okay?"

"Yep. Just edgy today." It was true enough for me to pull off. "Go on. Tom said...?"

"That you stayed as late as anyone else, and that you provided some of the last minute additions to the project, such as the global message component. That was one of the selling points in the strategy."

Huh. There was nothing terrible or grumpy or embarrassing about that. I eased my weight onto my hip. "Really?"

"Yes. Really. I wanted you to know your commitment to your team didn't go unnoticed. Everyone seems to be responding really well to you. The staff likes you. Your team likes you, and I'm really glad you came." He reached out and tugged the same piece of hair I was holding.

"Thank you. I appreciate that." My nerves were still jittery with adrenaline. I hadn't expected to be complimented. I was flustered about it. "Was that everything?"

"Yeah, that's everything," he chuckled.

"Okay, then. Thank you again." I started to leave and then remembered. "Oh, and congratulations on the account."

"Congratulations to both of us." He raised his palm up in the air. I lifted mine up to give him a high five, and afterward, his hand lingered. As I pulled away to leave, he laced his fingers through mine, not letting go. "You're coming tonight, aren't you?"

My insides dipped and swerved like when I was trying to avoid a deer that had just run in front of my car. It felt wrong to be holding his hand like this. Dishonest—not just because of his arrangement with Elizabeth—but also because of all the things going on in my head about someone else.

But just then, Donovan walked into Weston's office, and even though his reasons for being there might have had nothing to do with me, it sure felt awfully coincidental.

And that made me feel awfully spiteful.

"Uh, yeah. Of course," I said to Weston, entwining my fingers in his.

"Good. I'll save you a seat." He held my hand until I was

out of reach. "Kincaid. Whatcha got for me? Budgets for the toothpaste campaigns, I'm hoping."

I brushed past Donovan as I left the room, letting my arm graze his, which sent sparks of electricity spinning through my body.

But no matter how nice the dizzying sensation was, it couldn't erase the shock of seeing a flicker of pain in his eyes when he caught sight of my hand in Weston's.

SEVENTEEN

I thought about Donovan while I dressed for Red Farm later that night. He was definitely not who I wanted to get involved with. Today had proven that. He was confusing and cruel, and he was also right—I should be with Weston. Weston was safe and nice and decent.

And if it hurt Donovan to see me with Weston, too bad. He'd made his bed. He could be jealous all he wanted. I'd even help him by dressing for the part. I wore my favorite pair of La Perla underwear, a matching sheer nude-colored bra and panty set—not that I planned on getting naked for anyone. They just made me feel sexier.

The dress I chose had a split black skirt and a pale long-sleeved top in a style that made the dress look like it belonged in the office—if it weren't for the plunging neckline and the way too short hemline. It would drive Donovan crazy.

It wasn't an outfit I'd wear alone with him, but we wouldn't be alone. We'd be at an office party. With a ton of other people, including Weston. This was a night to have fun.

To be sure I was all the way on board with the fun plan, I tossed back a shot of scotch before leaving my apartment. Then I threw on a jacket and headed out to catch a cab.

The party had already started when I arrived at Red Farm, which was fine. I was the type who preferred being late to being early. I stepped out of the taxi and approached the front door of the restaurant.

Before I could put my hand on the knob, however, Donovan appeared from the shadows. Grabbing my wrist, he pulled me several feet to the side of the entrance.

"What are you doing?" he hissed, his eyes wide.

"What?" I had barely caught my breath. I could feel the thrum of my pulse at my wrist underneath his hand, and I didn't know if my heart was beating so fast because he'd startled me or because he was touching me. "I just got here."

"With Weston." He tightened his grip, on the edge of discomfort. "What are you doing?" This time the question was slow, each word emphasized so as to be sure I would understand.

And I did understand. Very clearly.

"I cannot even believe you." I was seething, my vision clouding in red. This was too much. I yanked my wrist away from him and turned toward the door.

"You cannot be with him right now," Donovan warned behind me.

Pissed off, I turned back and pushed him, hard, both palms flat against his chest. Immediately, my body tingled as it remembered pushing him like that once before, years ago.

"This is familiar," Donovan said, his voice a low rumble.

"Leave me alone." Once again, I made for the door.

"He's *engaged*."

I spun around. "It's a *fake* engagement that *you* pushed him into."

"He's a grown-up," Donovan spat back. "He can make his own decisions."

"That's right." I nodded. "He can. And so can I."

This time when I headed toward the entrance, I made it all the way inside without turning around.

But once I was out of sight from the door, I stopped to catch my breath. I was shaking from adrenaline, and I had to hold on to the wall to steady myself.

How dare he?

How fucking dare he?

That was all the time I allowed myself to recover. He could walk in at any minute, and I didn't want him to think he'd affected me because how the fuck dare he?

Our group was comprised of nearly thirty of the staff members and their guests who were working on the Phoenix campaign and took up a full table across the restaurant as well as some side booths. Weston saw me before I saw him and called me over. He was seated at the main table next to Nate at the head. The chair next to him was empty.

There was still no sign of Donovan.

"Told you I'd save you a seat," Weston said, hugging me a little tighter than was maybe appropriate for a man who was engaged.

He lingered in the embrace too, which was actually nice after the altercation I'd had outside. Unlike Donovan who was still in his suit, Weston had changed from work clothes to jeans and a T-shirt with a gray button-down sweater.

I patted the fold of his shawl collar. "You look nice."

His gaze flickered to the very low cut of my dress. "Not as nice as you. I'm glad you made it." He let his hand trail lightly down my backside then helped me with my jacket.

We were doing this then—flirting. Playing around. It was likely going nowhere considering Weston's current situation, but that didn't mean we couldn't have a little fun if we kept it low-key. He probably needed it after weeks of being cooped up, so to say. I needed it to prove once and for all that he was exactly the kind of man I wanted to be with.

Once we were both seated, Weston draped his arm over the back of my chair. "We've already ordered a ton of appetizers. We were thinking about getting a bunch of dumplings too and just sharing them all family style. Or you can get an entrée if you'd rather."

"No. Dumplings are good." I honestly didn't have much of an appetite. I was restless and distracted. My blood was still soaring with adrenaline and my skin felt itchy. "And a drink. A martini please."

Donovan finally came in from outside, which was a strange relief. When I'd thought he'd left, I'd wondered why I was even still out myself.

Then he saw me, saw who I was sitting next to, and his expression grew hard and defiant, and my irritation returned.

I put a hand on Weston's arm and feigned excitement. "Look who's here!"

"Donovan!" Weston and Nate said in unison along with a few other employees.

Donovan smiled tightly as he greeted and congratulated people, but one eye was always on me. I felt it even when I didn't see it.

I'd thought I'd lucked out when there weren't any seats by us, but Tom and his wife had been sitting across from us, and now they had tickets to a show so they got up to leave just as Donovan was looking for a place to scoot in.

Weston checked something on his phone, and I leaned in closer to him, just to show that I could, and Weston, who still had one hand on my chair, moved it closer so his fingers brushed against my shoulder.

It was obviously intentional, and Donovan noticed so I shivered. On purpose.

It might have been my imagination, but I swore I heard him growl.

Weston had quite a different reaction. He moved his arm from behind me to *in front of* me—beneath the table. On my knee.

Only the truly perceptible would have noticed.

"Scotch. Straight," Donovan said, his eyes still pinned on me, when the waiter took his order. *He'd* noticed where Weston's hand had gone.

Not that I was paying attention to anything Donovan said or did.

We continued like that for a while—Donovan noticing me, me "not" noticing him, Weston playing with his phone and playing with my thigh. Without words, I could tell Donovan was more than displeased. Even across the table, the tension wrapped around us, as though we were a set, bound together by Cellophane. It smothered, making it hard to breathe. Making it hard to see anything outside of him.

Then things really got interesting.

Shortly after the first round of community dumplings arrived, so did Weston's fiancée.

"Elizabeth." Weston's hand left my leg for the first time since Donovan had arrived. He stood to greet her, surprise written all over his face. "What are you doing here?"

He bent in to kiss her, but just before his mouth met hers, she moved and his lips landed on her cheek, which left him disgruntled at best.

"My fiancé had a celebration," she said gruffly. "Thought I should be here."

"I'll move so you two can sit together," Nate said, offering to slide into the spot across from Weston.

Elizabeth waved him off. "Don't be silly. I don't need to sit by him. I'd much rather sit by Donovan."

Anyone who heard her would think she was teasing her groom-to-be, but to those in the know, it was obvious the level of tension between the couple had risen significantly.

I almost exchanged a glance with Donovan about it but remembered he was an asshole so I exchanged one with Nate instead while Elizabeth climbed over to the open spot.

"Now. Next time the waitress comes by, I'm going to need a drink." She put her arm on Donovan's back and ruffled the hair at the base of his neck. "So. I'm here!"

Donovan responded by bending forward to take a bite of a dumpling, acting as though the hand on his neck didn't have any effect on him at all.

I scowled. Elizabeth's fondling of Donovan was irritating, even if she and Weston weren't really a couple. No wonder he was having problems with her.

Weston seemed to find it annoying as well, if his actions were any indication. His hand found its way back to my knee, but only once he was sure that his fiancée was watching.

Now it was Elizabeth's turn to scowl.

"You said you weren't coming," he said, low enough so that only those in our corner could hear.

"I hadn't planned to. But." She turned and looked at the man next to her. "Donovan called and told me I needed to be here."

I clamped down so hard on the shrimp in my mouth that I bit my tongue. All the sound in the room seemed to whoosh by my ears, and my vision turned red.

Donovan called.

That's what he'd been doing after I'd left him outside. When he'd realized I was going to come in and be with Weston, Donovan had called Weston's fiancée.

"Wasn't that thoughtful of him," Weston said through gritted teeth, though I was sure he believed Donovan's intervention was about looking good for business or about not losing a bet on whether or not Weston could keep his pants zipped.

He had no idea that the real reason his friend had interfered had to do with me.

God, I was so mad I wanted to throw something.

Or fuck something.

It was strange to be so angry and so aroused, but that was how I was around Donovan—always excited and ready to go off in any way possible.

Under the table, I wrapped my leg around Weston's.

He took my cue. Or else he had his own battle to win. "Sabrina," he said, scooting his chair closer. "Have you tasted the seared pork and shrimp dumplings yet?"

"No. Where are they?" I had barely tasted anything, but that was beside the point.

"Have some of mine." He lifted his chopsticks to my lips, feeding me a bite of the morsel. I made sure to groan.

"Donovan, the pan-fried lamb—" Elizabeth started to say.

"You can have it," Donovan said, picking up the dumpling on his plate with his chopsticks and dropping it on her plate before she could ask him for a bite.

She frowned but quickly recovered. "Guess that's better than swapping germs." More importantly, she finally stopped playing with Donovan's goddamned hair.

"Elizabeth's a germophobe," Weston said snidely.

"I am not." She moved a dumpling around on her plate, apparently struggling with her chopsticks. "Just because I'm concerned about the diseases that come into my house doesn't qualify me as a germophobe."

"She's asked for a report of clean health." There was no doubt as to what kind of clean health report Weston was referring to.

Elizabeth shrugged, chopsticks poised in the air with the small bit of food she'd managed to wrestle between them. "I think that's reasonable." She lifted the bite to her mouth, dropping the dumpling just as it reached her lips. "Goddammit."

"Guys," Nate hushed them, trying not to laugh as he did. "Lovers' spats are fun and all..." He trailed off, probably figuring that Weston and Elizabeth would get the hint and remember that there were other people around.

Apparently, Weston didn't. "Why do you even care when there's no way I'm sharing anything I've got with you anyway?"

Nate winced.

Under the table, Weston's hand moved farther up my thigh, as if to spite Elizabeth.

Donovan remained stoic, his gaze on me, reading me. Watching me.

Elizabeth was the only one who seemed unfazed. Reaching

over to steal the unused fork from Weston's setting, she said, "Big words, King. Just remember the thing you want out of this relationship isn't as replaceable as the thing I want."

That seemed to silence Weston. In fact, it silenced our end of the table for a few thick minutes, but then Nate told a story and soon everyone was laughing and smiling like a bunch of people out for a celebration.

Weston's hand stayed on my leg though, brushing up and down my skin every now and again. Then, when everyone around us was preoccupied with other conversations, he leaned close and whispered, "In a few, I'm heading to the back of the restaurant. Toward the kitchen. Wait five. Then follow."

He shifted to joke with Nate, not waiting for me to answer. If I showed up, that would be my answer.

But what was my answer?

I turned to my drink and noticed Donovan watching. Again. He'd probably seen the whole exchange. He couldn't know what Weston was saying, but he had to guess the nature. There wasn't much he missed.

As if confirming my suspicions, Donovan narrowed his eyes, giving me what could only be called a warning glare.

Fuck him.

He'd wanted me with Weston. So he could fuck right off.

I threw back my shoulders and threw back my drink and five minutes after Weston disappeared from the table, I followed.

The restaurant wasn't large, and the kitchen was easy to find. I headed in that direction, even though Weston was nowhere in sight. I'd almost made it when, for the second time in one night, I was pulled unexpectedly off my path, this time into a cubby filled with shelves full of linens and table settings, closed off from the public by a thin curtain. Firm lips met mine, asking permission, as my body was pushed against the narrow wall.

I opened my mouth, letting Weston's tongue meet mine. It was easy to kiss him. It was familiar and safe. He tasted like gin and curry sauce and misbehavior. Not the fun kind of misbehavior, but the kind of misbehavior that left regrets in the morning, if not even the night before.

He broke the kiss and leaned his forehead against mine. "I'm going to be completely honest, Sabrina—this is a booty call and nothing else. You have every right to slap me and walk back out there. But I hope you don't. I'm sensing you need a release right now too."

It was what I'd come back for, but now that I was here, it felt wrong. Weston's body felt staged against mine, as if we were two mannequins propped up in a window display. He wasn't even pressed up all the way against me. His hand was caressing my arm, but it was awkward and mechanical. And while I'd been wound up for weeks, aroused and restless, I didn't feel turned on now. I just felt tired.

And Weston seemed tense.

Outside our hiding space, a rustling caught our attention. He leaned away so he could open the curtain and peek out.

"What is it?" I asked.

Weston shook his head, but I'd caught sight of someone in a suit. It could have been Donovan, I decided. Because I wanted it to be Donovan.

And because I felt more thrilled wanting it to be Donovan than I did hiding in a makeshift closet with Weston, I knew it wasn't where I was supposed to be.

Now I just had to tell Weston.

I lowered my head and stared at the buttons on his sweater. He was solid and sexy and sweet, and still he wasn't the guy I wanted, no matter how much I tried to want him. No matter how much I tried not to want someone else.

"I can't do this," he said.

My head snapped up. "I was just going to say the same thing."

He let go of me and ran his hand through his hair instead. "I'm sorry." My words registered a moment later. "You were?"

"Yeah. It's not..." *I'm not*, was the better phrase. *I'm not right for you. You're not right for me.* But maybe that wasn't the kind of thing meant to be discussed in restaurant closets. "The timing," I said.

"The timing," he agreed.

"I'll go out first."

When I got back to the table, Donovan was gone. I didn't bother pretending to myself that I didn't notice. I was past that. After grabbing my jacket, I thanked Nate for the party, said goodbye and went home. There couldn't be any more loneliness waiting for me there than there was here.

EIGHTEEN

I was exhausted by the time I reached my building, so I waved to the doorman instead of stopping to give my usual hello. Inside the elevator, I kicked off my heels and leaned against the back of the car and remembered the night I'd gone to Gaston's with Donovan. Remembered being in an elevator with him. If I hadn't pushed him away, would he have taken me home that night?

If he had, he'd have fucked me and been done with me. I'd still be alone tonight.

But maybe I'd be over him by now too instead of just finally realizing that I wanted him.

And, oh, did I want him. Like I hadn't wanted anything in a long time. Like I hadn't wanted anyone since I'd wanted him back then. Like I'd always wanted him but was too proud to admit.

Some fatalistic part of me was sure that it was a realization that made no difference. Whatever I wanted didn't matter because I would do what was best, like I always did, and Donovan was not it.

The elevator opened on my floor before I'd reached any conclusions, not that there was anything to conclude, and I trudged barefoot out into the carpeted corridor and froze. Down the hall, standing by the door to my apartment, was Donovan.

For the smallest fraction of a second, less time than it took to inhale a full breath of air, I got excited. I didn't care if he was there to tell me why Weston was the perfect guy for me or lecture me about not seeing him until he wasn't engaged. I didn't care if he was there to ask for my thoughts on Phoenix or the campaign. I didn't care if he wanted to borrow a cup of sugar. He was standing at my door, and that was everything.

But then I remembered that I was mad at him, and the thrill faded. Donovan Kincaid had been an epic asshole. Not only that, but he'd been an epic asshole *to me*.

With a solemn expression and my eyes forward, I strutted toward my apartment. Even as I refused to look at him, though, I saw him. On the surface, he looked composed and put together like he always did, but there was something about his posture, something about the way his foot tapped and the way his jaw stuck out like it was flexed that suggested he was keyed up.

Well, that made two of us.

"That didn't take long," Donovan said when I stopped at my door and pulled my key from my purse.

So he thought I'd hooked up again with Weston. Maybe he actually had been the suit I'd seen outside the closet at Red Farm. Or he'd just put two and two together. He wasn't dumb.

I wasn't ready to admit anything, so I simply shrugged.

Really, he had balls to bring it up. He had balls to even be here. The only reason he made it past the doorman was because he owned the building.

"You didn't have your own key?" I asked, half joking as I stuck my key in the lock.

"I would have had to go home for that first," he muttered.

I twisted my head back to look at him and found he was serious. He really had a key at his place? Wasn't that something the building manager took care of? I felt twisted up inside to think that Donovan had the very real ability to walk into my place whenever he felt like it.

I felt even more twisted up to realize how near he was standing behind me, so near that another slight shift of my body would bring me into his arms. My eyes traced a path from his Adam's apple up his throat and over his jawline to his mouth... Would he taste like sin and scotch, secrets and sweat?

What would it take to make me stupid enough to find out?

"Thank you, I guess, for waiting for me instead." I pushed my shoulder against the door and stepped inside when it opened.

Surprise, surprise, he followed.

"By all means, come on in," I said, switching on the light, not sure anymore if my irritation was feigned or real. I wanted him here—I just wanted him here for me, not for some other nonsensical agenda he'd concocted.

He closed the door with his foot and trailed behind me as I turned on lights and made my way to the coat closet.

"Are you going to tell me anything?" he asked while I hung my jacket on a hanger.

My eyebrows furrowed. "About Weston?" So that was

honestly why he was here. I was irritated. And hurt, which was stupid. "You want all the details? Pictures too?"

I threw my purse on the dining room table and breezed past him into the kitchen to grab a bottle of water from the fridge. I took a long cold swallow, imagining how good it would feel to throw the whole thing in Donovan's face.

Correction—Donovan's *smug* face. His shoulders had relaxed visibly in the past few seconds and his expression had gone from agitated to confident.

"Nothing happened, did it," he said, like it was a statement, so sure he was of the answer.

Fuck him for being so sure.

And fuck him for being so ridiculously sexy while we were at it.

This was impossible. I was thirsty but not for what I was drinking. There was only one thing I wanted to taste on my lips, and if I couldn't have that then I didn't want anything.

I slammed the bottle on the counter, exasperated. "Why are you here?"

He crossed his arms in front of him. "Because I can't not be. Are you going to meet up with him later?"

I considered dicking him around, but I was tired of the games. All of them—his and mine.

"I'm not," I said. "But guess what. It's not any of your business. None of this is. And yet you keep showing up, playing God like it's your job. Thinking you know best what everybody wants."

"You don't want Weston." Matter-of-fact. Plain light of day. No room for arguments. He said it like it was reality as we knew it.

And I about went off.

"Oh my god, I can't..." With my hands to my heart, I pushed past him to get into the living room. I needed space. Did he even hear himself?

Spinning back toward him, I pointed accusatorily in his direction. "For weeks now you've been trying to convince me that I *do* want Weston."

"Well, you don't." It was infuriating how calm he remained while both my head and my chest felt like they were going to explode.

"How do you *know* what I want?" My voice was louder than my neighbors would probably have preferred, but if they had a problem with it, they could take it up with the building's owner. "You assume and assume and assume. You've never even bothered to ask!"

He came toward me so we were only an arm's length apart. "What do you want, Sabrina?" he asked earnestly, his hazel eyes holding me captive. "Tell me."

Weeks of torment and denial had built up inside me. *Years* of it. My skin itched on the inside, and the want of Donovan had grown so acutely sharp and specific. It didn't even occur to me to try to lie or pretend that I didn't know the answer. I could only think in terms of transparency and truth.

"I want you to touch me!" I cried, desperate and willing to lay it all on the line.

Donovan's reflexes were quick. He grabbed one of my wrists in each hand and twisted one until it was pinned behind my back and bent the other until it was trapped between us.

"Touch you like this?" he asked brusquely, yanking my arms uncomfortably and pushing me until my back met the wall.

"No," I said, meekly. Except I meant exactly like that.

It was just the way I'd been yearning for him to touch me. Like he controlled me. Like he owned me. My nipples were already tight knots.

He raised an eyebrow. "No? Because I can't touch you like Weston touches you."

Jesus, I was so tired of hearing that name. Tired of that being the thing between us. Even now, Donovan had me against the wall but the only place we touched was where he held my hands. And everywhere around us, in the space between us, the imaginary being holding us away from each other was Weston.

"I don't want you to touch me like Weston," I said, once and for all. "I don't want *Weston*! I want *you*!"

Donovan let loose the smallest hint of a smile. "I know. I was waiting for you to know too."

I had the impulse to slap him, but it was lost when his mouth crashed against mine. Then I couldn't think about anything but him—his hands, his body, his victory over me.

It was such an easy surrender.

He took complete command. With the length of his body pressed against me, his erection pushing firmly at my pelvis, his lips molded mine. He sucked alternately on my bottom lip and then my top, leaving no part of my mouth untouched or untasted. When this wasn't enough, he let go of one of my hands and grabbed a fistful of my hair in its place. Then he yanked my head back, opening my mouth wider. I let out a cry that he lapped up with a long swipe of his tongue.

I'd remembered this about him. I'd remembered that he'd been a kisser, and there was something validating about having the memory confirmed. Something surreal about living again a time that had only been lived through recollection for so long.

Experiencing it for real with all of my senses fully engaged already had me wild.

And I needed more.

With my hand free, I urgently pushed his jacket over his shoulder and down his arm. Then I tugged at the empty sleeve until he let go of me long enough to finish taking it off. Now I had both hands free, and I stroked them up and down his torso, clawing at his chest through his shirt, frantically, wanting it gone, wanting to be able to scratch at his skin.

But Donovan was in control, and he had a free hand too, which he used to plunge inside my dress, inside my bra, and clutch my breast. It was painful, and I groaned into his mouth as he squeezed harder. Harder still.

Then he let go, and as soon as he did, pleasure vibrated straight down to my pussy.

"Oh my god," I gasped. "Do it again."

"No," he said, pulling his hand from the cup of my bra and moving it lower to play with my belt sash.

He was an asshole even now.

It was such a turn-on.

Releasing his other hand from my hair, Donovan pulled the tie at my waist, and my dress fell open. He pushed it off my shoulders and took a step backward so that he could see my whole body.

I felt a blush run down my skin; his gaze was the sun and everywhere his eyes touched I got burned.

"Were you thinking of him when you put this on tonight?" His breaths were quick, his gaze feral. He was rabid and ready to bite.

I told him the truth anyway. "I was thinking of you."

He practically groaned. Pressing in closer, he cupped my pussy. "You're so wet, I can feel it through your panties."

"Donovan..." I begged, bucking into his hand. This was torture. I'd wanted him to touch me, but I needed him to touch me in every way. I needed him to never stop.

Unexpectedly, he slapped my pussy. Hard. Then he slipped a finger inside the crotch of my underwear, gathered some of my wetness, and brought it to his nose and sniffed. "Just like I remember," he said before licking his finger clean.

I couldn't take it anymore—I lunged for him. Wrapping one hand around his neck, I brought his mouth down so I could kiss him while I rubbed my other palm along the outline of his dick. I could taste myself on him, and I wanted to devour every last drop.

He let me kiss him like this for a minute. Then abruptly he captured my hands again and drew them up against the wall above my head.

"You're dangerous with your hands free," he said then bit along my collarbone, marking me.

"Dangerous how?" I moaned as his teeth sunk into my skin, but if he hadn't been biting me, I might have laughed. Me? Dangerous? He was the one who wore that warning in my book.

"Dangerous like you always are when I let you touch me." He kissed me deeply, distracting me from the topic.

By the time he pulled away, I was dizzy and desperate for what words couldn't provide. My eyes flicked to my room and back to him.

"I know," he said, reading my mind. He circled one large palm around my wrists and tugged me into the bedroom where he tossed me onto my bed.

The light was off, but the blinds were drawn and the outside light spilled in across his torso. His dress shirt stretched tautly over his muscles, and though I wanted to see them in the flesh, I also loved the way it felt to be nearly naked while he was still dressed. It made the whole thing dirtier. Kinkier.

Especially when he ordered me around like he had a right to tell me what to do. Like he was still my teacher. Like he was my boss.

"Get naked for me," he commanded, loosening his tie.

Goose bumps spread along my arms and stomach. My hands trembled as I reached behind me to undo my bra. I threw it off the bed then scrambled out of my underwear.

He watched me as I did, his eyes dark slits. "Give me your hands."

I held them out to him, palms up, not sure what to expect. His authoritative tone along with the not knowing had my breaths coming double time, and I was pretty sure there was already a wet spot underneath me.

Looping the tie around my wrists, he tied a knot and pulled my arms until they were lying flat on the bed above my head. Then he looped the remainder of the tie around the corner bedpost and positioned my body so that I was stretched diagonally across the mattress.

He stood back and examined his captive. "How many men have you been with like this, Sabrina?" he asked, as he began undoing his belt.

"I've been with five men besides you." My number felt large, even when I was sure that Donovan had likely had plenty more lovers than I'd had. "But I've never been with anyone like this."

His eyes flared. "Never been tied to the bed before?"

"No." I'd never been so thrilled I nearly came without being touched before either.

And it was more than that. Except for that one time in a small office at Harvard, I'd never been with a man who made me feel so completely turned on, as though every single one of my arousal buttons had been hit and not just one or two.

And now his belt was off and his cock was out, hard and thick and purple in the moonlight. I tried to sit up, wanting it in my mouth. Wanting to taste him the same way he'd tasted me.

But Donovan put his hands on my thighs, and with the bindings on my wrists, I couldn't move very far. I definitely couldn't get to him. It felt like all the years of yearning for him were compounded in this one moment and the torment was nearly unbearable.

I wriggled and pled. "Please, Donovan!"

"What?" He knew exactly what. There was even a hint of a laugh, as though he found my misery amusing.

"You're cruel."

"So you've said." With a smile, he flipped me over so I was on my stomach and propped me on my knees. Then he stroked his hand down my back, pressing my head down. I peered back at him through my legs and saw him put one knee on the bed next to me, the other foot he left on the floor.

I heard the tear of a condom wrapper and watched as the foil fell to the floor. Again he ran his hand along my spine. This time when he reached my ass, he gave it a firm slap that made me jump. When I relaxed again, he was waiting with his cock to slam inside me.

"Fuck!" I cried into the pillow. Or I meant to, but it came out as some strangled sound I didn't recognize.

The feeling, though—now *that*, I recognized. Donovan

filled me so uniquely. Like no one else ever had, completely and totally, but it was also *how* he filled me that made my pussy crave him, how he *moved* inside me, how he bucked and raged, how he managed to go wild and yet master me all at the same time.

It was some form of magic or manipulation or maybe he just made me insane. I couldn't say which. All I knew was that with each thrust of his cock, I felt myself slip further under his spell.

My first orgasm hit almost immediately.

The second took longer, growing torturously as Donovan drove into me, hitting me at just the right spot, and with each thrust, my nipples rubbed against the ties of the quilt below me. It couldn't have been more agonizing if he had planted the quilt there. The yarn tickled my breasts and no matter how much I tried to adjust my position, I couldn't get the pressure to be enough. Every time I attempted to raise my torso even an inch off the mattress, he would push me back down. As if he knew the torment I was suffering. As if he wanted me to suffer more.

And I loved it.

When my second orgasm hit, my body fell into spasms, writhing with ecstasy.

I was still thrashing when Donovan put both of his legs on the floor. He shifted me so that my body was now perpendicular on the bed, and just my wrists were bent at the post. With his fingernails digging into my hips, he hammered into me, chasing his own orgasm, which he found quickly.

Exhausted and overwhelmed, I fell on my side.

Immediately, my head started working, like it always did, but I forced all thoughts and judgment and regret from my mind. Those would come later. I knew that well enough from experience.

Donovan collapsed on the bed behind me, his breath ragged.

I closed my eyes and listened as his breathing evened out. It was a peaceful sound, and I wondered how long I'd get to hear it. He wasn't the type to spend the night. He'd leave soon.

But I didn't think about that. I just listened and breathed.

I was only vaguely aware when he shifted a few minutes later, only vaguely aware of the loosening of the binding at my wrists before I slipped into the contented haze of unconsciousness.

NINETEEN

I woke with a start, as if I'd been dreaming, but the only images in my mind were from real life. Images of Donovan over me, inside me. I could still feel him even though I knew immediately that the bed was empty.

It felt worse than I thought it would to wake up without him. I guess I hadn't thought it would feel like anything, but it did. It felt hollow, like I'd forgotten to eat all day, yet my appetite was completely gone and the hollowness was both higher and lower than my stomach.

Other than the emptiness, though, I felt kind of amazing. Post-sex hormones lingered in my bloodstream, and my head spun in a weird euphoric haze. I stretched and my muscles screamed in protest, reminding me they'd been used in ways they hadn't been used in quite some time. I rubbed my eyes and blinked. It was still dark, and I'd woken in the position I'd fallen asleep in, so I knew I hadn't been out long. I rolled over to look at my alarm clock and nearly jumped out of my skin.

I wasn't alone after all.

Donovan sat in the chair in the corner of my room, his elbow propped on the armrest, his chin in hand, watching me.

The clock said I'd been asleep for more than an hour. Had he sat there the whole time?

I shivered at the thought, but I didn't pull a blanket over me. If he wanted to look, he could look. As far as I knew, it was the only thing keeping him here, and now that I had the choice, I wasn't ready for him to go.

But he would go. I knew that. He'd told me before that he was the quick-to-escape kind of lover. If he were staying, he'd be naked in the bed with me. Instead, he was just as dressed as he'd been when he'd fucked me. His pants were still unfastened and now his tie was looped around his neck.

But maybe that's why it thrilled me so much to find him still here, why it warmed me to think he'd been sitting there the whole time I'd slept—because he hadn't left *yet*.

I sat up and tried to pat down the bird's nest that had once been my hair.

"Were you even going to say goodbye?" I asked, pretending to balance accusation with acceptance when really I was hoping he'd say he'd changed his mind about going at all.

He smiled lazily. "I don't know what you mean. I'm still here."

"You're just as much already gone."

His face was in the shadows, but I could feel his expression sober even if I couldn't see it. "I'm less gone than you'd imagine."

My inner thighs clenched with desire, but the sincerity in his tone tugged at some emotion beyond lust. It made me brave. "Get in bed, then. Stay."

He chuckled. "Sabrina, Sabrina," he scolded. He stretched his legs out in front of him and crossed them at the ankle. Then, distinctly changing the subject, he asked, "Where did you get your name?"

Casual conversation wasn't where I thought this was going, but his attention had a way of engaging me whatever the form. I swung my knees to one side and leaned my weight on the opposite hand. "My father. When they were thinking of names, he was reading the Milton poem about the nymph who saves the virgin."

"Can't say I read that one. Is Sabrina the virgin?"

"Sabrina is the savior."

There was a beat of silence. "Huh. That wasn't the answer I was expecting."

For half a second, I wondered if I should be offended, but it was kind of amusing to think of myself as anyone's savior. "I guess in our version of the story, Sabrina was the virgin."

He didn't say anything. Didn't respond at all, just kept looking at me in the same piercing way he would all those years ago in Business Ethics class.

I used to hate it when he looked at me that way. I still did. Hated it because he seemed to see things I didn't want him to see. Seemed to see things I didn't even know about myself. Mostly I hated it because I liked it so much.

I cocked my head, wondering if I could see him the same way he saw me, but all I saw was a fiercely attractive man with the devil's smile and dangerous sex appeal.

I'd let a dangerous devil in my bed. A dangerous devil who'd once been my savior. Could Donovan be any more of an enigma?

I let out a sigh. "Where did you get your name?"

He didn't answer right away. "It was my great-grandmother's maiden name. She claims that's why I have the name, but I think my mother just liked the sound of it."

It occurred to me that this was one of the only things Donovan had ever told me about his family or his personal life. It was small, but in some ways it was also really big, and I held it like it was precious.

"What does it mean?" I asked, hoping not to sound too eager.

"Dark warrior." He shook his head. "I think she was expecting an entirely different kind of son."

"But that fits our story. Dark warriors are totally the guys who save the virgins." It was maybe too fitting. Too easy to romanticize. And I knew even without being able to clearly see his sneer that he didn't appreciate the analogy.

Or maybe he didn't like that we had an *our story*.

Now that I'd said it out loud, I wasn't so sure I liked it either.

I tugged at my hair and stared out the window. What was I doing with this guy? What the hell did I imagine could happen next? Coworkers with benefits? We weren't really friends, and it wasn't like this could lead to anything romantic.

Could it?

"You're a beautiful woman, Sabrina," Donovan said, pulling my focus back to him.

It was the kind of statement that was usually followed by a *but*. When it didn't come, I couldn't resist questioning. "Am I?"

"Very." His voice was thick and rough, like heavy sandpaper.

I glanced down at where the moonlight hit his lap and saw

his cock bulging, its head peeking out over the band of his underwear.

Oh. So not a *but*.

Wherever this was going tomorrow, it was still tonight right now. And tonight I was wet and wanting and Donovan was hard and here.

I straightened, purposefully showing off my breasts. "Do I make you think dirty thoughts?"

"Mm," he moaned. "Very dirty thoughts." He kept his hands braced on the armrests, his eyes pinned on me.

"When I was younger, I used to have all sorts of dirty thoughts about you." I didn't know why I said it. I'd told him I'd had inappropriate thoughts about him back then. The information wasn't exactly new.

"And not now?"

"Now too." God, it was my last secret. How much I thought about him. How much he invaded my mind. "All the time."

His grip tightened on the armrests, and my pussy fluttered in response. I liked telling him, I realized. I liked him knowing, just like I liked knowing he had dirty thoughts about me.

"Do you get yourself off when you have these dirty thoughts?"

"Yes." I pressed my thighs together, seeking relief. I was so turned on.

"Show me."

"*Show* you?" I'd heard what he'd said. And I knew what he meant. I just needed a second to process what I thought about the idea.

"Yes." He sat up straighter in his chair, obviously eager. "And tell me. Tell me what I do to you in your imagination.

Show me and tell me. Show and tell." He smirked at his own pun.

"Well." I'd never played with myself in front of someone else before. I'd never wanted to. Donovan was different though. He brought out different things in me, and saying no to him never crossed my mind, much less felt like an option.

I lay down on the bed, propping my head up with pillows so I could see him when I opened my legs. Now which scenario would I share? "There's a few different..."

"Tell me your favorite," he interrupted.

Variations on a rape. That was my favorite and most played out. No way was I telling him that. I'd stick with one of the more generic fantasies. Maybe the one where he threw me across his desk...

I closed my eyes and prepared the scene in my mind. Then I opened my mouth to begin.

"Now, be honest, Sabrina," he said, cutting me off before I'd started. "It's no fun if you aren't honest."

My heart thumped louder against my ribcage. Could I really tell him the truth about this? It was so dirty. So wrong.

I opened my eyes just enough to peek at him. He wouldn't know if I lied, not if I made it good enough. But he was right—what would be the point of that? Wasn't my whole fascination with him about this filthy daydream of mine anyway? Wouldn't it be best to tell him so I could finally get this sick perversion out of my system?

No. I should tell him because it might be my only chance to live out this deepest, darkest fantasy. And feeding that need, that craving, that endless hunger, was reason enough to be worth it, humiliation and all.

And, honestly, as humiliating as the act was to think about, it was equally as hot. Hot *because* it was humiliating.

I took a deep breath. This time I didn't close my eyes—I met Donovan's instead. "You hold me down." My voice sounded slow and monotone, like a narrator stripped of emotion, but even just that much of my story was enough to make Donovan's eyes flare. "I can't get away. You've muffled my screams. No one can hear me. No one can help me. You manage to get my pants down—"

"But you struggled first," he added, in a similar matter-of-fact tone.

"Yes." His addition to my fantasy surprised me, but it added to my arousal. My nipples immediately budded. I brought my hands to my breasts, caressing them, easing them from their sudden heaviness.

"*How* did you struggle?"

"I kneed you, but I didn't get you where I aimed." I lowered my glance to his cock and saw it had grown even bigger, which made my breath catch. "Fighting just turned you on more. You punish me with a hard bite on my nipple."

He raised his brows, and I realized he wanted me to act this out how I would if he wasn't there. Taking a nipple between my thumb and forefinger, I pinched and pulled as hard as I could.

"Harder," he taunted.

I tugged harder and tears formed at the corners of my eyes. "Until it makes me cry."

He adjusted slightly in his seat, as though his erection was growing uncomfortable, but he didn't even touch himself. It made me antsy that he didn't. *I* wanted to touch him. Wanted to rub my palm across his crown. Wanted to wrap my fingers around him and feel him throb in my hand.

If I couldn't have that, then at the very least, I wanted to watch him do it.

Then I remembered—I had myself to touch. Spreading my legs wider, I pressed two fingers between my folds and began massaging the bundle of nerves in quick, aggressive circles. "You're rubbing my clit now. You're rough and you're relentless, working me to orgasm." I could already feel it building. This fantasy always brought me to climax fast. "I'm close."

"Close to coming?" His voice was threadbare and ragged, a reflection of how I felt.

"Yes," I panted. "You're glad because you're impatient and you want me to come. Not because you want me to feel pleasure, but because you hate going in dry."

He grinned like he was admitting something. "Nice detail."

I had my own confession to admit. "But what you don't know is that I'm already wet."

He threw his head back and groaned in the back of his throat. "Show me."

Though I was teetering on the edge, I pulled my hand away from my clit and moved it lower where I dipped two fingers inside me. When I withdrew them, I held them up so that Donovan could see them glistening with my wetness.

"Jesus, Sabrina." His expression tightened, and he bucked his pelvis in the air. I could feel his control abandoning him. Especially when I brought my fingers to my mouth and sucked them clean. "Are those my fingers?" he asked.

"Yes. You shove them so far down my throat I think I'll gag." I stick my fingers in my mouth again, shoving them in as far as I can.

"Fuck, the things I want to do to your mouth right now." He shifted once more, and I could see his thighs tightening through his pants. "Then what?"

"Then you fuck me." Watching him get aroused made me even more turned on. I writhed on the bed, trying to rub my pussy against the mattress. We were both miserable—surely we'd played enough of this game. I needed him inside of me. Now.

But he didn't move.

"Fuck me, Donovan," I begged. "Please!"

"No. You have to do it." He was cold and in charge. "Show me how I fuck you."

I whimpered, but I didn't protest. There was no use arguing with him, and I knew it. Reaching down, I rammed several fingers inside my pussy, thrusting in as far as I could go.

He sat abruptly forward in the chair. "Three fingers—is that what you always use?"

"No," I gasped, drawing my fingers back out. "Sometimes I use a toy."

"What else?" He was on edge. I could feel it in the air between us.

"Nothing else."

"If I couldn't fuck you with my cock, I wouldn't use a dildo." His eyes began to frantically search the room. "Next time, use that bottle over there."

I followed the line of his gaze to my moisturizer sitting on the nightstand. The bottle was thicker than my toy. It would be an uncomfortable fit, but because the order to use it had come from Donovan, I was more than eager to comply. "Okay. I will."

Seemingly satisfied with my response, he returned his focus

to me, to my hands and what they were doing, what I was pretending he was doing to me.

He stood up, as though to get a better view. "Now," he said, finally, *finally* drawing his cock out. "Tell me how I fuck you."

"Hard. Brutally. It hurts." I couldn't take my eyes off his cock, hard and thick in his palm. It made my mouth water, made my cunt wetter.

"Show me," he said, stroking himself lazily. "Show me how much it hurts."

I thrust my fingers inside of me again and again, rapidly, the way I always liked to imagine him fucking me. The way I always remembered him fucking me. The pressure of my hand helped relieve my discomfort, but it wasn't perfect. I wanted more. I wanted him. I stared at him, stared at his cock as he ran his hand up and down his shaft, wishing again that I could touch it. Wishing it was closer.

Without realizing what I was doing, I scooted closer to the edge of the bed. He still wasn't close enough. "Show *me*!" I cried. "I want to see you too. Please!"

For once, he didn't argue. He walked to the end of the bed and scooped some of my wetness from my pussy. Then, standing over me, he matched my tempo, jerking himself off inches above where I finger-fucked myself. It was so hot, so dirty, watching his hand moving briskly over his thick cock while I imagined he was holding me down, plowing into me instead of his palm.

I couldn't take more than a minute of it before my orgasm ripped through me. My back arched and my toes curled and my vision went black and then spotted with lights. It was the kind of orgasm that I felt everywhere in my body. The kind I'd never had with another person other than Donovan.

Donovan watched intently throughout my climax—I felt his eyes on me the entire time—and when I was finished, he was ready with his own. As soon as I could see again, I threw my focus back to him. His hand quickened and he moved to tug on just his tip. Suddenly, his tempo slowed and he came, spilling everywhere on my belly and my pussy.

It was one of the most erotic things I'd ever experienced in my life. Even as sticky with sweat and cum as I was. I probably looked like a worn-out porn star, but I felt fabulous.

Donovan was already tucking himself away and zipping up his pants when I gathered myself enough to prop up on my elbows and stare dazedly at him.

"Was this you marking your territory?" I asked, sure that I had the dopiest grin on my face.

"Is that the reason you came up with for your fantasy?" He kept his attention on his belt as he fastened the buckle.

"Is that not the right interpretation?"

"No, Sabrina," he said sharply. He met my eyes. "I came on you because it's dirty, and it gets me off. Don't attach anything more to it than that, fantasy or not."

My grin slid off my face. More like he'd knocked it off my face by what he'd said. There were a thousand responses that came to mind, too many to sort through in the moment. There was nothing I could do except to sit there, dumbfounded, naked and covered in his cum.

And what an asshole that he could say something so cold while looking me straight in the eye. To my credit, I wasn't the one who looked away first.

He finished putting himself together quickly. "I'm going," he said, dodging my gaze. He'd taken several steps before—as an afterthought—he asked, "Would you like me to grab you a towel before I leave?"

"No, thank you," I said bitterly. "I need a shower." I suddenly wanted to wash the whole night off of me, wanted to clean myself of Donovan Kincaid.

He nodded, as if his approval was necessary. At the door to my bedroom he stopped. "Make sure you lock up behind me."

Yeah, yeah. Like you care.

I stood up to follow after him, but when I heard the apartment door shut, the first thing I did was pick up the night cream by the side of my bed and throw it across the room.

Once again Donovan Kincaid had proven to me that he was a total asshole. It was not the first time. Not even the second time. Why, then, was I always surprised when he showed his true colors?

A Dangerous Devil, that's what he was. A Dangerous Dark Warrior Devil.

After kicking a few things and locking the door, I took a scalding hot angry shower. I was angry as I washed my hair. Angry as I scrubbed myself clean. Angry as I erased every trace of Donovan from my body.

And it wasn't just Donovan I was angry with. I was angry with myself. More than anything else, I was angry at getting caught in his trap. I was angry for caring. I was angry, because if I wasn't, then I'd be hurt, and I was pretty sure that would feel even worse.

TWENTY

I spent the weekend engaged in a teeter-totter of thoughts where Donovan was concerned. He pissed me off; he didn't piss me off. I cared; I didn't care. It was just sex; it was more than sex. It didn't matter; it mattered.

By Monday morning, the conclusion I'd come to was that I was a strong woman who'd had dirty sex with a powerful man. It had been my choice, and I owned that. I was grateful for that choice. It had been consensual, and there was nothing to regret or be ashamed of.

What I didn't own was the disrespectful way that Donovan had left, and that had nothing to do with me—that was on him. I refused to feel bad about it. He obviously had a fear of women growing attached to him. If he'd thought that I'd grown attached after one roll in the hay or that I'd misread the situation, he'd worried needlessly.

Or maybe he'd worried as he should. I'd thought about him

for ten years after the first roll in the hay—if that wasn't attachment, I didn't know what was.

The point was, I wasn't planning to cling, and if he thought I was then he needed to get over himself.

The only thing I hadn't decided was whether or not I planned to say something about his nasty departure. Yes. No. The answer changed by the hour.

It would have to be a bridge I crossed when I came to it. Luckily, I didn't see much of Donovan on a day-to-day basis without going out of my way.

Problem was, there were other people that I *did* see on a day-to-day basis. And, as I stepped into the elevator and found myself standing next to another man in a suit who was both my boss and had seen me naked, I realized I'd forgotten to consider how I planned to deal with Weston.

"Morning," I mumbled, unable to meet his eyes. What were the rules of etiquette in this situation? Did I need to tell him about Donovan? Did I owe Weston a heads up? We weren't together, but we'd almost made out just hours before I'd ended up in bed with his best friend. What was my obligation here?

While I bandied the two options—tell, don't tell; tell, don't tell—Weston fidgeted next to me. His eyes seemed focused on the dial watching as the elevator climbed from floor to floor when he abruptly burst out, "We need to talk."

Oh, shit.

My options suddenly seemed slimmer.

Or, maybe I was jumping to conclusions.

"If this is about Friday..." I paused, realizing that wasn't specific enough. "If this is about the restaurant, I don't think there's anything else that needs to be said."

"This isn't about the restaurant." He couldn't look at me either, I noticed.

"Oh." My hands were sweaty. He knew. He already knew. Donovan told him, and he knew. "Okay."

I took a breath.

This was fine. I'd tell him that I was planning to tell him today. He couldn't be that mad. We weren't a couple. He was engaged to someone else, for Christ's sake.

The elevator arrived, and I followed Weston onto our floor. Might as well get this over with. "Right now good?"

He looked at me as though he hadn't expected anything else. "If you're free..."

"I'm free. I'll just drop off my bag and be there in a few."

I took my time in my office, checking in with my assistant, and trying to decide what I'd say to Weston. But I could only dawdle so long, and there wasn't much I could think of to say except the truth, so it was only ten minutes later when I arrived at Roxie's desk.

"He more relaxed than he was the other day," she told me, which lifted my spirits. "But something has him on edge. Good luck."

"I still hear you," Weston called through the open door.

"Thank you," I whispered to Roxie. "I think I need it."

At least I looked good today. I'd worn something different than usual—a short black skirt and a white fitted button-down blouse with a ruffle. I'd paired the whole thing with stockings and black high heels. It was less of a power outfit and more feminine, more demure.

Ah, crap. Weston probably thought I'd worn it for Donovan.

Huh. Had I?

No way. I hadn't dressed for anybody but myself. Most likely.

I took a deep breath and walked into Weston's office. He shut the door behind me but kept the windows clear. Like he had the last time I'd visited, he sat behind his desk and invited me to take a seat in front.

And like the last time, I crossed one leg over the other and tried to stop the nervous tapping. Well, at least this would be out in the open once and for all. No more coming to Weston's office and fretting about what he knew about Donovan and me.

Silly, too, considering that Donovan and I had already dissolved into a big fat nothing.

I sighed.

Weston inhaled. "Friday night," he began, "after you left the restaurant..." He trailed off as though unsure how to finish the sentence.

And how *could* he finish it? *You left the restaurant and fucked my friend and now I'm confronting you about it.* Nothing he could say would come out politely.

I had to help him out. This was my burden more than his. He shouldn't have to be the one struggling to come up with the words. "Things change, you know, Weston. Things don't always happen the way we plan and—"

"I slept with Elizabeth," he blurted out.

I actually had to replay what he said in my head before responding. "Uh, what?"

Totally not where I saw that going. Not even a little bit.

"I slept with Elizabeth. I didn't mean to. And I don't know where things are headed in the future, but I thought you deserved the truth."

"I see." So he *didn't* know about Donovan.

Did this mean I had to tell him anyway?

"Are you upset?"

"No! Not in the least." Actually, I felt relieved. More relieved than I'd expected to feel. Now I didn't have to feel guilty about anything I'd done behind Weston's back. Not that I *had* felt guilty. "We didn't have an arrangement between us. I didn't expect anything from you." Hint, hint—he shouldn't have expected anything from me either.

"I know, but we were in a closet together." He moved his stapler from the corner of his desk to the center. "And I know I was acting weird that night, but it wasn't you." He pushed the stapler several times, shooting out a bunch of wasted staples. "It was because I was all wrapped up with her, and this bullshit that's going on between her and me." After fiddling for another few seconds, he returned the stapler to its original position.

I studied Weston. He did seem to be in a better mood than he'd been on Friday morning, and more on edge at the same time. His eyes lit up when he talked about Elizabeth, and his body seemed tense, but it was strained with electric energy, the kind of energy that came from feeling out of sorts in a new relationship.

The kind of energy that came from falling in love.

"So you and Elizabeth...?" I asked tentatively.

"No. God, no." He flipped a pen back and forth between his fingers. "I mean. I don't know. It's complicated. Anyway."

It's complicated meant *more than a fling*.

The nervous tap of my foot was back, and for the life of me I couldn't understand why.

I sat back in my chair and folded my arms across my chest. "What does this mean for the pool? I had good money on you holding out."

The pen stopped spinning abruptly. "You placed a bet too?"

I shrugged, trying to be elusive, but he seemed too affronted for me to carry the teasing any longer than that. "I'm joking. Any bet I would have placed seemed to be against my better interest."

He dropped the pen and put both palms flat on the desk. "But you're really okay with this situation?"

I smiled reassuringly. "I am." My conscience, which had been niggling at me since he'd made his confession, took that moment to get the better of me. "Actually, I slept with someone this weekend too." I paused to take a breath and decided I wasn't obligated to say more.

But I also decided I wasn't a dick. "I slept with Donovan."

The air between us thickened, and Weston squinted at me for a beat too long.

"Uh. Say something?" I prodded, suddenly concerned that I shouldn't have been so honest.

"I'm trying to decide if I'm jealous or if this relieves me of my guilt."

I reached across the desk and playfully punched his lower arm. "It relieves you of your guilt. Jerk."

He nodded. "Donovan, huh?" He inhaled. Nodded again. "I have to admit—I didn't see that coming."

So we were both stunned by the weekend's developments.

"Is this a bad thing? Should I have not told you?" I wasn't friends with Elizabeth. Maybe this was harder for Weston because of his relationship with Donovan.

"No, no! I'm glad you told me. It's just...weird." Immediately he realized his error in wording. "I don't mean it's weird because of *you*. It's weird because of *him*. He hasn't been with anyone that I've been on a first-name basis with since Amanda."

That was impossible. Donovan's fiancée Amanda died eleven years ago. Surely he'd had relationships since then. "What about Sun?"

"That model?" Weston brushed his hand dismissively in the air. "I guess he sleeps with her now and then. He sleeps with a lot of women now and then, but I'm telling you, Sabrina, he doesn't sleep with anyone that he has any interaction with outside the bedroom."

"Oh. That *is* weird." Goose bumps shimmied down my arms. What did that mean about me?

Nothing, probably. We worked together, but it wasn't like we saw each other that much around the office.

Still, something warm burrowed into my chest insisting I was different. Insisting that this implied I was special. Special to Donovan in some way.

Yes, Sabrina, you have the distinct honor of being a sex partner that Donovan has also seen with clothes on. Congratulations.

Right. I was being ridiculous.

But maybe this explained why Donovan was such a dick when he'd left my place. Maybe that's how he always left women's beds. Since he usually didn't see them again anyway, he had no reason to act differently.

"Although it's weird, this could be good." Weston started nodding again. "Yes. I think this is really good. You're the perfect woman to show him what romantic relationships are supposed to be like. You could domesticate him. Show him how to love again."

I burst out laughing. "There are so many things funny

about that statement, I don't know what to laugh at first." Like, who was Weston to talk about relationships? Was he suddenly an expert because he'd banged his fake fiancée?

And even more hysterical—a romance between Donovan and me? Show him how to *love*? Ha. Ha. Ha.

"I'm serious," Weston said excitedly, seeming to have warmed up completely to the idea of our coupledom. "You're right for him. You're already in his world. You won't take his bullshit. I already approve of you, which is essential. The whole thing is brilliant. I should have thought of this before."

I rolled my eyes. "Right. In between making your own moves on me, it totally should have crossed your mind." The whole thing was insane. "It's not happening. That's not where this thing with Donovan is going."

Weston stared at me skeptically. "Are you sure?"

"Positive. With a capital P."

"Okay, okay." He didn't appear entirely convinced. "Wanna talk about it at least?"

I brushed a loose piece of hair behind my ear and considered. It might be nice to have some insight on Donovan. But I didn't necessarily know if it was fair to ask about him when I hadn't tried hard enough to get insight from the guy on my own.

And what did it matter since Donovan and I were a done deal? "I don't," I said. "If that's okay."

Weston wasn't quite ready to let it go. "Just a one-night thing, then?"

"Just a one-night thing." Why did it make my stomach knot so tightly to say that?

"Fine, fine." Weston narrowed his eyes. "Even just a one-night stand, he better have treated you right."

Again, I laughed out loud. "Or else what?"

"Or else I'll have to kill him." The wink he gave as he made the declaration sort of ruined its power, but it was a nice gesture all the same.

"Yeah, I totally believe you'd kill Donovan," I said sarcastically. "Glad to know you got my back."

I didn't need Weston to take care of Donovan or any of the men I dated, but what the heck was going on? Was he treating me like a sister? Was that what happened when ex-lovers became coworkers and found other lovers?

After I left Weston's office, I was halfway down the hall toward my own when it hit me—if Weston was involved in more than just a fling, then that meant he would no longer be available to be my fallback guy. No longer my safety net.

I didn't want Weston. I'd never wanted Weston. The most attractive thing about Weston was that I'd believed he could keep me from Donovan. That he could keep me a "good girl", safe and content without the urge for dirty, kinky filth.

It hadn't been a very good plan anyway because somehow I'd still ended up naked with the wrong guy.

Well, lesson learned.

I couldn't depend on Weston to protect me. I could decide what I wanted for myself without hiding behind someone else. I could stand up for myself and, at the same time, teach Donovan a thing or two about how to treat women in case he ever *did* decide to have a romantic relationship again.

Feeling buoyed, I changed direction and headed toward the opposite side of the building right away before I had time to have second thoughts.

TWENTY-ONE

Donovan was standing by his secretary's desk when I got there, discussing his day's schedule with Simone. Despite the way my stomach flip-flopped when I saw him in his fitted black Armani, I kept my shoulders back and my head high.

"We need to talk," I said, stealing Weston's opening line. Then, without waiting for him to respond, I marched past him into his office.

I didn't look back, but after a beat, I heard him say, "Simone, hold my calls."

It took thirty painfully long seconds for Donovan to follow me in, hit the buttons to shut the door and darken the windows, and get situated at his desk.

Meanwhile, I paced, pulling my hair over one shoulder with both hands.

"Go ahead, Sabrina," Donovan said, making himself comfortable in his high-back leather swivel chair. "Tell me what's on your pretty little mind." He said *mind* but his eyes drifted down my legs, and he made no effort to hide it.

I scowled, but truthfully, it made me a little giddy. Especially when I'd never seen him look at the other women in the office like that, but thinking about that would get me off track so I shelved the giddiness for later.

"Look," I said as forcefully as I could while continuing to pace the length of his desk. "I can accept that Friday night was a one-time thing, but you—"

He cut in before I could finish. "Do you want it to be a one-time thing?"

I stopped mid-step, my pulse quickening. "That's not what I said." My cheeks suddenly felt warm.

"It's not what you said, but it's what I'm asking."

"I don't. I hadn't thought." I was flustered. This wasn't fair. Another round hadn't even been on the menu when he'd left the way he did.

And that's what I was here to discuss—how he'd left, not if I wanted to do more naughty, naked things with the man who'd given me the best orgasms I'd ever had in my life.

I shook my head to clear it of the filthy images that had begun to flood my imagination. "I'm not talking about that right now. Can I just finish what I was saying?"

"Yes, of course. Go on." He gave me that devilish smile of his. The one that made my panties wet every goddamned time.

Devilish smile or not—wet panties or not—I had a message to deliver, and I was going to get it out if it killed me. Aiming a finger directly at him for emphasis, I said sternly, "You don't get to leave like an asshole again."

Phew. I'd said it. And I felt pretty proud about my delivery as well.

Donovan rubbed his chin, considering. "Sex with me isn't always as easy as the other night, you realize."

Perhaps my delivery hadn't gone quite as spectacularly as I'd believed.

More likely, the fault was with my audience. "Are you listening to me?"

I tried to pretend that I hadn't been listening to *him*, but part of me definitely had. The part of me that was less concerned with respect and woman's pride and more concerned with primal needs and wants. There was a lot to question after a statement like that. Sex with him wasn't always that *easy*? My head wanted details. My body wanted demonstrations.

"Yes, I'm listening to you. In response, I'm explaining what a continuation of a sexual relationship with me could look like."

My breasts felt heavy and my thighs felt weak. I threw my hands up in frustration. "But what does that have to do with what I was saying?"

His eyes glinted at me, more green today than brown. "You said 'again', Sabrina. Which insinuates you foresee a time in the future in which this would be an issue."

Was that what I'd really said?

I replayed the words in my mind. "That wasn't what I meant," I said hurriedly.

"Wasn't it?"

I wasn't sure. Because maybe that was what I meant. What was the point in even correcting his behavior if I hadn't, on some level, wanted there to be another time?

Still, none of that mattered if he didn't hear me. "But did you get what I was saying?"

He sighed. "Yes, yes. *Don't be an asshole, Donovan.* I heard you." He swiveled his chair to the side. "Come here." He used two fingers to summon me.

Didn't sound like he took me very seriously though. And what he'd done had been a big deal.

Grudgingly, I trudged around his desk and stopped when I was a couple feet in front of him. "You heard me, but will you actually make an effort to change?"

He half-shrugged. "That sort of remains to be seen, doesn't it? Get on your knees."

"Remains to be seen? That doesn't sound very committed." Without thinking about it, I began to kneel down when my eyes hit the very large bulge in his crotch. "Wait." I shot back up and stepped away. "Oh, no!"

"Come on." He stroked his hand along his erection. "Door's locked. Windows are dark."

Goddammit. What was wrong with me? I was mad at this jerk, and he had the nerve to try to entice me to suck him off? In his office, no less? This was sexual harassment. This was inappropriate and indecent and such a fucking turn-on that I wouldn't be surprised if Donovan could smell my arousal from a yard away.

But respect! Women's lib!

"I'm not going to reward your bad behavior with a blowjob. That's not why I came in here." Though every second I stood before him it got harder and harder to remember why I existed if not for him.

"No, you came in here to tell me off. Which you did. More or less. Now we're moving on. I'm helping you decide whether or not the other night was a one-time thing with another look at what it can be like to have sex with me."

Donovan's expression got serious—the kind of serious that

said he was on the verge of losing patience, and I'd better listen if I knew what was good for me. "So, like I said before—get on your knees. I'm not going to tell you again."

I was a girl who knew what was good for me.

Immediately, I fell to my knees.

The office floor was hard, even with the carpet Donovan had under his desk. It was dark brown with a tight pile that rubbed against my knees. It would leave marks if I spent much time there, even through my stockings.

But honestly, I didn't give a fuck about my stockings. They could rip for all I cared. I was on my knees in front of Donovan Kincaid, and all I could think about, all I wanted was to get my mouth on him.

He was already undoing his pants. When he'd gotten both his belt and his zipper open, he dropped his hands to his sides. The crown of his cock peeked up at me above the band of his boxer briefs, much like it had the other night at my house. This time, however, I was eye level. This time, I was close enough to touch.

"Now this is where you make your choice," Donovan said, his hands gripping the armrests of his chair. "If this is what you want—and by the way you're biting your lip, I'd say this is exactly what you want—then you make the next move."

Way to save himself when it came to consent. It was probably a wise move on his part. Not that I was going to sue him for workplace harassment, no matter how many times I brought it up. I happened to like it too much. I probably even encouraged it at times.

But there was a bigger question here now—was this really what I wanted? Did I really want there to be an "again"? What did it mean about me if I did?

Maybe I really couldn't take care of myself. Maybe I really did need Weston or a safe guy to hide behind, someone who wouldn't be asking me to get on my knees in the middle of a workday. Someone who didn't get off on the idea of holding me down while he fucked me. Someone who didn't think it was necessary to warn me that sex with him wasn't always "easy".

Except this *was* what I wanted. All of it. The dubious consent, the dominant overtones. I wanted it with every fiber of my being, and if I was a big enough girl to know that about myself then maybe I could be a big enough girl to accept it too.

Hesitantly—only because I was nervous, not because I was reluctant—I wrapped my hands around the band of his briefs. Donovan raised his hips, and I pulled his briefs down until his cock sprung out thick and heavy.

Damn, was he always this big?

He was longer than I'd realized. Rounder too. And it only made me want him more.

I just wasn't sure where to start.

A drop of pre-cum glistened on his head as if signaling me, and I leaned forward and licked it off, slowly. Deliberately.

His cock stirred, but that didn't mean anything. It was too gentle of a movement for Donovan, too soft, and I knew without him telling me that I needed to progress my game.

I sucked his tip, then past that, drawing the top half of his cock into my mouth. When I started to wrap my fingers around his base, he stopped me. "No hands—just your mouth."

Okay. I could do that.

I rested my hands on his thighs instead, loving the way his muscles felt under my palms, and resumed the action with my mouth, bobbing up and down his shaft, hollowing my cheeks to make the suction tight. He tasted good—like clean and musk and Donovan, and as big as he was, he felt good. It made me horny, made me super aroused. Like the way he stretched my lips reminded my pussy how it felt to be invaded in the same way.

"Very nice," Donovan said after I'd spent a few minutes sucking him off. "Good girl. I like that." He brought both his hands to my head and wrapped them in my hair. "But now I'm going to take over."

That was all the warning I got.

After that, Donovan was the one in control. With my head held in his grip, he pushed me down over his cock, slowly at first, forcing more of his length in than I'd previously taken.

"That's it, that's it," he coaxed as his tip hit the back of my mouth. And still he pushed in farther. "Relax your throat, Sabrina."

My eyes went wide. I couldn't take any more. I was going to gag. I started to panic. I couldn't breathe.

Yes, I could. Through my nose.

I inhaled, and my throat relaxed, and he slid in farther, deeper than I'd ever taken anyone into my mouth before.

"Jesus." He held me there, with his cock down my throat, not moving.

After a few seconds, he let go, but immediately he pushed in deep again. "All the way. Good girl, good girl." This time he pumped my head over him, raising and lowering me only an inch or two above his balls. "God, it feels so fucking good. Fucking your mouth like this."

I didn't know how *I* felt. Aroused. Confused. Panicked. His thrusts brushed by my gag reflex, and I could only take it so long before I was sure I'd puke, but I couldn't do anything to tell him but claw along his legs and look up at him with watering eyes.

He read my cues and understood. He let me up to relax. Let me catch my breath. But as soon as I did, he urged me back into position and pushed me farther the next round. And the next.

It was intense. It was brutal. But I could feel his cock get thicker in my throat. I saw how wild he got when he pumped my mouth over him, and it only made me love it more. Made me want to please him more.

When he was close, he held my head still and instead drove his cock into my mouth, fucking my face with as much frenzy as he'd fucked my cunt.

"I could have anyone's mouth on me," he said, his breaths short. "Any woman I want. Money can buy the prettiest lips, the most famous mouths, the deepest throats. And still, for ten years, all I can think about is your mouth. It's only yours I want. Why can't I get over your goddamn lips?"

I clawed into him, hard. So hard I thought I might tear his expensive suit. But not because I couldn't take the pounding, but because I wasn't sure I could take what he was saying.

He let up, reading the signal the same way as usual, but this time he barely let me have a break before saying, "I'm going to come. Swallow it all, Sabrina."

He jerked twice, grunting as he shot into my mouth. Warm liquid coated my throat, as his thighs quivered beneath me. It was so hot. So fucking hot to see him so savage. Whatever I had to do to see it again, I'd do it. I'd have given my soul away.

I might have said something about it too, except the second after I swallowed, Donovan pulled me up and kissed me forcefully. Our tongues tangled, our tastes mixed until I could no longer distinguish the taste of his mouth from the taste of his cum in my mouth.

When he pulled away, our eyes locked.

"This doesn't help me figure out where things are between us," I whispered.

"It doesn't help me either." He sounded off-balance. Which threw *me* off-balance—more than I had been—because when had I ever seen Donovan unsteady before?

But no wonder he was bewildered. What had just happened? What he'd just said—I was pretty sure he hadn't meant any of it. He couldn't. It was impossible.

Wasn't it?

As though we'd simultaneously woken from a weird trance, I fell back on my ass at the same time he fell back in his chair. There was distance between us now. Not much, but enough to feel like I could think my own thoughts for half a second.

And the look on his face said he was now thinking his own thoughts. I could actually see him shutting down. See his expression tighten and his eyes become guarded.

"Don't," I said, putting a hand up in warning. "Whatever you're about to say, don't. You can ask for space without saying something terrible."

His brow furrowed. "Is 'I have to get back to work now' considered terrible?"

"When you say it directly after an intimate act, yes." I stood up and did my best to straighten my hair without a mirror. "So how about I just go."

Without any other movement, he nodded.

His gaze had a weight to it that I had memorized, and I could feel his eyes on me as I walked to the door.

Just as I was about to leave, he called after me, "Sabrina?"

I turned back to look at him, and the thing was, whatever he had to say, even if it was decent and not terrible, I wasn't entirely sure I was ready to hear it.

I put my finger to my lips. "Shh."

Then I pivoted and left, surprised I could walk as high as I was from the erotic scene.

But even dazed and confused, there was one thing I did know—the next move was on him.

TWENTY-TWO

I quickly learned the downside of having the ball out of my hands—Donovan was patient. Me—not so much.

Every day Donovan left me wondering anxiously if he'd make contact. And each day that passed without seeing him, I felt on edge. More and more, I worried he'd decided he wasn't interested in pursuing anything further.

And then what the hell would I do?

I was into this now. He'd made me choose. I'd chosen to play. And then he'd made me wait.

And wait.

Goddamn motherfucker made me wait until Friday before he made his move.

I'd just returned from a working lunch with my team. I'd been distracted through the whole thing because I'd caught a whiff of Donovan's cologne in the hall beforehand, and all I wanted to think about after that was how good he smelled when he was hovering over me. Somehow I'd gotten my head together, but I still felt dizzy when it was over, so I'd rushed back to my office. I'd barely had time to stow my purse in my locked drawer when Ellen, my assistant, called from her desk.

"Is my one thirty here?" I asked in lieu of greeting while trying to look at my teeth in my cell phone. "If he is, he's early, and he can wait."

Before she could answer, my door opened. And there was Donovan. Striding in like he'd been invited.

Guess Ellen hadn't been calling about my one thirty.

I dropped my cell. Thank god, my teeth had been clean.

Because, damn, Donovan looked hot. Wicked hot. Hotter than last time I'd seen him, which wasn't saying much because he always looked hotter than the last time I'd seen him. His suit today was light gray, his tie thin and black, his scruff thickening as afternoon rolled in.

But it was never what he wore or how recently he'd trimmed that made him sexy. It was how he stood, how he moved. Like he owned every inch of space that he took up. Like he *deserved* to own it.

It was how he looked at me. Like he owned me. Like he deserved to own me.

"I'm sorry," Ellen rattled on through the receiver of the phone I was still holding. "It's Mr. Kincaid. He just walked in. Obviously." She sounded flustered, but she couldn't possibly feel as flustered as I did with him in my office.

I mean, I got it. To her, he was The Big Boss. He held power over her.

That was nothing compared to the power he held over me.

"It's okay, Ellen." I started to tell her to hold my calls and cancel any appointments because, after four long days and nights of carnal thoughts about the man, I needed this encounter to get naughty. Just seeing him had ruined my panties.

But on the other hand, he'd put me through those four long days and nights of torture, and he didn't deserve to be greeted with me falling at his feet.

"Buzz me when Mr. Hoder arrives," I said instead. Reluctantly. Then hung up.

Without an apology for the intrusion, Donovan shut my door, fastened his eyes on me, and advanced to my desk.

"We need to have dinner." His tone was harsh, and the energy surrounding him felt heavy and dense.

"Dinner or dessert?" I teased with a grin, throwing back the same question he'd asked me when I'd invited him out. I was relieved he was there. Excited, even.

"Dinner," he said emphatically. "We need to talk. I'll send my driver to pick you up at eight." He turned around and headed back toward the door.

"Tonight?" I called after him. He was blustering around so fast I couldn't quite keep up, and the air he was blowing in his path was chilly. My excitement was starting to fizzle into confused agitation.

He stared at me sharply. "Tonight."

Everything about his delivery said there was no arguing.

"Fine. I'll be ready." As anxious as I'd been to see him all week, now I just wanted him out of my office and gone. Whatever was up with him, he'd better be over it by tonight.

"My driver will text you when he's there."

"Yeah, yeah, I know the drill."

"You don't," he said sternly. "But you'll learn."

The hair at the back of my neck prickled. It was a clearly

pointed statement. There was no way I could ignore that his annoyance was directed at me.

"Hang on a second," I said, stopping him before he stormed out. "Are you sure there's something you don't want to say now? It seems you aren't really happy with me, and if that's the case then maybe you should just tell me."

He only barely hesitated. "You told Weston about us."

Oh, that.

I hadn't considered that Donovan might not have been happy about that. "I did tell him," I began slowly. "He'd admitted—"

Donovan interrupted, taking an intimidating step forward as he did. "You told Weston about us, and you shouldn't have told him about us. You should never tell anyone about us because there is no us."

His speech hit like it had been a heavy sandbag that he'd thrown instead of a combination of articulated sounds. I felt the blood drain from my face, humiliated. Hurt. *There is no us* already stuck on a repeat loop in my brain.

"We have had sex a couple of times, Sabrina," he continued, as if I hadn't already been wounded sufficiently. "That's all. Nothing more. And since we are both decent people, I'm sure we can concur that it's no one's business but our own."

I blinked back threatening tears. We hadn't defined what we were, and I hadn't made any assumptions about what kind of relationship we'd have. I'd never thought we would be more than lovers. But it stung to have that confirmed outright. Quite a lot more than I would ever have expected, for no reason I could figure out. Probably because he was so fucking condescending. Because he was so self-righteous. Because, despite not being what I'd even wanted, it was rejection.

That was it—he'd diminished something that had been important to me. Maybe this relationship was just sex, but it still mattered. To me, anyway. It mattered a lot. For the first time in my life, I was beginning to see how I could feel comfortable in my body, comfortable with my desires, and it was only because of Donovan. It hurt to realize that it didn't mean anything to him the way it did to me.

Which was probably dumb and immature and a stupid girly emotion—exactly the thing he was trying to avoid dealing with by giving his *there is no us* routine.

But I had a right to be upset on a practical level too. I'd had a relationship with Weston as well. I had a right to tell him what I fucking wanted, especially when it fell on the heels of our closet encounter.

After a deep breath—when I was sure I wouldn't cry—I started in on my defense. "I didn't tell Weston be—"

But I was too slow and Donovan cut in once more. "Do you think you can handle that?" He barely waited before adding, "Well?"

I paused for several seconds. "Are you going to actually let me answer?"

He narrowed his eyes. "Go ahead."

Reminding myself that this wasn't the first time I'd sparred with Donovan and yet somehow survived gave me confidence.

"Look." I stood up and circled around to the front of my desk. "I told Weston that I had sex with you so that he wouldn't feel guilty for having sex with Elizabeth. It was the right thing to do. I wasn't informing him about 'us'. I've told no one else, and I have no plans to. But what I do with *my* life and *my* body, at times, affects people besides you, and when it does, I do intend to be open with them. Do you think *you* can handle that?"

Donovan was silent for a few beats, his features unreadable. Finally his head tilted questioningly. "Weston slept with Elizabeth? That makes things confusing for the pool."

I threw my head back. "That's what you got out of that? Did you listen to anything else I said?"

"I heard you," he said, flatly. "I'm glad we're in agreement on the matter."

"You're *glad we're in agreement*? What's that supposed to mean?" I was the one who sounded worked up now, but honestly, Donovan didn't appear any more relaxed than he did when he walked in.

He crossed his arms in front of him. "We both are on board with a just sex, no strings private affair. That makes things simple."

Fuck if anything felt simple. I still had fresh wounds; some that I was sure were going to leave bruises. Even if I didn't want Donovan to see the deeper injuries, the surface damage he'd done deserved an apology at the very least.

"Was that your way of addressing the subject?" I asked, bristling. "You accuse me of making a big scandal and when you find out you're wrong you say *I heard you*, that's *simple*, and that's all I get?"

His lips curled up slightly, but the smile didn't reach his eyes. "No. You get dinner. Eight o'clock. The driver will text."

"You still want dinner?" To say I was appalled was putting it mildly.

Before I knew it, he was in front of me. "Now I'm more interested in dessert." With his thumb and forefinger, he pinched my already erect nipple. "I believe you are too."

He pinched harder, and something about the cold, intense way he stared into me as he delivered the pain made me feel it was more than an erotic gesture. It was a warning. Or a punishment. Or proof that this situation wasn't as simple as he wanted to believe it was, and this was the outlet of his frustration.

It confused me more. Riled me up more. But as much as I wanted to pretend it didn't affect me, I couldn't help the whimper that escaped.

"I like that," he whispered against my mouth then kissed me quickly, ending with a painful nip of my lower lip.

"See you later," he said then started to go, leaving me a mess. Leaving me unsteady and turned on and annoyed and pissed off, and somehow, out of everything up in the air, my head went back to *there's no us*. If there was no *us*, what was this? What was it when he and I were together like this, surrounded by such a strong field of electricity that we were practically wired together? Wasn't that an *us*?

He meant a romantic us. I knew that and to make the argument would be to debate semantics, a battle I'd never win with Donovan.

But I had enough of a temper fuming that I had to direct it somewhere. "Didn't Weston explain why I told him?"

Donovan hesitated, his hand on the door handle. "He didn't say anything. He made a joke. It felt too direct to be a coincidence."

All the blood that had drained from my face earlier returned with a flourish. Donovan hadn't even had any proof that I'd said anything at all. He'd accused me on a fucking whim. I'd been pissed but now I reached a new level. A level that was somehow more intense and yet eerily calmer.

"I don't even know what to say to you right now." The flatness of my tone scared even myself.

"Wasn't like I was wrong." His sneer looked sexier on him than it should.

No, that wasn't what happened. "You said..."

When I trailed off, he finished for me. "I said 'You told Weston'. I never said *he* told me anything."

I felt hot. Like my physical temperature was rising.

Donovan looked at me with a delighted smirk. "You know, the harder you glare at me, the more I look forward to dinner."

Dinner? "You've got quite the balls, Kincaid." I was amazed I could talk so steadily. I was seething. "I can't believe you expect me to still show up tonight. I'm so pissed off right now."

The smirk turned into a grin. "Take it out on me later. You'll feel better. I promise." He slipped out the door before I could respond.

I ignored the phone as it began ringing on my desk and stormed after him. "Donovan!"

I'd opened the door in time to see him disappearing around the hall corner. There was no way he didn't hear me call after him, but he didn't stop. Didn't turn around. Which was probably a good thing since there was another figure waiting for me outside my office.

"Oh, hi, Mr. Hoder," I said to my one thirty appointment, hoping I didn't look as agitated as I felt.

"I was just calling to let you know he was here," Ellen said, hanging up her phone. The ringing stopped behind me.

Dammit. There wasn't anything I could do about Donovan now. Clearly, I'd have to deal with him later.

THE NEXT TWO hours were spent in meetings with clients, but when I had a chance to breathe, I found that not only was I still mad, but that my anger toward Donovan had gone from simmering to boiling.

Maybe I'd be able to get over his jackass behavior, but I needed some time to process. There was no way I could see him as soon as tonight.

When I got a chance, I rang Ellen and asked her to get him on the phone.

"I'm sorry, Ms. Lind," she said when she called back a few minutes later. "His assistant said he's unavailable at the moment. Would you like me to leave a message for him to call you back?"

I almost growled, and not in the sexy way, but in the I'm-going-to-kill-something-with-my-bare-hands way, especially if that something was named Donovan Kincaid.

"What was that?" Ellen asked, trying to interpret the sound of my murderous rage.

"No message," I said and hung up loudly. Well, if he was avoiding my call, he couldn't avoid a text. He didn't usually have his cell phone out at work, but he'd get the message in time.

Canceling dinner, I typed and hit send.

His response came before I could even put my phone down. **Why?**

Did this really require an explanation? I made my answer as simple as possible. **You're an asshole.**

Neither new nor relevant. Dinner is still on.

I squeezed my phone so hard I probably almost broke it. There were so many responses rolling through my head, complete monologues of speeches I wanted to deliver.

I settled on, **Fuck you.**

Then I threw my phone in a drawer and ignored it so I could attempt to get some work done.

It didn't really help.

I was still mad. Still hurt. And now I wouldn't get the evening I'd needed so desperately, so I was also still horny as hell, which just pissed me off more.

Another thing that pissed me off? Donovan had been right —the fact that he was an asshole was irrelevant. I knew it from day one, and I was still drawn to him. I was drawn to him *because* of it, even.

What did that say about me?

It was just after six when I finally pulled the phone out of my desk and read his response. **The car will be there at 8. You choose whether or not you get in.**

The ball was back in my court. And I'd already decided I wasn't going, so it wasn't an issue.

Except, I was curious about what his dinner would entail. Or rather, his dessert. Last time had been impromptu. Would a planned rendezvous be different?

It didn't matter. He'd been a giant dick and a half. He hadn't trusted me, he'd manipulated me, he'd betrayed me. He'd hurt me.

What if he tried to make it up? If I just gave him a chance?

Clutching the phone to my chest, I threw my head back against my chair and sighed. For a relationship based only on sex, these kinds of choices should have been no-brainers.

Why, then, did this one feel so hard?

TWENTY-THREE

I got in the car.

It wasn't a last minute decision either, though I tried to pretend that I was only doing a quick shave because that was standard behavior for a Friday evening. And the expensive lingerie and stockings that I put on after my shower? Well, sometimes it's nice to be alone and pretty.

And when I took the elevator down to the lobby, I convinced myself I was only checking my mail, even though I'd checked it earlier, so when the driver texted he was outside, and I was down there, it was easy to say, *Well, I'm already here.*

I stewed the entire ride, but it was harder to validate being as pissed as I wanted to be with Donovan when I was on my way to meet him. It gave me less credibility. If I were really mad, I wouldn't have gotten in the car. Or so logic said. Reality, on the other hand, said differently. I still felt the way I felt, and yet I was driving toward him when all instincts said I should be running the other direction.

Maybe I was mad at myself the most. Either way, I still planned on being a bitch when I saw him. I wasn't sure I could be anything else with Donovan at the moment. Luckily, I didn't think he'd mind.

The drive was farther than usual. This time, I was dropped off in Lower Manhattan. I hadn't been there before, and I didn't see a name anywhere on the building, but it seemed to be a hotel.

So Donovan had rented a room?

Practical, I supposed.

Cold and efficient, as well. Were we even having dinner? From what both Weston and Donovan had said about his sexual relationships, it made sense if there was only one thing on the menu. Donovan did straight-up sex, nothing else.

Why was that having such a hard time sitting in me?

"I'm not sure where I'm going," I said to the driver, after he let me out and shut the car door behind me.

"Inside the main doors. The hostess desk for the restaurant is to your left. Wait there for Mr. Kincaid." He got in the Jaguar and drove off before I could think to ask anything else.

Then we *were* eating dinner. And the hotel was just a coincidence. Or it wasn't. We'd see.

I found the restaurant easily. According to the sign, it was a Japanese place called Okazu. I checked in at the hostess desk. They didn't have my name down, but they did have Donovan's —who hadn't arrived yet. I scanned the lobby and didn't see him anywhere.

"You're welcome to wait in the bar," the hostess suggested, a pale young woman who looked one hundred percent like she'd come from East Asia but talked like she'd lived one hundred percent of her life in the Bronx. "I'll let him know you're there."

Fine. I'd wait at the bar. But his tardiness wasn't helping my already sour mood. He knew I was pissed at him. Shouldn't he be trying harder than this to be smoothing things over?

Apparently the rules of social etiquette weren't foremost on Donovan's priority list.

With a sigh that could be construed as grumbling, I sat down at a high-top and considered ordering a martini to settle my nerves. Before I'd decided, I got a text. **On my way. Take off your panties while you're waiting.**

I grumble-sighed again, though this time butterflies did a bunch of aerial tricks in my stomach simultaneously.

He really wanted me to take off my panties? Why? Just so he'd know? That was kind of hot. Thinking about sitting, bare, next to him did a bunch of fantastically scandalous things to my mind.

Or was he planning on more? Like fingering me discreetly at the dinner table?

I blushed at the completely impractical idea.

And then was struck with a totally practical thought—take them off and put them where? My purse was exactly big enough for my phone, my house key, my credit card, my ID, and a tube of lip gloss. Was I supposed to carry them? Stuff them down my bra? Leave a hundred dollar pair of La Perlas in the trash?

Nope. I wasn't doing it. Besides, I wouldn't reward him for his tardiness. I wasn't even sure I was staying.

Another quarter of an hour later, he still hadn't arrived, and I was irritated. Especially since I had decided against ordering the martini. This was beyond rude. He could have just let me cancel when I'd told him I wanted to. This was intolerable. I refused to wait another minute.

I stood up and headed out of the bar toward the front of the lobby, and walked smack into the most delicious smelling man wearing a fitted suit over a solid chest. I recognized him by the feel of his torso and the way he gripped my arm to steady me. I didn't have to look up to know it was Donovan.

But I did look up. So I could shoot poison-tipped daggers with my eyes.

"I apologize," Donovan said with a decidedly unapologetic smirk. "I got wrapped up in something last minute at work and lost track of time."

I jerked my arm away. I would have understood if an emergency had come up. He was one of the CEOs. He sometimes had to put out fires. That he'd just "lost track of time", however, added insult to injury. I'd been irritated with him all day long and not for a single moment had I been able to forget that I had plans with him later.

Was I that unremarkable? Was that the point he'd been trying to make when he'd told me we weren't in a relationship?

I crossed my arms over my chest and frowned. "I think it's interesting that you can't even leave work when you have plans. Nothing's important enough to tear Donovan Kincaid away from his office before he's ready."

He raised an amused brow. "Want to know what I think?"

"Fine. Let's hear it." I prepared myself for a matching pot and kettle remark. It was true I worked a lot of candlelight hours myself, but I never had places to go afterward. Never had anyone waiting for me.

"I think you think about me too much." He backed it up with the grin he used when he'd won an argument.

My cheeks flooded with warmth. The statement was hard to refute, and thank goodness, I didn't have to, because the hostess interrupted just then.

"Mr. Kincaid, your table is ready." She started to lead the way back toward the restaurant.

Donovan put his arm out, waiting for me before he followed her. "Sabrina?"

"I haven't decided if I'm staying yet." He'd made it clear I wasn't important or significant to him. On top of that, he believed I cared about him more than I should. Now I wasn't just mad and hurt, I was also humiliated.

His expression said he found my emotional turmoil a bit boring or at least unnecessary. "Yes, you have. Why else would you have come at all?"

He'd caught me. Because of course I wouldn't have shown up if I weren't going to stay for *something*. And he'd only just arrived, so I couldn't go now. Things were just getting started. Who the hell did I think I was fooling trying to pretend otherwise?

It didn't make it any easier to accept. In fact, it felt like a trap. Like I'd been bullied, even though, of course, I was here of my own accord. Which was probably the worst part of all.

My frown deepened. "Fuck you."

"We'll get there." This time his smile was a promise, and that was something I wanted him very badly to make good on in very bad ways.

As if sensing my defenses weakening, he pressed on. "At least stay for dinner. You're here. You're hungry. So am I." This time he backed up the promise with his eyes—they were dark, more brown than green, dilated with desire, telling me his hunger belonged to more than just his stomach.

Yeah, I was hungry too. Very hungry.

But he'd made me feel shitty. Then been late for our dinner. And then made me feel shitty *again*.

"I know you didn't eat much for lunch. You really should stay." There was a note of concern in his tone that disarmed me.

"How do you know what I ate for lunch?" I hadn't had much. I'd shoved a few bites of a salad in between agenda items, and I was ravenous.

"Because you had a team meeting, and you never eat much when you're working."

Damn, he really did still notice everything. My anger melted as my chest warmed.

"Fine. I'll stay. Because I'm already here." I let him put his hand at the small of my back and lead me to the front of the restaurant. It didn't matter that I had two layers of clothing between his palm and my skin. The power of his touch came from the pressure he wielded as he directed me past tables, around this group of drinkers, around that crowd of lingering bar patrons.

It felt like a form of surrender, and for a few minutes at least, it seemed like I could give everything over to him—not just the path I walked, not just my body, but these stupid tangled up sentiments dwelling inside of me. I could give him my anger. I could give him my embarrassment. I could give him my hurt. And maybe he didn't know any better what to do with them than I did, but for however long he held them, I wouldn't have to feel them. And what an amazing gift that could be.

That alone would be worth staying for.

But then we were led beyond the hostess station to the coat check where two dark wooden benches lined the sides of the room. Donovan dropped his hand and my jumbled up emotions flooded back like a dam had broken.

"Please. Take your shoes off here," the hostess said.

I knew about the Japanese formality in households, but I hadn't been to a restaurant that had required it. Donovan sat down to remove his shoes. I hesitated, too consumed with the absence of his hand on me. I missed it already. Missed its heat. Missed its authority.

God, what was my problem?

And of course I was still standing there, shoes untouched, looking like an idiot when Donovan was already done. He looked up at me, his head tilted, then tapped his thigh, indicating I put my foot there. So I did.

After he undid the buckle of one strappy sandal and removed it slowly from my foot—which, holy hell, was maybe one of the sexiest things ever—he gestured for me to switch feet. When I did, my skirt caught on my garter, and though I fixed it almost right away, I saw Donovan staring before I did.

As fussed as I'd been all afternoon, the buzz I had from catching him checking me out was amazing. It was especially amazing when he had to adjust his pants when he stood again.

After we checked our shoes and coats, we followed our escort downstairs where the restaurant was actually located. As we walked down the narrow hall, we passed individual dining spaces, each separated by sliding shoji doors. Another set of doors was available to shut the rooms off entirely, but most of them were open. In each room, the dining table was low to the ground, and instead of chairs, they were surrounded by cushions for guests to sit on. Kneel on, actually.

I'd seen those kinds of tables in movies but never in a

restaurant. In fact, they were exactly what I imagined when I thought of dining in a Japanese home.

"The tables are those kind," I said, not knowing how else to express my surprise. "All little and low."

"They're called chabudai. I have one at my apartment."

"That's interesting." Kind of cool was what I meant, but I wasn't all the way ready to be friendly yet. Especially now that he no longer had his hand on my back.

"Okazu is a traditional Japanese restaurant," he explained. "These are called tatami rooms, named for the straw mats, which are easily damaged and hard to clean. It's why we took off our shoes."

I smiled as we passed a little boy who waved at me over his soup bowl.

"Hard to clean but they're kept under people when they eat food?" I was willing to bet that little kid alone had as much rice under his feet as he did in his belly.

The hostess stopped and gestured for us to enter our room.

"Have you never eaten Japanese before?" Donovan asked smugly from behind me as we walked in.

"Yes," I said, offended. In fact, my first experience eating it had been with Weston back at Harvard all those years ago. Not something I intended to bring up now. "I might not be as experienced in the world as you are, but I am a somewhat cultured eater."

I knelt where I was directed on the cushion near the far end of the table. "Now I haven't eaten at a Japanese restaurant anywhere as fancy or as traditional as Okasu, but the food's essentially the same, I'm sure."

The hostess gasped while Donovan, who was unbuttoning his suit jacket so he could sit down, broke into a grin.

My eyes darted from one of them to the other. "Okay. What did I say wrong? Is the food totally different?"

Donovan knelt at the head of the table next to me. "It's Okazu . Not okasu. The first, which is the name of the restaurant, is a word that means food that accompanies rice. The second is a verb. That means rape."

I rolled my eyes, taking a menu from the hostess before she scurried out of the room. "Who would name a restaurant something so close to a word that you'd never want the place to be called?"

Donovan bent over his own menu. "Both could be appropriate depending on how well our dinner goes."

I scowled, but something hummed deep in my belly and spread between my thighs. And I was pretty sure my scowl didn't look as sour as I'd meant it to, so I hid behind the menu for as long as I could.

Which was about three seconds.

Then I sighed when I couldn't read a single word. "This might as well be Chinese," I said, throwing it down in front of me.

"It's Japanese."

"Oh, yeah." I managed a smile at my stupid word choice. "I guess you can order for me."

"I already planned to." It was another remark that deserved a glare, and I was sure to deliver.

When the waitress arrived a few minutes later, she brought a porcelain container and two cups, which she set down on the table in front of us. Then Donovan proceeded to order in fluent Japanese, which was also a lot sexier than I could have imagined. As was seeing him sitting so comfortably on his knees. Basically, I was learning that almost everything where Donovan was concerned was a lot sexier than it should be.

Which made things complicated. I could understand a sex only thing between us, but if he made everything so sexy, then what did that leave as not sex?

The whole thing was frustrating, and that wasn't helping my underlying mood.

When the waitress left, Donovan poured the liquid from the container into one of the cups and turned to me.

"We need to talk about why you're still wearing your panties."

I hadn't told him. And my little mishap with the skirt upstairs hadn't been enough to show off the goods. He just knew. Like always.

"I bet you're still wearing your underwear too," I said as sassily as I could. Though I was pretty sure his weren't nearly as wet as mine were at the moment.

He handed the cup out to me. "Drink this."

"Why? Did you spike it when I blinked?"

He glowered at me. "I don't need to spike it. I'm trying to help you with the stick up your ass."

I let that sink in. "Never in my wildest dreams could I have imagined *you* accusing *me* of having a stick up my ass."

He dipped his thumb in the cup and then smeared my bottom lip with the liquid. "That's how wound up you are. You're the uptight one tonight."

A shiver ran down my spine and my lungs suddenly felt constrained, like my bra was too tight. I licked the liquid from my lip—sake—and wished I could suck the rest from his thumb.

Except I was still feeling all the other things I was feeling, too.

"Did you consider that I might have reason to be wound up? That the reason might be you?" I took a swallow of the sake, finding it more acidic than I'd expected, which fittingly matched my mood.

He leaned close and the warmth of his breath at my neck accompanied his next words. "I don't care *why* you're wound up. I care what you're wearing."

Yep. Panties definitely weren't dry.

"There's a restroom in the hall to the left," he said, believing he had me under his command.

Apparently, he wasn't wrong. "I'll be back."

In the bathroom, I slipped into a stall, undid my garters and, while continuously shaking my head at myself, removed my panties. I still didn't have anywhere to put them, so I wadded them into a ball in my fist and stopped at the mirror to check my lip gloss and give myself a silent pep talk.

Being mad wasn't making the night better for me. Nor was being confused or frustrated or hurt. And none of it was meant to make the night better for him. So what was the point of holding on to these miserable emotions?

No point. No point at all.

With my panties still hidden in my fist, I returned to the table, knelt at my place, and dropped them discreetly in Donovan's lap.

He held them up like they were treasured lace and swept them under his nose as though attempting to identify the bouquet of a wine cork.

"Oh my god!" Nervously I glanced around the restaurant. The people across the hall weren't paying attention to us, thank goodness, and no one was walking by. The lights were dim and shadows could be seen through the thin walls between rooms, but I couldn't make out what our neighbors were doing. No one would be able to tell that Donovan was showing off my panties.

"I didn't have anywhere to put them," I explained, when I felt less panicked about his display.

His eyes narrowed in on my mouth. "I can think of somewhere I'd like to put them."

I took a breath but only managed a shallow one. It had been an element of some of my fantasies—Donovan stuffing my panties in my mouth to keep me from screaming. The image was already burned into my mind from previous daydreams, but now I had a feeling that the image was burned into his mind as well.

And, Jesus, there'd been a good reason I'd been wearing panties. Was I leaving wet stains on the cushion now?

Someone walked past our room. My hand shot out over Donovan's forearm and pushed it below the table, into his lap. "But we're in public. So you can put them in your pocket and return them to me later."

"Yes," he said, with a victorious smirk. "I can put them in my pocket." He knelt higher so he could stuff them in his pants pocket then fell back on his feet.

I had a pretty good feeling I was never seeing that pair of underwear again.

With my panties no longer a source of distraction, I noticed something new had been placed on the table since I'd been in the restroom—a silver platter with a lid. Next to it was a pair of metal tongs.

I nodded toward the dish. "What's that?"

He took off the lid and steam rushed out. Several towels were rolled up in a pile inside. With the tongs, he picked up a rolled towel and set it on the table long enough to replace the lid. "It's customary to wash our hands before the meal."

He picked up the towel and unrolled it, bouncing it from hand to hand a few times until it cooled enough to hold. Then he gestured for me to hold out my hands toward him. Carefully and attentively, he cleaned between each of my fingers and washed my palms and the backs of my hands.

It was strangely erotic and sensual, but it was also intimate. Tender, even. And so while it made my thighs clench and my blood rush hot, it also made my breath stick in my chest. My head felt dizzy.

The moment was too heavy. Like a weightlifter trying to hold a barbell that's too weighted, I couldn't hold it without it pressing down on my chest. Without it crushing down on my heart. Without it meaning something that it wasn't supposed to mean.

I giggled, trying to lighten the mood. "You're washing my panties off my hands."

"Such a shame." His tone remained thick and humorless, and instead of letting the moment ease, he bore into me with a gaze so intense, it carried its own gravity.

Was he like this with everyone? Just sex. No relationships. Could he really look at a person—look at *me*—and not intend the burden that was clearly in his stare? Could he really witness this extreme force between us and say it didn't connect us in any way except sexually?

Was it only me who felt the weight at all?

He finished with my hands and moved to his own then dumped the towel on an empty plate that seemed to be for discarded linens. He poured himself some sake, and we each drank in silence.

I took the moment to knock myself out of the stupid trance I'd been in.

Of course it was only me who was feeling these things. That was why he'd given me the speech about no relationships in the first place. And, in all honesty, I wouldn't even be thinking along these lines if he hadn't yelled at me earlier about it and put the idea in my head.

Just sex. Got it. I was all for it. I wasn't into anything more than that myself. Bring the waitress back. I could order this without help, no menu required—just sex. No adornments, no side dishes, no appetizers. Just plain sex.

What else would I want with a man like Donovan anyway? Overnights? Romance? Marriage?

I almost laughed at the idea.

No. There were men who were intended for futures, and there were men who were intended for filth. Donovan was intended for filth, and he was wise to lay it out from the beginning.

I tried not to think about the fact that he'd had a fiancée once upon a time. Because what did it mean Donovan was intended for then?

In all honesty, it probably wasn't that simple, and I needed to accept that. Otherwise I'd kill myself wondering if what it really meant was that he just wasn't intended for me.

TWENTY-FOUR

When the waitress returned, she brought someone else with her to help carry the trays of food. Together, the two servers placed dishes of soup and sushi and tempura and fish on the table. Afterward, they stood back with their hands in front of them and seemed to wait for something. For what, I didn't know.

Maybe we were supposed to taste our food before they left? Tell them everything was all good or something.

I looked to Donovan for guidance.

He brought his hands to his lap, and I mirrored him instinctively. "In Japanese culture," he said, "before we start eating, we say *itadakimasu*."

He'd only said it one time, but he looked at me expectantly.

I gave him my you've-got-to-be-kidding-me look. "I can't say that. What did you say? Say it again. Slower."

He started to answer and then seemed to have another idea. Reaching into his jacket, he pulled out a marker from an inner pocket and took off the lid with his teeth—another super sexy move.

"Give me your hand," he said around the lid, though he needn't have said anything because he'd already tugged it over to him and had started writing.

"You just happen to have a Sharpie in your pocket? Of course you do. Did I mention you were a workaholic? Also, this is never coming off." Thank god we were coming on November, and I could get away with wearing long sleeves. Sharpie was impossible to wash off as it was, and as I stared at his neat print handwriting on my skin, I wasn't sure I was planning to try that hard.

"*It-a-dak-i-ma-su*," I read slowly from my arm when he was done. It came out better than I'd thought it would on the first try, which wasn't saying much. I glanced up and found him trying to hide a grin. His eyes twinkled, though, and he couldn't hide that. "You're laughing at me."

"No, you did pretty good. It was *cute*." He said the word cute as though he'd never had a reason to say it before.

I rolled my eyes. *Cute* was not what I wanted him to think of when he thought of me. "What does it mean?"

"It means, 'I receive this food'. You're thanking the preparers for their work, telling them you appreciate what they've done for you."

"Oh!" I turned to the waitress and her helper who were still standing in a bowed position, politely waiting to be dismissed. "Itadakimasu," I told them.

They smiled and nodded.

Donovan followed up with a whole bunch of Japanese words that were not *itadakimasu* and also seemed to be somewhat instructive in tone. When he'd finished speaking, they bowed and exited the room, shutting the sliding doors as they left.

They shut the doors.

We were alone.

And I wasn't wearing panties.

"What did you say to her?" I asked, pretending to be more interested in reaching for the miso.

"I told her to shut the shoji on the way out. And not to return until I'd opened it myself."

"Who knew that dining was such a private event for you." I picked up the bowl and blew across the top.

"It's not the dining that I was concerned about keeping private."

My stomach did a flip-flop. Thank goodness I hadn't actually sipped the soup yet because I might have swallowed wrong.

Donovan chuckled, as if he could interpret my every thought when I couldn't understand them myself. I drank from the miso and put the bowl down, and after I did, he was waiting with a piece of sushi that he'd dipped in soy sauce and was now holding out to me between chopsticks.

"Am I supposed to appreciate what you've done for me too?" I took a bite of the sushi. "Oh, man, I do appreciate what you've done for me." Like, really really. "Donovan, this is amazing."

I finished the piece then took the tempura he offered.

As he so often did, he watched me attentively. The amusement in his eyes was gone, and now they were dark and intense, not just with desire but with something else. Something heavier. Like the weight I'd felt when he'd washed my hands.

Whatever it was I saw—whether it was there or I just

wanted it to be there, it made me shiver. Made me not want to look away.

"Come here," he growled, abruptly wrapping his arm around my waist and pulling me into his lap. He picked up another piece of sushi, dipped it and fed it to me. "This is better."

Better for feeding purposes or because now my bare pussy was just inches from the outline of his stiffening cock, I didn't know. But yes, I agreed it was definitely better.

It was also easier for me to feed him. Since Donovan wouldn't relinquish the chopsticks and I couldn't find mine, I used my fingers, which he sucked thoroughly. He let me feed him one more piece like this. The next time he fed me, he reached down under my skirt and drew slow circles on my clit with his thumb at the same time.

"Mmm," I moaned.

"You like the sashimi?" His eyes taunted as his fingers teased me.

"Yeah, that's what I liked," I said sarcastically.

"In that case..." He drew his hand away from where I so badly wanted it.

"No!" I rubbed up against him, begging for his attention to return. "Please."

His eyes flashed with an idea. He reached behind me and grabbed the Sharpie that he'd tossed on the table after drawing on my arm earlier. Again, he removed the lid with his teeth —*unf*, super sexy. With my skirt gathered up around my waist, he bent low so he could write something on the skin at the top of my folds, just above my clit. Then he capped the lid and put the marker back in his jacket pocket.

"What did you wri—?"

But my question was cut off by the return of his thumb on my clit, and seriously, I didn't care much after that. I didn't care much about anything except the whirlwind building inside of me and trying to maintain enough composure to eat what he gave me when he offered it.

I managed for a while. I even managed to feed him most of the teriyaki salmon at the same time. But then Donovan abandoned the chopsticks, feeding me with his fingers instead, and with the thumb of his other hand still on my clit, he slid two fingers inside my very slick hole.

After that, I was a goner.

"Fuck, you're so wet." He pulled his fingers out and the next time he drove them in, he added a third. "You're so wet, you could take my cock right now. Couldn't you?"

I'd eaten the entire piece of sushi, but I clutched onto his hand, sucking on his thumb and forefinger as if they were his cock. "Uh-huh," I moaned, my mouth full.

"Take it out," he ordered. "Take out my cock."

I was dazed but I was still aware. Aware of where we were. Aware that we were in public, that the walls were thin, that I could hear the clatter of dishes and the buzz of conversation on either side of us. I could see the shadowed movement of other guests through the shoji. Could they see us? Could they hear us? Did they know what we were doing?

Probably not. But it was possible.

And that possible was all it took to be one of the hottest things I'd ever done.

Without further hesitation, I scrambled with Donovan's belt and pants. I pulled his underwear down far enough to release his erection. It sprung out, tall and thick and alert. By this time, he was ready with a condom he'd retrieved from his jacket pocket. While he continued to finger me, I unwrapped the latex over his cock.

As soon as I'd gotten him fully covered, he moved his hands to dig into my hips underneath my skirt. He hoisted me up a couple of inches, and even though he was working quickly, all I could think was that he wasn't moving nearly fast enough. I needed him inside me. I needed him now. Now. Now.

And then there he was at my entrance.

He was right—I was so wet, I could easily have slid down over him. But, like every time he'd been inside me before, he didn't hesitate or let me take the lead—as soon as he'd notched his head at my hole, he drove up into me without mercy.

"Ah, fuck," I whimpered, feeling like I was in the first car at the top of the big loop on a rollercoaster. Adrenaline and excitement surged through my veins, my body ready for the ride.

With incredible stamina, he hammered into me, pounding my pussy with such vigor and force that he was soon sweating. Even through his clothes, I could see the strain of his muscles as he struggled to hold me up. He bucked into me so hard I knocked repeatedly against the table behind me—not too loud that we caused a disturbance, but loud enough that people might have noticed. My breasts jiggled despite the fact I was wearing a bra. Something clattered to the floor. Sake spilled and dripped at my side.

I clung onto him desperately, wrapping an arm around his neck to steady myself. With my other hand, I reached down to massage my clit, which started me again toward the orgasm that had already been building.

I was close. He was too. I was tight in this position already, but I closed my knees in tighter against him and tensed my pussy, both to reward and to torture him.

He had his own version of reward and torture—it came in the form of kissing. When his rhythm was established, and our positions were perfected, he leaned forward and claimed my mouth with his. His lips were frantic and frenzied against mine, as though no matter how much I gave him—and I gave him everything—it wasn't enough. It could never be enough. His tongue plunged deeper. His pressure grew stronger. Still, it wasn't enough.

But it was enough to send me soaring. Higher, higher, higher.

When I came, he came with me, brutally, like two savage animals fucking in the wild. I practically screamed, and he had to push my face into his jacket to muffle the sound. He wasn't quiet himself, grunting his release into my hair. My legs trembled and my muscles stretched with the fierceness of my climax. Instead of rolling over my body in waves, it hit me like a truck, smacking out of me in one terrible, amazing rip of ecstasy. It hurt how it crashed through me, as though it was too much pleasure to be experienced at one time. As though my orgasm didn't know about Donovan's rule to fuck and run, and it had built up expecting that it would be dispensed in bits and pieces and not all in one dose.

I fell on his shoulder and closed my eyes to let myself catch my breath. When it didn't feel like the world was spinning anymore, I sat up. He was waiting to kiss me once more, slowly this time, with his hand holding my cheek. It was a sweet kiss, even as he controlled it. It was soft. It was something much lighter than the heaviness that every other intimacy with him carried.

Too soon, he was finished. He lifted me off of him and stood me on the floor beside him.

He tied off the condom, wrapped a napkin around it and stuck it in his pocket. After he'd put himself away, he got into the platter with the hot towels and grabbed one to clean me up.

"Turns out the hot towels are just as useful after the meal," I joked when he lifted my skirt and swiped the wet rag over my pussy. "More like warm towel now, but perhaps that's for the best."

He didn't say anything, and I realized he was already pulling away, as he always did afterward. I wondered how difficult it was for him to extend this courtesy, to help me clean up. Did this bother him because he'd made rules about his life? Or did the rules about his life come because things like this bothered him?

Whichever it was, I sensed it anguished him to have to deal with me now. We were done, and I should be gone. I already knew that about him, but after today's message I understood even better how, for him, sex was not a way to connect with others. Sex was something separate. Connecting was something he didn't do at all.

So I practiced disconnecting too.

I didn't watch him while he cleaned me up, didn't think too hard about its intimacy or its eroticism. I let it just be an act. Like sex was just an act. Without meaning, without attachment. Without emotional interpretation.

When he'd finished, we silently wiped up the spilled sake and picked up the platter of tempura that had clattered to the floor. In a few minutes, the room looked fairly decent, considering.

Donovan nodded for me to kneel in my spot, and once I had, he opened the shoji. "I'll be right back," he said, turning in the direction of the restrooms, presumably to dispose of the condom.

While he was gone, the waitress came to leave the bill, which Donovan took care of right away on his return.

"When the meal is over, you say *gochiso sama deshita*," he said when she returned with his receipt. He said it slowly, and I listened carefully the first time, ensuring that my other arm wouldn't soon be marked up.

I turned to the waitress and put on a grin. "*Gochiso sama deshita.*" I brutalized the pronunciation. She nodded politely all the same.

"Perfect," Donovan said. He stood then gave me his hand to help me up.

"What's it mean, anyway?" I asked.

"'It was quite a feast.'"

The waitress bowed to both of us as we stepped past her out into the hallway. Donovan led the way out, which was fine with me. Then I wouldn't have to feel his distant stare at my back.

But before we'd gotten too far, he stopped and peered over his shoulder. "Sabrina?" His small smile nearly reached his eyes. "*Gochiso sama deshita.*"

Yes, it definitely had been quite a feast.

AS USUAL, Donovan didn't ride home with me. He had his driver take me, and he took the car he'd driven himself. Never mind that he could have given his employee the night off and taken me instead. I understood. It didn't mean anything. I'd given him what he'd come for. Just sex. Good sex, but just sex.

I'd almost forgotten entirely about the marks he'd made on me until later in the shower. I spent most of the time trying to scrub at the ink on my arm, when suddenly I remembered to look at what he'd written lower. I hadn't thought much about it, assuming he'd written something else that had to do with Japanese culture. Now when I examined the marks, I saw they were actually English and they formed two letters—D K.

Donovan had written his initials on my flesh.

He'd said, in every way possible, that I meant nothing to him beyond sex, and then he'd written his initials on the most private part of my body.

It was another way to mess with me. It had to be. Like how he'd signed off on my grade back in college, the grade I shouldn't have needed to "make up". This time he'd signed off on my skin.

It was infuriating and shitty and a turn-on and also...

Also, it hurt.

The problem was, for the first time since I'd known Donovan, his fucked-up games and how much I loved them weren't the most dangerous parts of our association. The most dangerous part was how much I wished that his brand on my skin meant something different than what it surely did.

The most dangerous part was how much I wished it meant he thought of me as his.

TWENTY-FIVE

"**B**ut Thanksgiving is almost a month away," my sister grumbled the next morning over the phone. "You've been on the East Coast six weeks, and we still haven't seen each other."

I resisted the urge to apologize. To be fair, it wasn't just my job that had been keeping us apart, but also her class load. Actually, if I spent the rest of the day knocking out some tasks, I could probably take the train up to see her later and come back the next day.

"I wish I could," she said when I offered. "But I have a group project that's due Monday, and we're working on it all day tomorrow."

"Oh. It was just a thought." I hadn't realized how much I'd wanted to see her until right then.

Audrey seemed to pick up on my melancholy. "Are you okay? Is there something you need to talk about? Guy stuff?"

Guy stuff. Yes, actually that's exactly what it was.

I was both confused and hungover from sex with Donovan the night before, and while I hadn't particularly been looking to talk about it before, now that she was on the line, I yearned to have someone to sort through the strange non-relationship.

But also I wasn't ready to put my feelings about it into words.

I shouldn't even be having feelings about it in the first place. I was sure that was against the rules of his Just Sex policy.

"Nope. I just miss you." It was true too. I tried to think of an alternate way to get more sister time. "When you come for Thanksgiving, can you come earlier than Wednesday? I'll have to work some of the time, but we could make up for lost time that way."

"I have the whole week off," she said, sounding instantly on board. "I could come up Friday after class. And maybe we could see some shows! Will there be ice-skating at Rockefeller Center by then?"

"Probably." I didn't honestly know, never mind that Audrey couldn't ice-skate to save her life.

"We definitely have to go ice-skating, Bri! And we can do the MOMA. And One World Trade Center..."

She spent the next twenty minutes giving me a list of all the things we should do on her vacation to Manhattan, about a month's worth of activities. There wasn't any way we'd get through even a quarter of them, but it was good to talk to her.

It was especially nice to have a few minutes when I wasn't thinking about Donovan. Not that I spent *all* of my free time with him on my mind.

When we hung up, he was there in my mind though, immediately. I pulled down my yoga pants and panties and stood in front of my bathroom mirror. His initials were faded with the scrubbing I'd given them the night before, but they were still clearly visible.

Why did I like the look of them on my skin so much? It was erotic and it turned me on, yes. But there was more to it than that. It felt like he'd given me his letterman's jacket. Or like he'd asked me to wear his class ring. It felt like he'd claimed me, and if that was his intention, then I really didn't understand the terms of Just Sex.

There were other terms I didn't understand. What were the rules of this arrangement? Was there even an arrangement? Could I call him up for booty calls if I wanted to or was he the only one allowed to do that? Was there a length of time I was supposed to wait in between dates?

Was he sleeping with other women right now too?

My stomach suddenly dropped like a ball of lead at the thought of him in the arms of another woman.

Because it was tacky and it made me feel slutty, of course. Because it created health risks. Not because I had an emotional attachment to him. Not because I was jealous.

Point was, this no strings, private affair of ours needed to be further discussed.

Taking my phone, I snapped a picture of his artwork on my pussy. Then I typed out a text message to him—**Can we talk?**

Pretty sure that he wouldn't respond unless I spoke his language, I attached the photo and pushed send.

DONOVAN STILL HADN'T RESPONDED by Monday.

I'd come to the conclusion that either I was not allowed to reach out to him, our arrangement was over, or he wanted to make me squirm—something I knew he enjoyed doing.

Well, if that was the goal, it was working. Not only was I antsy waiting for his reply, but I was also missing him physically. I was desperate for the taste of his lips. I longed for the roughness of his grip. I yearned for the overwhelming way he rode my cunt.

It made me desperate and distracted all through my day. A few times I even tried walking by his office, but he was always in a meeting, and he was gone by the time I got done with my work.

Lying in bed that night, I tried texting him. **I'm thinking dirty thoughts of you.**

I attached a picture of the bottle he'd told me to use as a dildo sometime when he'd fucked me in my apartment.

I brought myself to orgasm three times before I was finished.

Donovan never replied.

"TOM," I said, stopping my employee from leaving the conference room after our Thursday morning team leader meeting. "I'm really impressed with the way you've handled all the details for SummiTech's presentation at the Think Expo tomorrow night. It was thrown at you without much notice, and your team has taken it on without missing anything."

I hadn't spoken to Tom Burns one-on-one since he'd walked in on Donovan almost kissing me weeks ago in the strategy room. Even after he'd spoken kindly about me to Weston, I hadn't wanted things to be awkward. But he'd shown consistently good work on his team, and when SummiTech had asked Reach to put together an ad and materials to unveil their latest products, I knew Tom was the guy to head up the marketing side.

"Thanks," he said, seemingly surprised about the acknowledgement. "I appreciate the compliment."

"You're welcome. I'll stop in tomorrow night, but I'm sure you won't need me."

He gathered the items he'd brought for the meeting and started to leave but suddenly stopped and turned back to face me. "You know, Sabrina, I have a confession to make—I didn't think I was going to like you."

"I'm listening." I straightened, bracing myself for what he'd say next. The rest of the room had emptied, and it was just the two of us now. This could go anywhere, and this wasn't starting out very promising.

"Especially after I found Donovan Kincaid trying to get cozy with you that night we were working on the Phoenix campaign. I was sure that must have been why you were hired."

"What do you mean? Like you were sure I was sleeping with him?" I hadn't been at the time. But hadn't I gotten the job by sleeping with Weston?

Guilt knotted in my stomach. I'd deny it. I was qualified to be here. I might have gotten his attention by taking my clothes off, but that didn't mean I didn't deserve my position.

At least that's what I told myself.

"It's shitty," Tom said, regretfully. "I'm sure that sounds sexist, but it was how it looked. You know?"

I nodded because I knew exactly how it looked, and yes, it

was sexist. But the truth wasn't much better, so I couldn't say a lot to defend myself.

Tom, however, could. "You've really proven yourself, though. You put a lot more time into the team than I expected you would. I know I'm not the only one who appreciates it."

"Thank you." The knot loosened slightly in my belly. "I appreciate the compliment as well."

Again, he started to go, but with my anxiety a bit settled, I realized things didn't quite add up. "Wait a minute, Tom. I'm confused. Didn't you put in a good word to Weston about me back then?"

He scratched at his neck, his eyes averted. "Yeah, but that was just because Kincaid threatened my job if I didn't."

Um. "He did?"

He looked up, studying my reaction, which was utter shock. "You didn't know. I wasn't sure."

No, I absolutely didn't know that Donovan had talked to him about anything. "What did he say to you?"

"He said that he was the one who had come on to you and that he had been out of place for doing so. Then he said you deserved to be respected for all your hard work, and he made it clear that spreading rumors about you would not be respectful. He suggested I get the rest of the team to support you if I wanted the department to continue running smoothly."

My heart was beating rapidly, my hands shaking. "And he said he'd fire you if you didn't?"

"Not in those exact words, but I knew what he meant."

My cheeks flushed. "Oh my god, I had no idea. I'm so sorry!" It was so unfair for him to threaten my employee. Tom was innocent. I was mortified.

But at the same time...

What did it mean?

I ran my hand along my forehead, wiping the bead of sweat that had gathered along my brow. Why would Donovan have done that? Was he worried that Tom could make my job hard for me? Had he been concerned about my reputation?

"You didn't know," Tom said consolingly. "Why are you apologizing? *I* should apologize. I assumed I understood the situation, and I never even asked to make sure you were okay." He took a cautious step toward me and lowered his voice. "I don't want to cross the line, but do you need any help with him?"

"No," I assured him. It was almost laughable, thinking I needed rescuing from Donovan. "No, I'm fine. We're fine." I shook my head, wishing I hadn't said *we*.

And because I had said it, I felt the need to say more. To explain the situation so that there was no doubt in Tom's mind that there was absolutely nothing to be concerned about. "It was a strange night you walked in on. Donovan and I have known each other since college, and..."

I trailed off. How the hell did I think I could explain any of this? It wasn't something I even wanted to explain.

Just then, I looked out through the glass walls of the room, and my eyes caught sight of someone familiar on the other side of the floor. Someone who, after this most recent information, I was desperate to speak with.

"I'm sorry. Can you excuse me? I see someone I need to talk to."

I picked up my files and brushed past Tom, running out into the hall to catch Donovan. He'd disappeared around the corner, and when I followed after, I saw he'd gotten on the elevator. He looked up as the doors started to close.

"Wait!" I called.

His eyes met mine, but he didn't hold the doors.

I chewed my lip for several seconds, trying not to jump to conclusions. Donovan was not transparent, and there were so many possibilities of what was going through his mind. But I had to get this sorted out. I wanted to talk to him about Tom Burns, and I wanted to know for sure if he was evading me.

I caught the next elevator and went to my office and called Donovan's secretary on the company line.

"Who may I ask is calling?" Simone asked after I requested to speak to him.

"Sabrina Lind in Marketing."

"And what is it regarding?"

"An employee in my department who I'd like to speak with him about." He was in charge of Operations. If he wouldn't talk to me about our non-relationship, he should at least talk to me about work.

"Hold just a moment, please."

I waited for several long seconds, tapping my foot nervously to the company's nineties-era hold music.

Eventually, Simone returned. "Mr. Kincaid asked if you've spoken to HR about the matter."

"No, I haven't spoken to HR," I snapped. "It's not an HR matter. It's a Mr. Kincaid matter, I assure you." I knew Simone was just doing her job, but I was getting angry, and she was the one keeping me from talking to the person I was angry with.

"Of course, Ms. Lind. Just a moment, please." The hold was shorter this time. "I can schedule an appointment for you to see him if you'd like."

"Yes, please." Finally!

"His first opening is next Thursday at two."

My chest felt tight. "He doesn't have anything sooner? All I need is a phone call. Can you tell him directly that I just need a few minutes with him?"

"I'm sorry, Ms. Lind. I already did. He said to give you his first available."

"Never mind." I hung up before she had a chance to respond.

Well. There was my answer. Donovan was definitely avoiding me. I'd known he was an asshole, but this had gone too far.

I sat back in my chair and pinched the inside corners of my eyes, refusing to cry at work. I could understand why he'd want to treat me like any other employee, making me wait until he had an opening in his schedule so that it didn't look like I had preferential treatment. But it sure hadn't seemed to be a concern of his the day I'd walked in and let him shove his cock down my throat. Why was it protocol he was all of a sudden interested in following now?

Playing with my emotions in the bedroom was one thing. At the office was a totally different story. Especially when I had so much more to lose than he did.

In fact, he didn't have anything to lose at all.

Was that why it was so easy for him to blow me off?

Whatever the reason—whether it was because he wanted to play a game or teach me a lesson or because he was over our tryst—it didn't matter.

I was done with him.

TWENTY-SIX

The next evening, I rushed home after work to change into something appropriate for the Think Expo. Tom and his team didn't need me, but I wanted to show my support and make sure that everything ran as planned. I chose a simple black ruched body-con dress and some strappy heels and headed to the Financial District.

I took a cab to the hotel and followed signage to the Expo, which was conveniently being held in the ballrooms on the first floor. All day, innovators had presented new ideas in the world of technology to investors and tech enthusiasts. A cocktail party in the ballroom topped off the evening. The hallway leading to the event was set up with major exhibiters displaying their products. Large screen TVs battled for the attention of guests dressed in tuxedos and fancy dresses as they made their way to the party. Our client was among these competitors.

I found SummiTech's exhibit quite easily, the bold media production easily drawing my attention to their display.

Employees for the company handed out brochures and spoke to guests as they passed by. I spotted a couple of my team members hanging back to monitor the situation and checked in with them to make sure they'd brought enough marketing materials and to gather some initial feedback on the items Reach had put together.

After I was satisfied that the event was running smoothly and that everything we'd provided was working as intended, I set out to locate Tom.

"Here you are," I said, when I found him inside the ballroom with a flute of champagne in hand. "I was looking for you."

His brows rose. "Am I in trouble?"

"Of course not. I watched SummiTech's presentation on my way in. The entire setup looked great. How do you think it's going?"

His shoulders relaxed visibly. "I spoke to Munns about fifteen minutes ago, and he was pretty stoked, so I'd say it's going great."

"Excellent." Robert Munns was our client, the CEO of SummiTech. "As long as he's happy then Reach should be happy."

"Exactly why I'm drinking." Tom held his glass up for emphasis. "You should join me."

A glass of champagne didn't sound like a bad idea. It had been a long day. Correction—it had been a long week. While my workload had been pretty manageable, there had been mental and emotional stress that had worn me out, and I longed for an escape.

Alcohol wasn't the kind of escape I had hoped for, but since

I'd banished my non-relationship from my life the day before, I had to take what I could get.

"I will definitely join you if I can find a server." I scanned the ballroom for the closest waiter.

"I'll find one." Tom, who was much taller than me, even as I wore heels, did his own survey. "I didn't know Kincaid would be here."

My heart stopped. "He is?"

"I just saw him talking to that Hudson Pierce guy."

As soon as I turned, I saw him. He was impossible to miss. He'd obviously come straight from the office because he was still wearing what he'd been wearing when I'd glimpsed him from across the hallway earlier in the day. And damn did he look good. Donovan Kincaid wore a suit better than a room full of men in tuxedos.

Which was not a good thing considering my whole resolution to be done with him.

Suddenly I wished I'd chosen my outfit better. Black was so boring. I hadn't even added jewelry. My underwear was fine but nothing fancy.

And none of that mattered because I wasn't sleeping with him.

What the hell was he even doing here anyway? There was no reason someone of his level needed to attend this sort of thing on behalf of Reach. He wasn't even dressed for the event. He'd obviously come here last minute. Had something gone wrong? Was he checking up on my team?

Was he coming here for me?

"Oh, god." I turned my back toward him. I couldn't settle the flutters in my stomach. I wanted him to be here for me, despite everything he'd put me through, and not only was that setting myself up for the worst kind of disappointment tonight, it was setting me up for the worst kind of disappointment in the long run.

I had to get out of there.

"Do me a favor, will you?" After our talk the day before, I was pretty sure Tom would help me out. "If he asks about me, tell him you haven't seen me."

I was already mentally mapping my escape. The ballroom was small, and I'd have to go past Donovan to get to the front doors, but I had to go that way because the coatroom was down that hall.

"Yeah. Sure. But..." Like he had the day before, Tom's voice filled with concern. "Is there some sort of problem that you need help with?"

"No. I promise. And you're a great guy for asking. Just, like I said, Donovan and I have a complicated..." I searched for a word that wasn't *relationship*. "Acquaintanceship, and I'm just not in the mood to deal with him tonight, so I'm going to slip out before he notices me."

"Ah. Got it. I had one of those myself." He lifted the champagne flute again, but this time he tapped the finger where he wore his wedding ring indicating the courtship with his wife had been *complicated*.

"I think I've given you the wrong idea," I said, dismayed by the conclusion he'd settled on. "Donovan and I are barely friends."

"I get it, Sabrina." But he was grinning like he had a secret. "Now go before he sees you."

"Okay. Thanks, Tom."

Still unsure about leaving my employee with the wrong

impression, I hesitated a moment longer. Then I got my priorities straight and took off.

I hurried out, a woman with a mission, racing down the exposition hallway as fast as I could to get to the coatroom. Luckily, there was no one in line when I arrived, and I was able to present my ticket and get out of there quickly. But as soon as I turned around, I saw Donovan had also left the party.

He still hadn't seen me, but there was no way that I could get out the main entrance of the hotel without crossing his path, so I slipped down a smaller corridor beyond the coatroom and discovered a side door. I pushed through the exit and found myself in an alleyway.

Perfect.

Except, once the door closed behind me, I realized how dark and narrow the alley was and immediately regretted the decision to come this way. I turned back and pulled on the handle of the door. It was locked. Of course.

I sighed, kicking myself for not having my Mace and looked in both directions, searching for the best way to get to a main street. Several garbage dumpsters lined the wall to one side of me, but the streetlight seemed to be out on the other side.

I started on the path past the dumpsters.

Something rattled along the pavement to my right—like the wind blowing a pop can or something inane, but it was eerie nonetheless. I pulled my coat tighter around myself and walked faster. More sounds behind me begged for my attention. The sound of a door? Footsteps? My imagination running wild?

I was too scared to look.

No, there was definitely someone behind me.

The steps got louder and nearer. I hurried my pace, but my

heel caught on a crack in the gravel, and just as I started to go down, someone grabbed me at the waist.

I inhaled sharply, preparing to scream.

"What the fuck are you doing?" Donovan asked crudely before I could get sound out.

"Oh my god, it's you." I crumpled into his arms, relieved to find my stalker was someone familiar.

"But it might not have been," he said, roughly. His grip on me was both warm and possessive. His fingers dug into my waist as though he'd had to lurch to reach me. Or as though he didn't want to let go.

It felt good.

So good.

Then I remembered everything from the week. How he'd been a complete ass. How I'd vowed I was done with him.

"But it was you. So let me go." I wriggled out of his grasp, missing him instantly.

"Seriously, Sabrina. What were you thinking coming out here alone? If you wanted to get raped, you could have just called me." Even with the dark, teasing words, his delivery was a lecture.

"Actually, I couldn't. Since you aren't taking my calls or answering any of my texts. If you'll excuse me, I'll—" I started to turn away, but he grabbed my arm, digging his fingers into my skin painfully, even through the thick material of my coat.

"You aren't going anywhere out here alone." His eyes were black in the dimly lit alley, his tone final.

I yanked my arm away. After a week of avoidance, now he was going to give me his two cents? No fucking way. "You don't get to tell me what to do."

He put his hands in his coat pockets and scoffed. "I don't

know about that. I have a pair of panties in my nightstand that says otherwise."

I stared at him incredulously for half a beat. None of this was serious to him. This was just like college when he fucked with my grades for his own amusement. "You goddamn asshole, Donovan," I seethed. "Don't talk to me. Don't touch me. Don't stick up for me at work."

His eyes narrowed. "You're so angry. It's making me need to fuck you."

Fury bubbled up inside. Before I could think about what I was doing, my hand flew up to slap him.

He was too quick. He grabbed my forearm before I reached his cheek. A smile spread devilishly across his face. "Save it for the bedroom. I like it when you struggle."

"This isn't foreplay!" I pulled my hand free. "You can have your non-relationship rules, and I'll follow them, but you don't get to avoid me like I'm nothing and still expect me to walk into your arms the minute that you're in the mood."

"I don't expect that at all. I'd much rather you crawl."

There was nothing to say. He wasn't listening. He never did, or when he did, he didn't care. Words meant nothing to him. The only thing he cared about was his goddamned games.

With my eyes burning, I spun away from him once more.

"Sabrina, you're not walking out here alone." He followed right behind, but when he tried to reach for me, I snatched my hand away.

I heard him sigh. "I wasn't avoiding you."

"Like hell you weren't," I grumbled, pissed that he'd gotten me to engage. I kept walking though, only yards now from the street.

"I wasn't *exactly* avoiding you. I had a major deadline this week. It required my full attention."

I couldn't help myself. As angry as I was, as done with him as I was, I couldn't stop myself from reacting. That's what he did to me—that's what he always did to me—he made me *feel*.

I pivoted toward him. "Then you act like a decent person— remember how you said that's what we both were? And you take ten seconds to explain that to me in a motherfucking text."

Before he could say anything in response, I spun right back around to continue my advance to the road.

But this time Donovan caught me, wrapping both arms around me from behind. I struggled with determination, elbowing him sharply.

"Jesus Christ, Sabrina," he exclaimed, tightening his grasp. "Stop!"

I wrestled for another several seconds then surrendered, hating myself for giving in so easily. But I was no match for his strength, and the longer he held me the more I loved the feel of his firm arms, and the way he pressed his body tight along my back, pressing his head next to mine.

"What?" I asked, broken. "What do you have to say?"

He exhaled, his breath warming my neck, his mouth right at my ear. "You distract me," he said quietly, honestly. "If I spend any time around you, I can't focus for days. You sent that picture of your pretty little cunt, and I couldn't even look at my phone all week without getting hard. I avoided you because it was the only way I knew how to deal with you."

I closed my eyes and let his words sink in, let them settle in between the facts I already had and the things I'd decided must be true and the things I wished were true and the things he'd said were true before, but I couldn't get them to make a pattern that made sense.

I couldn't get these words to mean what I was pretty sure he was saying and still exist with what he'd said in the past.

And these were the words I wanted him to mean. More than I'd realized.

Afraid to make the wrong move, afraid to guess wrong, I told him, "I don't know what you're telling me right now."

"I'm telling you to come home with me."

TWENTY-SEVEN

Donovan's car was parked with the hotel valet. It wasn't the car that his driver normally drove me in. Instead it was a silver Tesla. I couldn't say definitively since I'd always sat in the back of the Jag, but I was pretty sure this was the most sophisticated and modern car I'd ever been in, and watching Donovan handle it expertly through the city streets was captivating and stunning.

We rode in silence, the energy between us electric and barbed, making it painful to sit in. My breasts ached. My pussy throbbed. My skin wanted to touch and be touched, my body wanted to be fucked and roughed up and bruised and bumped around.

I still had anger in me. And pain. They were strong emotions that heightened my arousal, and they needed an outlet. Donovan had wordlessly promised to provide one when he'd invited me home with him, and the anticipation grew exponentially every second that passed.

As we headed toward Midtown, the anxiousness drove my brain into overthinking mode. I wondered about trivial things, like did he only have a chauffeur for the women he didn't want to deal with or did he sometimes use those services himself? And where did he keep his cars?

There were so many things I didn't know about Donovan Kincaid. So many things I wanted to know and yet didn't need to know. And if I knew them, would I lose the attraction? Knowledge banished fear. If I understood him, would I lose the fear that drew me to him in the first place?

I already knew the answer, and it was almost as frightening to face as the question.

Because in between the banal thoughts, others wove in, more vague in form and heavier in weight. Thoughts like how the things I felt sitting next to this man right now were wider and deeper than lust and desire. They didn't stop at what we'd already shared—the dirty sex, the filthy fantasies. They moved further into other realms. He'd looked out for me at the office. He'd worried about me in a dark alley alone. He'd come for me tonight—I was sure of it even though he hadn't said so outright. I *cared* that he'd come for me. I *cared* that he'd worried. If he suddenly didn't, I'd hurt.

Donovan Kincaid had the power to hurt me.

And not just with his hands or the rough way he treated my body—those possible ways had always fascinated me. But he could also hurt me by not caring, could cut me so much deeper. Could scar me so much more permanently. I realized that now. And that was terrifying.

So I was still scared. He still scared me. Now he just scared me for different reasons.

Eventually, we pulled off in front of a luxury building in

Upper Midtown called the Baccarat. I hadn't been there before, but it seemed to be a hotel. A small thread of disappointment entered the weave of emotions inside me. I'd gotten the impression that Donovan was taking me to his home, that we were moving toward something more intimate between us.

But that hadn't been exactly what he'd said.

It was already happening. I was already opening myself up to be hurt by assuming that we were becoming something other than what he'd so adamantly stated we were.

I was too vulnerable.

Panic started to twist and braid in my chest.

We left the car with the valet, and as we walked through the elegant, crystal-adorned lobby, he took my hand in his. I stared at our fingers interlaced, suddenly aware of how thick the air felt in my lungs and how my heart sounded as loud as my heels on the marbled floor. After a nod at the doorman, we got in the elevator. The doors had closed, and we were on our way up before I realized we hadn't actually checked in.

The car stopped at the fifty-sixth floor, and Donovan led me to the suite doors almost immediately across from the elevator. He dropped my hand to retrieve a key card from his wallet and let me in.

As soon as I crossed the threshold and he turned on the lights, I realized I'd been wrong about the hotel situation.

"You live here?" I asked as he helped me with my coat. I didn't let him answer before heading toward the floor-to-ceiling windows at the other side of the open space behind him. It was a luxury residence, not a hotel room. The main space was white and large with a huge fireplace, furnished sparsely with modern sofas and a conversation area. The floor was dark wood covered with rich-toned rugs.

But the highlight was the view. Even in the dark, I could tell that the windows framed Central Park in the near distance.

The place was both elegant and masculine, and though I would have expected Donovan to have more black in his color scheme, I knew it was his house before he responded.

He responded anyway. "Yes. I live here."

He lived here. These were his windows, his sofas. This was his view. This was his fireplace.

I studied more of the apartment. There was a formal dining room at the opposite end of the main space and the kitchen beyond that. A staircase led to an upper floor where I imagined his bedroom was located. There weren't any portraits, but a few art pieces decorated the walls. An impressionistic ink painting of pine trees hung above the fireplace. An abstract oil canvas of orange water lilies filled the wall of the dining area.

The paintings could have been chosen by an interior designer, but neither of the designs were what I'd imagine for a man like Donovan. And there was something about each of them—the stark loneliness of the pine trees, the frankness of the lilies—something about their honesty that made me certain that he'd picked them out himself.

I shouldn't know that about him.

I shouldn't know something so intimate about a man I was supposed to have just sex with.

These things exposed him, but they made me feel like the one who was exposed. As if he understood that the more I knew about him, the more I'd feel for him. And the more I felt for him, the more he could use my emotions as his toy.

My heart started racing. My palms began sweating. I wanted to run. I wanted to stay. I needed escape, but I needed him too—with every part of me, I needed him. Needed him to fill me and fuck me and bend me and break me, and, oh god, it was going to hurt when he did.

I needed to run.

I spun around and found him standing behind me, watching as I scrutinized his quarters. He'd taken off his jacket and loosened his tie. His eyes narrowed and glistened, pinned on me like I was a rabbit through a riflescope. As though he could read every minute thought racing through my mind. As though he knew I wanted to escape. But every crease on his face said he was determined that he wouldn't let me.

He took a slow step in my direction.

I took a cautious step away.

Another step from him. Not really a step even, more like a prowl.

I kicked off my heels, ready to take off. A quick scan of my surroundings said I wouldn't get far without him catching me, which didn't matter. I *wanted* him to catch me. Just...I couldn't stand still anymore, couldn't stand frozen in his trap while the panic and the fear and the lust and desire overwhelmed me. Couldn't stand there waiting for him to take me. I needed to move.

So I ran.

Adrenaline surged through my veins as I took off around the coffee table and slipped past the sofa. He was right behind me as I darted across the open space. There were two routes out of the main room—one that seemed to lead to the kitchen and the other that went up to the second level. I headed toward the stairs.

He followed practically on my heels as I rounded the corner after the first flight. He lunged for me then, and his hand grabbed my hip sending a thrill through me, and I fell.

He had me, but I tried to pull away, my fingers clawing at the carpet of the step above me. I couldn't get a good grip, and his other arm came around my waist, twisting me to my back as he dragged me down two stairs so that he could hold me beneath him.

"You can't run from me," he said cruelly, pinning my hands above my head.

"Fuck you," I spat. I didn't know how I was so certain that he knew this was a game, but I was. Just as I was certain that he knew that part of it was real too.

"Don't worry, you will."

With one knee bent on the stair next to me, he held my wrists with just one of his hands so that he could start pushing my dress up.

My pussy throbbed with anticipation. He was so close to touching me there, and it couldn't come fast enough.

But this game required that I give it my best fight.

I wrestled again, just like I had in college when we'd sparred in his office. This time I tried to go down, but he grabbed my hair and yanked so hard I cried out as I fell forcefully back on the stairs.

Automatically his hand came down to cover my mouth. Clamped over it tightly. Exactly the same way Theo had covered my mouth when he'd tried to rape me.

The physical recollection of Theo's attack was so vivid, so close to the surface of my mind, that it was hard to differentiate between Donovan and the memory. My heart raced like I was actually being raped, my throat tightened, but everywhere we touched I was on fire, burning with need and arousal. My panties were soaked. My nipples were painfully erect.

Donovan stilled, and I worried that he'd stop. Especially

when he lowered his hand from my mouth. I was already preparing all the things to say to get him to go on.

"How much do you want me to hurt you?" he asked.

God, I almost came. He *knew*. Knew that this was edgy, that this brought up difficult memories, but he knew I still wanted to play.

"Do you want me to tell you to stop?" I'd never tell him to stop. I was sure I'd take whatever he wanted to give me.

He lowered himself over me so that I could feel his erection, hot and hard against my pelvis. "I want you to *beg* me to stop."

A shiver ran down my body.

"Safe word, then." I'd never used a safe word. Never even thought about safe words. In all my fantasies, they'd never been necessary, and it wasn't like I'd ever thought I'd play these games for real.

I knew the concept though. I just needed to pick a word—any word—the first that came to mind, that wouldn't normally come up in a sexual situation. But, put on the spot, it was weird what things my brain came up with. Maybe it was because the scene brought up so much from the past. Maybe that's why my mind finally settled on what it did.

"MADAR," I said, firmly.

His jaw flexed, but other than that slight change of expression, he didn't move.

"Donovan?"

He stayed frozen. "Why did you choose that?"

Of course he didn't know how the MADAR Foundation had taken away my Harvard scholarship. He might not have even ever heard of the foundation. He'd been born with wealth and privilege and didn't need the services of such an organization.

There was no way I was going to explain right now. "It's a long story. It's the reason I couldn't come back to Harvard. It's a word that means 'end' for me." All that mattered was that I wouldn't say it without meaning to.

He continued to look down on me strangely, making no move to continue.

"Just. Go on."

Still he didn't move, as though he were lost in thought or busy analyzing my safe word choice.

I wriggled underneath him. "Please, Donovan!"

Abruptly he was in motion. He clamped his hand back over my mouth, harder and tighter than he did before. "If you can't talk, you snap." His tone was cruel and cold now. "Snap now to show me you understand, but as soon as you do, this starts. Got it?"

I didn't even hesitate. I just snapped.

Immediately, he was back where we left off. He pushed his hand up under my dress, reaching up toward my pussy. I gripped my thighs together, trying to deny him access, but he managed to get where he wanted easily enough. Once he had the front panel of my panties in his fist, he twisted hard and pulled, causing the waistband of my thong to cut painfully into my back and then break. He tossed the ruined panties over his shoulder.

Holy shit.

It had been so primal and raw to witness, I'd stopped fighting for a moment, awestruck and turned on. But then I started fighting even harder, because as arousing as it was to see his strength, it was also exactly the right amount of frightening.

I kicked. I bucked. I twisted and scratched. All my squirming only helped him—my dress gathered up around my waist, baring my pussy to him completely. His eyes glinted in the dimly lit stairway, like an animal. Like all he could see was this target, this prize that wasn't a being or a person at all but just a thing to dominate and fuck.

And in every way that it was vile and wrong, I loved it. In every way that it meant I was sick and shameful, I embraced it.

I made one last attempt at escape when he loosened his grip to undo his pants. But I only managed to scoot up one stair before he pounced on me with his entire body. I'd have bruises in the morning, I was sure. Marks I welcomed and longed for. The next time he went to work his zipper down, he was smarter. He put his knee on my chest, pinning me down. It hurt. I couldn't breathe. I felt lightheaded like I'd pass out.

As soon as he moved his knee off of me, I sucked in air in desperate gulps. But I didn't have long to recover. His cock was out now—massive and threatening—and I felt a sudden flash of the fear I sometimes felt in my nightmares, the ones where Donovan didn't stop my assault, and I was forced to face Theo's terrible excuse for a dick. Those were the worst dreams. The ones that woke me in a cold sweat. The ones that I had to erase with fantasies of Donovan fucking me and claiming me instead.

Just like he was about to do now.

I was so scared and turned on I couldn't even explain myself anymore.

"You want this," Donovan taunted in the same menacing ways Theo had taunted me. He rubbed his crown along the skin at the top of my folds. "Girls like you always want it."

I did want it. In all the ways I hadn't wanted Theo, I

wanted Donovan now. Even though I meant to fight him until the very end.

I hit him. I scratched. I heard my dress tear. I bent my knees and clamped them together, denying him entry to my hole, but he dug his fingers into my knees, pulling them apart. The next time he tried, he wedged his thigh between my legs, and then settled his body in the space he created while he once again gathered my wrists in his hands.

"Now fucking hold still," he growled, angry and aroused. With my wrists secure, he used his other hand to notch his cock at my hole and then pushed in bluntly.

I was so wet, so turned on, so high on the enactment of a fantasy I'd had for years, that I came instantly, the intensity of it taking my breath away. He shoved in again as the strength of my orgasm tried to push him out. He continued to thrust with belligerent determination, fighting against my body's tightening around him.

As soon as I thought I was done, I came again, my body shuddering as the second climax rippled over me.

"Jesus Christ," he swore in awe. He forced himself inside me once more, plunging in deeper and with more aggression than he ever had.

He worked up a pace that was uneven and unrelenting and too frenzied to call rhythmic. I lay almost completely still, letting him invade me in whatever way he wanted. I was delirious and dazed and already wrecked, but I was still so sensitive and aroused that he brought me to orgasm twice more before he slowed and then stilled, emptying himself into me with a long grunt.

He fell on top of me with a thud, as though all of his energy had been exhausted. The weight of him felt heavy and welcome, like a thick winter blanket, and in the comfort of that moment I thought that if this had been what had happened that night, if this had been the outcome—if Donovan had tried to rape me, if he'd succeeded—would I have loved it like this? Would that have changed everything about what happened then?

What did that mean about me? Did it mean I *wanted* to be raped? I was sure there was a difference. Sure there was a reason why the fantasy wasn't the same as the reality, but in my euphoric cum-drunk bliss, I couldn't sort it out in my mind.

As long as Donovan was lying on top of me, I didn't feel like I had to. I was satisfied. Protected. I was vulnerable, but only to him.

But he didn't stay there long. After a few minutes, he rolled onto his back next to me and lay there staring at the ceiling until he caught his breath.

"Sabrina?" he asked eventually, turning on his side with a sense of urgency in his energy.

He was checking in, and I knew what he needed to hear. "I'm all right."

Except, I realized, that there were tears streaming down my face. I'd cried a bit through our struggle, but these were fresh. As soon as I recognized them, they fell faster, quickly turning into rivers.

Wordlessly, Donovan sat up and quickly scooped me up in his arms, cradling me as the weeping turned into sobs. He let me cry like that, running his hand through my hair, smoothing the tangles he'd created, neither trying to shush me nor question me.

I couldn't have explained if he'd asked, but I did know it had to do with Theo. Partly I was still confused. Confused about what was wrong with me that I wanted Donovan to reenact this terrible thing that happened to me. Why I liked it when he was rough and mean and animalistic. Why it turned me on so goddamn much.

And partly it was that I was actually remembering Theo. My body remembered him in ways my head didn't. My fear remembered him. My panic remembered him. And as much as I didn't want to think of him while I was with Donovan, I had. How could I not? I'd nurtured and groomed this fantasy over many years, and it had come to grow independent of that night. But the roots were still entangled with that other thing—the thing that Theo had planted with his assault.

But I didn't know how to tell that to Donovan.

I had to tell him something, though. So when I calmed enough to get out words, I said, "I wanted that. I did. I'm not crying because I didn't want it."

"I know." He kept strumming his hand through my hair.

I lifted my chin from his chest to look at him. "How do you know that?"

He let out a soft breath and met my eyes. "Because it's what I've always recognized in you."

"Because it's in you too?" It was almost a whisper. Almost like I hoped it more than I believed it could be true.

He wiped several tears from my cheek before answering. "Yes. Because it's in me too."

We were quiet again, me cradled in his lap, my head tucked under his chin. I rubbed absently at his cheek, knowing I needed to start to think about pulling myself together. We didn't have the kind of relationship where I could stay. We didn't have the type of relationship where he would hold me.

We didn't have a relationship at all.

But we were both naked and bare right now, even though we still had most of our clothes on. I was already raw. How much more vulnerable could I be?

"I don't want to leave," I said.

Not even a beat passed. "I don't want you to go."

"Okay," I said.

"Okay."

TWENTY-EIGHT

Donovan led me upstairs and into a master bedroom with hardwood floors and an entire wall of windows. The king-size bed faced the view which overlooked the city and, in the near distance, Central Park. There was a fireplace on the far wall, and a gray headboard behind the bed, but the rest of the design was white, clean lines like the main room below.

The bedroom wasn't our destination, however. I was led next to the en suite where he started a shower for me. While I undressed, he pulled towels from a linen closet and set them on the counter.

"Take as long as you like," he said when I was naked and steam began filling the room.

I wanted to ask him to stay. There was a part of me that thought I needed him to help me recover from whatever it was that was going on inside of me. And from the searching way he looked at me, I had a feeling there was a part of him that wanted to stay too. Or wondered if he should.

But I didn't ask. Because I didn't know what was going on in his head at the moment, and there was a possibility that he needed time alone. He usually did after we had sex, after all.

And maybe I needed time alone too.

Honestly, I didn't know *what* I needed. But I knew I didn't want to go home yet, and I was grateful that he'd given me some time before he kicked me out, even if it was time spent without him.

I lost track of time in the shower. I lost track of thoughts. I didn't worry about sorting out my brain or my emotions. I just turned the water as hot as I could stand it and stood under the rain showerhead and let it pour over me until I felt like I could move again. Then I used some of Donovan's shampoo and body wash, cleaned up quickly, and got out smelling like him, which made me smile unexpectedly with every inhale.

After drying off, I realized that my dress and bra were missing. Donovan must have taken them out with him when he'd left. I squeezed the water from my hair as best I could and, with a towel wrapped around myself, left the bathroom to look for him and/or my dress.

I found him first, in the bedroom looking out the window, one arm braced against the glass, a tumbler of scotch in the other, and as soon as I saw him, the breath left my lungs. He'd changed out of his suit, and now he was wearing a pair of dark sweats that hung loosely around his hips, and nothing else. His feet and chest were bare, and I couldn't stop staring at the toned ridges of his abs, at the dips and curves of his biceps, at the sharp V lines that disappeared beneath the waistband of his pants.

It was a relaxed version of Donovan. As relaxed as he ever

got, I suspected. And there was something so sensual about it. Something so inviting and intimate and alluring.

It did strange things to my body to see him like that. Made my blood hot like I was still in the shower, made me shiver as if I'd been out in the cold.

He turned when I opened the door and studied me as I studied him. I was probably the one who should speak, should thank him for the shower and all that, but I'd lost thoughts of everything but the way my heart felt racing in my chest like it did.

So he was the one to talk first. "If you keep looking at me like that, I'm going to get you dirty again."

Goose bumps erupted along my arms. "I've never seen you with your shirt off." I sounded like a lust-driven teenager. Felt like one too.

He didn't seem to mind. "If I'd known it would elicit such a reaction, I would have stripped sooner," he said with a smirk.

"Would you really?" I had the distinct feeling he liked the power it gave him to be dressed when I was not. Or maybe that was just me.

"Probably not." *As I'd thought.* He pointed to a small tray on the ottoman in the sitting area. "I brought some cheese and grapes. What can I get you to drink? Wine? Gin?"

I gaped for two seconds. I'd expected to come out of the shower and be sent home. This hospitable side of Donovan surprised me. Elated me. How long did this mean I could stay?

With a glance at the tumbler already in his hand, I said, "Scotch, please."

If he was startled by my choice, he didn't let on. He simply smiled. "Scotch it is."

He set his own drink down on his nightstand, but I stopped him before he disappeared out of the room. "Where did you put my dress?"

"I hung it up. You can get it later."

So he really wasn't kicking me out...yet.

When he left the room, I was the one that was smiling.

Spotting his discarded clothes draped on the back of a chair by the fireplace, I exchanged my towel for his dress shirt. I rolled the sleeves up and grabbed the tray of cheese and grapes and scanned the room for my seating choices. The chairs faced the fireplace. Eating on someone else's sheets was tacky.

I ended up choosing the floor at the bottom of the bed. The area rug extended far enough that I wasn't sitting on hard floor, and this was the best way to enjoy the view.

Donovan returned a few minutes later and seemed mildly surprised to find me where he did. He handed me my drink, his brow raised.

"Thank you," I said, taking it from him. Without him pressing, I rushed to explain my choice. "I wanted to look out the windows."

Apparently that wasn't the cause for the brow raise. "I offered food and drink. I didn't offer clothes." Though the way he looked at me now, his gaze searing as it traveled down my bare thighs, I didn't think he really minded all that much.

"*You're* dressed," I challenged before bringing a grape to my mouth.

His eyes flicked from my own to my lips. "My house, my rules."

"I guess you're going to have to enforce them then. Because I'm kind of comfortable as I am."

His jaw ticked, but he didn't push further. Instead, he retrieved his drink and took a seat next to me, stretching his long legs out in front of him.

God, those legs. Those arms. That body. Just sitting next to him made me crazy with desire. Made my pussy pulse with want and—

"We didn't use a condom." It hadn't occurred to me until just then. Quickly, gears shifted from lust to panic.

Donovan, however, remained calm. He picked another grape from a stem. "You're on birth control," he said, before throwing it in his mouth.

I *was* on the pill. Not that I'd ever told him that. But pregnancy wasn't the only reason to use a condom. I bristled. "And you assumed...?"

He tilted his head toward me. "You had a safe word. You didn't use it."

I had to think about that for a minute because the thing was that protection hadn't occurred to me while we were having sex either. Which was weird. I'd never had unprotected sex.

But if I *had* thought about it, would I have interrupted the game to tell him to suit up?

No. I wouldn't. Part of the fantasy was about letting Donovan do whatever he wanted to me. Letting him take me however he wanted to take me. And if he wanted to take me bare, then he would take me bare. It wasn't up to me.

"I didn't want to use my safe word," I said after I'd thought it through.

He gave me the devil's smirk, the one that said he'd known I'd come to that conclusion all along. "Then what are you fussing about?"

"I'm not fussing. Just..." I trailed off. How was I supposed to ask about STDs? The deed was over and done. The only thing I could do now was get tested. I wrapped both my hands around my tumbler and took a sip, trying not to wonder about how many women Donovan might have slept with previously without a condom.

The thoughts slipped in anyway, making my stomach twist. It hurt to think about him having sex with anyone else, let alone to imagine him being so intimate with someone that he'd go bare.

Which meant I shouldn't be thinking about it.

But how could I stop?

"I haven't had unprotected sex in over ten years," he volunteered.

My head snapped up to see if he was kidding. His expression said he wasn't.

"Oh." Since Amanda, probably. He'd used condoms with every woman he'd been with since his fiancée? I liked hearing this. I hated how much I liked it.

"And," he went on, "I haven't fucked anyone else since you came into town."

While the first announcement had been a surprise, this one was a shock. "Why?" I asked, my voice thin.

"You know why." He pierced me with his gaze. Unflinching. Unapologetic.

My pulse sped up, and I wasn't sure if I was excited by his words or alarmed. I *didn't* know why he hadn't slept with anyone else. I could make guesses and all of them were dangerous answers to dwell on. They didn't fit into a Just Sex relationship, and that made this conversation thin ice. The safest thing to do would be to ask him point blank to explain, but I wasn't ready to skate out that far on this pond.

But I was ready to skirt the edges. "I haven't slept with anyone else either," I confessed.

"I know." He grinned as he devoured a piece of Gouda.

"You're so cocky."

"I'm perceptive." He picked up the tray of food, holding it out as if to ask if I wanted any more.

I declined it, too focused on the topic. "You can tell I haven't been with anyone else? How?"

"Because I just can." He reached over to the ottoman, grabbed a leg and dragged it until it was close enough to put the tray and his now empty glass on top.

I watched, trying not to drool as his back muscles stretched and flexed. "Like I said—cocky." Confident was more accurate. Conceited, even. But he made it sexy. Made me want to shed my clothes at just the nod of his head.

Or, in this case, *his* clothes.

He returned to his spot next to me, our backs propped up by the bed. Our arms lightly grazed each other as I brought my tumbler up for another sip of scotch, and I had a feeling the warmth running through my veins had more to do with him than the liquor. Though I'd barely been nibbling at the tray of food, I felt suddenly awkward without it between us. There was no longer something to "do". No longer an object to build a pretense around, and now there was nothing to distract me from the sexual tension that constantly surrounded us.

If he felt it too—and I was sure that he could—I knew he wouldn't let it sit long before addressing it; before either deciding this night was over or deciding I needed to be beneath him. Donovan was a guy who took the reins, which was some-thing I admired about him, and I waited anxiously for him to do so.

That motherfucker, though, was as patient as the day was long.

Sure enough, it seemed like forever before he leaned over to me and put his mouth so close to my ear that I could hear him inhale and feel his exhale rush along my skin.

"How are you doing?" he asked, trite words spoken in the sexiest rumble.

I bit my lip and pressed my thighs together, as if that could ease the need between my legs. "I'm okay."

He circled his nose around the shell of my ear, not exactly touching it but almost, sending a shiver down my spine. "I'm absolutely going to fuck you again, and I'm going to need a better answer than okay first."

"It's kind of hard to think of more complicated words when you say things like that. When you're this close."

"Let me fix that." He sat back against the bed, and I had to stop myself from pulling him back down toward me. The only reason I didn't, in fact, was because he rested a hand at my lower back, anchoring me. "Earlier tonight, we had what some might call rough sex and afterward you cried in my arms. Now I need to know—how are you doing?"

Ah. He meant earlier.

My cheeks quickly heated. How unsexy was a woman who couldn't take the kind of sex she'd insisted on having? "God, this is humiliating."

"You've let me choke you with my cock, fucked me for a better grade, and sat without underwear in a formal restaurant, and *this* is what you find humiliating?"

That earned him a small smile. Lower, unbeknownst to him, my stomach flipped. I'd done all the things he'd mentioned, found them crazy hot. Would do them again in a heartbeat.

But what had happened with Theo...

I didn't even know what was the most embarrassing about it. That the assault had happened in the first place? That I had fantasies centered on it? That I still thought about it so much now?

I set my tumbler down, drew my knees up and put my hands in my lap. "He probably doesn't even remember me," I said, staring at my French tips. "He was drunk, and I wasn't important. Just a nobody girl from a college party that happened over ten years ago."

"You mean Theodore Sheridan," Donovan said smoothly.

The hair at the back of my neck stood up at the mention of his name. "Yes. Him." Donovan had the luxury of talking about him without his blood turning cold. Without his throat going dry. "I know he doesn't think about me when he walks down dark alleys. He doesn't wake up in a cold sweat with me on his mind. He doesn't worry that I'm out in the world; that he could bump into me at the bank or at the airport or at Starbucks. He isn't afraid that I'll look him up one day on a whim and try to find him."

I'd almost searched for him so many times but always stopped myself in the end. It would only give me something new to resent or fear or worry about, and I suspected that wasn't healthy.

Still, the restraint didn't make me *well*. And maybe he was the real reason I hadn't kept pushing to get back into a good school after The MADAR Foundation pulled my scholarship.

Because he didn't just make me scared of *him*—he made me scared, period.

I leaned my chin on my knees and refused to look at Donovan, determined not to let him see my eyes filling again. "I'm sure Theodore Sheridan doesn't live a single day afraid at all."

Though his hand had remained steady at the small of my back, Donovan had been quiet the whole time I'd talked. After I finished, he let only a few beats of silence pass before he said, adamantly, "He's not going to come after you. You know that, don't you, Sabrina?"

I shrugged.

"Sabrina?" He leaned forward, trying to get my eyes on him.

I turned my head and rested my cheek on my knee. "I know it," I said, forcing a smile. "In my head, I know it. Just, sometimes it still feels like he could."

"He's not. I promise you that he's not." He searched my eyes, as though if he searched hard enough he could find the way to make me believe it. "It was years ago, and Theodore Sheridan is not looking for a random girl he came across at a party. Like you said, he probably doesn't even remember you."

They were harsh, true words. I was forgettable and nobody. I got it. "You're right. You're right. I know you're right. He scared me though. The kind of scared that runs several layers deep. It doesn't go away easily, and it comes up sometimes. When I don't always expect it."

I sat up and wiped the leaking tears from under my eyes. "So, I'm okay. Really. What we did tonight just stirred up that fear and brought it to the surface, but I don't regret it, and I'd do it again."

I blushed; this time it spread down my neck, not because I was humiliated but because I'd brought up what we'd done. The game where he forced me to fuck him. The game that I loved.

Moisture pooled between my legs just thinking about it.

It had been the best sex of my life, and I'd done nothing but cry about it. Donovan probably didn't even know how much I'd loved it.

With cheeks still red, I side-glanced at him. "I *want* to do it again. Not right now. Not always. But definitely. It was everything I'd imagined it would be. More, actually. I'm sorry that I ruined it."

With a mischievous lift of his lip, he reassured me. "Trust me, you didn't ruin it."

I stayed locked in his gaze, and I realized then that he had me. Really had me. Like a fly caught in a web. From the outside, it seemed so much more tenuous and fragile, this hold of his. Like getting near him was risky but wouldn't do any long-term harm because I'd manage to break free. What was a web anyway but mere strands of thin silk?

But I was inside his trap now. Stuck. And his hold wasn't fragile at all. I was going nowhere until he cut me loose. Any moment now he would—he'd decide that he was no longer interested in feasting on his captured prey, and he'd cut me from his web. But I'd become too wrapped up in his spinning to escape undamaged. My wings would tear and break. I'd be destroyed.

On a sudden impulse, I climbed into his lap, straddling him. He brought his knees up behind me, creating a natural seat. Marveling at the smoothness of his skin, I ran my hands over the firm peaks of his pecs and down the ridged planes of his abs.

"You scare me, too," I whispered. A thrill ran down my spine as his cock stirred beneath me.

He ran a single finger from my cleavage up to the base of my throat. Lightly he pressed against my windpipe. "I like that I do."

"But it's different."

He continued trailing his fingers up my neck until he got to my chin. There he stopped and rubbed his thumb back and forth across my lower lip. "Because I stopped Theo? That doesn't mean I'm any less vile."

"Because I want you to scare me, and you know it. Because the way you're vile fits the way I'm vile." I sucked hard on his thumb.

"You're not vile," he groaned. He drew his wet thumb from my lips and placed his hand firmly behind my neck so he could pull me down toward him.

"Then neither are you," I managed before his mouth crashed against mine.

Our lips played with each other's. Our tongues tangled. He licked deep inside my mouth, getting lost behind my teeth. He bruised me with the pressure of his nips along my jaw.

He was content to just kiss me like this for a long time. Well, not *just* kiss me. I lost my shirt—*his* shirt—right away, and his hands wandered up and down my body. Everywhere. Fondling my breasts. Pinching my nipples. Teasing past the crack in my ass.

I touched him as much as I could in return, sweeping my hands across his torso and bucking my hips against the growing

length of his cock. But mostly, I clutched onto his neck and held
on for dear life. Because though this wasn't the first time I'd
kissed him or rode him or coiled my fingers in his hair, this was
the first time I was truly aware of what I was doing. That no
matter what Donovan wanted this to be, I was not just having
sex with him. This was not a non-relationship. Not for me.

And while I didn't know what he wanted anymore or what
would come next, I was sure that I needed to hold on.

Eventually, he tightened his arms around me and stood up.
I wrapped my legs around him, locking my ankles at his waist.
Without breaking his kiss, he carried me over to the bed and
laid me on it. He undid the drawstring on his sweats, and I
moved up to my knees so I could get a good look when he
dropped them to the floor.

Jesus, he was hung.

I'd seen his cock before. Of course, I had.

But somehow seeing him completely naked, his firm thighs
a mouthwatering background to the centerpiece, made his erection seem even fuller and heavier and more substantial than it
ever had before.

I licked my tongue along my bottom lip. His eyes shone, the
green flecks shimmering with satisfaction at the way I looked at
him. With my eyes glued to his every move, he wrapped his
hand around his shaft and tugged upward.

"Please," I begged, my voice trembling, and I didn't even
know what I was begging for, but Donovan knew what I
needed.

Wordlessly, he pushed me onto my side and curled up
behind me. I immediately missed being able to watch him, but
any objection I had to his chosen position was swallowed when

he turned my chin toward him and devoured my mouth as he entered me with a long, slow glide.

He fucked me at a leisurely pace, his strokes pulling all the way out to the tip before pushing in again, deep. So deep. Balls deep. My nerves hummed from the intensity, but my orgasm couldn't build enough to take off at this speed. It was luxuriously tormenting.

Soon, Donovan rolled onto his back, pulling me with him so that I was tight against his chest. It was harder to kiss him like this, but he had full access to my body, and he took advantage of it, playing with my breasts and rubbing at my clit in lazy circles, drawing my climax closer and closer and closer—

"Don't come," he commanded.

"I have to. I'm so close." I was already on the edge.

"Don't, Sabrina. I mean it." His teeth sunk into the shell of my ear, a warning.

The haze around me dulled enough for me to think. "Then stop touching me like that."

He was still massaging my clit, still tweaking my nipple in his other hand. "Uh-uh."

The tension continued to build like a pressure cooker. I tried to sit up, tried to pull away from his attention, but he held me in place. "This isn't fair."

"My house, my rules. Remember?"

"Ah, fuck," I moaned as his cock hit a particularly sensitive spot. "I. God. I can't."

"You will."

Without him telling me what they were, I knew that my disobedience would have consequences.

And I wanted to obey him, for whatever reason.

Because I was in his bed.

Because it would make him happy.

Because it was natural.

So I fought against the growing tension, even as Donovan made it more and more impossible, increasing the tempo of his thrusts, pressing harder on my clit.

All the while he threatened at my ear, "Don't do it, Sabrina. Don't you dare come. Don't you dare," and he might as well have said, *"Don't you dare fall for me,"* because pretty soon I realized it was just as pointless. Everything he did was leading toward that anyway. Everything he did was pushing me up, up, up and eventually, where else was I going to go? Eventually I'd—

"Now," he growled.

—fall.

Just like that, on command, my orgasm tore through me, sending me spinning and spinning and spinning like a top— out-of-control and frenetic. Whirling so fast I was dizzy with euphoric, chaotic bliss.

He was right there with me, grunting out his climax in symmetry with mine. Both of us joined physically but experiencing our own separate rapture like we were two spiral galaxies revolving around each other in harmony.

It was beautiful. And perfect. And so much more than anything we'd shared before.

At least, it was for me.

It was a good feeling, a sweet ecstasy, and I didn't want to disrupt it by thinking about what it was for him until I had to.

I closed my eyes to catch my breath.

It felt like a minute later, but it must have been longer because I was half asleep when Donovan pulled me under the covers and tugged me into his arms, spooning me. He was the only person I dreamt about that night, and my head wasn't filled with images of rape or sex or assault or violence.

Instead, in my dreams, Donovan held me tight and whispered words that made me feel things. Beautiful things. Things he could never feel in return. Words he could never mean if he were awake.

TWENTY-NINE

The smell of freshly ground coffee brewing woke me up the next morning.

I lingered for several minutes, letting consciousness chase sleep away. With wakefulness, I remembered—I was different today than when I'd woken up yesterday. I breathed that in; let myself adjust as my emotions spread their wings inside me like a butterfly emerging from its cocoon.

I was different.

But who was Donovan?

There was only one way to know. With a yawn, I stretched my well-used muscles and stumbled out of bed to find him.

First, I had to find some clothes.

The shirt I'd worn the night before had disappeared so I had no choice but to invade his walk-in closet in search of my dress. As he'd said it would be, I found it hanging on the rack in front of a row of sharply tailored suits. It was obviously out of place, yet I liked the way my clothing looked next to his. I trailed my hand along the jacket sleeves as I walked toward the back of the room and inhaled. It smelled like him in here. Like his aftershave and the brand of shoe polish he used. I'd never get tired of that smell.

In the back of the closet, next to rows of neatly folded ties, I discovered a shelf of plain white T-shirts. I decided he wouldn't mind if I borrowed one. Or, rather, I decided that I didn't care if he did mind.

After stopping in the bathroom to freshen up as best as I could and swish with some mouthwash I found in his cabinet, I padded downstairs toward the smell of the coffee.

My nose led me to the kitchen where I also found Donovan. He was standing with his back to me at the island, reading on a tablet. He wore a light gray T-shirt and a different pair of sweatpants than he'd worn the night before, and though I liked this look on him as much as any, I was slightly disappointed to find his beautiful torso once again covered up.

He didn't turn around when I walked in, though I was sure he heard me coming down the stairs. Sure he felt my presence the same way I felt the heat radiating off him in my direction.

He was going to make me be the one to break the Morning After ice.

Okay. No big deal.

"Hi," I said, feeling my cheeks redden for no reason other than I was in the same room with Donovan Kincaid.

Slowly, in his own time, he turned around. He narrowed his eyes as he looked me over. With a frown, he crossed over to a cabinet and pulled out a coffee mug. "I don't recall setting a shirt out for you." He handed me the cup.

I smiled, sure he was teasing, but quickly sobered when he didn't return it.

"I was cold," I said in my defense. Now that it was daylight, he could want me gone as soon as possible. "I'll change into my dress after I shower, if you don't mind."

Or did he want me naked?

I held my breath waiting for a clue.

"I suppose I don't mind." His tone was neutral, though, and didn't give me anything to go on.

I went to the coffee pot and poured myself a cup, trying to ignore the knot in my stomach and the tightness of my chest. The air between us was charged, but it felt like razors when I inhaled, I was so unsure of what we were. What would happen next.

Usually, I took my coffee with both cream and sweetener, but I didn't want to push his hospitality so I spooned some sugar from the bowl and stepped away from the counter.

Donovan was waiting for me with creamer from the fridge. "It's plain. It's all I have."

Goose bumps rode down my skin.

"Thanks. Plain is great." I held my cup out and let him pour some in, wondering if I'd ever told him that I usually drank my coffee with hazelnut or if he'd just guessed.

"I had a protein bar for breakfast myself. But I can get you anything. There's toast. Or fruit. Or eggs." He opened the refrigerator and reached inside.

"I usually just have—" I stopped abruptly as he handed me an individual-sized cup of Greek yogurt.

"Or yogurt," he said.

"Yogurt," I said at the same time. "Thanks."

"Spoons are in the drawer behind you."

I didn't move. Guessing that I took flavored creamer was one thing. My choice of breakfast food was another. "How did you—?"

"You eat your breakfast at the office most mornings." Reaching over, he removed the foil lid on the yogurt. "Same thing every day." He pulled on a lower cabinet handle and a recycling can emerged. He tossed the foil inside and shut it.

"You *are* perceptive." I hadn't even realized he'd ever seen me eating my breakfast. I was obviously the one who wasn't perceptive.

"I said I was." Since I hadn't moved to get a spoon, he reached around me to grab one and stuck it in my yogurt cup for me.

"You're *also* cocky." This time when I grinned up at him, his eyes twinkled as though grinning back, even though his lips remained straight and even.

I stared at those lips, wanting them. He was already so near, his hand resting on the counter behind me, and who cared that I had yogurt in one hand and coffee in another? I only needed my mouth to reach up for a kiss.

I took a step in toward him, but he blinked and abruptly backed up.

"Look." He scratched the back of his neck, evading my eyes. "I have some work I need to attend to."

...and there it was. The brush-off.

Disappointment fell through me like an elevator with cut cables.

"I'll take a quick shower and get out of your hair." At least he'd been more polite about the way he'd asked for space this time. He'd made progress there. It just hurt that he still *needed* space.

I set my mug and untouched yogurt on the counter and, with my back to him, babbled on awkwardly. "I have stuff to do today anyway. I have to review the ROI on the social media campaigns for last month, and I'm behind on my opportunity analysis reports. I should really get started as soon as possible if I expect to put a dent in those."

"No need to rush out. At least finish your coffee first." His inflection portrayed nothing but poise.

I nodded and took a sip from my mug. He'd turned back to his tablet, so I could watch him as he drank his own coffee and flipped through the pages of the online *Wall Street Journal*. As though today was life as usual. As though everything was normal. Was this really still no big deal to him? Were we really in just a physical relationship? Did last night mean nothing more than every other time we'd been together?

After several heavy minutes of silence, he turned his head slightly in my direction. "Weston still has you doing the long-form OARs?"

He wanted to talk about work then. Fine.

"Yes. They're time-consuming and the bane of my existence." I hated the several-page analysis that Weston required monthly for every account that I worked, but I'd do a million of them if it meant the uneasiness between Donovan and me would disappear. "If they were helpful, that would be one thing, but mostly they just reiterate information from month to month."

He nodded once. "Agreed. When you report to me, I'll reduce the requirement to semi-annually." He flipped another page on his tablet.

My brow furrowed and alarm bells rang in my ears. "I'm going to report to you?"

With his back still to me, he explained. "We have lax fraternization rules, but even so, you can't report to Weston once you're dating him."

I almost dropped my coffee mug. "You're kidding, right?"

He turned to face me. "No, I'm not," he said gruffly.

Of course he wasn't kidding. Donovan wasn't the type to kid and everything about his tone and body language said he was serious.

"Weston and I discussed it before you started working for Reach. We decided to wait until you were officially dating to make the assignment transfer, but it will be necessary."

I set my mug down and ran my hand across my forehead. "Wait...what?"

"When you start seeing Weston," he said slowly, patronizingly, "you will report to *me* instead of *him*."

There was something familiar about this. When I'd first arrived, Donovan had joked about me reporting to someone else, but the conversation had gotten dismissed. This was what it was about. They'd made arrangements in case Weston and I decided to see each other seriously.

God, that was a lifetime ago.

And Donovan thought it was still a possible scenario?

"No," I said, shaking my head emphatically, which was suddenly pounding as heavily as my heart. "No."

"No?" He crossed his arms over his chest and leaned against the island behind him.

"No!" I was vehement this time. "Never mind that we'd have serious conflicts with you as my supervisor." Okay, sometimes I found his power games hot, but that wasn't the point. "I am *not* dating Weston."

"Not now, you're not. This is after he's annulled his marriage that we're talking about."

I threw my hands up. "I am not dating Weston! Not now. Not ever. How can you even think that I would...?" I trailed off, realizing that I might have never fully clarified this.

Shit. Had Donovan been thinking I was still hung up on Weston all this time?

"Okay." I exhaled, trying to remain calm. "I *said* I was going to go after him, but I'm not. I'm not interested in him. He is not the guy I'm interested in." I couldn't make it any more clear without saying it outright.

Donovan thought about it then shrugged. "That's a shame." He grabbed his coffee mug and carried it over to the sink where he dumped out the remains. "You two seemed right for each other."

"We are not even a little bit right for each other!" I blared. *Besides, I'm seeing you!*

Calmly, he filled the mug with hot water from the faucet. "I wasn't aware your feelings had changed."

He was being such an incredibly hurtful ass. I wanted so much to grab the mug and throw the hot water in his face. "My feelings *haven't* changed, and you know goddamn well they haven't. I never had the feelings in the first place. You were the one who pushed me to him, and that was only because you were trying so hard to push me away from you."

He shut the faucet off and turned to me, his stare confrontational. "What was that?"

His icy tone and the cold way he looked into me sent a chill down my spine.

I folded my arms across my chest, willing to stand my ground but not sure I was brave enough to say it again. "You know what I said."

He took a step toward me, his eyes narrow. "Are you under an impression that something else is going on between us other than what is?"

My hands felt suddenly clammy, and my throat had a lump in it the size of a tennis ball. It was my chance. My opportunity to tell him things had changed. This *was* a relationship. This was more than *Just Sex*. Not just for me—for him too, I was almost sure of it. He hadn't slept with anyone else since he'd been with me. Wasn't that what a relationship was?

But I could tell how this would go. I could feel it in the energy vibrating off his body. As soon as I admitted it to him, he would either have to embrace me or end things, and there was no way he was embracing me. Humiliation was the only thing to be gained by that admission.

So, jutting my chin forward, I gave him the easiest answer for both of us. "Nope. There is no '*us*'. That's the right impression, isn't it?"

He held his offense posture a moment longer. "It is."

"Then we're good." My hands were shaky as I turned back to my coffee and my yogurt, but my appetite was gone. "I'm actually not hungry. And I'm just going to shower at home. You can get back to whatever it is that your life is."

Five minutes later I was changed. Thankfully my coat covered the tear in my dress. But even with my hair thrown up in a knot and my coat wrapped tightly around me, I would be making a very obvious walk of shame through his lobby.

Though we weren't really speaking, he saw me to the door. "My driver is waiting for you downstairs," he said.

"Thank you," I mumbled.

He stayed at his door and watched from across the hall, so when I got in the elevator and turned around, my eyes locked on his. The last thing I saw before the elevator doors closed between us was his expression wrinkle with regret.

I just couldn't tell if he regretted letting me leave or that he'd ever let me in in the first place.

THIRTY

I threw myself into work the rest of the day. Getting caught up on Weston's lengthy, redundant opportunity analysis reports was an excuse to ignore thinking about Donovan.

Even with my mind busy, I couldn't stop from *feeling*. And my feelings were like a swarm of bumblebees buzzing inside of me. I felt so much for him. So much *about* him. And all of it stung when I examined it too closely.

Maybe I wasn't cut out for this.

When I'd first let Donovan into my bed, I hadn't thought it would be more than a one-night stand. I hadn't realized that I'd fall so hard, so quickly. I hadn't imagined that he might show feelings for me and that every time he turned cold afterward, I'd be shattered.

It was better not examining any of it. If I did, I'd have to make a decision about what to do. So, instead, I kept my head in my laptop and focused on revenue pipelines and investment costs.

By Sunday afternoon, I'd knocked out a significant amount of work and had managed to distract myself from random crying jags with a marathon of *Community* playing on the TV in the background. My Chinese delivery had just arrived, and I was about to sit back and enjoy my Kung Pao chicken when my phone alerted me that I had a text.

I want dessert. When can I pick you up?

The bees took flight in my belly, fluttering in that way that made me want to respond with ***Now*** as fast as I could type it. But their stingers were out, needling along my ribs and heart and everywhere, everywhere, wounding me with even the thought of being in Donovan's presence while having to pretend that he didn't mean as much to me as he did. How could I lie beneath him, how could I be naked in front of him, how could I let him move inside me and not fall even deeper than I already had?

But what was my other option? I wasn't ready to end things with him either. That likely made me a masochist, something Donovan probably already knew about me, but it wasn't a label I could live with for long. I was too strong. Too ambitious. Too willing to go after what I wanted.

Which meant that eventually I'd have to confront this.

Just.

I wasn't ready yet.

Without responding, I turned my phone on silent and tossed it on my coffee table. He'd blown me off for an entire week. I could ignore him for at least one night.

FOUR HOURS LATER, I emerged from a shower to the sound of pounding on my door.

I already knew who it was. A hot rush swept through me while goose bumps pebbled along my skin.

He'd shown up at my apartment!

Fuck. He'd shown up at my apartment.

With a sigh, I wrapped my plain, fluffy terrycloth bathrobe around me and headed to answer it.

"What are you doing here?" I asked when, as suspected, I found Donovan on the other side of the door.

He was wearing tan khaki pants, a dark gray pullover, and a scowl that made my heart race and my toes curl with trepidation. "You didn't answer my texts."

"Texts" as in plural. He must have sent more.

This was the part of my plan that I hadn't thought through. He'd already proven my secretary wasn't a barrier. I should have expected this.

I leaned my face against the doorjamb. "It's not fair that I can't avoid you as efficiently as you can avoid me. I'm pretty sure your doorman would never let me up without your clearance."

His jaw ticked. "You're avoiding me?"

Obviously not anymore.

Resigned, I opened the door wide enough for him to enter. "Come on in."

As he had last time he'd shown up at my apartment, he walked in as if he owned the place, which, of course, he did. Openly he surveyed the workspace I'd made for myself on the couch, my leftover Chinese still sitting next to my open laptop.

I closed the door and made my way over to the coffee table

to pick up my phone, which I hadn't looked at since I'd silenced it earlier. There were a total of seven texts from him.

I hated how that made me feel special somehow.

"Why are you avoiding me?" he asked, reminding me that he was here in the flesh.

"If I wanted to talk about it, I wouldn't be avoiding you." I threw the phone down and headed to the kitchen to pour a glass of merlot. I'd had one earlier, but the buzz had worn off, and I definitely needed something now.

Donovan leaned against the back of my couch and watched me, shaking his head when I offered him a glass of his own.

"Well, I'm here," he said, hands curled into the sofa, "and I'm not leaving until you explain. Or until I've emptied my cock down your throat. The choice is yours."

My knees buckled at the sight of his devilish grin. I quickly threw back half my glass to help steady my resolve. "I cannot have sex with you, Donovan."

He seemed about to argue until I shot him a glare from hell.

"Fine. Sex is off the table," he conceded. "For now."

Thank god he'd agreed to that. Because I was already wavering. I felt warm everywhere, from my shower, from the merlot, from the way he looked at me—like he wanted to nibble every inch of my skin.

God, how I wanted to feel those nibbles turn into bites...

No, I couldn't think about that. I couldn't think at all with him in my house. I needed him to leave.

"I'm not talking about this with you, Donovan. You don't want to talk about this with me either. I promise you don't." With my glass in hand, I stormed past him and gestured toward the door. "So you might as well just go."

He didn't move except to tilt his head in my direction. "You can't possibly know that."

Except, I could know that. I was sure of it.

"Donovan..." I pled.

"Talk, Sabrina. Talk or I'll find a way to make you talk, I swear to god." Both his tone and expression were serious. The kind of serious that scared the shit out of me and made my pussy clench and drip.

I didn't want to do this. I didn't want to say this.

But it came hurling out of me like bad food that had sat in my stomach too long. "How can you be sleeping with only me and say we aren't in a relationship?"

"What?"

I circled around in front of the sofa and started pacing. "You aren't fucking anyone else. And I'm not fucking anyone else."

He turned around so he was facing me. "Do you *want* me to fuck other women?"

"No." I stopped mid-step, panic bubbling in my chest. "Do *you* want to fuck other women?"

His face told me nothing. "Not at the moment."

That was a relief, at least. "Then how can you say we aren't in a relationship? We've stopped using condoms."

He shook his head slightly as though he thought the conversation was ridiculous.

Then, meeting my eyes, he came around the couch toward me. "We're in a *sexual* relationship, then. Are you happier with that definition?" He grabbed the glass from my hand and took a swallow. "It's just semantics, Sabrina." He held the wine toward me, but I ignored it.

"What about the rest? What about the things you say?" I

was happier with the word *relationship,* but this was so much more than just semantics.

"Like what do I say?"

I began pacing again. "Like when you tell me that you can't work because you can't stop thinking about me. Or when you go behind my back and tell Tom Burns to stick up for me at the job."

"That was about keeping things running smoothly at the office. He could have caused a whole hell of a lot of trouble that we didn't need."

I stopped pacing and studied him. "I can't tell if you're only lying to me or if you're also lying to yourself."

"Oh, please. I'm not lying to anyone. I've been very truthful and forthright about what this is with you." He took another swallow from the glass and set it down on the coffee table. Then he rested his hands on his hips and stared at me as though willing me to deny what he'd said.

Pulling my damp hair over to one shoulder, I tugged on it nervously. "You have. I won't disagree." He'd been forthright, if not always polite.

I just wasn't convinced that he was facing the truth himself, which was most of the problem.

I dropped my hands to my sides. "But see, after you say that there's nothing between us, you contradict it with actions that suggest exactly the opposite. You showed up uninvited at my apartment tonight when I didn't answer a few texts! That's not the behavior of someone who thinks this is just sex. It's confusing and not fair, and I don't know what I'm supposed to do or believe anymore."

We were face-to-face, both of us frustrated, and so far the conversation hadn't gotten us anywhere at all.

With his eyes never leaving mine, Donovan sat on the arm of my sofa and seemed to let everything I'd said so far sit or settle or stir. The charge between us was a thick wall, and there was room to stand between his legs. I wanted to go there and lean against him. Wanted to smell him and touch him and fall into him like I had so many times before.

But I stayed where I was, my feet planted in the firm realization that it wouldn't be enough anymore.

After what felt like forever, he asked the most important question of the night. "Sabrina, what is it you want?"

I closed my eyes briefly. It felt like déjà vu, but of course it wasn't. He'd actually asked me that question before and then the answer had been so easy. I hadn't known that the need and desire I had for him could take root inside me, could sprout into something bigger.

So I'd been honest when I'd told him then that I wanted him to touch me. And I was honest now. "I want what we already have."

His shoulders relaxed visibly, and he reached out, grabbed my hand, and pulled me unexpectedly in between his legs. "Then I don't understand what we're arguing about." He slipped a hand inside my robe and found my bare breast. Rubbing my nipple between his thumb and finger, he said, "Now is there anything else that you need to say?"

I gasped, arching with the pleasure. Another couple seconds of this and I was a goner. I had to fight to stay focused. "Yes. I want you to acknowledge that what we have is more than what you say it is."

His hand dropped immediately, and he mumbled something incomprehensible under his breath.

He stared at me for several long seconds. "Acknowledge

that it's *what* exactly? We have a *committed* sexual relationship. Is that what you want to hear?"

"It's a start." Hope began to bud in my chest. He was listening, at least. He was talking. He was trying.

"And what else?"

I swallowed. "The ability to let it grow into more."

"No," he said adamantly. He pushed me away so he could stand and pace toward the fireplace and back. "Absolutely not. It can't grow."

I could feel the pain of his words between each of my ribs. How could he say that? It had already grown so much.

I tightened the belt of my robe around my waist and pretended that my eyes weren't pricking. "I don't believe that."

He put a fist on his hip and stepped toward me. "You mean *love*? Is that what you're asking for?" He said the word *love* like it was a disease or a piece of garbage to be held as far away as possible.

"If that's where it goes," I said meekly.

He scoffed. "This is not going there."

I took a slow shuddering breath in, hoping he didn't see how much his words hurt. Years of buried fears and insecurities came easily to the surface. A lifetime of not being enough.

If that's what it was, he was going to have to tell me to my face.

"Why?" My throat sounded tight. "Just say it. Because I'm not good enough? Because I'm not the right girl? Because you could never love someone like me? Just say it. I need to hear it."

His hand fell to his side, his posture softening. "Because I can't love anyone, Sabrina." His voice was softer, too. "I can't fall in love."

"You can't?" I challenged with a trembling lip. "Or you won't?"

"Both." His intensity began to escalate again. "I can't. I won't. I don't. I live my life so that it's an impossibility. So that there is no chance that someone will get that close, and I'm not changing that for anyone. Not even for you." He pointed an aggressive finger in my direction. "*Especially* not for you."

It was another series of stings. This time, instead of just making me want to cry, it made me want to sting back. He might not be willing to say it was because I wasn't good enough, but I was willing to say that it was because *she* was too good. "Because of Amanda?"

He shook his head, vehemently. "We're not talking about Amanda."

I'd honored his wishes regarding his dead fiancée for the most part and asked very little about her.

But those were his rules. Under his rules, I was automatically set up to lose. If I wanted a chance to win, I was going to have to challenge them.

Refusing to back down, I took a step in his direction. "You loved her, and you lost her so you won't love anyone else now. Is that it?"

"I said we aren't talking about Amanda." He walked away, circling my sofa, seemingly going nowhere except to escape.

I followed right on his heels. "Are you just so afraid that if you love you might get hurt again? Is that what it is? It is, isn't it?"

"Stop, Sabrina," he warned. He wouldn't turn around. Wouldn't look at me.

I pressed on. "We lose people sometimes, Donovan. We can't stop living when we do. Just because she died—"

He spun around suddenly to face me. "She's dead *because* of me!"

His words echoed through my apartment, sounding ominous yet somehow hollow without context. How could he possibly say that Amanda was dead because of him?

I quickly went through what I knew about her death. She'd died in an accident the year before I'd met him. Another driver hadn't checked his blind spot when he'd moved to her lane, forcing her into oncoming traffic.

That's what Weston had told me. He hadn't said Donovan had been involved at all. Which meant Donovan was just trying to scare me. And succeeding. But he hadn't said anything I could truly grasp onto. "I don't know what you're trying to tell me."

"Amanda's car accident happened because of me, Sabrina," he said, struggling for his usual control and failing. "That's what I'm trying to tell you."

"That doesn't make any sense. Were you driving with her? Were you on the road too?"

"No. It's not like that." He ran his hand along the back of his neck. "When I fall in love, I become so consumed, so preoccupied with the person I'm in love with that I do things I shouldn't. I get involved. I intervene."

"I don't understand." But I wanted to. The way he talked about being consumed—I wanted to be the one he talked about like that.

"I was so obsessed with her that I hired a private detective to follow her. I needed to know where she was—always. She found out, and we fought. She told me she'd call off the wedding if I didn't stop. But I couldn't stop. For no other reason except that I was addicted to her. I was addicted to knowing everything about her."

His eyes were wide and alight, like he was rabid. Like he was alive.

But wasn't that what young love was? Feeling that passion? That preoccupation with another human?

"I told him to keep on her. Her death wasn't an accident. She swerved into the opposite lane of traffic because she was trying to lose her tail."

My hand flew up to my mouth. "Oh my god."

"Exactly."

"Does anyone else know about this?" I asked tentatively.

"The P.I. does."

I nodded, taking it all in. Tugging on my hair, I made my way to the couch and sat down, trying to process. So the cops had called the incident an accident. The way Donovan spoke, he sounded like he believed he was culpable of murder.

And was he? What he described was...well, it wasn't normal. It certainly wasn't healthy. But who was I to be the therapist? I liked to play rape with the guy who'd saved me from being raped myself.

But hiring a P.I. wasn't a crime. Whatever they'd fought over, whatever his jealousies had been or his insecurities were that had driven him to feel like he needed one—those belonged to a different Donovan. He'd been so young.

And even if there had been an investigator on the road that night tailing her, someone that Amanda had been trying to escape, wouldn't it still be an accident? It wasn't like the P.I. had *tried* to run her off the road. It wasn't like he'd meant for this to happen.

Donovan was taking too much of this on himself.

And the more I thought about it, the more I understood how he felt—I really did. Death did that, skewed things, built nests of guilt out of twigs of misdeeds and neglect. When my father died, and I'd been across the country at Harvard, I'd blamed myself for not being around. If I had been there to help carry the burden of raising Audrey earlier, maybe he wouldn't have felt so much pressure. Maybe he wouldn't have had the heart attack that had killed him.

I did blame myself. A lot of the time, at first. It didn't mean I'd actually killed him. And even though Donovan had been overzealous in his passion, he hadn't actually killed Amanda.

Maybe no one had ever told him that before.

I looked up to find Donovan watching me with hawk eyes, probably trying to read my mind. "I know you feel responsible, but this wasn't—"

He cut me off. "This wasn't my *fault*? I paid that driver to be there. I told him not to lose her. I told him to be aggressive."

My heart pinched. All these years he'd been holding this inside. Been carrying this weight himself.

I shifted so I was facing him with my entire body. "Donovan..." I said gently, tenderly, wishing I could take his pain away.

"And it won't happen again," he stated emphatically. "Do you see now? How I can't let it happen? How I won't be that person again?"

I couldn't stand it anymore. I jumped up and ran to him. "You can't do this to yourself." I threw myself against him, running my hand over his chest. "You can't keep holding yourself hostage over something that happened over ten years ago. It was an accident."

He refused to hold me in return. Refused to even touch me.

"It wasn't an accident. It was my fault. She's dead because I loved her."

I reached up to cup his cheek. "You can't spend the rest of your life punishing yourself for something that you didn't intend to happen. You can't spend the rest of your life alone."

He stepped back, pushing me off of him. "I'm not punishing myself for anything." His expression was hard, his tone harder. "I'm making sure that no one else gets hurt. I'm keeping yo—" He cut himself off. "I'm keeping *others* safe. Like I should have kept her safe."

We stared at each other, unmoving. We were at a strange stalemate. In simple terms, I wanted something that he refused to give. If it were really that simple, I could walk away. I could recognize the futility of fighting for him and walk the hell away.

But it wasn't that easy. It was thread upon thread of complicated, so many strands between us that wove us together. Even when he'd first taken my virginity, back when I'd been naïve and innocent, I knew that his broken fit my broken.

I ached for him now. I agonized for every day he'd let himself believe he deserved to be alone. I anguished thinking that he might walk out of my apartment without me changing his mind.

I couldn't let that happen. I refused to let him leave without a fight.

But he'd already pushed me away, already withdrawn. There was only one way I knew to reach him.

"Donovan," I said, untying my robe and letting it fall to the floor. "Touch me." I approached him and wrapped one hand around his neck and rubbed the other over his cock, which instantly came alive under my palm. "Touch me," I whispered again, as I pulled his mouth down to cover mine.

He hesitated only a few seconds before he tangled his fingers in my hair and yanked it until I moaned against his lips. Then he devoured my cries with his tongue, licking them up, savoring them.

Soon he began biting down my jaw and neck.

I pressed my mouth against his ear and told him what he needed to hear. "I know you've been carrying this weight around for so many years, and it's hard to put it down because you don't know how not to carry it anymore, but you have to put it down now. Put it down and let me make it better." *Let me love you.*

His kisses slowed as I spoke, and by the time I'd finished, he'd completely stilled.

Then, suddenly, he yanked my head back again, hard. Harder than he had ever before. With his other hand at my throat, his eyes pierced into me. "Who could forgive a man for something like that? Who would want a man like that?"

"I would!" I cried, meaning it with everything I had in me. "I do! I forgive you!"

He searched my face, and for half a moment I thought I had him. Thought that he got it. Thought that we had a chance.

But suddenly the green flecks disappeared from his eyes and they turned dark.

"Well, I can't," he said roughly. "I'm not risking anyone, Sabrina. This is the life I've chosen, and I'm not changing it for you."

Without another word, he pushed me away and walked out the door, leaving me naked and broken and alone.

THIRTY-ONE

Monday morning I woke up with puffy eyes and a pounding headache.

Coffee and a long shower helped with both, but even though I knew makeup would fix the rest, I called the office and said I'd be in a couple of hours late so I could miss the operations meeting scheduled for that morning. I knew I'd have to deal with seeing Donovan eventually, but it didn't have to be first thing on a Monday.

Though we hadn't said it outright, I'd gone to bed knowing that the way our conversation had ended probably meant the end of our short-lived relationship. Even if Donovan intended to continue our sex-only situation, there was no way I could. I'd already fallen so hard. It already hurt so much to let him go. I couldn't risk getting any more entangled if he wouldn't give me anything in return.

In the morning light, however, I found clarity. While he'd been resolute in his conviction to not let anyone in, it was possible that Donovan could change his mind. I was pretty sure we'd already grown into something more than he'd intended, and now that he'd heard me—now that someone had finally told him that he didn't need to keep punishing himself for Amanda's death—maybe he could start to get over it. Things change. People change. I was mature enough to know that. After all, I'd been determined not to let him in my panties when I'd first started at Reach, and look how long that lasted.

Just.

I couldn't wait for him to come around. I could hope, but I needed to be ready to move on.

Today was not that day.

When I did finally make it into work, I spent the day locked in my own office putting together summary reports for Summi-Tech. What better way to nurse a broken heart than to throw myself into work? Plus it was a surefire way to not bump into Donovan in the hall.

Late in the afternoon, though, I had to venture out to get Weston's approval on a project and it required a physical signature.

"Yeah, yeah," he said, seemingly distracted as he flipped through the pages of the proposal, and two different people walked into his office to set things on his desk before he'd finished perusing it.

"It looks good," he said finally, signing his name on the designated pages. "Can you email a copy of the projected expenses to Audra?"

"I already sent it to Barrett." Barrett held a similar position as me, only he oversaw Operations and Finances. He reported to Donovan. "Is this a procedural change?"

"Just for the time being. We're still trying to figure out how to reshuffle duties. I'm taking most of the load, as you can see." Another employee walked in with a stack of mail and set it on Weston's desk and then hurried back out. "But I'll be out for the wedding and the honeymoon soon so I can't take all of Donovan's tasks."

I was about to tease him for the millionth time about taking a real honeymoon for a fake wedding, but then I registered the rest of what he'd said.

My throat suddenly felt tight. "What do you mean? Why are you taking Donovan's tasks?"

He wrinkled his forehead. "Oh, that's right. You missed the meeting this morning. I announced everything then. Donovan left for France today."

I could feel the color drain from my face even though my heart was all of a sudden working overtime. "What? Why?"

"To take care of the merger with Dyson Media. With the wedding approaching, he decided he should be there to make sure everything happened smoothly. I mean, he just decided last night that he has to be the one to go, and that it has to be now. He must have sensed a change in the economic winds or something."

"Just decided last night," I repeated, my stomach knotting. He'd left because of me. It couldn't be a coincidence.

Then he wasn't going to give us a chance.

I swallowed past the lump in my throat. "How long will he be gone?"

Weston ran a hand through his hair. "Depends. He might just stay to handle the merger, which could be a month, two months? Or he might stay longer if he thinks that's necessary. He has to read the situation when he gets there."

He put his hands behind his head and leaned back, his eyes

suddenly narrowing. "I'm surprised he didn't tell you. I'm guessing that means things aren't going well between the two of you?"

I turned my head and stared out the transparent walls of his office so he wouldn't see my lip tremble. "There isn't anything between the two of us."

"Come on, Bri. Don't give me that bullshit. That's coming from Donovan, not you."

A day ago I'd have agreed. Even that morning I might have confessed more of the situation to Weston. But that was when I still had hope that something might change. That was before I knew for sure that Donovan had no interest at all in working anything out.

I met Weston's eyes and said sincerely, "It's the same answer coming from both of us."

Standing up, I gathered the reports I'd brought in and headed out of the office. Before I got out the door, though, my curiosity got the better of me. "Weston, when Amanda died, did Donovan ever say he blamed himself for her accident?"

He tilted his head, thinking. "No. Not that I remember. Did he say that to you?"

I shrugged. "I think it was just survivor's guilt." It was pointless to wonder about this further. "But..." As pointless as it was, I couldn't stop myself from asking. "Did he ever mention working with a P.I. back then?"

"He had a P.I. look into the accident?" Weston asked, misunderstanding me.

I didn't bother to correct him. I was already sharing too much of Donovan's secrets. "Something like that."

"Never told me anything about it."

I nodded. It was my cue to go.

Except I didn't go. I took another step toward Weston. "If I wanted to try to talk to the detective..." Maybe if I saw the report myself. Or if I talked to the guy that he had hired, I could better understand why Donovan blamed himself.

It was stupid.

Because even if I could find the detective—unlikely since I had no name to go on and it had been more than eleven years since he'd been hired—and even if he could shed light on the accident, what did I think I'd do after that? Fly to France and demand that Donovan give a real relationship a chance?

Laughing silently at myself, I dismissed the idea. "Never mind. This is an impossible task. I don't know why I'm asking."

I started to leave again, but Weston stopped me. "You know, if Donovan did ever hire a P.I., he'd have hard copy records. He's funny about the Internet with that kind of stuff. Hacking and privacy and all that. Which is why he uses more cabinet space than anyone in the building. It's annoying as fuck."

Ah, something else I didn't know about Donovan. There was so much I didn't know. Why I ever thought we'd be a good fit was beyond me.

I forced a smile anyway.

"Point is, I don't know if he'd have anything that far back, but you could check his files. Let me get you a code to his office."

It was useless—I'd already determined that.

But what if it wasn't? What if there *was* something to find?

I waffled for several seconds. "Are you sure? I wouldn't want to overstep."

Weston winked. "If he didn't want me to use it, he shouldn't have given me his code."

WESTON WAS RIGHT—DONOVAN did have more cabinets than anyone else in the building. But it didn't take me long to realize that most of them contained standard documents for the office, so I didn't spend much time perusing them.

It was the two-drawer cabinet behind his desk that interested me because it was locked.

"I don't suppose you have a key to the small file cabinet?" I asked Weston when he answered his phone.

"Sorry. I gave you everything I got."

"It was worth a try." I hung up the phone and swiveled back and forth in Donovan's chair. My eyes landed on a picture on his bookshelf—the same one that I'd seen the first time I'd talked to him in his bedroom back at Harvard. It was a picture of him and Amanda, an engagement photo, I remembered thinking.

This was the woman he'd been obsessed with. The woman he'd been addicted to. The woman he'd loved.

I wanted to see it closer. Wanted to see *her* closer.

The photo was on a high shelf, so I couldn't examine it well where it was. I reached up on my tippy toes to grab it and bring it out for a better look. As I pulled it down, I found the frame was loose, and something fell from the back.

A small, drawer-size key.

No. It was too coincidental.

I was already laughing at myself, but I had to try it. I walked over to the cabinet and slipped the key in the hole. I turned it and tried the top drawer.

It opened.

It was wrong to look through his files—I knew that before I

put the key in the lock. This wasn't like Weston giving me the code to the office. This was crossing the line. This was going through Donovan's personal things, and I'd pretty much convinced myself that I wasn't going to actually look at any of his files. I just wanted to see if the key fit and all.

But once the drawer was open, the label on the very first file caught my eye. And now I couldn't stop looking because it said in black, bold letters: LIND, SABRINA.

The folder was thick, and it definitely wasn't an employee file. Those, I knew for a fact, were kept in HR. There was no reason for Donovan to have a file on me. So why did he?

With my heart pounding, I pulled it out of the drawer and carried it to the desk. I sat down and opened it up.

Inside, there were pages and pages of information on me. All kinds of information. My transcripts from college were there. A copy of my rental lease for my first apartment in California. Another document appeared to be an invoice from the headhunter who had found me my job at NOW in Los Angeles. The bill, it appeared, had been paid for by Donovan Kincaid.

There was more. So much more. Candid photos of me over the years. Copies of articles I'd had published in various marketing magazines. Receipts for security installations in places I'd lived. An itemized list of all the things the movers had packed up from my house and moved to New York City on Reach's dime.

And then there were the papers regarding Theodore Sheridan, a slim stack of court documents that showed he was serving time for a sexual assault. The date showed he'd been prosecuted three years ago. There were invoices from the victim's attorney. These were also paid for by Donovan.

It took me almost half an hour to go through everything in the file. When I finished, I sat back in the chair, my skin tingling, my chest tight, my mind buzzing.

There was too much to think about. Too many emotions to sort through. I didn't know where to begin, and even if I figured that out, I sure as hell didn't know where to go from here.

But, as messed up and confused as I felt, there were two things I now understood without a doubt about Donovan Kincaid.

Number one—this was what he meant when he said he got obsessed with women he loved.

Number two—Donovan was in love with me.

EPILOGUE

"Can I get you anything, sir?"

The stewardess was attractive. Big tits and blonde hair. Barbie doll attractive. Not beautiful like Sabrina. I'd never used this stewardess before. Flying last minute like that, I took what I could get.

"I'll have a scotch, neat. Nothing else." I added the last part, hoping she'd get the hint that I didn't want to be bothered. It was a long flight to Paris, and she was the kind of woman who liked to think that meant it was okay to get cozy.

"Yes, sir." She gave me the kind of coy, innocent look that only the dirtiest women know how to give. That one was going to be trouble. I was already planning for it.

To be honest, there was a time when I might have taken her up on whatever I was sure she was going to offer, though I preferred to be the one doing the propositioning. But I didn't have an interest in it anymore. Not when I could still taste

Sabrina on my lips. Not when I could still feel the weight of her pleas tugging at my chest.

The stewardess brought me my drink, and I thanked her with enough of a growl to set her scampering. I took a hard swallow, letting the burn dull all other feeling. Then I pulled out my phone and loaded up the only picture I kept of Sabrina on my cell. I had hundreds of her, sure, but this one I'd taken myself, while she'd been sleeping in my bed. It was my favorite. She was naked, the sheet only pulled up to her waist, but what made it special was that she was curled up in my arms.

It was the only picture that had ever been taken of us together.

If I wanted to keep her safe, there would never be another one again.

"We're ready for takeoff, Mr. Kincaid, as soon as you are."

I looked up to see the pilot standing in front of me, waiting for my command.

I wasn't ready to leave her. I'd never be ready.

But I knew what I had to do.

After finishing off my scotch in a single swallow, I nodded to the pilot. "Let's go."

Donovan and Sabrina's story concludes in Dirty Filthy Rich Love.

Did you love this book? Enjoy reading it again on ebook or audio!

DIRTY FILTHY RICH LOVE

PROLOGUE

I brought the tumbler of scotch to my lips, taking another sip as the Frou Frou song playing from the Spotify app on my phone started up again. How many times could a song be listened to on repeat? If there was a limit, I was approaching mine.

I pressed my cheek against my bedroom window and watched the lonely street below. The glass was cold against my skin, a stark contrast to the liquor burning in my chest. Winter had set in just in time for the Thanksgiving holiday. The few people still out this late were well bundled in gloves and scarves, and hats pulled down over their ears.

I still didn't have enough winter wear. There'd been no need for warm gloves in L.A., and I'd only been in New York since September. My sister had already given me a hard time about it when she'd arrived earlier in the evening, and a shopping trip was on the agenda for the next day.

My wardrobe would soon be remedied. Audrey would

make sure of that. In one night, she'd already rearranged my living room furniture and put up the rest of the framed photographs and knickknacks I hadn't bothered to unpack.

If only she could fix the inside of me as easily as she addressed the outside.

No, I had to be the one to fix this mess.

I thought back to the conversation I'd had with Audrey before she'd slipped off to bed in my guest room.

"Will you press charges?" she'd asked.

"I don't want to press charges." I wanted explanations. I wanted theories confirmed. I didn't want more distance between us.

I didn't want any distance at all.

She'd smiled as though she got it, and because she was my sister, maybe she did, even without me explaining. "So you'll go to France, then. Make him tell you what's up."

"He doesn't deserve that either. He can run all he wants. I'm not chasing. I have more respect for myself than that."

"Good. I respect you too." She'd laughed then. "Probably not the best idea to chase someone who's obviously been stalking you for ten years anyway."

"Probably not." Though I wasn't really worried about him. He was dangerous, yes. Dangerous *to me*. But he wouldn't hurt me. Not like that. Not the kind of hurt that anyone else could see.

"You'll figure it out," she'd said in the end. "You always do."

I knew what I had to do already. Just...being bold enough to do it.

Another sip of scotch. Another full listen to the old song on repeat.

This time when the silent pause came at the end, I put

down my glass and reached over for the phone instead. I turned off the music, pulled up my contacts and only shivered slightly when I found his name.

Two weeks had passed. I didn't have to do this now.

But it might as well be now.

I hit the CALL button and waited.

It rang once. Twice. It was after midnight here. He'd just be waking up. Another ring. Was he alone? One more ring.

Then his voice.

His voicemail, actually. I hadn't exactly expected him to answer, and it was easier leaving a message.

Still, somehow it was disappointing. As though a small part of me had hoped he'd see my name and rush to hear my voice. Wouldn't I rush to answer if he'd been the one to call?

Maybe not.

Probably not.

The beep sounded and caught me off guard. But I was ready with what I wanted to say.

"Donovan. It's me. I know about the file you have on me. We should talk."

ONE

"There's nobody here," Audrey said as we stepped out of my office.

It was Monday evening and wrapping things up after a hectic afternoon had taken longer than planned. It was hard enough getting everything done in a short holiday week. On top of that, I'd lost my weekend to visiting with my sister—time I would have usually spent behind my desk.

It had been three days now since Audrey had arrived.

Three days since I'd left the message for Donovan.

Three days and no return call.

But I wasn't thinking about that. Or rather, I was trying as hard as possible not to think about that. Trying as hard as possible not to let on how much it hurt.

Work was a good distraction. Audrey was an even better distraction.

"When you got here it was almost five," I said, locking my

office door behind me. Thankfully, there was plenty to occupy her in the city while I worked. It would be a miracle if she got even a quarter of her agenda crossed off before she had to go back to school on Sunday. But even with the many other exciting items on her list, I'd convinced her to stop by my office so I could show her around.

More like so I could show off.

I glanced at the clock on the wall. "That was an hour ago. Most everyone's gone home now."

"Do you always work this late?" The question was accusatory.

"I usually work later." I didn't mention that part of the reason we'd stayed late tonight was because she'd had to tell me all about the bus tour she'd taken earlier in the day.

Crossing her arms over her chest, she glared in my direction. "Workaholic."

I rolled my eyes. "You're a workaholic too. Your work is just more artsy so you can more easily disguise it as a hobby. Come on." I threw my keys in my bag and hitched the strap on my shoulder. "Let me show you around."

She followed me to the main hallway. Out of habit, I glanced down the dark corridor leading to Donovan's office, feeling a pang in my chest before leading her in the opposite direction to the large open section of the executive floor. Usually, the floor-to-ceiling windows there would be a feature worth pointing out, but the sun had already set and the cleaning crew had turned on the lights so the glass just looked black.

Another light shone farther down the hall, and I steered us in that direction.

"Roxie," I exclaimed, when we came upon my boss's assistant gathering her things at her desk. "You're here late!"

"Just leaving. You caught me." Eyeing Audrey, she set her purse down and thrust her hand out, introducing herself before I had a chance. "I've heard wonderful stories about you. Sabrina is very proud of her sister."

"Thank you. Great to meet you," Audrey said, trying not to appear stunned by Roxie's brusque hospitality.

"You look alike," the Hungarian native said after studying us for a beat. "Light and dark versions."

Audrey and I laughed as we exchanged glances. She wasn't just a lighter version of me in coloring with her chestnut hair and almond eyes, but also in temperament. She was bubbly and romantic. I was serious and practical. She liked men who adored her and were into public displays of affection. I liked a man who enjoyed rape play and apparently had a serious problem with stalking.

It was something we joked about often.

"Night and day," I said.

"Chocolate and vanilla," Audrey agreed. "That's us."

"Is Weston in there?" I asked nodding to the office behind Roxie. The door was still open and the lights were on, but I didn't see him at his desk.

"No, but he be back any minute. You can wait inside for him." Roxie buttoned her coat and picked up her purse. "He in a good mood today. He won't mind."

We said our goodbyes and after Roxie went her way, I ushered Audrey into Weston's spacious corner office, switching off the light as we walked in.

The effect was immediate. "Holy bananas!" Audrey

exclaimed. "This is insane!" She ran to the closest wall of glass and gazed out at the city. "It's an endless sea of lights! I bet you can see everything in the daytime."

"Not everything. But a lot." I stood back, watching her with a smile. My reaction to the view had been quite similar. It had been exhilarating, not just because of how much I could see, but because I finally felt like I was on top of it all.

And then Donovan had walked in, putting my new world in a spin. Reminding me it had been his world first.

Whatever. It was my world now. He wasn't here, and I was. I wasn't going anywhere.

Audrey craned to look farther out the window. "If this isn't everything then you're too greedy. Hey! It's the empire! Why isn't this your office?"

"It will be soon enough," Weston's baritone sounded behind me. "With the work she's producing."

I rolled my eyes while he came to stand next to me. "Oh, hush."

He frowned as though I'd offended him. "I'm serious. You're the first name on a short list to replace me if I ever leave."

Weston was a sweet talker. All the smart women knew it. Still, I was warmed by the compliment, even though it wasn't one that mattered. "You'll never leave," I said dismissively. "I hope you don't mind we were in here. I was showing my sister the view. This is Audrey."

The lighter, younger version of me had already abandoned the windows and was prowling toward us, her hands behind her back. "Let me guess—you're Weston."

Weston stuck his hands in his pockets and lifted his chin proudly. "You've told her about me."

"We're close." I watched apprehensively as Audrey circled my boss, sizing him up. I knew full well she wasn't evaluating him as my superior, which would have been embarrassing enough. No, she wanted to figure out what it was about him that had lured me into his bed for an entire weekend earlier in the year.

Not that it wasn't obvious—blue eyes, blond hair, built like he was a personal trainer rather than a CEO. He was eye candy for sure. Add the charm and a smart head on top of that?

Yeah, my panties dropped.

"Nice," she said appraisingly. "Whoa. Real nice," she said when she got to his backside. "Good job, sis."

Weston's eyes widened as he interpreted her comments. "Ah, you've really told her about me." He turned his attention to my sister. "Maybe Sabrina didn't get a chance to tell you I'm involved with someone else now. I'm engaged."

"*Fake* engagement," Audrey corrected.

His head spun around to glare in my direction. "*Everything* about me. Wow."

"Audrey!" My face flushed. "She won't tell anyone. I promise." I shifted to scold her again. "That was supposed to be top secret."

Weston's engagement and impending marriage to Elizabeth Dyson was all an arrangement to get Elizabeth her trust fund money and to get Reach, Inc.—our company—access to an advertising firm in France she owned. Once married, Elizabeth would get her inheritance, sell the firm to the men, and the two would divorce.

At least that had been the plan.

That was supposedly why Donovan was in France—to

pave the way for an easy merger. Only Weston and I knew it was really just an excuse to get away from me.

Very few people knew about the fake marriage—only Elizabeth, the five guys who owned Reach, Inc., me, and now, my sister.

Weston chuckled. "It's fine. I mean, you're not a secret spy for the Dyson's, are you?"

Audrey lifted a brow. "No."

"Then we're cool. Besides, it's not a fake engagement anymore. Or, it's not a fake relationship anyway."

She raised both brows now and looked at me accusingly. "Now I didn't hear this."

"Weston and Elizabeth like each other for real now. There. Are you happy?" I didn't give her time to respond. "It didn't have to do with me so I didn't fill you in," I added, unapologetically. Also it wasn't really fun to talk about someone else being lucky in love when my own heart was hurting like it was.

She clapped her hands. "Of course I'm happy. I adore a good coupling! Tell us more, Weston."

"She left today to go to her grandmother's for Turkey Day," he said, directing this to me despite Audrey's eagerness. "I'm joining her Wednesday night, and we're supposed to do the whole pretend, pretend thing, but all I keep thinking is *I'm going to meet her grandmother*. This is the single most important person in her life. Which shouldn't matter because this is all temporary. But maybe it's not temporary. Maybe it's something more."

The last Weston had talked to me about his relationship with Elizabeth, they'd slept together. He hadn't said anything about *more*. "Then things are still going well?"

He sighed, running a hand through his hair. "Honestly, I don't know what things are. It's a mess. I want to wring her neck most of the time and she doesn't really seem to like me much either, but I kind of can't stand to be away from her for more than a day. Whatever that is, it's that."

"That's love," my sister said, her voice all swoony.

I groaned. "Audrey's a hopeless romantic. It's her only flaw."

But she made me think, too. Things between Donovan and I were a mess too. I wanted to wring his neck, and I was aching inside with him so far away. Was I so far in that I was in love with him?

Well, wasn't that going to be a bitch if it was the case? Because next time I saw him, I was planning on killing him.

"Weston, I can call my driver anytime you're ready to—" The man who'd walked in stopped when he saw us. "Oh, excuse me. I didn't realize you had company."

I stood up straighter, immediately on guard. I didn't know the man. His suit was expensive and he had brown wavy hair and a British accent. He appeared older than us by at least a dozen years, but was quite attractive and distinguished. What was odd was that a stranger was wandering the office halls after hours.

"I can go anytime," Weston said in reply. "But this is perfect. You haven't met Sabrina yet, have you?"

The man frowned. "Can't say that I have."

Weston shifted to me. "Sabrina, this is Dylan Locke. He's in the States this week to visit his son."

That explained things. Dylan Locke ran Reach's London office. He was one of the founders of the company. There were five of them in total—Nate Sinclair, Weston, Donovan, Dylan, and Cade Warren, who ran the Tokyo office.

"It's a real pleasure to meet you," I said, shaking his hand. "I'm the director of marketing strategy here."

"Ah, you took Robbie Wise's place when he came over to our office in London," Dylan said. "Robbie's fine at his job but he isn't as lovely as you. And he smells." He turned to Weston. "Is it entirely sexist if I say I think you got the better end of the deal?"

"Donovan got the better end of the deal actually." His subtext suggested he'd mentioned me to Dylan before. That this was his way of saying, *This is her. The one that Donovan was involved with.*

Which was fine. But I didn't want to talk about Donovan right now. "Weston, please..."

"He called earlier," he said soberly. Simply. As though he knew the words would knock the wind out of me, and still he'd thought the best way to present them was plainly and without a fuss.

"He called you?" I hoped no one noticed the hitch in my voice.

"He told me not to say anything."

"To anyone? Or to *me*?" Fuck, I shouldn't have asked. I didn't want to know. I *already* knew. If he'd wanted to talk to me he would have called *me*.

Weston lowered his head, confirming my suspicions. "I'm sorry."

It was sweet that he cared how I felt. And nice, I supposed, that he'd bothered to tell me about it at all. Though Weston and I had formed a friendship over the last several weeks, he was Donovan's friend before mine. He didn't owe me any loyalty.

I couldn't bring myself to thank him at that moment.

"I don't care," I said, when he took a step forward to comfort me. "He can do what he wants. I don't care anymore." Lies. But maybe if I kept saying it, someone would start believing it. Maybe even me.

And now things had gotten awkward.

"Hi! I'm Audrey. Sabrina's sister."

I wanted to shoot her a thank you glance for breaking the weird mood, but her attention was completely on Dylan. The way she flipped her hair and threw her shoulders back told me she wanted his attention on her too.

"I see the resemblance." Fortunately for Dylan, he kept his gaze on her eyes, the place any decent man in his forties should keep them when he meets a girl half his age.

If he'd looked anywhere else, we may have had to have some words, owner of my company or not.

"Do you work here as well?" he asked.

"Nope. Just getting the tour. It's my first time in the city. It's exciting."

Dylan seemed to be taken by surprise by her enthusiasm, though not exactly put off. "Yes. I'm sure it is exciting the first time."

"Been too long since your first time, Locke? Have you forgotten what it's like to get your cherry popped?" Weston teased.

"Apparently I've forgotten what it's like to spend an evening with you and your innuendos." The look he gave his partner made me think he'd appreciate those innuendos more if he weren't in mixed company. Spending time with Weston would be a lot more fun for the older man if he wasn't worrying about offending his young female employee and her even younger sister.

Which was why I didn't expect it when he next said, "We were just going to dinner. We'd love it if the two of you would join us."

TWO

"Art conversation?" Weston asked, an hour later, his fork paused mid-air.

Of course we'd accepted the invitation to dinner. Audrey seemed so smitten with Dylan's British dialect that she likely would have killed me if I'd suggested we do anything else. And I wouldn't have anyway. When your employers invite you somewhere, you try to go.

Though if I'd known the destination planned was Gaston's, I might have considered my options, for no other reason than I didn't want to be at a restaurant that Donovan owned.

Perhaps that was the reason I'd gotten so tipsy. I didn't know why the others had.

"Art *conservation*," Audrey repeated, over-enunciating in that way that told me she was also not quite sober. She was only a little more than a semester away from completing her master's at the University of Delaware in their art conservation program, and Dylan had just asked about her degree.

Weston swallowed his bite of foie de veau and nodded. "That makes a lot more sense. Is that like the people who work in museums to preserve the paintings?"

"That's some of it. It's a little chemistry, a little archeology, a lot of art, a whole lot of art history. Not nearly as exciting as your jobs." She was way too modest, in my opinion.

"I'm not sure what Weston does day-to-day, but it sounds a hell of a lot more exciting than my job," Dylan said.

While Weston had gotten louder as the wine had poured, Dylan's lips had gotten looser. It was a great way to learn about the new man, actually. Though I'd only gleaned surface details —born in Southampton, lived in the US for a number of years, back to London, secretly loved Metallica, played electric bass in a local pub band—he was turning out to be quite fascinating.

"That's because you handle finance. There is nothing creative about finance," said Weston, obviously quite smug about the fact that he handled marketing.

"I think your father finds finance to be quite creative," Dylan retorted.

"Rumors. No one can prove anything." Weston took a swallow of wine. "But also why I don't work for him."

Donovan and Weston's fathers dominated the financial industry. I'd never gotten a straight story on why the guys had decided to go into advertising instead of following them in the family business.

This breadcrumb was one I ate up eagerly.

"Corruption at King-Kincaid?" I scooted my chair a little closer to him. "Am I allowed to ask?"

Laughing, he shooed me away with a soft pat of the back of his hand. "No. You are not allowed to ask."

I continued to stare at him. Apparently drinking made me shameless.

He let out a sigh. "It's nothing that hasn't already been suspected by someone at one point or another. Your guess is as good as mine. It was definitely one of the reasons that D and I wanted to do our own thing, though. So we can genuinely say we don't know."

While I doubted that Donovan ever preferred being in the dark, Weston probably truly did. "Well, that was smart, I suppose. And boring. Who's going to give me gossip now?"

I turned to my other employer. "What about you, Dylan? How did you end up part of Reach with these bozos?"

He smiled and wiped his mouth with his napkin. "I'd had previous experience managing operations at another advertising firm. Donovan wisely saw the need for another rational man to balance out the unruly ones."

"*Another* rational man? Who are you counting as the first?" I regretted the question immediately because I knew the answer was Donovan. He was the man who formed Reach. The one who brought everyone together. The impetus behind all of it.

So I didn't bother waiting for an answer. He was the one I really wanted to know about anyway whether I wanted to admit it or not. Might as well just go there. "How did you know Donovan? I don't really picture you running around in the same circles."

"Ha. No. We don't exactly," Dylan admitted. "We met years ago. I used to be married to the mother of his fiancé."

My skin went cold despite the alcohol warm in my blood. I hadn't been expecting that. "Amanda?"

"You know about her."

"Yeah. Donovan's told me." The bare bones anyway—that he had loved her, that he'd been obsessed with her, that he blamed himself for her death. He'd told me that she'd been trying to outrun the private investigator that he'd hired when she got in the accident that killed her. I'd been searching for more information on *her* when I'd found his file on *me*.

"He did?" Dylan was openly surprised. "That's good he's talking about her. He tends to not mention her at all. He took her death very hard. As we all did. Sweet girl. So young."

I glanced at Weston, ready to let him jump in. But he seemed to be happy to let me be Donovan's spokesperson.

"I think he still takes it pretty hard," I said. Besides blaming himself, Donovan had told me he couldn't love anyone after her. Because of whatever it was he'd done to her. Which, if I had to guess without any real proof, looked a lot like what he'd done to me.

"Not surprising," Dylan said, disappointment in his tone. "Tortured son of a bitch. That relationship was doomed from the start."

"Why do you say that?" I tried not to sound too curious, not the easiest of tasks considering how desperate I was to know everything. Anything.

"He was too in love with her." He set his fork down and began pouring the last of the bottle of wine around the table.

Audrey frowned. "*Too* in love?" She said each word deliberately. "How can someone be *too* in love?"

"He obsessed over her." Dylan filled my glass, and I took a swallow. Okay, a gulp. "Knew everything about her. Cared everything about her. He hung the moon for her."

It was ten years ago and the woman was dead and still I ached with jealousy.

I shouldn't ask any more.

I couldn't stop myself. "Like, what did he do?"

God, I was so pathetic.

"Dylan," Weston leaned over to his partner. "She's. You know. With him." As if I wasn't sitting right there. As if I couldn't hear him talking.

"I'm not with him," I snapped a little too defensively. "He's in France. And I'm here. By no definition am I *with* Donovan." I pressed Dylan. "What did his too much love look like? Was it obvious?" *Did it look like what he does to me?*

Or, what he *did* to me. I had no reason to believe he was still having me followed and watched. No reason to believe he still cared about me at all.

Dylan seemed to consider Weston, but answered me anyway. "Not flagrantly, no. I'm sure most people didn't notice. It was subtle. The way he was always in control. Always a step ahead where she was concerned. I remember once she'd wanted this specific Tiffany bracelet. It was a piece the company didn't make anymore but she'd seen one up for a charity auction and had convinced her mother to try to bid for it. She failed. Her mother didn't try very hard, to be honest, and someone else bought it. Donovan found out and tracked down the person who'd bought it or something. A week later, Amanda had the bracelet."

Audrey sighed next to me. "That's actually quite romantic."

I concentrated on Dylan's eyes so that I didn't shoot daggers with mine at my sister for her obvious betrayal.

"Another time," he continued, almost as eager to share as I was to learn, "she'd gotten in an argument with her advisor at Harvard. A class she'd taken didn't count like she'd thought it would. It wasn't too long before her advisor was dismissed from the school on allegations of credit fraud."

Weston scoffed. "Are you saying that was Donovan too? Because I heard about that and there was nothing tying him to it."

Dylan shrugged. "King-Kincaid Financial couldn't alter credit reports? All I know is that Donovan didn't seem a bit surprised when it happened and Amanda's next advisor had no problem accepting her course credits. He also drove a brand new Jaguar. What do you want to bet his loan had been approved through a King-Kincaid bank?"

Weston shook his head, unconvinced.

But he hadn't seen the file on me. I had, and there were many things Donovan had done for me that had been just as extreme. And I wasn't his fiancée.

"And you think those were signs that he loved her?" I asked Dylan, desperate for those acts to mean something.

"Those are definitely signs that he loved her," Audrey said dreamily. She looked pointedly at me. "Anyone who did those things for someone else is obviously in love."

I ignored her. I already knew her opinion on the matter. Already knew what she hoped would happen between Donovan and I.

"Loved her too much," Dylan repeated. "If she'd lived, it wouldn't have worked out."

"You don't think so?" Weston asked. He'd always said that Amanda and Donovan had been the real deal.

"Because he'd eventually smother her?" I asked, making my own guesses.

"Because it's not real," Dylan said matter-of-factly.

"What isn't?" I asked, confused.

"The whole thing. Love. Marriage. It's an outdated arrangement. Amanda seemed to know what was what and had reasonable expectations. But Donovan bought into the pitch. He bought into the *feelings*."

"You don't believe love is real." Audrey's statement was a mix of shock and disbelief.

Weston waved his hand in the air. "Don't listen to him, Audrey. He's a bitter divorced old man."

"Bitter, yes. Divorced, thank God. Old..." Dylan scanned the faces of his companions. "Well, maybe that's true in the present company. It doesn't mean I'm wrong. In fact, by default, I'm the wisest one here, experience points and all, and I'm telling you: love's not real. It's a card trick. It's a marketing ploy. It's a term we use to pretty up a rather dull and worn out social system built entirely on the tradition of coupling off. Weston's fake relationship is probably the smartest arrangement I've seen in a long time. That's about as true as it gets, kid. Enjoy it for what it is and stop trying to figure out the mess. There's nothing to figure out. It's messy because it's fiction. And for some insane reason, modern western civilization has decided that the messier the story, the better the tale."

Audrey finished off her wine and set down her glass. "That was really sad."

Sad but probably wise, I thought. I was already twenty-seven years old and had never come close to finding a relationship that I would have called the real deal. Donovan had been the closest I'd come, and that was only because he'd been the first man to force me to be honest sexually. We hadn't had a chance to get any further than that. Maybe there wasn't any further to go.

"Wow Dylan," Weston said, setting down his napkin.

"That was a major downer. You're not getting enough pussy, man. Should we talk about your Tinder options across the pond?"

Dylan glared at Weston. "Perhaps this isn't the most polite conversation for our dinner guests."

Weston glared right on back. "And trampling all over America's number one reason for living is?"

"You know what?" I turned to Weston. "You're whipped." He wouldn't have defended romantic relationships a month before. Elizabeth Dyson had gotten under his skin.

He shook his head. "You're on his side. Of course."

I wanted to disagree, for Audrey's sake. Say I still believed in the happily ever after. Our parents were dead. I was her example of what adulthood should be. I didn't want her to grow up to be a cynic.

But after everything tonight and the last few weeks, I didn't know if I believed in happily ever after anymore.

And she was already grown up.

"I'm not on anyone's side," I said. "I'm on my own side."

Dylan raised his wine glass toward me in a toast. "Thatta girl."

We'd finished our meal by then. Weston charged the bill to a company account, then stood and helped me with my chair.

"Go on ahead," I said to the men. "I need to use the restroom before we leave. Audrey?"

"I'm good." More like she didn't want to miss a single second with Dylan. I wanted to attribute her fun and flirty nature to her age, but I had never been that easy with people. It made me jealous sometimes.

But also, good for her.

"We'll meet you by the elevators?" Weston asked. "We'll get your coat."

"Be right there."

On my way back from the restrooms, I took a different pathway through the restaurant than I had on the way there. I hadn't planned it. I'd just gotten my directions mixed up and suddenly I was walking past the table that Donovan always used when he ate at the restaurant. It was a total accident.

At least, I told myself it was an accident.

It was definitely an accident that I happened to catch the eye of the woman dining there as I passed by.

"Sun?" I'd only met her once, but her face was unforgettable. She was a model who Donovan used to sleep with. "What a surprise."

She smiled in greeting, her eyes darting from me to the companion across from her.

I turned to follow her gaze and found myself face-to-face with Donovan Kincaid.

THREE

The ground beneath me suddenly felt unsteady, as though the floor had been yanked away. My mouth gaped, but nothing came out. No words. No sounds.

He was here.

With fucking Sun, the most gorgeous woman on the planet.

All I could do was stare.

"This isn't what it looks like," Donovan said quickly. The long blink of his eyes afterward and the quiet curse under his breath told me he understood how trite and canned he sounded.

At least he was ruffled too.

It made it possible for me to speak. "It doesn't matter what it looks like. It doesn't matter what it actually is. I don't even care." And then, just to prove how catty I was, I said, "*Weston*'s waiting for me. So if you'll excuse me. Nice to see you again, Sun."

I left before he could say anything else. Before he could

touch me. Before he could look at me another second with those fucking green-brown eyes that saw everything inside me. Those eyes made me confess secrets I never wanted to share. Those eyes made me *be* and feel and try, and how the fuck could he see all that he'd seen and still be able to look away so goddamn easily?

"Sabrina!"

My legs almost gave out when he called after me. Even now, even after this, there was a part of me that wanted to go to him. Just to talk. To show him that running wasn't the way to handle conflict.

But I didn't look back.

Because I didn't want to do this here.

And I'd turned around too many times for him before.

I realized a second later that walking away was going to be a short-lived victory. As soon as I got to the front of the restaurant, I'd have to wait for the elevator. He'd catch me there.

He'd also catch Weston and Dylan, though. Maybe they could distract him. Or keep me from causing a scene.

But somehow I got lucky.

The elevator opened as I approached. Weston caught my eye, and I nodded for him to go ahead and hold it. Then I slipped in and turned around in time to see Donovan's face just as the doors were closing.

"Was that...?" Weston asked when the car started to move.

"Yep." I was shaking so bad, even that one word sounded tremulous.

"That was Donovan?" Apparently Dylan had seen him too. "I thought I was seeing things."

"Donovan was here? *Your* Donovan?"

I glared at Audrey. "He's not *my* Donovan." Especially not now. "He was with someone else."

"I'm sorry," she said quietly, helping me on with my coat. "That must have been a shock."

"I didn't even know he was in the States." I looked down at my trembling hands. I hugged myself to still them.

"Uh," Weston said, already sounding guilty. "I probably should have told you..."

My head snapped up. "You knew he was here?"

"When he called earlier he said he'd just landed. I told him your sister was visiting. I didn't know he was going to be at Gaston's. Hell, at that point, I didn't even know we were going to be at Gaston's."

I stared at him incredulously. "Why didn't you say he was here?"

"He told me not to. Remember?" A simple reminder that he'd betrayed Donovan to tell me about the phone call at all.

The sting of that snub returned on top of the newer pain. "Right. Probably because he didn't want me to know he was in town seeing his lover, Sun." My voice cracked. "That was sure polite of him."

He shook his head. "Sun is *not* his lover."

Yeah well, Weston also didn't want to believe his father was corrupt or that Donovan had framed a college advisor.

I wasn't going to argue about it. "Whatever she is, he's with her tonight." *And not me.*

Well, I didn't want to see him either.

The elevator stopped. The doors opened, and I hustled out, half expecting to see that Donovan had run down the stairs to meet us. But the lobby was empty.

"I've texted my driver," Dylan said. "We can try to make a speedy getaway, if that helps."

"That does. Thank you."

Outside, I pulled my coat tighter around me and paced the sidewalk, keeping one eye out for Dylan's limo and the other eye on the doors to the building in case Donovan showed up. The cold temperature sobered me up and left me with a throbbing headache.

"Here's the car," Dylan said as the limo drove toward us a few short minutes later.

This was it. We'd done it. Escaped. He hadn't even come after me. If I was disappointed about that, I wasn't admitting it to anyone.

But no sooner had the car parked then I heard my name again.

"Sabrina, wait!"

All of us turned together to see Donovan rushing toward us from the building. Rushing toward *me*.

"Oh, Christ," I mumbled. Though inside I felt a little relieved.

And also a whole lot pissed off. And hurt. So hurt.

Dylan spoke first, greeting the man who had no business looking as outrageously handsome as he did. "Donovan!"

It took Donovan a second to pull his eyes from me to the man at my side. "Dylan?" He seemed almost unable to process his friend's presence. "I didn't realize you were in town."

"I'm visiting Aaron. He has the holiday weekend. I'll be in the office tomorrow, though." He snuck a glance at me, and I realized this banal small talk was meant to diffuse the situation.

Thank you, I mouthed silently.

Not that Donovan was deterred for long. "We can catch up

tomorrow, then. If you don't mind, though, I need to just borrow Sabrina for the rest of the evening. Don't worry. I'll drive her home."

Before I knew what was happening, he had his hand on my back and was pivoting me away from everyone else.

"Hold on," Audrey ordered. "She's not going anywhere with you unless she says that's what she wants."

Donovan dropped his hand and turned to her. "You're protective of your sister. That's very sweet. We haven't met, Audrey, but I work with everyone here."

She lifted her chin and took a step forward. "I know who you are too, Donovan. Don't try to bulldoze me."

I bit back a proud giggle.

Donovan took a beat, and I could tell he was trying to remain calm. "Then if you know who I am, you likely also understand that I need to talk to her."

"I don't want to talk to you," I barked. Which wasn't true. I wanted to talk to him so bad I'd called him all the way in France.

"Then you'll listen." He shifted his focus back to my sister. "I promise to have her back to you in one piece."

I didn't understand why he was so insistent to talk now. Why did he care? He was already dating other women. Defending himself was needless. It wasn't like we had a relationship to save.

But we would need to talk at some point, and before Audrey agreed it was a good idea, she'd have to approve of Donovan's motives.

"You need to talk to her as her *boss*?" she asked, obviously poking at his choice to introduce himself as one of my coworkers.

"I need to talk to her as her boyfriend," Donovan corrected.

"Whoa," Weston said, echoing my thoughts. Audrey grinned, the traitor.

"You are *not* my boyfriend," I growled, though deep down inside of me I already knew I was going to replay those words over and over again later on. Analyze them. Dissect them. Cut them up and see if there was any possible meaning to them besides as a tactic to grab my attention.

Donovan let out an impatient huff of air. "Then I need to talk to you as the guy you've been fucking."

Dylan cringed visibly.

I fumed. "Not anymore. You made sure that was over when—"

"Sabrina," Donovan interrupted, his low authoritative tone impossible to ignore. "Give Audrey the keys to your apartment and tell her you'll meet her at home in an hour. I'm sure that you trust both Weston and Dylan to make sure she gets there safely."

God, I hated everything about him right then. The way he'd inserted himself into my evening plans. The way he made my skin prickle and buzz. The way he made me think I might actually be someone who mattered to him.

It was too cold to continue standing on the curb arguing, and it wasn't fair to keep everyone. I was giving in.

I met Audrey's eyes. I didn't have to say anything for her to know what I was asking.

"I'm fine," she said confidently. "You should go."

"I'll be less than an hour," I said, handing her my apartment key. I wasn't sure I could keep that promise, but I made it anyway.

She shook her head, nonverbally telling me not to worry.

"You have the History channel. That's enough entertainment to last me quite a while."

I waited until the three of them were in the back of the limo, and the door was shut. Then I took a deep breath, turned away from the curb, and stepped toward Donovan.

Donovan. Fucking Donovan in his tailored suit and five o'clock shadow.

Walking toward him was like deciding to walk through fire when I was already covered with first-degree burns. It hurt like I couldn't describe.

But I was a girl who lived in darkness. His fire sure looked bright.

He took my arm. It was a polite gesture, and the pressure of his hand felt comforting through my coat, but I pulled away immediately.

"Don't touch me. We can talk, but you don't get to touch me."

I know I didn't imagine the flicker of pain I saw in his eyes even if he refused to acknowledge it.

"We'll just talk then." He gestured to his Jag, which had pulled up along the sidewalk ahead while we'd argued. "After you."

FOUR

Halfway to Donovan's car, I realized we were leaving without Sun.

Not that I minded. But I sure as hell was going to make a point to mention it.

"You just abandoned your date?" I didn't want to seem like I cared about his response, but I glanced over at him from the corner of my eye.

His mouth tightened. "It was a business dinner. Not a date. We came separately. She'll get her own ride home."

That did make me fairly gleeful. Whatever happened tonight, at least I wouldn't have to wonder if Sun would be dropping her panties for Donovan in the backseat like she had the last time he'd driven her home from one of their dates.

I knew because he'd later told me about it in detail. It was months ago, and I still writhed with jealousy when I thought about it.

At the car, Donovan reached down to open the back door, and then held it so I could get in.

I paused at the curb and met his eyes, the door a barrier between us. "So no going down on Sun in the car tonight then. What a pity."

He didn't flinch. "You're the one I'm putting in a car, Sabrina. If that's how you want to spend the drive, I'm more than happy to oblige."

A shiver ran down my spine that I hoped he didn't see.

"I'm getting in the car to talk." But maybe I didn't mean that.

Did I? How strong could I be in Donovan's presence? Could I be as strong as I needed to be?

"Get in the car then."

I guessed we'd find out.

I slid across the backseat until I got to the other side and buckled myself in. It was a sad excuse for a barricade, but I pretended it would keep me safe. As long as I stayed on my side, and he stayed on his side, everything would be fine.

But then he got in next to me, his long legs taking so much more space, his very being taking up even more space. He *filled* the car. There was no escaping him. He was everywhere—beside me, in my skin, on my tongue. I couldn't breathe without inhaling him.

I needed to do or say something to remind myself what the situation was.

"Just because I'm leaving with you doesn't change the fact that you came with her," I said, bitterly as the car pulled away from the curb.

He studied me a moment. "I came here for you."

"Because you just happened to know I'd be at Gaston's tonight? That makes perfect sense. Bring along your girlfriend. That will show Sabrina what's what."

"I came *to the States* for you."

My heart tripped.

It had to be bullshit. "And you proved it by going out with Sun the minute you got here. I completely believe you."

"I didn't go out with her romantically," he said tersely. "I called Weston when I landed. He said your sister was in town. I didn't want to interrupt your evening. I planned to see you tomorrow. Meanwhile, I needed to negotiate some terms with Sun. We've hired her to be the face of the campaign for the merger in Europe, and she's playing hardball with some additional requests."

"So you thought you could wine, dine, sixty—"

He cut me off sharply. "It was dinner, and I'm in the goddamn car with *you*. I came back *for you*."

I looked over at him. The car was dark, but there was enough light from the street to see his face. His crushingly handsome face. He seemed tired. Jet-lagged, probably. His scruff was maybe older than a day. His jaw was also tight, like it got when he was frustrated. I wanted to reach out and run my hand along the muscle. Wanted to feel the warmth of his skin burn my fingers.

I didn't really have any reason not to believe him.

He'd called her first, but his reason made sense. If he'd really wanted to be with Sun instead of me, wouldn't he be with her now? If he said he'd come back to the States for me...

I'd been so wrapped up with Sun I'd forgotten about the rest. This was the first time we'd been together without the veil.

I knew about the file. And he knew that I knew. There were so many bigger things than Sun between us, and if he'd come back for me, was it to...explain? To try to make up a lie? To convince me not to press charges for invasion of privacy?

"Why?" I asked outright. "Why did you come back for me?"

"Don't play dumb, Sabrina. *You* called *me*."

"I called you, but there could be a dozen different ways to interpret your response when you show up like this. You could have just called me back."

"I thought this discussion deserved a face to face, don't you?" His tone was controlled and even and a little bit threatening, and I wondered for a moment if I should be scared of him.

But I was always a little scared of him. Didn't I like that about him?

I crossed my legs, trying to ignore the pulse between my legs. "Face to face so you could seduce me into believing whatever you wanted me to believe?" If that was his plan, he needed to come up with a new one. I had my seatbelt on and everything.

"I thought it would be easier to talk honestly."

Something in my chest pushed out, like it was reaching. Like there was a part of me that was still holding out hope that we could put everything out on the table, and there'd be a way in there that we could be together.

But I knew better.

A of all, given the lengths he'd gone to, putting together my file over the years, I couldn't be entirely sure he wasn't a psychopath.

B of all, I'd already tried the honest approach and it had failed.

Besides, I knew the truth. I didn't need him to admit it, and I didn't believe for one minute that he would. But if he wanted to play the honesty game, then fuck it, I'd play his game.

I'd tell him his truth before he had a chance to tell me any other story.

I twisted in my seat so I could stare him dead in the face. "You want honesty? How about this for honesty—I know what it means. That you have all that stuff on me. I already know what it means, so don't bother trying to come up with some story to excuse it."

He tilted his head in my direction, humoring me. "Really. What does it mean?"

I stared him right in the eye. "You love me."

"I do."

He'd spoken them no louder than anything else he'd said, and yet those two words echoed through the car like he'd shouted them into a canyon.

"Oh," I said. My chest felt heavy. And hot. I was hot. "Oh," I said again.

I looked down, suddenly feeling dizzy and shaky and a little like I was going to throw up.

"Can you handle that?"

I looked back up at him, jolting when I met his eyes again. "I don't know." *Fuck.* I hated that he could see how vulnerable he made me. "I mean. You don't even know me."

He raised a brow. "Are you sure?"

"A file of papers about me isn't knowing me."

"I realize that." He leaned closer, close enough that I could smell the faint scent of his aftershave. "But I knew you then and I know you now. And I know."

My entire body vibrated in agreement, as though the cells within me were able to admit something that my brain refused to acknowledge.

Donovan Kincaid loved me.

I'd believed it, deep down, I'd thought it was the only thing that made sense. He'd loved Amanda and he'd done the same things with her. The pieces added up. It was a rational conclusion.

But emotionally I hadn't been so sure.

I dropped my gaze. My head was rushing back through everything, putting this new frame on every experience we'd shared together, seeing it through the lens of *he loves me*, trying to feel if it made sense.

Two weeks ago all I'd wanted was a chance that he might feel *more* one day.

He'd hurt me. Pushed me away. Pissed me off.

"If you're so in love with me, why did you insist that a relationship between us was impossible?"

He pressed his lips together. "You've discovered that I've been stalking you and meddling in your personal life for the last ten years, and you're concerned about why I didn't want to have a relationship?"

When he put it that way, it did sound kind of ridiculous.

I chuckled. I was losing it. *Yeah, he's a psychopath, but it's okay because he loves me.* I wanted him to tell me more about how he felt about me, but he was right. I needed to get my priorities straight.

I looked away for a moment to get my bearings. "I'm concerned about all that too." There'd been so many things I'd wanted to say about that when I'd called him. "I'm really bothered by it. I'm mad. I'm confused. I'm freaked out. I feel...violated."

"Of course you do. You should feel all those things." He wasn't patronizing, but not apologetic either.

"You're damn right I should feel those things." I was irked at his lack of remorse. "I think I hate you for it."

"Do you?" he challenged.

I opened my mouth to answer when he added, "Remember it's no fun if you're not honest."

"I hate you for it," I repeated, softer this time. I closed my eyes, scared of the next part, the words I hadn't said aloud to anyone, not even Audrey. "But I'm also fascinated. That you're fascinated with *me*. That does things to me. It makes me feel safe. And wanted. And looked after. It turns me on." I opened my eyes and looked at him. "I don't mean sexually." But I did mean sexually too. "Does that mean I'm crazy?"

He laughed softly. "Probably."

He stretched his legs out, more relaxed than he had been when we'd first gotten in the car. He scrubbed his hand over his face and let out a sigh. "I forget how much I can trust you. I should have done that."

There it was. Remorse. He felt remorse.

"Before running away to France?" I clarified.

"I didn't...run away. Exactly." He smiled ever so slightly, and my pulse beat double-time.

"You did run away. Because you didn't want me to find out about that file?" I was still putting pieces together, slipping them in where they seemed to fit best.

"When Amanda found out about *her* file, she was the one running away."

"So you thought you'd be the one to run away first this time?"

"I don't know, Sabrina," he said with a frustrated huff. "Yes." After he'd thought about it a second. "Okay, yes." He looked somewhere in the distance. "I don't trust how I would handle losing you. It's better if the ties are cut on my terms. It's safer for both of us. For you, especially."

"But you're here..."

His eyes returned to mine. "Because you called."

"Which means you're willing to consider the possibility of *not* losing me."

He searched my face. "Is that a possibility? *Not* losing you? Even knowing what you know now?"

Fuck, we weren't ever actually together and here we were talking in such enormity. Donovan had done that. Had put all this weight on our entire relationship by having been there for parts of my life I hadn't realized he'd ever been part of.

So even though I wanted to crawl into his lap or kneel at his feet, even though I ached to touch him, I couldn't. Not yet.

"I need to process this," I said, not allowing myself to sound regretful.

"Whatever you need. Just tell me." His eyes darted to my lips, and I wondered if he'd kiss me.

Or I wished he'd kiss me.

But kisses weren't what I needed. "I need answers. There's so much I still don't understand."

"I'll tell you anything you want to know."

I studied his eyes. "I think you actually mean that."

"If you're going to test me, Sabrina, just test me." He sounded almost annoyed, and I had to bite back a laugh. He'd tested me so many times, but turn the tables on him, and he couldn't take the heat.

"Not now. Now I need to go home." I glanced out the window. We'd been driving around Midtown aimlessly while we'd talked, but we were only a few blocks away from my apartment. "You should drop me off."

Donovan waited a beat as though he wished I'd asked for something else. But then he leaned forward. "Next time around, John."

"I won't be able to get out to open her door here with the snow piles," the driver warned.

"That's fine," I said, before Donovan could say otherwise.

We were quiet for the next few minutes, but both of us were right there, present, aware of each other's every move. Every breath. I wondered what he was thinking. But I couldn't ask because I didn't have room for anymore on top of all that I was thinking.

And then we were almost at my apartment, and I already missed him.

"We can talk after Audrey's gone," I told him, feeling terrible that I wished it wasn't a week away.

"When does she leave?" Was I imagining how eager he sounded?

"Sunday morning at ten-thirty."

"I'll be at your place at ten-thirty-one."

I chuckled. It felt good to laugh. No, it felt good to have a date planned, to have something to look forward to, to know that we weren't yet done.

I peeked over at him and found him staring at me. Really staring.

"What?" I asked suddenly self-conscious.

"I'm thinking about asking if I can kiss you."

My heart did the sort of acrobatic flip it hadn't done since I was a teenager.

God I wanted that kiss.

But I wasn't ready to admit that. "You say you know me, and all of a sudden you think I want to be asked?"

He smirked. With that devil's smirk that had taunted and teased me for so many weeks.

The car pulled over to the side of the road, angled next to a bank of snow.

I undid my seatbelt.

Then Donovan undid *his* seatbelt. And he leaned across me, caging me in without touching me. I was suddenly too hot again. My heart beat too loud. My breathing grew faster as I waited for him to bend down and press his lips to mine.

But all he did was pull the lever on the door and push it open.

My eyes pricked unexpectedly. I was going to blame it on the rush of cold air. It didn't matter. This was a start. We'd made a start.

I put one foot on the ground and bent forward to step out. Suddenly Donovan's hand was cupping my face, pulling me back, and when I turned, my mouth crashed into his.

I sighed into his kiss, letting his eager lips tell me all the things he hadn't had time to say. Letting his mouth remind me that he'd confessed feelings I had yet to absorb. Letting his tongue make dirty filthy promises of nights to come.

When he broke the kiss—much too soon—I stared at him with glossy eyes.

"You hold the cards right now, Sabrina," he said, his nose

almost touching mine. "But don't begin to think I've forgotten who's in charge."

He brushed his lips across mine once more, then pulled away entirely. "You better go before your sister worries."

I was in the building and he'd driven away before I was sure I remembered how to breathe.

FIVE

"He kissed you?" I did not think that I'd be the one saying that tonight.

Turned out I wasn't the only Lind sister who'd gotten kissed on the way home by a Reach executive.

"More like *I* kissed *him*," Audrey said dreamily.

"You *kissed* my boss?" Jesus, I hadn't even gotten my coat hung up before she'd attacked me with this information, let alone gotten a chance to tell her anything about my car ride with Donovan.

She pulled her knees under her on the couch. "Dylan is not actually your boss. He's more like your boss's equal, if you want to be technical."

I threw my coat on the back of the sofa next to her along with my purse. Forget making it to a hanger; it wasn't happening. With my hands free, I put a fist on my hip. "If you want to be technical, he's old enough to be your father."

She rolled her eyes. "He is not. He's just experienced and wise."

"He's twenty years older than you."

"Maybe I have a thing for dads. Don't knock my kink. I don't knock yours."

That shut me up for a second. I hadn't actually ever told her my kink, but Audrey wasn't stupid. She could probably figure out enough to guess that I at least liked a good spanking.

"Fine." I dropped my hand. "I won't knock the age difference." I circled around to the front of the couch and plopped down next to her. "I don't actually care what you're into anyway, as long as it's consensual." It was the truth, too. I wasn't just blowing sunshine up her ass. "I just don't want you getting hurt. Dylan doesn't seem into relationships. You get that, right? Not to mention that you live on entirely different continents."

"It was just a kiss! God," she huffed, shifting so her legs were out in front of her. "I'm not planning to marry the guy."

"Just a kiss." I sounded skeptical only because, with Audrey, it was never *just a kiss*. The minute she decided she liked a guy, she *liked* a guy. She started doodling their initials on the back of napkins. She changed her Facebook status to *In a Relationship*. She gave her heart when she swapped saliva. She didn't do one-night stands. She didn't do casual hook-ups. She didn't do *just a kiss*.

Audrey sighed up at me with doe eyes. "I felt bad for the guy. All that doom and gloom. 'Love's dead. Grump, grump.' He needed something nice for a change."

Uh huh. "So you thought you'd kiss him and that would show him. Make him magically believe in hearts and romance again?"

"Shut up," she said with a pout.

That's what I was afraid of. Just a kiss and now she was head over heels for Dylan-love-is-a-myth-Locke. Thank God she was leaving in six days. And he was leaving. She might not even get a chance to see him again.

Audrey sank further into the couch beside me. "You think I'm naïve."

I looked over at my baby sister, ready to tell her all my worries, but stopped myself at the last second. I couldn't tell her to change how she felt any more than she could tell me to change how I feel about Donovan.

And she'd never try to tell me to change how I feel in the first place. She'd just encourage me to feel it.

So instead I kissed her hair. "I think you're amazing."

She peered up at me and grinned. It had been the right thing to say. Score a sister point for me.

She nudged me with her shoulder. "Hey. Tell me what happened with Donovan. He wasn't on a date with that woman, was he?" She said it with certainty, as if she had an inside scoop.

"He said he wasn't." I threw my feet up on the coffee table in front of us. "How did you know?"

She shrugged. "The way he looked at you." She followed me with her feet on the table too. "What else?"

"He said he came back to the States for me."

"To talk to you? To be with you?"

"That's what I don't know yet. We have more to talk about, obviously." I pulled a lock of hair down and twirled it between my fingers, replaying everything he'd said. There was so much I wanted to remember. So much I wanted to obsess over and hold too preciously.

"He said he loved me," I said softly. Well, he hadn't actually said it. I'd said it, and he'd confirmed. Was that the same thing? I was counting it as the same thing.

"Wow. That's big." Her excitement was hard to contain, but she was doing a pretty good job being cool about it. For me, I guessed. Probably trying to figure out how I felt about it before she let loose her own enthusiasm.

I nodded. It *was* big. But...

"But you already knew that he loved you," Audrey said, filling in the blank that I couldn't.

"Yeah. I did." That was the problem. Everything he'd said had only confirmed things I'd already suspected were true. I wasn't any closer to a solution where he was concerned. And it was going to be another several days before we got a chance to make any more progress.

"Still," Audrey said, "it had to be nice to hear."

I had a list of arguments why *nice* didn't matter. Then I remembered that I should just feel it.

"Yeah," I said, genuinely. "It's really nice."

I'D HEARD Donovan tell Dylan he'd be in the office the next day, I just hadn't really thought about it until it *was* the next day. Suddenly I was nervous and anxious and totally unprepared. All night I'd tossed and turned, and that was believing there were several more nights before I'd see him again. Now that there was a possibility I'd see him sooner, I was going out of my mind.

I settled on the simplest game plan—I'd hide.

My office was nowhere near Donovan's and since I was

taking Wednesday off to spend with Audrey, I had a lot of work to keep me busy anyway. I just had to stay on task, holed up in my little corner, and everything would be good.

The plan worked well for the most part. By late afternoon, I'd gotten all my must-complete projects done and had gone the whole day without leaving my office.

All I had left to do was drop off some forms that needed to be signed off on. Forms that couldn't be emailed because they contained client payment information.

I walked down to the edge of the hall and glanced toward Donovan's office. It was dark, which should have made me feel relieved. And it did. Mostly. I didn't even know if he'd actually made it in like he said he'd planned to. Now I wouldn't know at all because I'd been too chicken to look for him.

I was seriously ridiculous.

I wanted to see him; I didn't want to see him. It was confusing even to me.

Anyway, Weston's office was in the opposite direction and it didn't matter if Donovan was in or not.

So I headed toward Weston's.

Halfway there, I passed the glass-walled conference room and realized it wasn't empty. Weston, Nate, and Dylan were sitting around the far end of the long table. And standing behind them, as though he might have just walked in and hadn't sat yet, was Donovan.

As soon as I saw them, I snapped my head away, back to the hallway in front of me. They hadn't seen me. They were wrapped up in their conversation. I didn't need to interrupt them.

God, my stomach was fluttering like a teenager's. Just because Donovan was nearby. I didn't want to see him, but I wanted him to see me. My face was flushed, and I couldn't think and—

"Sabrina," Weston called through the open door, eyeing the stack of files in my hands. "Are those for me?"

Adrenaline shot through me at the shock of being "caught." I looked down at the pile, having almost forgotten what my original agenda had been. "I was dropping them off at your office."

He used two fingers to gesture me toward him. "I'll take them."

My heart was beating so loud I could hear it, and shit, I suddenly couldn't remember how to walk in heels. Somehow I made it to him without falling on my face, and without obviously staring at Donovan the entire time.

"Executive meeting?" I asked as if speaking would make me look somehow more collected than I was.

"Just shooting the shit, really," Weston said.

"Ah." Dumb, but fine. It was all fine. I'd gotten through it just fine.

But after I set the files next to Weston, I looked up, and Donovan was right across the table from me, staring at me in that way he always did. That way that saw into me and knew me.

It always rattled me when he looked at me like that. But today when he saw me, I remembered that he loved what he saw and the butterflies fluttered again inside me.

"Hi," I said quietly. Like a dork. Like a lovesick kid.

The corners of his lips pressed up just slightly, just for me. If we were alone I'd kiss him there. One kiss on each corner before—

"Donovan," Nate said, interrupting my daydream. "I meant

to tell you—I saw the early footage from the France campaign. Sun Le Chen looks stunning."

And then it was all gone—the butterfly flutters, the racing heart, Donovan's smile. Left was stark, bleak reality.

"Sun was with you in France?" My voice was even because this wasn't shocking. This made much more sense than any of the amazing things he'd said last night.

He didn't answer. The silence in the room was answer enough.

"Excuse me, fellows." I turned and walked on steady feet out of the room, but not before hearing Donovan mumble "fuck" under his breath.

Unlike at the restaurant, he was right on my heels. "Sabrina, stop."

I didn't want to stop. But I could feel the eyes of the other men on me, and who knew who else was watching from their offices? So I stopped.

"What, Donovan?" I said through gritted teeth. "Go ahead and tell me what you're going to say. You're going to make sure I hear it one way or another anyway."

"I explained last night that she is the spokeswoman—"

I interrupted him, my voice escalating. "You said you were negotiating terms. I didn't know she'd been with you all along."

"She wasn't *with me*." He was obviously frustrated. "She was—"

I glanced toward the conference room. Weston wasn't even pretending not to gawk. "People are watching us."

"I don't care who's watching us."

"*I* care."

Of course he didn't care. He owned the goddamn place. I

was the one who'd be laughed at in this situation. Not him. Never him.

Half a beat passed. Then without any warning, he grabbed me by the elbow and roughly escorted me down the hall. At the first open room, he dragged me inside and shut the door behind him. After a second, he locked it.

I folded my arms across my chest and fumed, my eyes locked on his. At least now we were in the privacy of the copy room, and I could say what I really wanted to say. Ask what I really wanted to ask. "Did you fuck her?"

"I haven't fucked anyone since I last fucked you. And before that the only woman I'd been with was you since you showed up in town." He stood in front of the closed door and braced his hands in the frame, barricading me from trying to go past him.

"You were only in France two weeks. Seems her campaign got arranged awfully quickly to get her there that fast. And then she got back to the States when you did? That's awfully convenient." Models were scheduled months in advance. They didn't do shoots at the drop of a hat unless they were fucking someone.

But he had an answer for this too. "She'd been booked to do the campaign since Reach proposed to Elizabeth for Weston. You can look up the contract information yourself and check out the date. She was already in France when I got there. She left a week ago."

Okay. More plausible. "Still gave you lots of time together there."

"We weren't together at all." He took a step toward me. "What else? Ask me what you want to know."

I inhaled then exhaled, my cheek twitching. "Did you kiss her? Stick your face between her legs?"

He shook his head sharply. "I barely saw her off the set. And I never touched her."

God, it was maddening! There was no reason not to believe him. We weren't even technically together, and even without a commitment, all signs had pointed to him being faithful.

It was just that we were unbalanced in our relationship in general. We were on a teeter-totter with him solid on the ground, and me dangling in the air. He had so much more of the picture than I did, and it left me to grasp and reach at anything and everything.

"Too bad I didn't hire a PI to follow you around Europe," I said, acting petty and rash. "I have to ask you these questions instead of reading a report. How am I supposed to know you're not lying about all of this?"

"I guess you'll have to trust me."

I pouted. "Well that fucking sucks."

"That does suck. Having to trust me." He sounded a little annoyed and a whole lot dangerous.

He took another step toward me, and I started to step back, but there was a counter behind me, so I had to stay put. And maybe I wanted to stay put. He was only a foot and a half away from me now.

"But I haven't lied to you, Sabrina." His gaze never left mine. "And I'm not lying when I say I don't give a fuck about anybody else's cunt but yours."

We stood there, not touching, not speaking, each of us standing our ground. But I had no basis to keep my position, and it felt like he'd won so much already.

I couldn't back down.

"Prove it," I said.

His expression flared, his eyes growing dark and mean, and I realized what I'd done. Donovan wasn't one to be provoked.

I'd just invited the devil out to play.

"Unzip your skirt and put your hands on the counter behind you."

My heart hammered and my belly twisted. My panties were embarrassingly drenched all of a sudden, and I *wanted* him. But I stood completely still. "I didn't—"

He cut me off. "No talking and unzip your skirt."

My mouth slammed shut, but I still didn't move. If I moved, I'd be asking for this. But if I talked, I'd be telling him to stop.

And I didn't want this to stop.

I just didn't want to ask for it because I was stubborn and stupid for wanting him in the first place.

But he would give it to me without the words, without my obedience. Because he knew me. He knew what I needed.

With his eyes never leaving mine, he found the zipper at the side of my waist and pulled it down. After that, the skirt was loose enough that all he had to do was tug it once and it fell easily to my feet. He nudged his knee against my inner leg, and automatically I stepped that foot out of the pool of material on the floor, widening my stance.

He gave a nod of praise, sending a jolt of warmth through my entire body.

Then he bent down in front of me.

Suddenly, breathing was harder than it should have been. My chest moved up and down, air passed through my mouth, but I couldn't get enough of it to my lungs.

And he hadn't even touched me yet.

The sight of him alone—Donovan Kincaid, one of the most

powerful men in the world, down on his knees in his black Ermenegildo Zegna suit—it was overwhelming and erotic, and by the time he put his hand at the back of my knee, I was already trembling.

He smiled up at me with his devil's smile, trailing his fingers up the back of my thigh, higher and higher still, to the round curve of my ass. His constant gaze kept my eyes pinned to his, and I knew he could read every thought, every emotion that ran through me. He knew exactly what he did to me with this caress of my skin, with that pinch of my flesh.

Finally breaking eye contact, Donovan brought his other hand around me and squeezed both of my ass cheeks as he buried his nose into the crotch of my white lace panties. My knees buckled when he inhaled audibly, and now I had to reach for the counter behind me. Just to keep myself from collapsing.

"I'm going to believe you wore these for me," he said before licking slowly up the center panel.

It wasn't a question so I didn't comment. Besides, I was too busy stifling a moan. If he'd made me answer—if I'd been able to speak—I'd have told him he was full of himself. It wouldn't have been a lie, but it wasn't all the truth. Of course I'd worn them for him. There was a chance I'd see him today, and I dressed thinking about that, thinking about all the dirty filthy things he might do to me if I let him.

I just hadn't actually planned to let him.

Keep telling yourself that, Sabrina.

"Fuck, you're already wet." He said this so quietly I was almost convinced it was for himself, but the gleam in his eyes told me differently. It told me I wasn't fooling anyone. I was at least as turned on as he was whether I wanted to admit it out loud or not—and judging from the way he kept having to adjust himself, he was pretty goddamned turned on.

He sucked my clit into his mouth through my panties, and this time I couldn't keep my moan inside. There'd been too much want, too much need, and he sucked eagerly, driving me quickly to a frenzy.

But the material was an unwanted barricade. Like a condom, dulling the sensation, and I wasn't getting where I needed to be. Not all the way. I was still dangling. Always dangling.

Just when I thought I couldn't take it any longer, he dragged his mouth lower, and found my hole. With his thumb now on my clit, he used his tongue, to push the fabric of my panties inside me.

I jerked forward, caught off guard by how fucking good it felt, my hands landing on his shoulders.

Immediately, he sat back. "Hands behind you."

The rules, right.

Did he want my hands behind me because it was part of the game? Or because he didn't want me touching him? Or just because he said so?

It didn't matter. All that mattered was that he finished, that he made me come, and I was far enough along now that I didn't care about what I conceded in giving him my obedience.

I put my hands on the counter.

His mouth was back on me in an instant. This time he nudged my panties aside with his nose and resumed his attack on my bare cunt in earnest. With one hand wrapped around the back of my thigh, his other hand used the bunched material of my panties to cause extra friction on my clit.

He pinned my eyes once more, and maybe that was the

most erotic part of the whole thing—the way he looked at me. The way he always looked at me.

I was whimpering now, bucking into his face, so close to coming.

Suddenly the door handle behind him jiggled as though someone was trying to get in.

I tensed in absolute panic, but Donovan didn't ease up at all.

A second later, the person knocked. "Anyone in there?"

I recognized the voice. It was Ted from creative. And Jesus, I was so close to coming.

"Melissa?" Ted called out to someone. "Do you have a key to the copy room? Does anyone know where a key is?"

I tried to push Donovan away, but his grip on me tightened. Without ceasing the massage of my clit, he took a break with his mouth long enough to say, "I'm not stopping until you come. So either relax and let it happen or be prepared to give them a show."

I knew enough about Donovan to not question his sincerity on this.

Giving my eyes back to him, I forced myself to ignore the commotion outside the door and focused only on the feeling of his mouth. Of his lips. Of his tongue. Of his fingers, and the expert way they played me—like he knew how to make me sing; like he had me memorized.

I didn't think I could relax enough, that I could come with Ted outside and the door locked and the lights off, but suddenly my orgasm shot through me like a freight train at a railroad crossing. Even though I knew it was coming, its speed still surprised me. I saw stars, my knees buckled, and a burst of pleasure ricocheted through my body. I didn't recognize the wail coming from me, low and unfurling like a ribbon of sound. Immediately, Donovan jumped to his feet to swallow my cry with a kiss, his hand still rubbing me through my climax below, and all I kept thinking was *yes, yes, yes, yes*, yes!

I was still shaking when he broke away a minute later. Thankfully, I still had my hands on the counter behind me or I might have slumped to the floor. Donovan bent down and straightened my panties, then went to the floor, and picked up my skirt. I stepped into it, moving my hands to his shoulders for support while he pulled it up and fastened the zipper.

He didn't complain about the touch this time, and even gave me a half-smile as he wiped at the makeup under my eye. He leaned in and kissed me once more, hard, his tongue sweeping deep inside me. As deep as I wanted him to be. Even after he'd just made me come.

"I love the way your jealousy tastes," he said.

I frowned, remembering all of a sudden how this whole interaction started. "I'm not sure that—"

The doorknob twisted. Donovan dropped his hands and moved away from me just as the door opened and Ted walked in.

"You guys were in here the whole time?" he asked, confused. "The door was locked. I had to find a key."

"I didn't realize you were trying to get in," Donovan said without apology. "It's all yours."

He slipped out around Ted before he could say anything else. Before *I* could say anything else.

Maybe it was for the best. I didn't know that Donovan wanted to hear what I had to say anyway.

SIX

I spent the next day devoted to touring the town with my sister. I'd only lived in New York since September and hadn't made much effort to see any sights beyond those tied to spots used in the marketing campaigns I'd put together. Before that, the only other trip I'd taken to The Big Apple had been spent in Weston's bed. It was time that was remedied.

Together, we'd hit Macy's and much of the fashion district over the weekend. Today we hit One World Trade Center, The Met, and Rockefeller Center. It was warm enough that Audrey managed to convince me to get on the ice skating rink. I fell several times and didn't last long before calling it quits, but I laughed a lot more than I'd expected, despite the aches and bruises the adventure earned me.

Outside the office, it was easier to pretend that there weren't other things weighing on my mind. That Donovan didn't occupy my every waking thought. That every joke I made and every smile I gave wasn't laced with him, as though he had been grafted onto my DNA and every part of me contained a fragment of him.

I thought I did a pretty good job of hiding it, anyway. If I didn't, it wasn't until the intermission of the Rockettes' Christmas Spectacular that Audrey said anything about it.

"Is it a new thing? Or just all the old things?" she asked.

"Huh?" I'd been lost in my head, sure I must have missed the first part of what she'd said.

"You've been staring blankly at the stage for the past several minutes. And there's nothing happening up there at the moment. I'm guessing it's Donovan that's on your brain. Is it a new thing he did that's bothering you? Or all the old stuff?" Before I could answer, she clarified. "The old stuff is enough, by the way. I'm just curious."

I groaned and threw my head back on the seat. Which hurt more than I'd expected. So I groaned again. "Am I that obvious? Have I been a terrible drag all day?"

"No," she laughed. "You've been awesome. Now spill."

I grabbed a lock of hair and twisted it around my finger. "It's the old stuff. But there's new stuff too." I hadn't told her what had happened the day before, and I didn't plan on telling her. Not all of it, at least. "I found out that Sun—the woman from Gaston's—was in France with him."

"Not *with him*, with him, though. Right? Working together probably." She was so certain. It was enviable how certain she could be.

I studied her, wondering if she'd developed psychic powers while away at college that I was unaware of. "How do you know that?"

"I told you how. He came after you, Bri. He ran out of that restaurant for you. He looked at you like if you didn't hear him out he was going to be lost for a long time."

Oh, right. My sister wasn't a psychic. She was a *romantic*.

I closed my eyes so that I didn't roll them. It wasn't that I didn't believe what she said. I just couldn't base truths in our relationship on how he *looked* at me.

I couldn't base them on anything physical. Which was the current problem.

I opened my eyes. "Okay, yes. He said she was there for work," I admitted. "And then I..." I hesitated, looking for a way to convey the situation without telling her the actual situation. When he'd knelt in front of me and brought me to a mind-blowing orgasm with his tongue. "I let him...*kiss*...me." Yeah. That was a good way to frame it.

She tilted her head. "You let him kiss you? Why is that a problem?"

"It was a really serious kiss." I watched her to see if she understood. "Serious enough that he might think things are better with us than they are."

"Ah. I see." Her face got inexplicably red. "One of those kinds of kisses."

I didn't know exactly what kind of kiss she was thinking of, or what *kisses* she'd experienced herself to start her fidgeting the way she was, but I had a feeling she got what I was talking about.

"Well, you're just going to have to tell him the situation then," she said. "Set him straight." It was something she'd never do herself if she was in my shoes, but I would, and we both knew it.

"Set him straight," I echoed as the lights dimmed for the second act of the show. "Yep. That's what I have to do."

I might have already known that's what I needed to do. But doing so would require reaching out to Donovan.

Again.

LIKE LAST TIME, I waited until Audrey had gone off to the guestroom for the night. With a glass of scotch in hand and wearing nothing but a T-shirt and panties, I curled up under the covers with my phone.

After the show at Radio City Music Hall, Audrey and I had gone out for drinks at a piano bar. It was late now. Past two-thirty. Before when I'd called Donovan, it had been morning his local time. It was too late to call tonight.

But I could text.

Can you call me soon? We need to talk. It was embarrassing how long it took me to come up with those nine words. I pushed SEND, dropped my cell in my lap and sat back against the headboard to take a sip of my drink. Hopefully that would get him to call. If not tomorrow, which was Thanksgiving, then the next day. I didn't want to get my hopes up too high. The last time I'd texted him, he hadn't responded at all.

Thinking about the possibility of him not responding this time made me need to take another sip.

And then my phone started ringing in my lap.

I answered it quickly before it woke Audrey.

"You missed me," Donovan said, his voice as smooth as the Macallan 12 Year I was drinking.

My chest felt warm and fluttery. "What are you doing up?"

"What are *you* doing up?"

"Don't you already know?" I teased.

"Touché." There was a smile in his tone. "I'm nursing a scotch and talking to my girlfriend on the phone."

I suddenly felt dizzy, like I'd fall off the bed. I wrapped the fingers of my free hand tightly into the comforter. "You can't keep calling me your girlfriend."

"Because you're not? Or because you'd prefer a different term?"

"Because I—" I broke off. He always threw me like this. I didn't want to answer. I didn't *know* the answer. "Because I don't think we should be talking about that right now."

He let a full second go by. Then two.

"Fine," he conceded. "What *should* we be talking about?"

I said a silent prayer of gratitude, thankful to have been given the reins. "Yesterday." Then, because I did not want to start arguing about Sun Le Chen again, I clarified. "We need to talk about what happened in the copy room." I took another sip of my drink. I needed it.

"Ah. The copy room." His chair creaked like it was made of leather. A recliner? A desk chair? I didn't know. "I assure you, Ted doesn't know anything. He thinks he knows. He doesn't."

"That's not what I'm worried about." Though, now I kind of was.

"What *are* you worried about, Sabrina?" He didn't sound curious—he sounded annoyed. As though he already knew the answer to his question, but he had to go through the procedure of asking before he could challenge the response.

I didn't like that feeling. The feeling that he was two steps ahead of me.

But there was no turning back now.

I took a deep breath. "I'm worried that because I didn't stop you, I let you think that you can use sex to fix this. Fix us."

"I see." The reply was tight.

"And you can't. You can't use sex to fix this." There. I'd said it.

I swirled the liquid in my glass, waiting for him to say something. Anything.

But he sat silent, and I had to nudge him. "Are you going to say something?"

"Okay."

"Okay?" It hadn't sounded like he was challenging me, but it was so hard to figure out what a person truly meant from a two syllable word. "Can I have more than an okay?"

"I'm actually impressed you made it more than a day before you let this bother you."

And I was impressed that I thought for a minute he wouldn't be a dick about this.

"I am not predictable," I grumbled. Though admittedly, I might have given him grief about sex at times in the past.

But that wasn't this. This was different.

He chuckled. "I never implied that you were."

"You're implying that you knew I'd eventually complain about it," I huffed.

"*Are* you complaining?"

The low rumble of his question made me shiver. Add to that the memory of his hands on my thighs, his eyes pinned on mine, his mouth buried in my pussy...

"No." Except it never should have happened. "Yes. It won't fix things."

"But did you enjoy it?" Of course he wouldn't let me get away without the exact truth.

I closed my eyes as if that would make it easier to give this to him. "You know I did," I whispered.

"I just wasn't sure you remembered."

I bit back a groan of frustration. Donovan was not an easy person to interact with, but I wasn't a cakewalk either. I had my own issues. I was too proud. Too serious. And I had a border-line unhealthy comfort level with the kind of sex I liked.

We were both works in progress. I needed to be better about remembering that.

I set my drink down and pulled my knees to my chest. "I do remember," I said, softer now. "Which is why it took so long to make myself do the right thing and call. I want you, Donovan. I always want you. But we have to sort things out before anything like that can happen again. It can't be what we use to make this better."

"Okay." There was that damn two-syllable response again.

"I'm serious," I said, solemnly.

"All right. Got it." Without missing a beat he moved on to a new subject. "Where's your sister?"

"In bed. In the other room." I still wasn't sure if we were on the same page or not.

"Good. Now." There was a rustle like he was shifting the phone to his other ear. "What was your favorite part of riding my face?"

"Oh my God." Against my will, blood rushed to my lower regions. "Did you hear me, Donovan? We can't do this."

"I heard you." Unconcerned. As though he hadn't just been talking about eating me out.

The calmer he was, the more worked up I got. "You're not taking me seriously!"

"What did I do?" he asked innocently. "I just want to hear

you tell me what you liked most about having your cunt pressed up against my face. Then I can tell you what I liked most. Would you rather I go first?"

"So basically you want to have phone sex." I pressed my thighs together, wishing I didn't want that as well.

I could hear the shrug in his voice. "I might pull out my cock later. Depends on how good you make the details."

"Donovan!" I rubbed my hand across my forehead, trying to convince myself I wasn't tempted. But I was tempted. And was it really that big of a deal? If we just talked about how good it felt to come with his fingers inside me pressing at just the right spot?

My resistance was waning.

But this relationship—whatever this relationship was turning out to be—was important to me. So I made another attempt at keeping my ground. "This can't be anything real if sex is the only thing you want from me," I told him pointedly.

"Think about it and tell me if I'm the only one who seems to want just sex from this relationship," he said just as pointedly.

I wrinkled my face, about to protest. Then I did think about it. Thought about the fact that I'd been involved with him in a pretty much sex-only relationship for less than two months. Even when I'd known him back in college, every thought I'd had about him, every instinct that had drawn me toward him had been sexual.

Donovan on the other hand, had noticed me before I'd ever really noticed him. He'd stayed involved with me for over ten years. He'd been there. Watching. Interfering. Manipulating. But he hadn't even tried to take advantage of me when I'd been most vulnerable—when he'd rescued me from being raped by Theo Sheridan.

Donovan was right. I was the one who appeared to be only interested in him physically. It was a blow to the gut to realize that so much I'd perceived about us was a misconception.

And it made me feel terrible.

It wasn't quite that simple, though. "To be fair," I said, trying to make myself feel better, "since I've been in New York, you haven't made anything else seem like an option."

"That is fair," he agreed. His breath came so clearly through the phone. I wished it were his thoughts, that I could hear what was in his head.

Then he told me. "I thought that somehow if I just fucked you it would be enough."

"Me too." That was exactly it. It wasn't that sex had been all I'd wanted from Donovan—it was that I'd thought that if I at least had that, I could live without the rest. "I thought that it would be enough if I, uh, did that too."

"Say it."

"Say what?" But I knew what he wanted to hear.

"No games, Sabrina," he said, impatiently.

"If I *fucked* you. Are you happy?"

"I'm hard." And so fucking smug.

"God, you're so..." I trailed off, too infuriated to find the words I wanted.

But as always, he wouldn't let that stand. "I'm so...what? You act like you're mad, but you also act like you like it, so tell me what it is that I am?"

"I don't know what you are!" That was the problem. I had no fucking idea.

I took a deep breath, and then more calmly repeated, "I don't know. Whatever it is, I can't stop coming back to look. I can't stop coming back, wanting you to tell me what it is that I am too."

I didn't know why I said it. Maybe because it was dark and we were on the phone, or because I was lonely, or because I really wanted him to know everything inside me.

Whatever the reason, I'd said it. It was out there. I couldn't take it back.

He was quiet a minute, and I imagined him stretched out in that leather armchair, I'd decided—his legs propped up on an ottoman in an office I'd never seen. He had to have a place like that in his apartment. A place where he was completely comfortable. Just one of many Donovan rooms I'd never seen.

He let a beat pass, and it didn't feel awkward because it was so full.

Then he asked, "Remember when you applied for that internship at BellCorp the final year of your graduate program?"

Of course I remembered, but how did he know about it?

Oh, yeah. He knew everything about me.

It was irksome, mostly because I didn't know what he knew and what he didn't, not because I minded that he knew things. I didn't really have anything to hide. It was also irritating because sometimes he'd made my only options seem silly and insignificant.

"You mean the graduate program at the *little school* that I attended after leaving Harvard? *That* internship?" I asked, bluntly.

"Yes, Sabrina, I've been a dick. Let's make sure we don't forget that."

"I won't." It was a small victory, but it was my turn to feel smug.

"Now can we talk about the internship?"

"I didn't get it." I'd been fairly disgruntled about it at the time. BellCorp was a financial industry giant and their internship always went to the top student in the master's program, which was me. Somehow, though, I'd been overlooked, and given a position at Citi Health while BellCorp's internship had gone to Abraham Decker, the cocky know-it-all who actually didn't know shit, but you definitely couldn't tell him that after he scored BellCorp. His ego had barely fit into a room before that.

The animosity hadn't lasted too long however, because two months into the year-long position, it came out that several Bell-Corp executives had been involved in insider trading. Abraham Decker spent the rest of his internship trying to help the marketing team put the best spin on the situation rather than learning how to run a successful firm.

My internship, on the other hand, had gone amazingly well. The company was in a growth phase and I'd been part of several campaigns. Citi Health had even earned a statewide community award that my boss had credited in major part to me.

"Actually, you did get it," Donovan said.

"Uh. What?" Because I heard him. Just...what?

"You did get it. But I called in a favor and asked them not to give it to you and they listened."

"Uh, what?" I asked again. And this was a favor to him?

"I know BellCorp's vice-president—they do a lot of business with King-Kincaid. I also knew they were about to go down for that insider trading scandal. When they did, I didn't think it would be good for your budding career to be caught up in it. Plus, Jeremy Shotts, the guy at the Colorado office, is a major blowhard who likes to fuck the pretty interns."

"I can take care of myself around execs with grabby hands," I snapped defensively, though I was pretty sure my track record didn't speak in my favor.

"Jeremy Shotts wasn't the reason I made the call, Sabrina," he said, annoyance underlining his tone. "Denying him was a bonus. Did you hear any of the rest of the story?"

"Yes. I heard you." I chewed the inside of my lip, trying to decide how I felt about this new information.

No, that was a lie. I knew how I felt. I felt good. I felt really good. Protected and looked out for and...loved. Things I hadn't felt in a long time. Sure, Audrey loved me, and she'd go to the ends of the earth for me. But not like that. Not fiercely. Not violently. Not to extremes. Not because she didn't care enough, but because that wasn't how she cared for people in general.

But Donovan did.

It was dazzling.

His love dazzled me.

It was rich and fierce and dazzling.

I could also name at least ten women right off the bat without thinking too hard who would tell me this was sick. That I was a victim of this or that misogynistic/patriarchal agenda. That I was weak. That I was malleable. Blah, blah, blah bad feminist.

"Stop thinking too hard, Sabrina," he said when a whole minute had gone by in silence.

I shook my head. "I'm sorry."

I didn't know what else to say. There was so much I wanted

to say, but like the reasons he shouldn't call me 'girlfriend,' there were reasons I shouldn't talk about being dazzled. They weren't words for right now.

So I gave him what I could. "I guess I owe you a thank you."

He let out a frustrated sigh. "That's not why I told you about that."

"Then why did you?" I asked, just as frustrated.

"You wanted to know what you are."

"Okay."

"What you are is mine."

If there were such a thing as floating and sinking all at once, that was what I felt when I heard those words. Like I was one of the beloved giant cartoon characters that would be filled with helium and floated through the city in today's Macy's parade, and at the same time like someone who had just been thrown in a cold ocean with an anchor tied to her feet.

Mine.

His.

It was an answer to everything and nothing all at once. Something that seemed so unsure. Something that seemed so, so certain.

Could it be this easy?

I didn't know. I just didn't know.

"Finish your scotch and go to bed, Sabrina," he said breaking the silence. "You're not going to get any more of this figured out tonight. We'll talk more later."

"Okay," I said, still dazed. "Goodnight."

"Goodnight."

I put down my phone and picked up my tumbler, and wondered for a solid five minutes if I should text him back and ask him if he'd actually *known* I was drinking scotch too, or if he'd just guessed.

But I didn't because I wasn't sure yet if I cared what the answer was.

SEVEN

The things Donovan had said to me in the early hours of that morning stayed with me through the next day. So much of it was meaningless banter, but some of it was so poignant, so significant, that I played those words on repeat in my head.

What you are is mine.

I pulled that phrase out like a little pet. Stroked it and fed it. Listened to it purr. *Mine. Mine. Mine.*

I wondered how much he'd done behind my back. The story about BellCorp was a good one. It made me feel better about knowing him. But how many other stories like that were there? Would I feel the same about all of them?

I still didn't know if he was someone I could truly love.

But I was surer than ever that I wanted to find out.

We needed to talk. Really talk. And we would as soon as Audrey was gone. But a real relationship between the two of us wasn't just going to depend on what he had to say about the file he had on me. I couldn't pretend that was the only issue between us. I still didn't know him at all.

And then there was the idea that I only wanted him for sex. If I wanted that to not be true, I needed to show it. To Donovan, but also to myself.

Friday morning, before leaving the apartment for another day in the city with my sister, I gathered the courage to call him once again.

"There's this thing we do every year," I said, pacing the living room with nervous energy. "This lasagna dinner tradition on the Saturday after Thanksgiving. Do you already know about this?"

"I can honestly tell you that I have no idea what you're talking about."

"Oh. Okay." It made me relax a little to realize there were still things about me that he had yet to learn. "Well, like I said, it's this Lind family tradition. I'm going to cook lasagna and there will be garlic bread and tiramisu—"

He interrupted me. *"You're* going to cook?"

This I expected him to know. Lind women were exceptional, bright, ambitious women. But neither of us could cook. We'd gone out for Thanksgiving because of our lack of skills in the kitchen. Also what was the point of making a big meal for two people?

But while our Thanksgiving was less conventional, we'd been sure to keep our lasagna dinner tradition intact. The custom had been passed down from our mother, always set for the Saturday of the last week of November. And while neither Audrey nor I were good behind a stove, this was the one dish we could both cook without burning the house down.

"It's not a big thing," I said defensively. "It's really just one main dish. Don't expect it to be amazing or anything. And we won't be alone. Audrey will be there, of course."

"Sabrina. Is this your version of introducing me to the parents?"

There he was again, one step ahead of me. I hadn't thought of it like that, but now that he'd put it in those terms, yes. That's exactly what this was.

I suddenly had to sit down.

"This is just something we do every year," I lied, unable to admit the truth out loud. "And since you're under the impression that I'm only interested in you for your—" I stopped.

He'd said something while I was talking, and I'd missed it.

"What was that?" I asked.

"I said I'll be there. Just tell me the time." He even sounded like he was looking forward to it.

"Awesome." My stomach had flutters and I couldn't stop grinning. Or shaking. "Seven o'clock."

"It's a date."

"HOW DID you spend your Thanksgiving, Donovan?" Audrey asked, as she filled the water goblets on the table.

I listened to the conversation from the kitchen as I pulled the food out of the oven. The evening had gone well so far, despite my anxiety about it. Donovan had shown up on time with an expensive bottle of red wine, looking more than amazing in his gray slacks and maroon sweater. I'd been an awkward hostess, too nervous to know how to handle small talk with a man who knew everything about me, who'd been inside me, who'd said I belonged to him.

So instead of trying to talk about the weather or rehash the Macy's Day Parade, I'd hidden in the kitchen, pretending that the salad needed more tossing and the vinaigrette needed whisking. I'd only come out once to grab a glass of wine after Donovan had popped the cork. He and Audrey had moved to sit around the dining room table, and from what I could see and what I'd overheard, my sister seemed to have the conversation more than handled.

But dinner was done now. I'd have to sit at the same table with him and hope I could contain the torrent of emotions that kept me flustered and prevented me from having coherent thoughts.

"I had dinner at my parents' apartment on the Upper East Side," Donovan answered casually.

"Is that a good time?" A question I probably wouldn't have been brave enough to ask.

"No. It's not. It's thirty or so of the richest, snobbiest, cattiest people that my mother feels socially obliged to impress, crowded into a Central Park mansion to celebrate what they own, who they own, and who they fucked over to own it. It was my first Thanksgiving in the U.S. in a long time. I'd forgotten how awful it was."

Steam rushed up to glisten my face as I opened the foil around the garlic bread. Despite it's delicious smell, it suddenly seemed like such a simple side. Embarrassingly simple.

How different this dinner must be to Donovan, who was used to servant-prepared meals and glamorous surroundings. And here we were in a two-bedroom in Hell's Kitchen that he owned and rented to people in much lower tax brackets, furnished almost exclusively from a Pottery Barn catalog, serving him a dinner that was heavy and rich with refined carbs.

I didn't even think I could pronounce the wine he'd brought.

This whole idea had been ridiculous. What had I been thinking?

If he hadn't realized by now how totally beneath him I was, he would after tonight. I might be making good money now with an executive job in his firm, but I was still the poor girl he'd met back at Harvard on scholarship.

Hell, I hadn't even managed to keep the scholarship in the end.

But I couldn't hide in the kitchen all night feeling sorry for myself. I quickly downed the rest of my wine then carried my empty glass and the garlic bread to the table.

"Can you grab the salad?" I asked Audrey. "We're ready to eat."

"Yep!"

She ran off to attend to her assigned task as I set my glass at my place and the bread in the center of the table. I avoided looking at Donovan, but when I turned to go back to the kitchen, he grabbed my wrist. Electricity shot up my arm. My skin burned under his fingers.

I looked back at him, my pulse speeding up when my eyes met his.

"Hey," he said.

"Yeah?" My voice cracked on the simple word.

He stroked his thumb along the inside of my wrist. "I want to be here. Okay?"

A storm of butterflies took off in my stomach. He never missed anything. Even behind a wall and a stove, he saw me.

"I mean it," he said when I didn't say anything. I couldn't say anything. "Okay?"

I took a deep breath in and let it out. It didn't completely relax me, but it helped. Expecting to be any more at ease was ridiculous with Donovan so close, touching me. Looking at me. Looking at me like he wished I were the main course instead of what I'd prepared.

"Okay," I said softly.

He didn't let go of me, though. He held on until my sister came bustling around the corner, her arms full with the salad bowl tucked precariously under one arm and the bowl with the vinaigrette I'd made in the other hand.

"Have you heard of making trips?" I hissed as I passed her on my way back to the kitchen.

"I think I'm doing just fine," she called back to me. "So if you weren't in the U.S. before, Donovan, where were you?"

"Tokyo," he answered. "Do you want to know the best thing about Japan?"

"Sure."

"No one gives you a hard time when you decide to work through the holiday."

Smiling, I shook my head and stuck a serving utensil on top of the lasagna dish.

Audrey giggled. "No wonder you and my sister get along. Workaholics."

"I heard that," I yelled, using hot pads to pick up the lasagna and carry it around the corner to the dining room. *He wants to be here*, I told myself. *He wants to be here.*

"Did she tell you that?" he asked, meeting my eyes when I returned to the room. "That we get along?"

Oh yeah, he wanted to be here. The way he looked at me

sent sparks through my body. Every cell inside me was charged. Every molecule.

Jesus, how was I going to make it through this night?

Audrey pursed her lips. "Hmm. I don't remember."

"We don't," I said, teasing. "We bicker like crazy. He's a pompous asshole, and he never acknowledges that I'm right." Maybe it was only half teasing.

"That's not true. You're just so rarely right," he taunted right on back.

I set the dish down on the table and stared at Audrey. "See? Pompous. Asshole."

My sister thought it was funny. Donovan only shrugged as if to say, 'you get what you get.'

It made my chest pinch. I wanted to *get him*, pompous asshole parts notwithstanding. For the first time, I started to believe it might actually be possible. That we might be able to work out everything between us, and we'd just get to *get* each other.

But that was for tomorrow.

Tonight I had to hope that my food didn't give anyone food poisoning.

After surveying the table for anything missing, I took my seat at the round table between Donovan and my sister. The next few minutes were spent refilling wine glasses. Audrey made a toast, and we all clinked. Then we began dishing up and digging in.

"How did the two of you spend the holiday?" Donovan asked Audrey as he passed her the salad bowl.

"Uh uh," I said before she could answer. "He doesn't get to know anything else about me."

Audrey looked from Donovan to me then back to Donovan.

It wasn't that we'd done anything secretive. We'd gone to the parade and then the Holiday Shops at Bryant Park before having dinner at The Dutch. I'd tell him if he really wanted to know.

He just knew so much already. It was my turn to decide what he knew. My turn to hear about him.

So when she looked back at me, I narrowed my eyes into a warning stare.

"Sorry," she said to him. "Sabrina makes the rules around here."

He raised a brow. "Does she?"

"She does." Even as I said it I recalled the kiss he'd given me in his car almost a week before, and his parting words that made me shiver from head to toe. *Don't begin to think I've forgotten who's in charge.*

I hadn't forgotten where and how Donovan was in charge.

I hadn't forgotten the ways in which he took charge.

My inner thighs tingled, my belly tightened, my body yearning for him like that now. For him to manage me. To control me. To dominate me.

"Hmm," Donovan said, the sound vibrating through me.

I crossed my legs, hoping to dull the steady ache. "Shut up and eat your dinner."

"Yes, boss." He was in on the joke, the fucker. It only made my want that much stronger.

I tried not to watch him as he brought his fork up to his mouth and took his first bite, but it was impossible not to. It was extremely intimate, watching him eat the food I'd made. Watching his lips. Remembering the last time they were on me.

"This is good," he said, and I blushed for so many of the wrong reasons. "Really good."

I kicked him lightly under the table. "Don't sound so surprised."

He only smirked and took another bite.

"It's our grandmother's recipe," I said, as if that explained why it was so delicious. It certainly wasn't due to anything I did.

"On your mother's side, I'm guessing." He took a swallow of his wine.

I tensed slightly. "You guess correctly." His guess was educated, probably based on the knowledge that our mother's mother was full Italian, the first generation born in the United States.

I exchanged a look with Audrey. I'd told her that Donovan had a file on me and that he'd obviously been watching me for years, but I hadn't given her many details about the contents. Had she realized there were places where her own life's information intersected with mine? Like our family tree? Had it occurred to her that my past was her past, that Donovan knew that too?

If it hadn't, she didn't seem too bothered by learning it now.

She had her own history on her mind, history that she also shared with me. "If it weren't for Nonna's lasagna, Thanksgiving would be a holiday that I'd be fine skipping all together," she said. "Our dad died over this week, so there are bad memories. But we had so many years of lasagna dinners with Mom that are tied into my memories of her—I can't get rid of this week and the bad memories of dad without losing the good memories of her too. It makes it a complicated time."

"I understand," Donovan said, piquing my full attention. "I lost someone over Thanksgiving too."

Amanda. I'd forgotten she'd been coming back to school from the Thanksgiving break when she'd died.

He looked only at Audrey as he went on. "But, a year later, I spent a really nice day in my office at Harvard with Sabrina. I can't wish one didn't happen without losing the other, too."

Audrey and I had talked repeatedly about this time being difficult before—losing Dad, remembering Mom.

And I often thought about leaving Harvard now too. About Donovan. About losing my virginity to him against a bookcase. About realizing I liked sex that was filthy and dubious and involved power plays.

I hadn't ever stopped to think about what this time might mean to him.

Yes. Complicated was right. For all of us. Then and now.

AFTER WE'D FINISHED DINNER, conversation was even easier. We didn't leave the table, choosing to stay there to pick at tiramisu and drink coffee and whiskey. Over a glass of scotch, I discovered that Donovan Kincaid was quite an expert in art history. He and Audrey debated long and hard the merits of modern art versus the classics—Donovan particularly liked the works of Jackson Pollock and Shiryu Morita while my sister preferred the romantics and gushed profusely about Carl Blechen.

I'd learned enough over the years from Audrey to add an opinion here and there, but I was happy to sip my drink and listen to these two very different, very important people in my life. It suited Donovan to favor the bold, abstract strokes of the modern expressionists, just as it suited Audrey to love the dreamy wistfulness of the romance period.

Did it suit me that I liked the pointillism of Seurat? Was I made up of small, distinct pieces that combined to form a bigger story? Was it easier to appreciate me from a distance? Was that what made a man like Donovan choose to love me so long from afar?

He was nearer now. In my life, in my home. Would he keep loving me when he saw me this close up?

Eventually, the discussion lulled and our glasses emptied. I got up to take our dessert plates to the kitchen. When I returned, I didn't sit, instead choosing to lean against the dining room wall.

The evening was ending, and I was unexpectedly nervous again.

Audrey stood and stretched. "It's almost midnight? I didn't realize it was so late. I need to get packed."

Donovan nodded toward her. "Thank you for letting me intrude on your last night in town. I hope I wasn't unwelcome."

She waved her hand, dismissing the idea. "Not at all unwelcome. We invite friends...and *boyfriends*...to this all the time." She glanced at me in time to see the death glare I gave her. "Besides, it gives me a chance to deliver the My-Sister-Is-My-Only-Family speech."

His brow rose. "I don't believe I know this speech."

"It's a good one," she promised.

"Audrey!" I hid my face with my hands. I was going to kill her later. I loved her, but I'd kill her.

She pivoted toward me. "This would have been a lot worse coming from Dad. Admit it. You can bear my version." She turned back to Donovan. "It's short. It's standard. But it's serious. Try not to hurt her. That's all."

Donovan focused on his finger as he ran it along the bottom of his empty tumbler. "Audrey, I'm going to be honest with you." He looked directly at my sister. "I've done and said a lot of the wrong things already in an attempt to not hurt her. But I came back from France to fix it."

"Okay then," Audrey declared. "Fix it."

Donovan nodded.

Satisfied, Audrey took his glass from him as well as her own and carried them to the sink.

I didn't move. Didn't breathe. Definitely didn't look at Donovan. I wasn't *in* this moment—I was outside it, looking on. If I let myself be in it, I'd feel it, and that would be too much. I'd hold it for later instead, bring it out when I was alone and try to feel it in pieces. Not all at once where it would too easily overwhelm me.

She came back quickly, announcing, "I'm going to my bedroom to pack now."

"I'll go," Donovan said with no motion to get up.

Audrey's expression grew panicked. "No! Don't! I'm going to my bedroom. I'll close the door. I'll turn on music. I'll pack. I'm not coming out. But I'm an adult. What that means is that you definitely don't need to go." She looked from me to Donovan and back to me, making sure that we both understood exactly what she was saying. That she was giving us permission to *be adults too.*

I wanted to crawl into the wall.

But God, I also wanted Donovan.

"Goodnight, Audrey," I said flatly.

"Goodnight." With a waggle of her brows she slipped away. A second later, music did indeed start playing from her room.

Now it was just us. Just Donovan and me. Alone.

I pulled a lock of hair over my shoulder and tugged at the end, trying to hide my flushed cheeks. "She's a meddler. I'm sorry. Protective but also overly sentimental. She believes that All You Need is Love and that kind of idealistic crap."

Donovan tilted his head, his gaze scorching every inch of me. "Whatever will you do with her?"

I shrugged. "Send her back to art school, I guess."

I dropped my hands and put them behind my back against the wall, hoping that might ground me. Because I needed to be grounded. I was floating right now, and I loved it and it scared me all at once.

Maybe I didn't need to be grounded. Maybe what I needed was to let go.

I forced myself to look directly at Donovan. "I'm really jealous of her right now, actually."

"How so?"

"Her head doesn't get in the way. Maybe if I were her, I wouldn't have all the noise in my brain that's preventing me from crossing the room and crawling into your lap."

I panicked the minute the words left my mouth. "I don't even know if you'd want me there." Then I panicked some more. "And that wasn't a desperate way of asking you to reassure me. Not at all."

Donovan's eyes darkened. "All I've thought about the last hour is bending you over the back of that couch, tying your hands with your apron strings, and fucking you raw."

I shivered. "Yes, please."

I became putty when he talked like that. In that gravelly

tone that rumbled through my bones. In that way that made me feel his words as if he were already doing those things to me, already bending me and tying me. Already fucking me raw.

His gaze raked over me. "You're tempting. Very tempting."

"But...?"

"But a wise woman once told me that sex doesn't fix things."

Karma. I probably deserved this.

I scoffed nonetheless. "Wise? That doesn't sound wise. That sounds annoying."

"In my experience, wise is often annoying." He smiled, like that was a concession prize. His grin in place of his body. His admission that this was comically torturous for him too.

It was a terrible concession prize.

My skin was buzzing and alive. My pussy was aching and wet. But more urgent than my body's arousal was the itch inside me that couldn't be named or explained. The spot that burned when he talked about fixing things and wanting to be here and when he called me his.

"I don't want you to go." It came out almost as a whisper.

"We're going to talk tomorrow."

"That's so far away." *You're so far away.* Six feet too far. Might as well be miles.

"And after we talk," he said gently, "you might not want to fuck me anymore."

I nodded because he was right—he had to go. "But you should know I can't imagine that right now," I told him.

He nodded back.

A beat passed. Then, as if we both felt the energy shift together, he stood up at the same time as I moved to the closet to get his coat.

"You still want me to come over tomorrow?" he asked as we walked to the front door.

"About that," I'd been meaning to bring this up. "As you've mentioned already, the apartment is awfully...distracting. I thought we could meet instead at the office?"

He looked at me carefully for several long seconds. "You really think it matters where we are?"

No, it didn't matter where we were. If he wanted to fuck me, he'd fuck me, and having him remind me like that made my pussy throb with need.

But I had my reasons. I needed to be at the office.

I shrugged. "Humor me."

"The office it is."

I opened the door and he walked past me out to the hall. When he turned back toward me, I wanted him to kiss me, but I knew he couldn't, that if he started, neither of us would be able to stop. Instead, he reached his hand out and traced his thumb along my jaw.

"Goodnight," he said.

"Goodnight."

I was glad he made me shut the door and lock it before he left so I couldn't watch him walk away. It already felt too much like when we'd said goodnight, we'd really meant goodbye.

EIGHT

With Audrey leaving and the talk with Donovan looming, I didn't sleep well. It was still dark outside when I finally gave up on sleep. I took a long shower. I shaved—everywhere. I plucked my brows. I gave myself a pedicure. I put on sexy lacy panties and a matching bra and stood in front of my bedroom mirror. If no one saw it but me, at least I knew I looked good.

I finished dressing, pulling on black leggings and boots and a cream sweater that fell to my thighs, and when Audrey woke up, we walked down the street for a last breakfast together.

Afterward, I'd planned to accompany her to Grand Central to see her off, but she vetoed that plan.

"That's stupid and out of your way," she said. "We can say goodbye here just as easily, and then you can get to Donovan sooner."

I wasn't usually the affectionate one of the two of us, but I pulled her into a tight hug. "I love you," I told her, worrying suddenly that I didn't say it enough, that she didn't know how deeply I felt it, that she would walk away now without understanding.

"I love you, too." When she pulled away her eyes were wet. I had a feeling she got what I'd meant. I had a feeling her words meant more than they said too.

Thirty minutes later I was at the office.

It was too early for Donovan to be there, which was a good thing. It gave me time to sit down at my desk and get my head straight. I needed to go into this with the right mindset. Like it was an interview. A trial, even, and I was the prosecutor.

Because as much as I didn't want to be cold or harsh, Donovan was on trial. He'd done things to me—he'd violated me in very real ways—and he was going to have to answer to that.

I just had to make sure I didn't let him in my pants before then.

But that wasn't the reason I'd chosen to meet at Reach.

Another half hour later, I heard the elevator open. My light was the only one on. I knew he'd find me, and I waited for him to do so. A minute more and there he was, standing in my doorframe dressed in another pair of dark gray pants, this time with a crisp white dress shirt and a black pullover. The scruff on his jaw was more rugged than usual, his eyes a little less green, and I wondered if he'd had a hard time sleeping too.

I wouldn't blame him. This was going to be hard for me. But I had a feeling this was going to be even harder for him.

"You want to do this in here," he asked without preamble.

My heart thudded against my ribcage, but I managed to keep my voice steady. "I was thinking the conference room."

He nodded, and I stood up, but before I'd moved out from

my desk he asked, "Do I need to go get it or are you already prepared?"

Now it felt like my heart was in my throat. He knew. He already knew what I had planned.

I blinked, unable to speak.

"Because you and I both know that I'd just as easily fuck you on the conference table as anywhere, so that can't be the real reason you wanted to meet here."

I nodded, acknowledging he was correct in his assumption. Acknowledging that we were here because I didn't just want him to tell me about it, I wanted him to go through everything *with* me. I wanted all the details explained.

I wanted him to get the file.

"I didn't want to go through your office," I told him earnestly, sounding timid.

He cocked his head. "I think there's some irony there, don't you?"

"I'm well aware." I swallowed. The air between us stretched taut and thick.

And his eyes, where they'd been so warm last night, seemed cold and shielded today. As though he didn't want me to see anything inside of him.

I might not have walked in prepared, but he did.

"I'll meet you in the conference room," he said. Then he turned to walk to his office, and I turned and walked the other way.

Five minutes later he joined me, the overflowing manila file tucked under his arm. He studied me for a second. I'd chosen to sit at the middle of the table, unwilling to choose the head for myself, not wanting him to choose it either. In his eyes I could see him deliberate—should he sit next to me?

He chose to sit across from me. It was the right choice. We weren't here together today. At least, we hadn't come together. We might *leave* together—that remained to be seen—but for now, we were on opposite sides.

Donovan slid the folder across the table in my direction. I reached out to take it from him, my fingers on the edge closest to me, so far from where his hand still gripped the side, and pulled. He didn't let go, and I looked up to meet his eyes. They were empty, and I realized that might be the closest to afraid that I'd ever seen him.

It almost made me feel sorry for him.

Then I glanced back at the thick folder, its contents practically spilling out from its seams. This would be hard for us. But if we had any chance together, we had to get through it all.

My eyes still locked on his, I tugged on the folder again. This time he let go, and the whole thing slid easily to my side.

With a shaky hand, I opened up the front cover and smoothed it down onto the table.

"So," he said. "Where do you want to start?"

God, there was so much in there. So many papers and photos I had questions about. So much I needed to know. "How about the beginning?"

"A very good place to start." He leaned back in his chair, but he was by no means relaxed. His shoulders remained tense, his jaw tight.

That wasn't my problem.

I took the first paper out of the folder and scanned it. It appeared to be a receipt for a wire transfer from Donovan's bank to the mortgage account in my father's name dated shortly after his death.

I turned the paper around and scooted it toward him. "What's this?"

Donovan glanced quickly at it. "It seems to be proof of payment of some kind."

I drew my eyes into narrow slits. "Is this really how you want to play this?" I asked. Admittedly, it was almost easier if he did want to be an asshole. Then I could be an asshole right back.

He cocked his head this way and that ever so slightly, and I understood it wasn't me he was wrestling with—it was his own need for control. His own drive to hold the reins. To deal the cards. To run the show.

Eventually he let out a short audible breath. "It's the payoff for your father's mortgage. I paid the balance after his death."

"Why?"

"For you." For him, the answer was plain as day.

When my father died, everything had been left in my name. I'd been as surprised then to find out my childhood home had no mortgage outstanding as I was now to hear Donovan proclaim his reason for paying it off. I'd expected to be paying that loan for ten more years. When I didn't receive a statement for several months after the funeral, I'd even gone to the bank and questioned it.

"The loan officer told me that my father had made extra payments over the years," I told Donovan. It seemed impossible at the time. My father had saved every extra penny to send me to Harvard. Where had he gotten the money to pay off his mortgage? But I hadn't been about to argue with the bank.

His mouth twisted. His jaw ticked. "I have friends," he admitted. "A friend. He made the register appear the way I wanted it to appear." He was about to leave it at that, but then, as if realizing I'd demand more, he added, "I knew if there'd been a lump sum, you would've gotten suspicious."

"You didn't want me to find out it was you." I couldn't decide if I was mad or grateful. Having the mortgage paid off had been a real blessing. It would have been really hard for me to go back to college and pay for my sister's expenses with house payments on top of it.

But he'd done it behind my back! He'd done it in secret!

"Are you wanting me to thank you?" My words were sour, poisoning whatever gratitude I meant to show.

"No," he scoffed. "That's not why I did it."

"Then why did you do it? Why did you care about me enough to do that? Because of what happened in your office? Because we had sex?"

He frowned as though offended. "Do you really think that was when this began for me?"

No. I thought it began that night at The Keep.

But I wasn't giving him that. I wasn't giving him anything.

"How can I have any idea when you haven't told me shit?" My voice was already raised. I was already swearing, and we were only on the first item.

Good thing I had nowhere else to be, because I was going to stay until this was done. Until I knew everything I wanted to know. I hoped he was prepared for it to be a long day.

"I noticed you the first day you walked into that classroom, Sabrina," Donovan said. "*That's* when it began for me. And it never stopped."

Goose bumps scattered down my arms despite the sudden warmth that filled me inside.

We'd barely known each other, and yet he'd noticed me. Out of everyone. Out of an ocean of people, he'd found me.

But I had to ignore that—had to ignore the way it made me feel. It didn't benefit me at the moment.

What I needed were facts. Details. Confessions. The more, the better. "So you anonymously paid for my house? So that I would...?"

"So that you would be taken care of," he said with pronounced candor.

I closed my eyes for a beat.

Then I opened them again. I couldn't spend too much time on this one thing, large as it was. There was simply too much to go through. I took the receipt back and put it face-down on the inside cover of the folder and moved on to the next item.

The next several papers in the file were related to school. Recommendations he'd sent that I hadn't known about, items related to the internship from my master's program. We went through every single document, Donovan explaining each connection and his reasoning for interfering. Every time, it had been for my own good. As though he'd been my secret fairy godfather, showering me with the best opportunities at every turn.

"If you were this determined to butt in," I said after learning that the article I'd been asked to write for University Today had been suggested to the editor by him, "why didn't you just bring me back to Harvard? I was certainly trying hard enough to get there. Couldn't you have pulled strings there?"

He stared at me with a dull expression. "I'm flattered that you think so highly of my influence. It was *Harvard*, Sabrina. I can pull strings, but I'm not a miracle worker."

On and on it went through piles of invoices, receipts, copies of contracts, and school papers and essays I'd written. The headhunter I used to find a job in California had worked for

Donovan. The management company that had overseen my first apartment was owned by Donovan. The new security system that had been installed in my second apartment hadn't been paid for by the landlord as I'd believed. It was all Donovan.

Memories reshaped and took on new form. It was like when I learned that Santa Claus wasn't real; that all those gifts I'd been given had really been from my parents instead of some magical being. Now I was learning that situations I had always attributed to good luck or good fortune, other situations that I hadn't even thought more than two seconds about, all had been gifted to me by Donovan.

I couldn't help but ask over and over, "Why? Why? Why?"

And always, always it was the same answer. "For you."

We'd been at it for a couple of hours when I came across a paper that didn't make any sense. "Why is there an employment contract for Brady Murphy in here?" I hadn't noticed it the first time I'd been through the file.

Brady Murphy had been someone I'd dated for a short time while working in California. The relationship had never been very serious, but I'd been more serious about him than most of the guys I dated. He was too nice maybe. Too soft in bed. But a good guy. We might've stayed together longer than the four months that we had if he hadn't gotten a job offer from an up-and-coming tech firm in Japan.

...and suddenly I had a feeling I knew the answer.

"Brady Murphy was never right for you and you know it," Donovan said in answer to my question.

"So you got him a job that took him out of the country?" I didn't bother keeping the incredulity out of my voice.

Donovan shrugged. "If I'd found him a job in the states,

there was too great a chance that you would have moved with him. And you needed to break up."

Indignation fumed inside me. "You sent my boyfriend away so that we would break up? Oh my God. I can't fucking believe you!"

"It would have been too easy for you to settle down with him. And that's exactly what you would have been doing—settling. It was for your own good."

I spoke over him, my words landing in unison with his. "Don't tell me it was for my own good. You didn't do that for me. That was for you. You were jealous."

Donovan gave me his version of an eye roll, a slight shift of his gaze. "Oh please. There is nothing to be jealous of about Brady Murphy. He's a weak, whiny sap. I was looking out for you."

I didn't believe him. "You didn't want me with another man." I was almost more flattered than I was mad. Or something deeper than flattered. Just like his jealousy was primitive —because he *was* jealous no matter how much he denied it— the emotion it ignited in me was equally primal. Equally base. It turned me on. It aroused me.

"How many other relationships did you meddle with?" My mind started to race through all the other boyfriends I'd had, the other men I'd casually dated. Donovan had messed with Weston and I by arranging for him to be part of this fake marriage with Elizabeth Dyer. I knew that. It only made sense that he would've interfered with others.

"Roger Griffin?" I asked. "His grandmother wasn't really sick, was she?"

"Are you accusing me of luring a man away from you with a fake sick *grandmother*?" Donovan stared at me unblinking.

"Okay. I didn't really think that one through."

"But if his grandmother *hadn't* gotten sick, I did have an arrangement in the works," he admitted.

My interest was piqued. "What kind of arrangement?"

"Turns out Roger had a weakness for high-priced call girls."

I scowled. "I don't even want to know how you knew that." I chewed on my lip, taking in this new information. It wasn't as if any of my previous relationships had really been ones that I'd wanted to continue. Every man I'd been with before Donovan had just been a placeholder, someone to fill my time while I waited and wondered if anyone could ever truly know and love me.

And all along there had been someone.

He just never bothered to tell me, instead choosing to watch quietly from the wings.

It took another hour to finish going through the rest of the folder. Close to the end, there were papers that showed he'd paid to move me to New York, that he'd negotiated the extra benefits in my employee contract. I was becoming numb to it by this point. I wasn't shocked anymore by new discoveries. I was overwhelmed, but no longer surprised.

Then I reached the final slim stack of papers that addressed Theodore Sheridan. I'd saved them for last on purpose. There was a narrative I had created about these documents, and I wasn't sure that I wanted to find out my story wasn't true.

I slid the pile across the table to Donovan. "Tell me about these."

"Those are the court papers for the trial against Theo Sheridan," Donovan said, gliding the pages right back to me. "He's currently serving time in a prison in upstate New York. He was sentenced to seven years. He's got four left."

A mystery that had been unsolved since college found its answer.

"You framed him at Harvard." It was an accusation, but it didn't carry judgment.

After Theo had assaulted me, he'd been arrested for possession of drugs with intent to sell. He'd had to drop out that semester. I'd never found out what had happened after that, though I'd searched online from Denver. I'd always had a feeling that Theo's arrest seemed too convenient. Too easy. But I hadn't ever really thought Donovan was involved.

"Those charges didn't stick," Donovan said dismissively, confirming my suspicion by not denying it.

"And so you set him up for a sexual assault charge seven years later instead?" I couldn't hide the hostility in my voice. I appreciated the intent. It was a sweet gesture, noble even. Of course he'd done it as revenge for me. But I had serious problems with sending a man to jail on trumped-up charges. I told him so.

Donovan tilted his head and stared at me with a strange expression on his face. "Those weren't trumped-up charges," he said slowly. "Theodore Sheridan *raped* Liz Stein."

And that was *exactly* what I didn't want to know.

"No," I said, shaking my head back and forth vehemently. I didn't want to believe it. I grasped for other possibilities. "You found someone, paid someone to say these things. For me. To get him back for what he did to me."

"Are you looking for honesty? Or do you want me to tell you what you want to hear?" It was remarkable how Donovan could be so obviously irritated and incredulous, and still retain a note of compassion in his subtext.

I didn't want compassion. I wanted the truth.

"I want you to be fucking honest. For fucking once. I want you to fucking tell me that you made this fucking happen."

His jaw worked. But he stayed silent, and the silence told me everything. That he'd already been honest. That he'd been honest all day. That the truth hurt.

I shot up from my chair and crossed to the window. I bit my lip and folded my arms across my chest, hugging myself. It looked cold outside, like the temperature had dropped. The snow banks at the side of the road lit up as cars passed them, the exhaust slowly discoloring their purity.

I didn't hear him, but I felt Donovan move up beside me. His hands were tucked safely in the pockets of his pants. He wouldn't dare touch me. Not after everything we'd gone through today. All the disclosures and revelations had been laid out, but had yet to be weighed. Who knew which way the scale would tip—in his favor or not?

Still, I could sense his desire to connect to me physically.

Or maybe that was me.

"I've only ever thought about myself," I said, my eyes never leaving the road below. "I thought about what people would say about me if I called the cops that night. What it would do to my life. I didn't once, for a single moment, consider what he might do to someone else." My voice was steady, but inside I was cracked. Theo hadn't even had his dick inside me, and he'd wrecked my life. What had he done to this woman? What had *I* done to this woman by letting him go free?

"You couldn't have changed anything. The only reason he's behind bars is because Liz Stein had a good case and a good lawyer. And she only got the good lawyer because I had people monitoring Theo so I could be there in case he ever got into trouble like this." He wasn't just being kind. It was rational. Somehow, I understood that.

It didn't relieve my guilt.

"I could have at least tried."

"I tried *for* you," he insisted, turning to face me. "I couldn't get the drugs to stick, even when he'd been caught with them. I had a better chance at that than you did with your assault case, and you know that. I'm sorry if it's hard to hear."

It *did* hurt to hear, even though I already knew. I'd always known. It was why I hadn't pressed charges in the first place. Because I'd always known that a girl crying assault at a college party—a scholarship girl no less, accusing a rich, white prep boy —never went anywhere.

Knowing didn't make it any less painful. Not then, not now.

I turned toward Donovan. "Tell me what happened to her. Tell me what he did to her. I need to know."

"If I tell you, are you going to hate yourself if you're turned on?"

Fuck you.

But I didn't say it. Because I couldn't promise either.

"Tell me how he did it."

Donovan regarded me briefly. "He worked on Wall Street. He met her in a bar that he frequented after work. Her friends abandoned her, so he volunteered to walk her home. He took the subway with her, walked her to her door, then asked to use her restroom before going home. Inside her bathroom, he saw her robe hanging on the back of the door. He pocketed the belt of the garment before joining her again. She offered him a drink.

"While she was making it, he came up behind her,

secured her wrists with the belt, shoved her up against the counter, pushed down her pants and penetrated her. He held his hand over her mouth so she couldn't scream. And when she fought too hard, he covered her nose with his palm as well so she couldn't breathe, until she settled down. He untied her before he left and threatened to ruin her and her family if she told anyone. She immediately went to a neighbor and they called the cops. He didn't use a condom. He came inside her which made it easy to collect his semen in the rape kit."

I wasn't turned on. I was sick.

I moved to lean on the conference table. It was horrible, and horribly true. Hearing her story brought back all the things that I remembered from my own night with Theodore. How he'd pushed down *my* pants. How he'd covered *my* mouth and *my* nose with his hand. How I'd fought. How it had been hopeless.

Until Donovan had shown up.

"He took her robe belt. She might've even just offered if he'd waited." And she might not have ever been there with him if I'd done something first.

"He's a predator, Sabrina. He's not interested in an offer."

Right. He was a predator.

But what about Donovan? Was *he* a predator? Was he interested in *my* offers? Or was he only interested in what he could take from my life without my permission?

I stared at my hands, angry with him, with Theo, with myself.

I walked back to where I'd sat, closed the file and slid the file across the table. I didn't want it anywhere near me anymore. I didn't deserve the good deeds inside it, and I didn't want to think about the mess that Donovan had cleaned up on my behalf.

"That wasn't so bad," he said, crossing back to where he'd sat, and I wasn't sure if he was saying that to me or to himself, but he did look a lot more relaxed than he had when we started.

Too bad I didn't feel the same.

"I'm not done yet," I said. I had one more question to ask, the question I'd been wondering for weeks. It felt even more relevant now that I'd wondered about the exact definition of a predator. "Are there cameras in my apartment?"

Donovan's skin seemed to sallow before my eyes. He paused. Then swallowed. "They're rarely ever on."

My stomach dropped like a boulder into the ocean. "But sometimes they're on."

"Sometimes they're on," he confirmed, heavily.

I knew this. In my heart of hearts, I knew this. Too many times, he'd known things. Things he shouldn't have known. About how little I slept. About the details of what I was doing.

"What do you watch?" I asked, my voice surprisingly steady, even though my heart felt like it was beating in erratic waves.

"I'm sure you don't need to ask that." His voice was low and warning.

"I'm asking because I'm imagining what you *could* watch. You might as well just tell me so I'm not imagining something worse." And I was very definitely imagining the worst, me at my most intimate. All the nights I'd used fantasies of him to lull myself back to sleep after being woken by nightmares from the past...

"You're not imagining something worse."

My skin prickled. My stomach twisted into knots. My skin

got hot, and my blood felt like it was boiling. A low level of rage had simmered beneath the surface of my emotions all afternoon. Now it bubbled to the top. It had been one thing when his violations were in the past. It was quite another to find out he was still invading my privacy, even now, even when we lived in the same city, even when all he had to do to be with me was *choose* to be with me.

I pushed my chair into the table so hard the other chairs rattled.

"Sabrina," Donovan implored. "Don't make this more than it is."

"Don't make this more than it is?" I echoed. "Which part? The part where you butt your way into every relationship I've had? Every job? Every situation I've been in—none of which you were ever invited to be a part of. That part? Or the part where you spy on me, like a common peeping Tom? Or did you mean the relationship that we have right now, the relationship where I actually wanted something with you, wanted something real with you? Where I asked you for it and I begged you for it, and you pushed me away? Is that what I'm not supposed to make too much of?"

I was trembling with anger and hurt.

Donovan rounded the table to approach me, reaching his arms out toward me in the way I'd wondered if he wanted to earlier. "Sabrina," he said again, softer.

"Don't!" I said, backing away. "I don't want this."

He lowered his arms, but he didn't move away from me. "You don't want what? You don't want *this*?" He pointed to the file. "Or you don't want *me*?"

I shook my head, unable to answer.

"Because they're one and the same, Sabrina. This file is who I am. You don't get one without the other." His tone was sharp.

It cut at me where I was already bruised.

"You never gave me a choice." The sum of everything I'd learned. My eyes were wet. I blinked to keep tears from falling.

"I'm giving you a choice now." He took another step toward me. "I fucked up when I pushed you away. But I'm here now. And you have to decide."

I shook my head again. He was so close I could reach out and touch him if I wanted to. And I had wanted to touch him for so long. The yearning and desire from the night before were still inside me, still layered just underneath my skin. Pressing at my edges, begging for his skin on mine.

But the wall that I had hoped would be gone after today was still there too, perhaps less thick than before, but a barrier just the same.

"I think this is enough for one day," I said, wrapping my arms around myself. "I'm ready to go home."

Whatever decision was going to be made, it was going to have to wait for another day.

NINE

I let Donovan give me a ride home. His driver was already at the curb when we got outside the building, and it seemed petty to refuse and wait for a cab. Especially considering how cold it was outside.

We were quiet as we drove through town. I couldn't even look at him. Instead, I stared out the window, my thoughts lost in the overwhelming scraps of discovery from the day. There were too many new pieces of information; too many things that startled me in beautiful and amazing ways. Pieces of my past I now had to look at through an entirely different lens, stories that took on entirely different meanings. Some of them moved me in ways I never thought I could be moved. As if I'd been a boulder stuck in mud that finally had enough rain washed upon it to sweep it down the mountain.

But some of it was too raw, or I was too raw. Donovan's symbols of affection felt like lemon juice against paper cuts.

He'd been well-meaning, maybe. But I never asked for that. I'd never asked for him. I'd never asked for his *invasion*.

The worst part was knowing how many times I would have wanted that invasion. How much of my life had been lonely? How many years had I longed for anyone, any *man* to love me? No, to *get* me. To understand. It wasn't fucking fair of him to love me in secret.

Dylan's description of the way Donovan had loved Amanda echoed in my mind. *Too much. Loved her too much.*

And now when we were finally together, Donovan pushed me away over and over in every way he knew how, all the while watching me, invading my most sacred moments...

Could I forgive him for that?

I didn't know if I felt betrayed or hurt or violated or desired, or all of those things combined. But I was wound up; my insides a whirlwind, a tornado.

Too much.

And next to me, Donovan sat still and quiet like he was in the eye of the storm. Like it didn't matter that I wasn't talking to him. Like it didn't matter that I had just put him on trial for the last several hours. Like it didn't matter that the jury was now out deliberating, and that the verdict didn't look good.

I was jealous of his ability to remain stoic. Of his ability to have no emotion.

Except it was a lie, and I knew it now. I had seen a whole file that proved how much emotion he had where I was concerned.

And yet sitting together in the backseat of his car, I felt further from him than I had in days.

I didn't know how to fix it.

I didn't know if I should even try.

When his driver pulled over to the curb in front of my building, I didn't wait for him to get out and open my door for me. I bolted. As if I could run from these volatile emotions within me. If I could just get far enough away from him, from Donovan, from the way he invaded and possessed and obsessed and cared...

Halfway to the front door of the building I came to a halt.

What was I doing? I was mostly angry because Donovan had kept himself away from me for so long, and now I was pushing him away further? How did that help things?

I didn't care anymore about what he'd done. As long as he didn't drive away. As long as he kept loving me *too much*. Maybe *too much* was *just enough* for me.

"Sabrina?" Donovan called from behind me.

I spun around and found his car still at the curb. He had slid across the seat. The back door was open; he was half out of the vehicle. "What's wrong?" he asked, his expression etched with concern.

"I don't care," I said testing the words out. Finding them true.

"What?" The note of hopefulness was unmistakable even in that one word.

"I don't care," I repeated, stronger.

He shut the door of the car, and in two strides he was at my side.

"Sabrina?" He said only my name, but I heard what he was really asking. I heard how eager he was for me to give him the words that I was feeding him.

"I don't care. I really don't. About any of it. I know I should. I should be mad. And I *am*, though not for the right reasons. I'm only mad because it took you so long to invite me in."

I had more to say, more to explain. But he cut me off, pulling me into him, his mouth crashing against mine. His lips were hot, his kiss desperate. Or maybe it was *my* kiss that was desperate. My hands were already all over him, wandering up inside his coat, stroking along planes of his chest, my hips grinding against his.

Too soon he pulled away. "I'm coming inside with you." Confident. Sure. As if it was his decision.

"I know."

There wasn't anywhere else I wanted him to be.

Donovan nodded to his driver, then laced his hand in mine and tugged me toward the building. We breezed past the doorman and caught an elevator that we shared with a father and his teenage daughter, the latter as distracted with her phone as I was with the heavy curtain of sexual tension between Donovan and me. I couldn't even look at him. I was certain that if I did, I would end up ripping off all my clothes despite the other people in there with us. Even the slight touch of his thumb rubbing up and down the length of my finger was almost too much, enough to make me wet and fully aroused. Ready to explode.

When we arrived at my floor, I stepped out, appearing calm and collected, despite the torrent of urgency inside me, with Donovan right behind me. But as soon as the elevator doors shut, I was rushing down the hall, swollen with need, my hand still laced in his.

At my apartment, he dropped my hand so he could move my hair from my neck. With his body pressed up behind me, his erection pushing into my ass, he kissed along my skin, nipping at the spot where my shoulder curved upward while I dug in my purse for my key. A door opened down the hall, and he stepped slightly away from me. He grinned politely at the elderly lady as she passed by us in the hallway, but under his breath he whispered to me in a low rumbling voice, "If you don't stop fumbling with that lock and get the door open, I'm going to fuck you in this hallway, and I don't give two shits about who watches."

I almost melted into the floor right there.

And hallelujah, the door finally opened.

I burst through the entry, not bothering to turn on the lights, dropping my keys and my purse and my coat as quickly as I got into the room. Stripped of my accessories, I spun around into Donovan who shut the door behind him with his foot. He tossed his coat on the floor.

And then we were there, in each other's arms, ravishing each other.

I moaned against his lips. His tongue was driven and aggressive, plunging inside my mouth, scraping against my teeth. I grabbed the edges of my sweater and pulled up, breaking from him only long enough to pull it over my head and toss it aside.

He took the moment our mouths were apart to push his hand under the waistband of my leggings, inside my panties to stroke along the length of my slit. When I met his eyes again, they gleamed with satisfaction, and I knew it was because of how wet I was. How drenched.

"Please," I begged, pushing into him. I got my hands under his pullover, plucking his shirt from his pants, desperate to feel his skin. "Please."

I was too frantic.

Donovan liked control.

With his free hand, he grabbed my wrists, and in one quick

motion whirled me around so that I was pressed against the wall. He held my arms stretched above my head, and I let out a groan of frustration. I needed to touch him. I needed to feel him.

"Donovan, I need—"

"I *know* what you need." Proving his words were true, his hand, which was still inside my pants, rubbed ruthlessly against my clit. My knees buckled at the intensity.

Jesus, I was going to come quickly at this rate.

"I've thought of so many ways I want to fuck you." He whispered in my ear. "So many ways I want to make you come. Every way I can imagine. That's how many ways I'm going to make you come. Every way I can imagine."

He maneuvered his hands so that his thumb was still pressing against my nub and his fingers could reach down lower, inside my hole. Two long fingers stroked inside me, massaging exactly the right spot. He didn't warm me up. He didn't need to. He didn't take his time. He went right for the kill, intent on making me come hard and fast.

And I did. Fast and hard, so hard I couldn't stand.

He let go of my hands so he could anchor his arm around my waist to hold me up while sonic waves of pleasure rippled through my body.

I hadn't even recovered when he turned me around again, turned us both around, so that he could walk me backward, his arm still around my waist, the other now snug in my hair. His mouth again claimed mine. Devoured mine.

And I was dizzy, dizzy, dizzy, and wanting more.

When I hit the back of the couch, Donovan lifted me up and set me on top. He broke away from me and pulled off my boots. Then I lifted my hips so he could pull off my leggings and panties. As soon as I was bare, I reached for the fly of his slacks, assuming the command before he gave it.

"Take out my cock," he demanded, his voice warm like scotch.

I was already halfway there, tugging first his pants down, then his boxer briefs, just far enough to get to the prize. Out he fell, heavy and thick, his angry pink tip dripping with pre-cum.

I threw my arms around his neck and wrapped my legs around his hips, pulling him toward me, pulling his cock toward the ache between my thighs.

He took his dick in his hand and dragged it down the length of my pussy, and for one terrible torturous second I feared he was going to torment me, tease me, make me beg before he filled me. But then his crown was notched at my hole, and, with his hands gripping my hips, he rammed inside me. Then again. And again. Over and over, pounding into me with a frenzy that matched the agitation within me.

"Fuck. There. Right there. Oh, shit."

I was an unneeded director. Even if he didn't know how to touch me, how to make me feel good, he wouldn't listen to me telling him what to do if he didn't want to. My commentary might even have provoked him to change tactics, because a moment later he was pushing my knees back so that my feet rested on the back of the couch. And now when he drove into me it was so far, so deep, it was as though he reached the very center of me.

He *did* reach the very center of me, I realized. Not just with sex, not just with his cock, but with everything he did. He was the only man I knew, the only man I'd ever met who could reach so far into me that he could see my darkest secrets and understand my most intimate self. Even before he'd manipulated my life and put cameras on me, even before he stalked me, even before he violated every bit of my privacy, he'd known me. He'd seen me. He'd noticed me.

Now he noticed me with his fingers tangled in my hair. He pulled my head back, exposing my throat, then with his free hand, he plucked down the cup of my bra and twisted my erect nipple between his thumb and finger until I squealed at the pain. Immediately he brought his mouth down to suck on it and soothe it, alternating licking with biting, sending jolts of shock and pleasure straight into my pussy, which throbbed and screamed, at the brink of coming again.

"No, I can't," I said, when he moved his hand down to brush against my clit. It wouldn't take much before I was erupting.

"You can," he insisted.

"No. No. I can't. It's too much." *Too much.*

"Keep saying no. That only makes me more determined." I could feel him grinning, even as he went back to nursing on my tit.

I clamped my jaw shut, intent on keeping silent, but my protests seeped out in high-pitched one syllable *no-no-no*'s.

Donovan angled his hips and rubbed his thumb and pulled at my nipple with his teeth in just the right, right way—that right way that only he knew. And then I was coming again, exploding. Trembling. Convulsing.

"Fuck, baby, that's it," Donovan urged. "Come all over my cock. Just like that." He shoved against me as I tried to push him out, his pace slowing as my pussy vice-gripped around him. He rode out my climax, a satisfied smile on his lips.

When he pulled out, his eyes moved down to stare at his cock, dripping with my cum.

"You look so pretty on my dick," he said. He stroked his

finger along the length of himself and rubbed my wetness along my lips. Hovering just above my mouth he whispered, "I bet you taste so pretty, too."

He kissed me, licking my cum into my mouth. I could taste myself. Sabrina-flavored lip gloss.

"Don't you think you taste pretty?" But he didn't let me answer, instead kissing the breath right out of me.

He didn't let it go on long, though. Soon he cut off sharply and pulled me down to the ground. When I was steady on my own, he let go of me and wrapped his fingers in the hem of his pullover. "Go to your bedroom. Take off your bra and your socks. Bend over the bed, your ass up, and wait for me." He didn't wait for me to leave before pulling both layers of shirts over his head.

I stalled, my eyes drinking in the sight of his naked chest. It had been so long since I'd seen it. So long since I'd touched it freely. I felt like an inmate who'd been newly paroled, drunk on the absence of bars between me and my man.

But that man didn't appreciate my delay.

"Go." He smacked my ass, and I dashed toward my bedroom.

Once there, I stripped the rest of my clothes off and situated myself on the bed like he'd asked—ordered, more like—tilting my head so I could peer in the direction of my door under my arm. I wanted to watch him walk in. Wanted to watch him see me. Wanted to watch as much as he'd let me see.

Was this how he'd felt all these years?

Maybe I understood that feeling more than I thought I did.

But even more than liking to watch Donovan—I liked it when he watched me.

He made me wait, arriving a long five minutes later, naked

now himself. He leisurely stroked his cock as he walked in, and I felt my jaw drop. He was magnificent. So magnificent to look at. Even in the dark, with only the light of the city streaming through the window. I'd already had two massive orgasms, and at the sight of him, all power and man, I was aching for him to be inside me again.

This time, he did taunt me. Instead of plunging inside me, he stared at me, his eyes glazed and filled with lust.

"Sabrina, you can't imagine the things I think about, seeing you like this." He came up behind me, and swiped his free hand across my wet pussy, dragging my cum up higher, to the rim of my asshole. "So, so pretty." He pressed his thumb just inside.

I bucked forward, surprised by the invasion.

But he persisted. "You'll let me in here, if that's where I want to be."

And I would. After every other invasion, it seemed almost inevitable. I did trust him. I had a safe word.

Still, I wasn't sure I was ready for that now. Not when what we had was still so fragile and, not *new*, exactly, but raw.

My heart sped up as he pushed in even farther. "Don't worry, Sabrina. Not tonight. But when I say."

Then his cock was at my entrance, sinking into me, slow this time, so I could feel the length of him as he fell in. His thumb remained where he'd put it inside my other hole, and with both parts of him filling me, I felt so full and tight, like I was inflating, like everywhere was being pressed against at once.

I let out a moan, long and low as he rode in and out, massaging all my nerve endings.

I couldn't think in words anymore. Couldn't think in details. All I was aware of was this feeling of abundance, a feeling that existed not just in my lower regions, but everywhere inside me. As though the tiny speck of contentment that existed in me at all times had suddenly ballooned, reaching out along every vein, along every bone to the ends of my appendages, from the top of my head to the ends of my toes. Tears gathered at the corners of my eyes, and the final orgasm that Donovan teased from me stretched and lingered like a new morning on a spring day, tightening and pulling, screaming from my being.

When everything was drained from me, I collapsed, listless, on the bed. Donovan secured his grip on my hips and pummeled into me, racing toward his own climax, eager to join me. Soon, his pace lagged and his thrusts deepened until finally he stalled. With a ragged grunt, he spilled his release inside me and fell on the bed at my side.

I opened my eyes, barely conscious, fighting against exhaustion. We had needed each other like this. Needed to let our bodies speak to each other in the dirty, filthy ways we knew best.

Now there were other things to be said. We had no course set for where to go from here. I needed a road map. I needed to know we were in this together. I needed to know exactly what *this* was. And I was afraid that if I let sleep take me, I'd be alone when I woke up later.

But when I met his gaze, steady and piercing, I realized the fear was unwarranted. Whether or not he was in my bed in the morning, I knew the truth now—Donovan was always with me. He never really left me alone.

TEN

"Have lunch with me," Donovan said, interrupting my daydreams.

I looked up to see him standing in the doorway of my office. I'd just been thinking about him, remembering the night before. When I'd stared into his eyes, dark and vague in color in the lightless room. *"What are you thinking?"* I'd asked.

"I'm thinking you probably want to be fed before I fuck you again. But I don't know if I care."

He'd left my house late in the night, but I'd seen him around the office already this morning. We'd brushed past each other at the Monday morning executive meeting, my body immediately going on high alert, and though our conversation had been benign, the tone and subtext of our meaning was heavy. *I belong to you. You belong to me.*

Even though we never actually said those words. We had barely said *any* words the night before, spending most of our time preoccupied with reacquainting ourselves with each other's physical landscape.

Which meant there was still part of our relationship in limbo. But wasn't every relationship in some form of limbo, until someone put a ring on it?

Shaking off the dizziness that the sight of him brought on, I rushed to see if anyone noticed him sneak into my office. Thankfully I saw no one but Ellen, my secretary.

"I can't go to lunch with you," I said, pulling him in and shutting the door behind him. God, just the touch of his hand on mine made my entire body spark.

"You can. Your schedule is free. I already checked with your secretary." His fingers were playing with mine, but my eyes were on his smirk.

"That isn't why I can't have lunch with you," I whispered, as if I'd be heard even behind the closed door. "People will talk."

He dropped my hand and crossed the room, turning to lean on my desk. "You have lunch with Weston, don't you?" He didn't look at me, instead poking nosily at the papers I had laid out on the workspace behind him.

"That's different. He's my boss." I walked over to my desk and straightened my papers as I spoke.

"*I'm* your boss." This time he gave me the full piercing weight of his hazel eyes, and I hated that I was going to have to defend Weston, but I was.

"You're not the boss I report to."

He let that sit for several seconds. It was impossible to refute. Weston was in charge of marketing. Donovan was in charge of operations. There wasn't a reason for me to have lunch with the chief of operations.

Unless I was banging him.

"So people will talk," he said, deciding where he stood on the matter.

I was flabbergasted. This was not the man I'd been with the last few months. That man had winced at the slightest hint of scandal between us. Yeah, things were different now, and he wasn't worried I'd find out his deep dark secret—that he'd been secretly in love with me for years. But just because things *were* different, I wasn't sure I wanted people thinking I was slutting it up with one of the presidents of the company.

"I—"

Donovan cut me off, apparently bored with the conversation. "Sabrina," he said, standing. "I don't give a fuck about other people. Come to lunch with me."

Twenty minutes later we were seated downstairs in the New York Minute Grill with our meals on the table in front of us. The restaurant had been Donovan's choice, proving how much he really didn't give a fuck about other people, seeing as how the New York Minute Grill was located in the very same building as Reach.

Quietly, I'd been on the lookout for anyone from the office for the first quarter of an hour, but despite the location of the restaurant, I hadn't seen anyone I knew and was forced to relax and admit it hadn't been a bad decision after all.

So a few bites into my pear pecan salad, I set down my fork, took a swallow of my ice water, and smiled at the man across from me. "Thank you for dragging me out of my cave."

It was actually really nice to be out in the open with Donovan. It was like a real date, and we hadn't really had one of those. Sure, we'd gone to the Japanese restaurant and Gaston's, but one had been a weird feeling-each-other-out scenario and the other had just been a precursor to sex. Today's meal was something else entirely. It was two people wanting to spend time together because they liked to spend time together.

"I had ulterior motives," Donovan said over his steak salad.

So much for two people wanting to spend time with each other.

"Of course you did." Why did I ever think anything different? "And they are?"

"Primarily, spending time with you."

Well, then. I felt my cheeks pink, delighted my initial feeling about our date was the correct one. Except, he did say *motives* in the plural.

"And?"

His grin made me feel he was impressed with my intuition. "And we left things unfinished last night."

I could feel the flush in my face deepen. I'd been thinking about last night all morning, but his mention of our carnal interlude made me as hot and weak as if he were undressing me.

"It sure didn't feel like we left anything unfinished." I shoveled a forkful of salad into my mouth, hiding my brazenness behind the act of chewing.

My body felt the aftermath of him. My thighs were sore; my stomach ached. The flesh between my legs was tender and raw from how he'd used me. How I'd let him use me.

"Oh, Sabrina." The rumble in his voice made my belly do back flips. "There are still a thousand ways I intend to make you come, and another hundred thousand I haven't thought of yet."

"Ah," I shivered, "I, uh, well. Sure." I drank half my glass of water just to cool down.

He laughed low in his throat. "That's not what I'm talking about, though. I think you know that."

"Actually, there *is* more to say." I'd meant to say more on the sidewalk before he'd come running after me and cut me off with that incredible kiss. "I said I didn't care. And I don't. But you should also know I felt a lot of other things too. Hearing about those things you did for me—for my family—it really stirred things inside me. Part of me is still pissed—"

"Understandably," he interrupted.

I ignored him, raising my voice ever so slightly. "I never asked you to do those things. I never expected it. You didn't have the right, but then, *didn't* you? Doesn't...*caring* about somebody give you a right?" He'd yet to say *"love"* himself since I'd brought it up that night in the back of his car, so I steered clear of that word in particular. "I don't know. I spent so many years as a girl with nothing in my pocket, daydreaming about a knight in shining armor. As so many young girls do. And don't we all wish the rich would give more to the poor?"

I laughed at myself then shook my head. "But this isn't about the money. Or this isn't *just* about the money. The time you invested... It means a lot. I know you're not looking for a thank you. I'm not going to give you one. I don't know if I'm exactly grateful. But I'm not exactly mad. And I am...moved. And turned on. In some way that I think is probably sick and unhealthy."

Donovan tsked. "You worry too much about what arouses you. If you're turned on, just go with it." His gaze drifted briefly down to the neckline of my blouse before returning to my eyes. "And I am not a knight in shining armor."

"No," I laughed. "You're not." I sobered. "And yet you are."

We held each other's gaze for several seconds. Something deep inside me tugged. Or tore. Or tightened. I dropped my eyes.

But I couldn't let him be a hero in this. That wasn't right either. "You're also the villain, don't forget that."

"Lucky for me you're the kind of girl who likes to fuck the villain."

I pressed my lips together hard, unwilling to acknowledge how true the statement was, even though we both knew it.

My stubbornness seemed to amuse him.

Then he grew serious.

"Fucking around is usually all the villain ever gets," he said, studying me to see if I understood what he meant.

I didn't. "I'm not sure what you're getting at."

"I'm asking what you see as happening next."

I sat up straighter in my chair, tension rolling down my spine. I'd been in this position before with Donovan. I'd laid it all out on the line, told him what I wanted. I'd gotten hurt.

"I don't know what to say," I said slowly, cautiously. "I don't know where to go next. What to—"

He helped me out. "Maybe start with telling me what you want."

I was silent. It wasn't—of course it wasn't—but it felt like a trap.

He shifted in his seat. "How about I start by telling you what I want?"

This. This sounded interesting. "Okay."

He wiped his mouth with his napkin then returned it to his lap before drilling his eyes into me. "I want more. I want a relationship. I want to be open about it. I want people to know we are together. No hiding or worrying about having lunch together. I want to be able to assume a blowjob comes with the meal." I bit back a giggle at that, which he noticed and acknowledged with a grin. Then, quickly, he was somber again. "What are the terms in order to get that?"

I blinked.

Just three weeks before, I'd proposed almost the same scenario, minus being open about our relationship and I'd said nothing about blowjobs—though I wasn't against them.

The whole idea made me giddy and lightheaded.

Terms, though. "What, we negotiate like a business deal?" I hoped he wouldn't notice how bothered I was by his choice of words.

Or maybe I hoped he did notice. I couldn't decide how passive-aggressive I wanted to be.

"If that's how you want to look at it."

Okay. Aggressive-aggressive then. Because that was not how I wanted to look at it at all.

"I don't. I mean, where's the romance?" I could hear myself, and it annoyed me. "God, I sound like my sister."

But annoyed as I was that I sounded like Audrey, I still wanted that. Still expected that. Still expected some sort of hearts and flowers from a man who supposedly loved me.

"Where's the *romance?*" His face wrinkled with disbelief. "I'm not asking you to prom, Sabrina."

I dropped my fork and threw my napkin on the table, no longer interested in my meal. The warm fuzzy feeling I'd had a few minutes ago had disappeared, leaving irritability in its wake. I was seconds away from going off, but before I said anything I would regret, I wanted to get full clarification. "What exactly *are* you asking?"

He pushed his dish aside and leaned over the table. "I'm asking who you need me to be in order to get you."

He was asking about the files. And the surveillance. And the ways he manipulated.

He was asking who he had to be to be with me.

My insides felt gooey like liquid chocolate. Goosebumps rose up my arms. I ran my teeth along my bottom lip, afraid I might get teary if I didn't keep myself together. After I'd caught my breath, I said, "I told you. I don't care."

I fiddled with the hem of the napkin and Donovan reached out to put his hand over mine. "You told me you didn't care about what happened in the past. You seem to care a lot about what's happening right now."

My brows pinched together. "I don't understand. If we are together, why would you need to do any of—"

My gaze landed on a Christmas tree in the lobby, the blue and gold ornaments as obvious as the realization that entered my mind. Even if we were together, even if we were a couple, Donovan had no intention of giving up his stalking, his interfering, his private viewing from the cameras in my apartment. He'd done all those things while he'd been with Amanda. It was how she'd ended up dead.

I moved my gaze back to his. "It's because that's who you are." He'd said it himself. Said it as plainly as he could.

He nodded, but doubled down by answering as well. "Yes, Sabrina."

"But you're asking who I need you to be..." I let out the air in my lungs, slowly. "So am I to assume that you're willing to give up some of who you are in order to be with me?"

He nodded again. "Or all of who I am. It's up to you to decide how much."

My stomach twisted and braided with both the intoxication of such crazy power and a little bit of disgust. Or a lot of disgust. And also something else—something sentimental and tender, some sort of emotion that would probably fit a lot better inside Audrey than in me.

But here it was inside of me all the same, and I had to figure out what to do with it and how to make decisions with it. I had to figure out how to answer the question that Donovan was waiting for me to answer now:

"So, tell me, Sabrina—who do you want me to be?"

ELEVEN

I needed a moment to process.

It had been less than twenty-four hours since I'd learned the extent to which Donovan had infiltrated my life in the last ten years. I still hadn't worked through all of the emotions I had about that. I hadn't been away from him long enough, hadn't had enough time to truly think and let it all sink in.

And here he was asking me to make major decisions based on those emotions?

It felt impossible.

Fortunately the waiter came then and left the tab at our table. Donovan swiped it before I had a chance to even offer.

"I don't expect you to pay for my every meal," I said. A prickly subject perhaps, but much safer than the one we were on before.

"I do." He pulled his gold card from his wallet. "I just told you I wanted a relationship. This is part of a relationship."

"Maybe in the 1950s. I'm a modern woman. You should let me take a turn now and then."

"Is that part of your terms, then?" He had me there. This subject was more related to the one before than I'd realized. He'd been my benefactor for years, hadn't he? Was that Donovan's idea of a relationship? Taking care of someone? Paying the bills? Coming to the rescue? Had he been taking care of me for too long? *Was* the ability to pay my own way part of my terms?

This was even more complicated to answer than it sounded. And it had already sounded complicated.

"You can pay for my lunch." I was chickenshit. It was easier than continuing the debate when I wasn't prepared to argue.

Donovan nodded with a knowing smile and caught the eye of the waiter as he passed by again. He handed him his card and I watched as the server disappeared, wishing I could look at the man across from me instead. Wishing I knew what to say.

"I can ask for his number when he comes back if you want me to," Donovan teased.

I glared in his direction. "I'm not interested in our waiter."

"He sure seems to have your attention."

I sighed. "It's not him who has my attention. It's you. Always you. I don't know how to answer you. I'm a bit overwhelmed here."

His forehead wrinkled as he considered. "Tell me what you need."

He sounded so sincere, and why shouldn't he? He was good at that. Good at giving me what I needed. I just never realized how good he was at it. I wondered if it was as hard for him to share it with me now as it was for me to understand the fullness of it.

"I need some time to think." I needed time to put things into boxes, sort out the good from the bad. Divide the right from the wrong.

Or maybe it was all wrong.

He paused, and in that pause I could see his doubt. I could feel his concern. I wanted to reassure him, but before I could, he gave me my release. "Take all the time you need."

———

AN HOUR LATER, I sat at my desk in front of ad sketches for a new electronics line, barely seeing them. I was supposed to be creating a timeline for product release, but instead I was reviewing my mental notebook of all the instances Donovan had interfered in my life. I was still collecting inventory and hadn't gotten to the point of breaking down which were good and bad when I realized my stupid mistake—I'd given him the wrong answer.

I didn't need time to think. I should have been able to answer instantly. I could kick myself over it. Immediately, I called down to his office but was told he was in meetings all afternoon. My revelation would have to wait.

So as soon as Ellen was gone for the day and the halls began to darken, when all but the most committed employees made their way home for the evening, I locked up my office and headed down to his.

His secretary Simone was at her desk, her purse on her shoulder, obviously about to leave.

"He's on the phone," she said, a fact that was evident since the walls to his office were currently clear and there he was behind his desk, the receiver cradled under his neck. "But you can go right in."

Uh...odd.

First, it was unusual for him to keep his glass clear. Was that because, as I'd always suspected, he'd kept them opaque to hide from me? Did his transparent walls now suggest a greater transparency than just the literal one in front of me?

Also strange was the permission to walk right in. The last time I'd tried to see Donovan in the office, Simone had, at Donovan's behest, requested I make an appointment.

Things really were changing between us.

Emotion lifted in my chest, a contradiction to the grimace on Simone's face. Apparently she wasn't as happy with the change in events as I was.

Yeah, I got it, sister. If I were his secretary, I'd have a crush on him too.

Ignoring her pout, I thanked her and moseyed over to the doorway as the click-clack of her heels sounded her exit down the hall behind me. I leaned against the frame, much the way he'd leaned against my doorframe earlier in the day. Simone may have instructed me to go on in, but I preferred to have an invitation from the man himself.

He looked up at me immediately, a sly smile forming on his lips as he continued his phone conversation.

Warmth spread within me. It was a nice thing to feel wanted.

"I'm glad I could help you out," he said into the phone. "Or *not* help you out, as the case may be. I'll pull my man off the case immediately."

He was quiet for a moment, obviously listening, but all the while he ate me up with his gaze. Slowly, he traced up my

Dolce & Gabbana knee-high boots, higher along my tight-fitting pencil skirt. Then he scaled the curve of my abdomen and the swell of my breasts to follow the arch of my neck, the line of my lips.

By the time he reached my eyes, my skin was hot and my panties were slick. He shifted in his seat and I wondered if he was turned on.

"I hate to interrupt you Cade, but an urgent matter has just made itself known." He paused, and I bit back a giggle. "No, no. Nothing to worry about. I can handle her. Er, it. I'll see you later this week."

I crossed my arms casually across my chest. "Cade *Warren?*" It wasn't my fault that I'd been eavesdropping. He'd been the one to leave the door open. "Was that the Cade you were talking to?"

Cade was the fifth founder of Reach. He ran the Tokyo office and rarely made it to the United States. As such, I hadn't met him yet.

"Yes, as a matter of fact. He was having a little trouble finding someone he used to know. I was helping him out with some of my resources." Donovan leaned back in his chair and crossed one leg over the other at the knee.

"You are good with those resources, aren't you?" Everything he'd done for me without me knowing? That took a man who knew people.

"That I am. But he's found who he's looking for now. So he doesn't need me anymore." With barely even a breath to note the change in subject, he said, "I'm hard."

"Because of Cade?" I teased. "Apparently he'll be here later this week for Weston's wedding. We'll have to make sure you two schedule some alone time."

Weston's *fake* wedding. It seemed silly that Cade was traveling halfway across the world for that. But I was looking forward to meeting him.

"Not because of Cade." With a nod of his head he gestured for me to come farther into the room.

I waited a fraction of a beat then pulled the door closed behind me. Anyone lingering around the office might be able to see us through the glass, but they didn't need to hear this conversation. It was private.

"Something on your mind?" he asked as I walked toward his desk. "Because if you just stopped by to visit, I am more than willing to occupy your time."

I had to clench my thighs together to distract myself from the buzz between them. There'd be time for that later. There'd be time for everything later.

First...this.

"I wondered if your offer was still on the table." My voice sounded breathier, more seductive than I meant it to. Or maybe it was exactly as seductive as I meant it to sound.

"Why yes, Ms. Lind." Even with his devilish grin, his statement managed to sound sweet. "Are you ready to get down on your knees?"

I rolled my eyes. "We're still negotiating."

He raised a brow. "Then you're ready to negotiate?"

"I'm ready, yes. I'm ready to tell you what I want." I felt shaky all of a sudden, excited. I was eager to say what I had to say.

If he was nervous, he didn't show it. "Sit," he said, and pointed at the chair across from him.

"Like a real business meeting." I slunk down in the chair. I crossed my legs, letting my skirt ride up my thigh. "Nice." I was being sassier than I needed to be simply because the business terms still prickled at me.

"Keep provoking me, Sabrina, and we'll both have a good evening."

A delicious shiver ran down my spine. I had to keep focused. Because the sooner I got through this, the sooner I'd have his mouth on me.

And I really needed his mouth on me.

"I hope that's a promise," I pushed one more time.

It was perhaps pushing a little too far because his response was serious. "What do you want, Sabrina?"

I swallowed, letting my tone match the somberness of his. "You. I want you."

My words hung in the air like the tinsel and the mistletoe of the season. Donovan heard them, absorbed them. I saw them sinking into his skin, saw the flicker of his eyes as they started to form meaning inside him.

I went on.

"I wanted you at Harvard. I couldn't admit it to myself back then, but I wanted you. I wanted you all the years we were apart. Every night in the dark, it was you I thought about. I wanted you when I got here, from the moment I saw you. I wanted you even when I was with Weston. I wanted you when you flew across the ocean to get away from me. And when I found the file showing me all the ways I had you? I wanted you all the more."

He tilted his head just a bit to the right, not enough to disturb my train of thought. Just enough to show he was listening.

"And if that file represents who you really are—which isn't

all of you, trust me, but let's say it's a significant part of you—then I don't want to change any of that."

Not any of it.

Okay, maybe some of it. Small modifications. But we'd get there momentarily.

Donovan's eyes narrowed. "I don't think you know what you're saying, Sabrina."

"Don't do that. Don't patronize me like that. I know what I'm saying. I'm saying go ahead and butt in. Interfere. Take care of me." Wasn't that what even Cinderella wanted?

He started to say something else, but I jumped in. "With some understandings in place."

"Right. Terms." He didn't sound angry about the idea. In fact, he seemed quite comfortable with this direction. "Name them."

I glared at his word choice but decided not to argue about semantics. "Mainly, transparency. I want to know what you're up to. If you're maneuvering things behind the scenes, I want to be behind the scenes with you." I winked, just because it sounded dirty.

"The benefit of maneuvering behind your back," he said purposely changing my choice of words, "is that I don't have to justify myself to you." Apparently he *did* want to argue over semantics.

"Oh, like you mean if I might not agree with your choices for *my life*?" I over-enunciated the words '*my life*'.

"Something like that." His lips were tight, his jaw tighter.

"Then I guess we'll argue about it until one of us wins, like all couples do. I think that's the very definition of a relationship."

I stared hard at him.

His shoulders loosened as he chuckled. "How very quaint."

My mouth gaped and I fluttered my eyelashes in bewilderment. "Were you not serious about negotiating terms? Was that just a thing to say to sound noble?"

"Were you not serious when you said you took me how I am?"

I scowled. He smirked.

I must've won because then he said, "Yes, I was serious. Very serious. If you need transparency, I'm happy to give it to you." His teeth were clenched as he said it, but his expression seemed sincere.

I believed him anyway.

"Thank you. I appreciate that." *Point for me.*

Scratch that. *Point for* us.

"Is there anything else you desire, Ms. Lind?"

There was so much I desired. And all that was wrapped up in on Armani suit and sitting two and a half feet away from me.

"Along with transparency, I think honesty is a given. But I'll mention it anyway because it's important." This was mandatory. I would not tolerate lying. "I need to know that everything is out in the open. That there are no more secrets. I don't care if you have someone tailing me and I'm unaware. I'm pretty much going to assume that for the rest of my life now, you know. But decisions that affect my life? Those things can't be kept from me. You have to tell me, or it's a deal breaker."

He nodded before I'd finished my monologue. "Of course."

"I mean it, Donovan. I know you're a secretive person. Things affecting me though, you have to keep completely out in the open." I sounded redundant. But it was well worth repeating.

"I get it. Complete honesty."

He was already looking me straight in the eye, and I didn't want to beat a dead horse, but I had to be sure. "And there's nothing from the past? Nothing left that I don't know? Now would be the time to tell me if there is."

He paused as if mentally going through a tally of the years, making sure that everything was checked off. It was a little unsettling that he couldn't answer right away. I would've been even more unsettled if he had.

"Everything was in that file," he said after a few seconds. "You know everything."

"Okay." I let out a slow breath of air that I didn't know I'd been holding. "Okay," I said again. We were really doing this.

"Then we've come to an agreement?" Donovan asked with a tone that hinted of hopefulness.

I considered but was already nodding.

"And exclusive commitment," I added, as he got up from his chair and walked around to lean on the other side of the desk just in front of me.

"We already have an exclusive commitment. So that goes without saying." He was semi-aroused. Hard to miss when his crotch was now at eye level, but let's face it, I probably would have looked anyway.

"Except we've never said it. I had no idea you weren't sleeping with anyone else." I pressed my hand along the inside of his knee. It was right there. It was impossible to resist.

"If you had any idea what goes on inside of me, Sabrina, you would know—I'm not sleeping with anyone else. There's not going to be anyone else."

I pushed my hand flat, on his inner thigh and stood so we were face to face. "You know that's what all cheaters say."

"I guess you'll just have to trust me." His thigh muscle flexed under my palm.

"And I guess you'll just have to... Well. You have private eyes on me." My hand drew closer to the bulge in his pants. He was now fully erect.

Before I could reach the prize, however, he grabbed my hand and brought it to his lips. He sucked one long finger into his mouth. "And are those private eyes going to bother you?"

"The private eyes won't." I shivered as he drew my next finger into his mouth along with the first. "I'd like the cameras off, though."

"We'll only use them to make dirty movies." Three fingers in his mouth now, and I wondered if I'd be able to come just from this. "And you agree we can be public?"

This one I'd been iffy about. On the one hand, we couldn't really have a grown-up relationship if we were sneaking around everywhere. On the other hand, his reputation was secure. Mine, not so much. I was still really new to the company. I didn't need my whole team thinking their leader was only here because she was fucking the boss.

Though it was kind of true. Just wrong boss.

"How about we don't announce anything?" I offered as a concession. "We can be private without being secretive. We don't need to be obvious."

He rocked his head back and forth, considering, then drew all four of my fingers into his mouth, sucking on them hard before answering. "I suppose I can agree to that."

Next, he licked his tongue along the surface of my palm. I shifted my weight from one hip to the other, entranced by the erotic tingles that traveled down my spine.

I had no idea how I had the sense to remember the last

thing I had on my agenda. But somehow I did. "Oh, and I'd appreciate a little more romance."

His eyes burned into me. "And I'd appreciate a few more hand jobs."

I nodded as his mouth closed down over mine. His kiss was teasing, nipping at my lips. He pulled my hand down to his pants, a silent command, and I began unbuckling him eagerly.

"Darken the glass," I whispered against his lips.

"I'll worry about the glass. You worry about my cock." He didn't darken it.

So much for not being obvious.

We'd played this scenario out before, touching each other when others were nearby. The risk of being seen thrilled me to no end. My heart was pounding. I was breathy, as though it were his hands on my sex organ rather than my hands on his. Some responsible area of my brain shouted a warning to me, begging me to ignore the high I was riding and demand some privacy.

But another part of me reasoned: it was late. Most everyone was gone. And hadn't I just agreed to let him take care of me?

So he'd take care of me. He'd watch out to make sure we weren't caught. And in return, I'd take care of *him*.

His cock was thick like steel in my hand, still wet from his attention. It was slick enough to run down the length of him, up and down. A burst of pre-cum formed at his tip and I drew it down his shaft, pumping him the way I knew he liked. Soon he wrapped his hand in my hair and pulled my face up so he could kiss me as I stroked him. Deep, lush, possessive kisses. Kisses that told me exactly the way he imagined fucking my cunt.

It was so fucking hot. His mouth. The low groans in the

back of his throat. Knowing there could be anybody walking by behind us made me moan along with him.

When he was close, he broke his kiss so he could ask, "Where do you want it?"

I was prepared to swallow, but I'd let him choose. "Wherever you want to put it."

"I want to put it on your tits."

My knees buckled. Thank God he was holding onto me or I might've lost my balance. The image sounded so sexy.

But the windows...

"Trust me, Sabrina." He could read my hesitation every fucking time. "Or don't. But you have to hurry." The strain of his voice told me, even if his words hadn't, how near he was to climax.

"Unbutton my shirt," I told him without another minute's pause.

He was fast, and my shirt was undone and my bra cups tugged down before I could second-guess myself. Then he put his hand over mine, taking over the action of the hand job. I knelt down as he stood, just in time. With a guttural moan, he shot his load over my bare breasts. Cum dripped along my décolletage, down over my nipples. I was covered with him.

I peered up and grinned, feeling as satisfied as if I'd been the one to orgasm.

He matched my grin with one of his own. After tucking himself away, he helped me to my feet. "If I offered to go get something to clean you up, would that count as romantic?"

Considering how sex had ended often for us in the past... "I'd say that's a good start."

THE NEXT AFTERNOON, I received flowers by delivery. A large beautiful mixed bouquet that was impossible to miss as the deliveryman walked in through the office. Everyone was talking about them, about who sent them. At least that's what Ellen said when she brought them in to me.

"Some are saying you have an admirer," she said. "But most are sure you must be seeing someone."

Yeah, the secret wasn't going to last. Particularly since it seemed like Donovan didn't care if it didn't.

Well, people could talk. It didn't mean they *knew*.

"Are they from Kincaid?" she asked.

Okay, she knew. And if *she* knew, it wouldn't be long before *everyone* did.

"I guess I should open the card." I found the envelope buried in the stems and tore it open. Inside was a simple note in Donovan's handwriting. He must have gone into the shop and ordered them in person. *Would you be my date for prom (a.k.a. Weston's wedding)? –D.*

He definitely had no intention of keeping our relationship low key. If I showed up as his date to Weston's wedding, everyone in the office would know we were together.

But, wow.

What a way to ask. Here was the romance I'd requested. My heart was racing and I could feel the flush on my cheeks.

Suddenly, I didn't really give a fuck who knew about us either. I would go to his prom with him. I would be his date.

In fact, I couldn't think of anything better.

TWELVE

"Holy shit," I exclaimed as we walked past the divider in the middle of the ballroom, leaving the ceremony portion of Elizabeth and Weston's wedding to go to the reception. Everything about the event was incredible, from the décor to the uniforms of the wait staff. The location itself was very highbrow—the Park Hyatt's Onyx Ballroom, a luxurious venue, steeped in glamor with floor-to-ceiling watercolor panels.

"That's what I said when I saw you walk out to the car this morning," Donovan said, squeezing my hand.

I heard him, and my chest did a silly little flutter, but I was too wrapped up in the scene in front of me. Though it had been an early evening wedding, hors d'oeuvres were the only food being served. There were probably too many guests to accommodate a full-service dinner logistically. But it was an open bar, and the food on the trays that the waiters passed seemed substantial. A live band played jazz music, and there was a table with a nice sized-gift bag for every guest to take upon their departure.

"All this for a fake wedding?" I wouldn't even do this much for a *real* wedding. Of course I'd always planned on eloping somewhere, so maybe I wasn't the best judge.

"Hush." Donovan scanned the nearby vicinity to make sure nobody had heard me. "You want to be careful what you say. Elizabeth apparently has a few family members suggesting this marriage is a sham. There's nothing like a fifty-thousand dollar wedding to say true love."

My jaw might have dropped.

Well, if that's what it took to access her trust fund... I assumed her inheritance was exponentially more.

"I guess I'm amazed she could pull it off so quickly." They'd only had a handful of months to plan the whole shebang. If I ever *did* get married, I was definitely hiring her wedding planner to handle everything.

And why was I thinking so much about my own possible wedding? Spending so many nights with Donovan the past week, maybe. Funny how having a relationship got me thinking long term, even when it was such a newly formed relationship.

"It helps to have friends." He pulled two glasses of champagne off a tray as a waiter passed and handed one to me. "The hotel belongs to the father of a friend of mine. Elizabeth knew the woman who brought in the flowers. Her wedding dress came from Mirabelle's. Mira is Hudson Pierce's sister. Hudson has done some business with Reach recently, as you know. They agreed to only one attendant each, which made the rehearsal quick and simple for everyone, especially when Weston realized Brett would be a more enthusiastic best man than I would. It all came together."

"You mean, *you* made it come together." If there was one thing I was learning about Donovan, it was that he knew how to maneuver. Knew how to pull strings. No wonder he'd once had the nickname The Puppet Master.

"I know what's important. And this is important." He took a swallow of the champagne then so I couldn't read his expression. Couldn't tell if the importance was because of the business merger this union created, because he believed in their marriage, or because it had made Weston unavailable to me.

Perhaps it was a little bit of all three.

"For what it's worth, I don't think you have anything to worry about on the believability front." I raised my voice just slightly in case anyone nearby was listening in. "It's obvious how much love they have for each other. They gazed at each other during the ceremony like no one else existed in the universe." I lowered my voice. "I actually mean that."

He frowned skeptically. "We'll see. There's already a pool going around with the guys on how long before they file for annulment."

"Isn't filing for annulment part of the plan?" I whispered.

He smiled and nodded at someone across the room. "It is," he said through his grin, "but a date hasn't been set for it yet. It was left to be determined. The guess is how long they'll last. Do you want in?"

It was my turn to frown. "No, I do not." I didn't know what bothered me so much about it. We'd made bets on Weston regarding Elizabeth before. But that was when I truly believed that they were just pretending their way through this whole thing.

Now I wasn't so sure that they were. "It doesn't seem right to bet against somebody's happiness."

My date swung his attention back in my direction. "Jesus. You really believe this could work out, don't you? That's cute."

"Thank you for being so patronizing. I truly appreciate it," I said sarcastically, folding one arm over my breasts so I could sip my drink with a scowl. So apparently he didn't believe in their relationship. It stung for some reason, as though he'd said he didn't believe anyone should get married, and as though I cared what he thought on the matter.

And maybe he didn't. He'd once been engaged, but he might have changed his perception of the ritual, but why I cared about his opinion was unbeknownst to me. It wasn't like we were getting married.

"No, I really mean that. You're adorable." He tugged my hand away from my chest and pulled me toward him. "I'm not saying I don't believe in marriage," he said, as though he knew exactly what I was thinking. "I'm saying that this marriage has obstacles. Weston is a playboy. He hasn't stayed with one woman for longer than two weeks in his life, and here you are with faith in him. I think that's cute."

His mouth was near mine but before he could kiss me, I said, "That's not true. He's been faithful for months to Elizabeth." I tipped my chin up, cueing him to press his lips to mine.

"Then the rumors are true," an unfamiliar voice exclaimed beside us. "Donovan Kincaid has found himself a girlfriend."

Instinctively, I backed away from the man I'd been about to kiss. I'd accepted that people were going to talk about us—I really had—but it was one thing to say I was cool with it and quite another to actually *be* cool.

"I'm the one who told you that rumor, you asshole," Donovan said clapping the back of the stranger in front of us. He was of average height; his hair cut short, almost military style. He appeared to be in his mid-thirties, bulky where Donovan was lean. Hard where Donovan was chiseled. Mean where Donovan was mischievous. "Sabrina, this is Cade Warren. Cade, I told you about Sabrina."

"No. You told me about our new Director of Marketing Strategy. *Weston* told me about Sabrina." He shook my hand in greeting—a firm shake, just gentle enough to prove he remembered he was shaking the hand of a woman. "Pleasure to meet you. Everything I've heard has been quite... complimentary."

I bit down the anxiety threatening inside. I hated not knowing what he had learned from Weston versus what he had learned from Donovan, but at least it had been Donovan who had told him we were together.

I also hated that I knew almost nothing about Cade except that he worked in the Tokyo office. It made it hard to make small talk.

Fortunately, Donovan knew things about him, and he came to my rescue.

"Cade's story that he's here for the wedding is only a cover," he said—a pointed jab at his partner. "He's really in the States to meet up with a woman from the past."

Cade's eyes narrowed. "Hey—"

"Payback's a bitch." Donovan wrapped his hand around my waist and pulled me in to his side, possessively.

I liked it. A lot.

"But that was supposed to be a secret," Cade said with a note of menace.

I knew good and well that Donovan wasn't afraid of Cade. But maybe he should have been. Cade seemed tough. The kind of tough that covered up that he had once been broken. Broken badly.

I knew that kind of broken.

But I'd never seen this kind of tough. It was a myth, as far as I'd been concerned. I'd never believed people could build walls that strong.

Apparently I was wrong.

People with walls that strong were to be feared. They didn't have anything to lose.

"Sabrina and I have no secrets," Donovan said, his thumb drawing circles on my hip.

Goosebumps shot down my skin from his touch and from the words he said. It felt good to hear them. To know that they were true.

"Well, isn't that precious?" Cade rolled his eyes. He seemed like the kind of guy who didn't believe in relationships that required no secrets. He probably didn't believe in weddings either. A hundred bucks said he'd made the first bet in the 'Weston and Elizabeth get an annulment' pool.

"Don't worry," I assured Cade, because I was more than a little afraid of the man, even if Donovan wasn't. "Your secret is safe with me."

He grinned. "It's a good thing too. With you dating this guy, you're gonna need all the friends you can get." He turned his focus to my date. "How long do we have to stay at this thing anyway?"

But I wanted to address what he'd just said about me.

I put my hand on his bicep, which was larger than it had first seemed under his tuxedo. "Oh." *Shockingly* larger.

Anyway. "Wait a minute—what do you mean 'I need friends'? Are people talking? People are upset that I'm dating him, aren't they?"

He took a swig of the beer he'd been holding and shrugged.

"You're dating one of the bosses. And you're fuckhot. And from what I hear, smart as shit. Of course people are talking. Have I heard anything? No. But look at them." He gestured at the crowd around us. "There's sure a lot of whispering and glances."

"It's because it's our coming-out party," Donovan said. "They're surprised. That's all. Ignore them, Sabrina. Ignore him." To Cade he said, "And you need to stay until the bride and groom arrive. They're getting their photos taken and then they'll be in."

"Fine." Cade took another swallow from his bottle, and when he did, I noticed the edge of a tattoo as his sleeve pushed up on his arm. "I'll stay until then. But then I'm out of here."

Yeah, this guy did not do weddings.

This guy did not do romance.

I made a mental note to ask Donovan where he found him later on. He seemed more like ex-military than a guy who ran an international advertising firm in Japan.

But I knew better than to judge by appearances. And I knew better than anyone that smart, creative people came from all walks of life.

"Maybe we should mingle while we're waiting," I suggested. I, at least, needed to say hello to the people from our office. I didn't want to appear stuck-up on top of everything else.

Cade let out a hearty laugh. "You're still trying to win their hearts aren't you? She's cute, Donovan."

I pressed my lips together tightly so they didn't say anything that I'd regret to the man that I just met, who was technically one of my bosses.

Donovan surveyed me, likely noting the glare I was holding back, and let out a laugh of his own. "I was just saying that." He moved his hand to my neck, just below where my hair sat tightly in a knot. His fingers on my sensitive nape sent shooting stars of want down my spine. "It looks like a bunch of the staff is gathered by the bar. We can go say 'hello.'" Then he bent in so that Cade couldn't hear him. "He's a dick, but he's a good guy. I'll make it up to you later."

I didn't know what exactly he was making up to me, or why he considered any of it his fault except that he'd been the one who'd wanted me to come with him to this thing. But the feel of his breath on the shell of my ear and the promise of something good to come was enough to make me relax. A bit.

"I'm holding you to that."

We'd just made it over to the bar when a buzz spread through the crowd, not just directly around us, but throughout the ballroom.

"Ladies and gentlemen," I recognized the voice that came across the speaker system as Brett Larrabee, Weston's best man and a fellow student from Harvard. "It's time to welcome, for the first time, Mr. and Mrs. Weston and Elizabeth King."

Applause erupted as the couple entered the room holding hands. Both were smiling, but neither looked at the other, each directing their attention at their guests.

Was it all an act? Were the glances passed between them just for show?

It was one thing to be sleeping together. It was quite another to be married and be serious about it.

Maybe Donovan was right. I'd likely spent too much time recently with my sister. Just because Weston was having a good time with his business arrangement didn't mean he'd found a happily ever after.

"They do a lineup or something, don't they?" Cade asked, finishing his beer with one long swallow.

"I think they plan to mingle," Roxie said, as our group joined hers.

"Fuck this. It will take forever for them to get through all these people. I'm taking off." Cade tossed his bottle into a nearby trashcan. "Can I borrow you for a moment, Donovan? It was nice meeting you, Sabrina. I'll probably see you around the office before I head back to Tokyo."

"Ditto." It seemed safe enough. Polite but noncommittal.

Donovan looked to me as if asking my permission. I scanned the faces of those gathered, noting who I'd be left with if he abandoned me. There weren't many staff members. Not many had been invited, mainly just the top employees who worked under Weston. My team members, Roxie, and a few other key staff members. Basically all the people who'd be the most pissed at the advantages I'd gain at dating the boss. In other words, I'd be alone with the wolves.

No. Not the wolves. My staff. My people.

"Go ahead. I'll be fine." I didn't know if it made things better or worse that he kissed me on the cheek before walking out to the lobby with his partner.

"You came with Donovan?" Roxie didn't even wait until he was out of earshot. He glanced back at me at the sound of his name, and I tipped my head up in reassurance. I had this.

I didn't have this.

"Uh, yeah. I did. He's my date. He's my..." *Say it. Just say it, Sabrina,* I willed myself. "I guess we're seeing each other." *Chicken.* "No guessing. We *are* seeing each other."

"Ah," Roxie said, a whole ton of subtext in the single syllable, and hell if I knew what any of it was.

Tom Burns, my lead team member, on the other hand, was pleasantly surprised. "Good for you." I hadn't really talked to him about me and Donovan, but he had walked in on an inti-mate moment and had a pretty good idea there was something going on between us besides a working relationship. He'd encouraged me to pursue it. "Glad to see you two together."

"Yeah. Me too." I didn't mean to sound so sketchy about it. I really was glad. Just nervous, too.

"Speaking of dates, this is my wife Daisy," he said, gesturing to a petite blonde with bobbed hair. "She just talked me and Frank into going off in search of more cream puffs."

"And more of those grilled shrimp kebabs," she added, eagerly.

"And shrimp kebabs. Got it. Would you like to add anything to the order, Sabrina?"

"No, thank you. You can take my empty, though, if you like." I handed him my champagne glass, which I'd been carrying around for the last several minutes even though it had nothing in it.

"Sure thing. We'll be back." He took off with Frank, Roxie's husband, in tow.

As soon as they were gone, Daisy's infectious smile disap-peared. "So. Sabrina. Tom's been with Reach since it opened. Worked his way up from the bottom. Then you came in and stole that top position right from under his nose. By all rights, that promotion should have been his. And now we find out you're sleeping with one of the main men? That's not fishy at all."

Every muscle in my body tensed. My throat felt like I'd swallowed a desert instead of Moscato.

"Not just *one* of the main men," Roxie added. "I still say she and Weston were together to begin with."

I gaped, unsure what to say. I wanted to defend myself,

defend my talent and resume, but nothing they said was untrue.

And I'd expected this might be a problem, but not from Tom Burns. Not from his wife. Not from Roxie. She was supposed to be my friend!

"I'm so sorry, Ms. Burns," I stammered. "I didn't—"

Daisy suddenly burst into laughter. "I'm just fucking with you. You should've seen your face." Roxie joined in the hysterics.

"Then ... you're *not* mad at me?" I was confused. Relieved, but confused.

"Mad?" She shook her head, her hair bouncing as she did. "I'm grateful. Tom wanted that promotion, but we have three kids. I would never have seen him, and I didn't want to be a single parent. I'm grateful they found someone competent instead of persuading him to make the jump. And Tom says you're good! Glad to see more women in those exec positions. Congratulations!"

Roxy was still laughing. "Her face. Her face!"

And now I was laughing a bit too. "Thank you. I think."

"I bet you get those kinds of comments all the time," Daisy said. "I should know. I work in an office with all men myself. Real estate. Men don't think we know how to sell anything except our bodies, am I right? But I have the second-highest sales in my team this year. Look at us go!" She patted me on the arm, as though we were old chums now.

"Go us!" I said awkwardly. I liked her. Despite her strange teasing and the fact that it was hard to get a word in edgewise, she was spunky and fun. I was neither. It was always nice to find common ground with someone different.

"If anyone gives you a hard time about dating that fine piece of Kincaid—which all the ladies are jealous about, by the way—don't you even listen to them. You do you, girl. Stand up proud knowing that you deserve to be where you are." Her eyes scanned the crowd as she talked. "Roxie, Frank got distracted by the fondue again. If we want our food, we're going to have to go get it ourselves."

With Roxie and Daisy gone, I looked around and realized the rest of the staff had dispersed too. I wasn't so sure that they were as unbothered by my relationship with Donovan as Tom and Daisy—I'd seen the uncomfortable exchange of looks as we approached—but Daisy was right. I needed to do me. And I did deserve to be there. Even though I *had* fucked not one, but two, men to get there.

Turning, I casually looked for someone to engage with. I spotted a client across the room, but I didn't want to end up talking shop, so I waved instead. Nate Sinclair was nearby, a woman I didn't recognize on his arm. He seemed engrossed in conversation with the couple standing next to him, and I didn't want to interrupt. Elizabeth was taking selfies with the trio of older ladies—aunts, if I remembered correctly from her engagement party. Weston was no longer with her. They must've separated from each other in their mingling.

I searched for him, looked for his face amongst the sea of tuxedos and suits, and then stopped suddenly, my heart racing faster, when it landed on a familiar profile. One I hadn't seen in ten long years. His face was fuller than I remembered, his hair shorter, his neck longer.

But I'd never forget that jawline. Never forget those eyes that invoked pure terror in me.

No way in hell would I ever forget Theodore Sheridan.

THIRTEEN

I was frozen. Torn between moving closer to be sure it was him and running far, far away. The oxygen in the room felt thinner. My lungs felt weaker. My legs were pipes of lead.

Before I could do anything at all, the man in question—Theodore—turned fully in my direction, and I could see for sure that it was him. The man who had held me down, who had covered my mouth and had stuck his hand down my panties, who had very nearly taken my virginity without my permission, was in the same ballroom with me, not twenty feet away.

Emotion bubbled up through me like vomit. My mouth dropped open in a soundless scream that heaved through me, causing sweat to bead at my brow. What was he doing here? He was supposed to be far away. He was supposed to be behind bars. He was not supposed to be drinking champagne and laughing with Elizabeth's maid of honor.

He was not supposed to be here.

I was struck with a sense of duty to go and warn her, the

woman I didn't even know. Melinda, I believed was her name. I'd never been good with names.

But even after what I'd learned about Liz Stein, I couldn't bring myself to do it. I couldn't bring myself to go anywhere near the fucker. I had to be away. Far, far away.

I needed Donovan.

I whirled toward the door he'd exited through half an hour ago, determined to go after him. At the very least, I intended to get as far away from Theo as possible. But when I turned, I smacked into a hard, warm, familiar body.

"Hey, hey, what's wrong?" Weston asked with all the concern and compassion of someone who cared about me.

"Theodore Sheridan." I was practically hyperventilating. "He's here. I have to leave." I tried to move but Weston had his arm on mine, securing me in place.

"He is? Are you sure?" His eyes swept the room behind me, his brows tightly knit. "With Melissa?"

Melissa, that was the maid of honor's name. I nodded, unable to speak.

"That's Theo's little brother Clarence. They sure look a lot alike, don't they?"

"What?" I still couldn't get a breath. I braved a pivot to look where I'd last seen Theo/Clarence and squinted at the man's face. There *were* differences from my memories of him, but it had also been ten years. "You're positive?"

"Yeah. I'm sure. There's no reason for Theo to be here. He's ... Well. He's not here. That's the polite way to say it. Clarence went to school with Elizabeth, though. Small world, isn't it?"

"That's not Theo," I said again. Weston probably thought I was crazy. I'd never told him about the assault, and I doubted it was something Donovan had ever brought up.

He looked me in the eyes. "That's not Theo. Swear on a bible."

"Oh." I believed him, I really did.

And I was relieved.

But the weight of my panic had been extraordinary, and now that I'd been reassured that fight or flight was unnecessary, I had to deal with all those extra endorphins the panic had produced inside me.

I started to cry.

Not a full-out sobbing, tears-rolling-down-my-cheeks kind of cry. But my eyes leaked and my lips trembled and my shoulders shook.

"No. Oh, no. This is..." Weston patted my arm where he held me, looking around, perhaps for someone to help him. Maybe he gave up, or realized he could handle me on his own, because a second later he pulled me into his embrace. "Don't do that. I mean, weddings are for crying, but not this one. Well, maybe this one. But not for the usual reasons, and that's not really a comforting topic right now. What I mean to say is, what can I do? I'm not really sure why you're upset. I am terrible with women crying. Are you okay?"

With my face buried in his lapel, I worked on pulling myself together. This wasn't the place to cry everything out of my system. I needed to just get the valve under control, put on a happy face, and get back to the event.

Weston was helpful thankfully, rubbing my back as he rambled. Both were soothing. Both distracting.

When I could finally swallow past the lump in my throat and get out a coherent sentence, I broke away from his chest.

"I'm sorry," I said, accepting the handkerchief he offered. "This is really embarrassing. I just really thought it was Theo.

Which I'm sure doesn't explain anything and you just think I must be truly bananas."

Weston continued to rub my arm. "I can actually fill in the blanks, I think. Elizabeth told me Theo is currently serving time for rape. Am I making unreasonable connections?"

"Um. No. Not unreasonable." I turned my face away, feeling another wave of tears threaten.

"Hey, that's not what I wanted." He swiveled on his shiny black shoes, trying to decide what to do with me. We were off to the side and out of the way of most of the crowd, but my display of emotion was definitely not well suited for Weston's wedding.

I was about to apologize again, tell him I wasn't his problem, when he said, "Oh, let's do this. Come join me on the dance floor. They just started a slow song. We can talk—or not —and sway, and no one will be the wiser."

As much as I didn't want to be his burden, I was still shaken up. "Okay."

I let him take my hand in his to lead me to the center of the dance space. It was warm, but nothing magical happened at his touch. It was funny that I once thought I might have a future with him. I'd always belonged to someone else.

And, maybe, so did he. "Aren't you supposed to have the first dance with Elizabeth or something?"

He shook his head. "We aren't doing any of the traditional things like first dance or cutting of the cake. It seemed strange under the circumstances."

Was I wrong or did it seem like there was a note of disappointment in his tone?

"Makes sense." I pressed easily against him, grateful for both the familiarity and the friendship. "While I'm disappointed to not see the two of you have a first dance, I appreciate this."

"That's what friends are for, right? Want to talk about it?"

"I prefer not to, if that's okay." The tears had stopped, but there was a layer of pure terror just under the surface, like heavy clouds after a rainstorm. There was more inside me waiting to get out. I was barely holding myself up, and it was with Weston doing most of the holding.

"Completely fine. I just have to say, I'm here for you. You have to know that. Things might not have gone the way," he lowered his eyes from mine and cleared his throat, "I once intended for us, but maybe this is better. Whatever *this* is, I have a feeling it lasts longer."

He sounded forlorn. More so than I expected a man on his wedding day might, even a fake wedding day.

"Uh oh. That sounds like there's trouble in paradise already. Things not going so well between you and the Mrs.?" It was nice to be able to have something to joke about. Not that I wanted Weston to be miserable. I just didn't want to focus on the reasons *I* felt miserable.

But Weston apparently wanted to play the same avoidance game. He shrugged. "It's a strange situation. I guess, all in all, things are going exactly as they should, and I'll leave it at that."

We shuffled together in silence for a little while, both of us lost deep in our complicated psyches. Then all of a sudden, Weston exclaimed, "Hey! You came to this with Donovan?"

I leaned back to look at him, smiling. "Oh, yeah. You've been preoccupied. I didn't know if you knew."

"Word gets around. Especially when it's juicy."

"I suppose it is pretty juicy," I said, not even caring anymore that I was the center of gossip.

"But is it good? Is he treating you right? Donovan's my guy, but if he doesn't take care of you I won't hesitate to kick his ass." He'd said words like this before, and while I didn't really believe Weston would ever take Donovan down, his intentions were sweet.

"Yes, Weston. He's taking care of me." Donovan Kincaid redefined what it meant to take care of someone.

"Good. You deserve it."

I wasn't sure I deserved it, but I wanted it. I wanted all that Donovan gave me and every way he gave it.

I also wanted the best for Weston. "You deserve it, too. To be loved. To be taken care of. To take care of someone."

He looked away as though he wanted to reject what I was saying, but I put my hand on his cheek and pulled his face back front and center. "I'm serious, Weston King. If that means growing up, do it. We aren't kids anymore. I know Donovan would want you to know the same."

He rolled his eyes. "I'm sure he would."

The song ended, and we parted.

"Speak of the devil..." He nodded toward sidelines where Donovan was standing watching us.

I headed toward him immediately, still worked up and eager to have his arms around me. Weston followed.

"You're here," I said, pressing into my date.

He paused a second, maybe surprised about my show of affection. Then he wrapped his arms around me. "I was only in the lobby with Cade. I've been here the whole time."

There was a slight hint of tension in his voice that I felt mirrored in his body, and I wondered what had happened between him and Cade to put him in this mood, but my curiosity wasn't strong enough to make that question a priority.

"I thought I saw Theo," I told him, desperate to share what had happened—even though it had turned out to be nothing. "I thought he was here, Donovan. I freaked out."

Immediately, his mood shifted. He was on high alert, my protector. "You saw Theo?" He scanned my face, urgently.

"I thought I did. But I was wrong."

"Clarence Sheridan," Weston explained. "He's friends with Melissa."

Donovan nodded, understanding.

"They look so much alike." My throat tightened again. "I thought it was him, and you weren't here..."

"I'm here now." Donovan drew me in tighter, wrapping an arm around my waist and placing a hand at the base of my neck. He kissed the tip of my head. "Are you okay?"

I nodded against him. "Weston helped calm me down."

"Thanks, King. Much appreciated." He didn't let me go as he extended his gratitude to his friend.

"It was no trouble, really," Weston said behind me.

I felt something transfer between them. Something that maybe only men understood—only men who were good friends. But because I couldn't see either of their faces from my position, I couldn't even see what it was to know.

I pulled out of Donovan's arms, uncomfortable with the feeling that I was being left out of the conversation. My eyes darted from one man to the other, but I was unable to read either of them.

"Congratulations are in order, I suppose," Donovan said, changing the subject. He took my hand in his.

Weston nodded his chin at me. "I hear the same should be given to you."

Donovan didn't say thank you, but for that matter neither had Weston.

They held each other's gaze for several seconds that might've been tense or might have just been seconds passing. I didn't really read men very well. I'd never been good at it, and I wasn't suddenly good at it now simply because I was dating Donovan.

Finally, Weston said, "So Cade already left? That mother-fucker didn't even wait to see me."

And the mood shifted.

Donovan shrugged with one shoulder as if to say *you know him*. "He's staying in the States a while. He might still be here when you get back from your honeymoon. I still can't believe you're actually going on one of those."

"Gotta make it look real." Weston waggled his brows, indicating the real reason he was looking forward to a honeymoon, despite the sham marriage between him and his bride. "Do me a favor and keep him out of my office. Last time he was here my signed copy of *Sandman* went missing."

I wasn't sure if that was directed to Donovan, or to me since I was the one covering Weston's job for the most part while he was out of the office.

Before either of us could respond, others were gathering around us to wish the newlyweds congratulations. Frank and Roxie, Tom and Daisy. Some of the guys from the marketing team. Soon there was joking and laughter and small talk that didn't require my full attention.

I was glad to let others handle the conversation. It hadn't been Theodore, and I should have recovered by now, but I still felt topsy-turvy. My stomach was still in knots. It was ridiculous.

Even though it wasn't Theodore, it wasn't just that I'd seen a man who looked like him that had been the reason for my turmoil. I hadn't been thrown into such fright simply because my memory had been jogged. I lived with those memories all the time. They were always in the corners of my mind. They haunted my dreams on a regular basis. It was almost a comfortable companion—the dreadful horror of those memories.

What threw me today—what had me still so worked up—was knowing how few degrees of separation there were between me and Theodore right now. If he were released from jail—*when* he was released from jail—his little brother would still be friends with a woman who was currently married to one of my bosses. To a man I was close to.

The chances were good that Weston and Elizabeth would be over in a matter of weeks; and that there would never be an occasion when I would even be in a room with Clarence again.

But what if I was? What if Weston and Elizabeth stayed together by some miracle, and a few years down the line, at a holiday party or a charity event or the launch of a new business venture, I turned unexpectedly and that time it *wasn't* Clarence?

It was a lot of what-ifs, and I'd learned not to live on what-ifs. But tonight the what-ifs were an infestation taking over the most vulnerable parts of me, wearing me down to just smiles and nods.

I lost track of how long I'd been disengaged from my companions when I felt Donovan's hand settle heavy on my hip.

"Come with me," he said with no further explanation.

Without giving excuses to the others, we slipped away through the open doors of the ballroom, out toward the restrooms in the lounge. I wondered for a moment, if we were leaving altogether, but he passed the coatroom and the stairs, and led me to a room across the lobby.

The door was slightly ajar, and after looking around to make sure no one was watching, he pushed it open and pulled me inside. He shut the door behind us and when he turned on the light I saw we were in what looked like an apartment of some sort, a series of rooms with a kitchen and dining room and living area.

"What is this place?" I asked, pretty sure we weren't supposed to be here, whatever it was.

Donovan unbuttoned the jacket of his tuxedo. "It's another event space, this one designed to look like a residence. The wedding party rented it as well. They used it earlier for the family breakfast and then later for last-minute prenuptial paperwork and photographs. No one is using it now though, and I for one, could use a break from all that chatter."

In my distress I'd forgotten that he'd been tense since returning from his chat with Cade. I wasn't going to pry. He would tell me if and when he was ready, and hopefully I would have my own shit together by then so I could be there for him when he did.

Meanwhile, a break from the chatter sounded like exactly what I needed.

I made my way to the closest couch and slumped down in the center seat. Donovan wandered around the room, checking out the décor. I watched as he fingered the heavy curtain sash, then as he crossed to the Christmas tree, decorated with large red and gold bows.

I closed my eyes and leaned back, opening them only when I felt the sofa cushion depress next to me a few minutes later.

"Give me your foot," he said, loosening his bowtie.

Without question I put one strappy heel in his lap. He unbuckled the sandal and removed it, then motioned for me to give him the other so he could repeat the gesture with my other foot.

"Do you need anything? A drink? Some water? Something to eat? Need to use the restroom?"

I rubbed at the inside corners of my eyes, thinking I could probably use a mirror but not having the energy to go look. "I'm good. You're being very hospitable." Maybe that hospitality would extend to a foot rub if I played my cards right.

"I am. Because if you don't need anything else, I'm going to make sure you remember your safe word. And then you're going to make me believe you don't want me to touch you when I do."

For the second time that night, I had a rush of endorphins. My heart sped up double time. My hands began to sweat. This time though, my blood was hot and the catch in my breath was excitement.

We'd played this game before. I liked this game. I was good at this game.

I bolted up to my feet, but Donovan was fast and he pulled me straight back down, hard, drawing me closer to him than I had been. I tensed my shoulders and slammed my thighs together tight. It wasn't hard to pretend I didn't want him. Not only did I have real experience with sexual assault, but I also practiced on a regular basis turning my fears of men into fantasies. How many times had I turned nightmares of Theodore into erotic indulgences, my head filled with thoughts of Donovan as I rubbed myself to climax?

As I said, I was good at this game.

Donovan moved his mouth to my face and licked along my cheek, which was somehow the perfect blend of smarmy and hot. It sent shivers down my back. With one arm keeping me tight against him, he pushed his other hand up the skirt of my dress, demanding access. I clamped my legs even tighter.

"Now don't be like that, pretty girl. You want me to keep things nice. Don't you?"

I turned my head away. He knew the perfect words to use. Substituting my name with misogynistic terms for women. Reducing me to nothing but my looks and my purpose, to nothing but what I did to him, what I did *for* him.

It made my pussy pulse with desire.

I fought not to moan.

Not earning entry between my legs, he found another way to violate me. My dress was mostly backless and had prevented the wearing of a bra. Now, the hand that gripped me at my waist took advantage of this, reaching under the material at my ribs to palm my breast.

His hold was tight, and it hurt, his trimmed nails digging into my skin. I would have bruises from this.

It was perfect. Such a perfect scenario. I could imagine it. I was a smart young woman trying to get a leg up, working extra hours with her seemingly detached boss, not realizing that his devilish grin was really dangerous. Not realizing that once he was alone with me, he'd want more from me than my reports on supply and demand.

God, I was dizzy, it was so hot.

Except, no.

Liz Stein hadn't had it this easy. Rape was rape—I wasn't saying that one rape was easier than another—but I needed this rougher.

And I was positive that was why Donovan was doing this—for me. Because he knew this was exactly what I needed.

So as he kissed my neck and continued to fondle my breast, I bent down and bit his arm, sinking my teeth through the layer of his white tuxedo shirt until I hit skin, until I hit blood.

He jerked away, shaking his hand. "Fucking bitch."

But in that brief moment that he was distracted, I escaped, crawling across the coffee table to get to the hallway that connected the residence rooms. There wasn't anywhere to run, really. The next room had more seating in a different arrangement but nothing else. Nowhere to hide. I breezed past it to the dining area, where a long banquet table ran the length of the room.

Donovan was right behind me.

I knocked over a chair behind me, stalling him, and running along beside the table. I would have to double back along the other side, I realized quickly, since this room ended in a wall.

The chair was barely an obstacle. I looked over my shoulder in time to see him jump it. Which was terribly sexy and wild. Then, as I rounded the table, he climbed up and across it, getting off on the other side. Before I could switch gears and go back the other way, he'd caught me.

"And now we're going to have to do it the hard way." Something told me he wasn't too disappointed.

I was panting like a dog, my panties so wet they were slippery as he pushed me toward the banquet table. But I struggled, kicking him high in the thigh with the back of my foot when he tried to bend me over, barely missing his crotch.

For a second he lost his grip again, but when he regained it, he was pissed. I could feel it in the way he clutched me, the way he slammed me against the wall. I'd have bruises from this too.

"You hurt me and you're going to hurt more." With that venom in his voice, I almost believed him. Or maybe I *did* believe him, that it came from somewhere so deep inside him that it was absolute honesty. That if I *did* hurt him, if I broke his heart, then he would, whether purposefully or unintentionally, hurt me more.

Or maybe I just wanted to believe that, that that's how much he loved me, because it turned me on to believe that.

He was actually hurting me now. My shoulder ached from how he wrenched it behind my back to tether my wrists. I could feel him fastening them together with a rope of some kind. His bowtie maybe, but he'd left that on the couch.

I glanced behind me and saw a flash of gold at my skin. *One of the ribbons from the Christmas tree.* When he was walking around the room he'd been preparing. Just like Theodore had done with Liz.

Perfect. Donovan was so perfect.

He knew that one day, inevitably, I would have nightmares about what Theodore did to Liz. I would create images where, instead of Liz, it was me that Theo wrapped up with the belt of a robe and raped. Especially after tonight, after seeing Clarence and believing he was the man who'd wanted to hurt me long ago.

Donovan was giving me images to replace those before I'd even created them.

I'd been hesitant to say I was in love. I'd been falling for so long, but I wanted to be sure before I told him. After all the years and energy he'd invested in loving me, I had to make sure my emotions were significant enough to match his. And I had to really understand what he felt before I could even make a comparison.

Right then, right there, with my hands tied behind my back, my cheek pressed against the wall, and his hand clasped at my throat, I finally understood the depth of what he felt for me.

And so I surrendered.

Even as I jabbed him in the ribs with my elbow. Even as he tore my thong and I wiggled and writhed. Even as he used his knee to separate my legs, and I flailed against him, I surrendered.

Surrendered everything.

And when he shoved inside me with his hot angry cock, he pounded all the tension and torment of the evening from my body, leaving me limp and weary and *his*.

We came together, both of us grunting out our releases like they'd been days coming. Like we'd been just practicing before, and this was the performance. A performance meant only for two.

Donovan let go of me, leaning back against the table to catch his breath. Meanwhile, I sunk to the ground, my hands still tied behind my back. I kept my eyes closed, my cheek pressed against the cool wall and allowed myself to revel in the blissful feel of nothing.

Suddenly, Donovan was kneeling in front of me, turning me to face him. He reached behind me to untie my wrists and then ran his palm down my cheek. "Talk to me."

He was checking in. Good man. Last time we'd played this I'd ended up sobbing in his arms.

"This was definitely a whole lot better than chatter. Just what I needed." It was a lot more complicated than that, but the point was, I was good. "How about you?"

His shoulders eased, his face relaxed, and words rushed out of his mouth like air out of a balloon that had just been untied. "I love you. I want to be the one to take care of you. I'm not going to share you anymore. Not even with Weston."

God, I was such a dummy.

He hadn't been tense because of Cade. He'd been tense because of *me*. Because he'd walked in and seen me in the arms of a man who'd once been a potential threat.

And all I'd wanted was Donovan. Wanted Donovan to comfort me, wanted him to say he loved me. How could he not understand that? Hearing it now for the first time for real shook me to the core. It was the balm I'd sought all night. He was the refuge I'd sought all my life.

I flung my hands around his neck and tipped my chin up to kiss him. Then I pressed my forehead against his.

"Okay," I said because there were no words for this, for all the words inside me. Just... "Okay."

FOURTEEN

The next morning, I studied Donovan across the kitchen bar as I licked yogurt off my spoon.

"Is it weird to have me here?" It was the first night I'd spent at his house since we'd been officially together, and what *I* was finding weird was how weird it *wasn't*.

Donovan looked up from his tablet, where he was reading the Sunday morning paper. "It's *nice* to have you here."

"But does it interfere with your routine? Am I in the way? Am I distracting?" I wondered what he had done with his days off in the past. Besides sit around and check up on me all the time.

His attention returned to his iPad. "I've thought about it enough for it not to seem too jarring," he said dismissively.

I set my spoon on the counter in front of me and leaned forward. "You've thought about it?"

He put his iPad down. "Yes, Sabrina. You aren't the only one who's had fantasies."

I bit my lip as I grinned. He really did have the romance thing down.

"Granted," he swept his eyes over my body, currently clothed in his tuxedo shirt from the night before, "in my fantasies, you were usually naked."

I shrugged with one shoulder. "Real life, man."

He was already coming around the bar for me. I shrieked with my hands held out to stop him from whatever wicked torments I was sure that he meant to implement.

"You've already attacked me once this morning."

"I've heard no mention of your safe word." He rested his hands on the arms of the kitchen barstool, caging me in, and bent down to kiss my neck. He normally had a bit of scruff on his face, but he hadn't yet shaved so his jaw was extra bristly, tickling my sensitive skin.

"No, no," I howled, laughing. "You can't! I promised to call Audrey. You have to stop!"

He lifted his head. "Okay." He kissed me, long enough and deep enough to get my lower belly fluttering, then he pulled away. "I need to work out anyway. Want to join me?"

I pretended to think about it for all of three seconds. "No thanks. I have that phone call to make and everything." Besides, hadn't we gotten enough of a workout last night?

A thought occurred to me. "You haven't bugged my phone, have you?"

"I have not bugged your phone. I told you, you know every-thing." He swatted the side of my bare thigh.

"Just checking," I teased. "But to be sure—there aren't cameras in *your* house are there?"

His expression, annoyed as it was, was also hot and searing.

"Make yourself at home, Sabrina," he said, refusing to address my last comment. "Join me in the shower later."

"I'll see if I can fit you into my schedule."

He threw me a warning glare over his shoulder. That, and the magnificent view of his backside—his torso naked, his ass covered with sweats hanging low on his hips—sent delicious tingles down my body.

I sighed, my gaze still fixed on the kitchen doorway long after he'd left. I was sore and exhausted, and I couldn't remember the last time I'd been this happy.

I waited until I heard the treadmill start in the other room before going upstairs to get my cell phone. I'd brought a small overnight bag with me and had included my charger so my battery was full. Lazily, I stretched out on Donovan's bed and perused social media, something I rarely indulged in. Elizabeth had posted a few candid pictures from the wedding and I wondered if they were more crumbs for doubting family members or if they'd been real moments she'd wanted to capture.

Maybe Weston would never change. Maybe he was a wild playboy who could never settle in one bed. But seeing him with Elizabeth made me want to believe it was possible.

Or maybe it was being with Donovan that made me want to believe that love was possible for Weston. Because I wanted it to be possible for *me*.

Did I love Donovan?

That was a question better left for the experts.

I closed out of the social apps on my phone, found Audrey's name in the favorites list, and clicked to call.

"Tell me everything," she answered.

I laughed. "Hello to you too." To be fair, I hadn't talked to her since I'd parted with her the week before, and a lot had happened in the last seven days. Not that I was going to tell her every detail. But I planned to tell her the major points.

"I wouldn't have to rush to the meat of the subject if you maybe called me a little more often," she berated.

"I know," I admitted guiltily. "It's been a busy week. But I do owe you a rundown." I stood up. This was going to require pacing.

I roamed the top floor of Donovan's apartment, giving Audrey the highlights of the last week. I didn't tell her that I had put him on trial, but I did tell her that we had gone through everything from the past, and that he had explained himself satisfactorily. That may have been somewhat simplifying the situation, but it was *our* relationship. Our business. Not anyone else's.

Then I told her we were making a go of it; that we were trying out something real.

"Has he said it yet? Has he told you he loves you?" Audrey's tone was as bright and eager as when she'd been ten years old asking me about Santa Claus.

"He has." I sounded especially young, too. Who was I? I wandered into the study. "Yesterday, he did. I didn't say it back. Maybe I should've said it back. Should I have said it back?"

"Did you *want* to say it back?"

"I wanted to say it back. I just wanted to make sure I meant it first."

"And you're not sure?"

I pressed my cheek against the cool window frame and switched the phone to my other ear. "I'm afraid that what I feel isn't worthy of what he feels for me."

It was the first time I'd said it out loud, the first time I'd formed it into words and I had to pause for a second to make sure it was what I meant.

It was.

"What have I done for him? Spread my legs? Sucked him off? Let him get a little rough? I can't be the only woman willing..." I trailed off, not wanting to make the conversation uncomfortable for my sister by discussing specifics of the kink I liked.

"He's not in love with you because you're a slut."

"I'm not a slut!"

I could practically hear her roll her eyes. "That's what I'm saying. You're *not* a slut, so that's not why he loves you. And people don't love other people because of what they do for them, anyway. If they say they do, they're wrong. That's not real love."

"Then why is he in love with me?"

"Oh, sister dear. You are wise and smart beyond your years, and yet you are such a fool."

It was my turn to roll my eyes. My sister's fountain of drama floweth over.

"The heart wants what the heart wants," she went on. "It is not ours to ask why. As for you and how you feel—there is no point in comparing your emotions with his actions. He did what he did because he wanted to do it, not just because he loved you. He didn't do anything that he wasn't completely comfortable doing whether you knew he loved you or not. He certainly wasn't waiting for you to give him something in return or he would've told you about his secret actions long ago. My guess is that he's out of his mind happy just having you wake up in his arms right now."

"Did you come up with that on your own or did you steal it

from Hallmark?" If I didn't mock her, there was a chance I'd tear up.

Besides, mocking her was my job as her sister.

But maybe she had a point. Donovan's comments from earlier replayed in my mind. He had fantasies about me being in his life. He'd said so himself. Maybe he really was just happy to have me here.

"I'm just giving you a hard time," I said now. "I appreciate what you're saying. I will keep that in mind as I go forth with my declarations of affection."

I walked over to the large wooden desk and plopped down in the brown leather chair in front of it. I meant to be present in the conversation with my sister, but at the same time I was thinking, *This is Donovan's desk. This is Donovan's chair.* Was this where he sat when he thought about me? When he watched me? When he called me and I imagined him nursing his drink?

Is this where I'd be sitting when I figured out my own feelings about him?

"It's complicated," Audrey said, as if reading my mind. "I get it. But I have every faith that you'll figure it out, and when the time is right, you'll say the right words."

I wasn't quite so confident, but there was a power in sitting amongst Donovan's things. It made me more wistful, and my hope less tentative. "I'm sure you're right."

We talked for a few more minutes about school and plans for Christmas and then we hung up with the usual *I-love-you*s and *keep-out-of-trouble*s. And when her voice was gone, for a few minutes I missed her more than I had before I'd called.

I sat in Donovan's chair and swiveled back and forth, flipping my phone absentmindedly against the desk while I thought about what Audrey had said, and about Donovan, about where I wanted our relationship to go. After the phone slipped through my hands one too many times, I got bored of the activity and let it lie. My eyes caught on the manila folder sitting on the desk in front of me, not unlike the folder that had contained all of Donovan's connections to my past. This one was thin, and I turned it to read the label that had been printed on the notch. *Sun Le Chen.*

I sat forward, my heart hammering against my ribcage. Why did Donovan have a file with Sun's name on it?

I opened it up.

There was very little inside, just a stack of black-and-white photographs. All were candid shots of the gorgeous model, seemingly taken without her knowledge as she shopped in a street market. I couldn't say for sure if they'd been taken recently, but they didn't seem to be in the United States. The style of the streets and the architecture appeared to be European, French maybe. And if it was France, it could have been recent. It had snowed here the last month but not there.

So Donovan had photos taken of Sun while she'd been in France?

"I'm sweaty," he said, suddenly standing in the doorway. "And I'm ready to make you sweaty."

I twisted my chin in his direction. "Why are there pictures of Sun here?"

He folded his arms across his chest and leaned one muscular shoulder against the frame of the door. "Have you been going through my things?"

"Is that a problem?" There was a hint of laughter in my agony.

He worked his jaw, not giving an answer. "They're part of

the France campaign," he said finally, thankfully choosing not to debate my snooping further. "They were delivered the day I got back. I've barely looked at them."

"They're candid." I flipped through them again. "She's unaware of the camera." I looked up at him, pleading for a more satisfactory answer.

He cocked his head with incredulity. "Sabrina, you can't be suggesting..."

"Can't I? Secret photos taken of a woman—"

He cut me off. "She knew about the camera. It's called acting. The whole shoot was taken in that style. It doesn't mean—"

"How am I supposed to know that?" I let that hang, our gazes locked. To his credit, his eyes were stormy and tormented. "Do you have feelings for her, Donovan? Is this folder like mine?" I couldn't help the tremble in my voice or the heat of the tears in my eyes.

He rushed to me, coming around the desk and turning the chair to face him. "No. No, Sabrina. You are the only one. You are the only woman alive that I have spent any time... The only one I've wanted to... watch and *know*. Everything has been you."

I'd never seen him struggle so much to get a thought across, and it made me want to climb into his arms and believe every-thing he told me.

But...

"You've slept with her." He'd told me that he had. He'd had his mouth on her pussy. He'd even described how he'd gone down on her.

And if he'd slept with her—like he'd slept with me—then couldn't he *feel* things for her too?

He didn't move, didn't lean forward or draw away, just stood there holding his ground with his hands planted on the armrests of the leather chair. "And you slept with Weston."

Ouch.

It felt like a punch.

I slumped back into the chair, absorbing the shock of his words. I knew what he was getting at—that I should understand that sleeping with someone did not equate to feelings. But what I heard was: *you hurt me, I hurt you.*

And he still had the upper hand.

"The thing is," I said, "you can just ask your private detective whether or not I'm sneaking off to see Weston behind your back."

Now he straightened. He considered for a moment, circling around the front of the desk. He was caught. If he asked me just to trust him, he would be a hypocrite.

When he was at the center of the desk, he turned to face me, placing both palms on the flat surface. "Is that what it would take to fix this? If you had someone watching me the way I have someone watching you?"

I turned the chair so it was pointed at him, and wrinkled my nose. "I can't really afford to hire a detective to follow you around everywhere, Donovan, if that's what you're getting at."

It was also dumb. If I wanted to know something about him, I'd just ask him.

Of course, he could always just ask me as well and that didn't seem to be good enough for him.

"No, it's not what I'm getting at. I take care of you, remember?" He reached over and grabbed the phone that was secured to the landline and dragged it over to him. Before I could ask what he was doing, he picked up the receiver and dialed a number he knew by heart.

As it rang, he said to me, "You're in luck. The guy I had working for Cade is free now, but he's still on retainer, which means he's—" He moved the mouthpiece to his lips. "Ferris. It's me. I have a new job for you."

I was beginning to understand where he was going with this. "This isn't necessary. Really."

He ignored me. "It's going to sound odd, but here's the details: your contact is Sabrina Lind. Yes, the same Sabrina Lind."

So, I'd been Ferris's subject before. Great.

"You're going to send the bill to me," he continued. "Anything she asks you to look into, you do it, no questions asked, even if the subject is me."

"*No*," I mouthed. "Hang up."

But he didn't hang up.

He moved his eyes so he wasn't reading my lips. "I don't want any copies of the reports. They all go straight to her. You got it?"

"Donovan..." I warned.

Stubborn and alpha-minded, the man disregarded everything I'd said so far and held the phone out to me.

"No!" I couldn't even entertain the idea. I wouldn't.

"It's already done. Just take the call and give him your information." He pressed the receiver toward my hand.

"I said no!" I jumped up from his chair, away from him and his stupid phone call. "I'm not doing it, Donovan," I hissed with finality.

It might be tempting to go along with the investigation—for somebody else. There was so much I didn't know about him, but I didn't want to learn about him from a report. I wanted him to show me who he was in person. I wanted to uncover him, layer by layer, the way that people do when they meet someone that fascinates them so entirely that they can't get enough until they hear everything from his own lips.

Donovan's jaw set, his mouth pressed together in a tight line as he held me in a hard unmoving stare. Several heavy beats passed.

Finally, he brought the receiver back to his own ear, and I let out the breath I'd been holding.

Until he started talking. "Ferris, the order is for a complete background report on me with surveillance. Solo surveillance only. No need for a tail if Sabrina is in my company. Photos. No videos. Send to the email that you have on file for her but send the invoice to me."

I crossed my arms under my breasts and tried to decide if I was angry or disappointed.

Donovan finished the call and hung up the phone with a sharp clack that suggested he was as frustrated as I was, and for some reason that lessened my irritation a degree or two.

"You don't have to look so wounded," he said, coolly. "You said I didn't have to give this up."

"That didn't mean that you should try and force me into the same behavior." How could he not understand?

"This is what I know, Sabrina. You wanted answers; this is how I know how to give them."

There was a sincerity in his tone that awoke something in me, made *me* the one to understand—he wasn't trying to make me mad. He wasn't trying to hurt me. He wasn't trying to over-rule my wishes. He was doing the best he could with what he knew, and *this* was what he knew. Surveillance. Stalking. Sneaking around.

It was up to me to teach him differently. I'd have to teach him trust.

And to teach him trust, I'd first have to show him trust.

"I don't need that report." When it came to my email, I'd just delete it, I'd decided. "But if that's what you need to do, I understand. Right now, what I need is for you to tell me once again that you don't have feelings for Sun." I took a deep breath —this was going to be hard. "And I'll believe you."

He came to me in three easy steps. Putting his hand on my chin, he tilted it up to meet his eyes. "I don't feel anything for Sun. I've never felt anything for her. She was always just a distraction so that I wouldn't go crazy from how much I loved you."

My chest tightened and a knot formed in the back of my throat. I pushed up to the balls of my feet and pressed my fore-head to his. "Thank you. I believe you."

FIFTEEN

M onday came faster than it seemed possible, as it often did. With Weston gone, my workload had doubled. On top of his absence, the end of the year always brought new campaigns. Existing clients wanted to get a head start on the new year; new clients were knocking on the door with resolutions for a better business going forward.

Fortunately, I had little time for worrying about office gossip or private investigators. I didn't even have time to eat lunch. By afternoon, I realized how easily I could be buried under the demands. I canceled everything unnecessary and came to terms with the fact that I would be running back and forth between my office and Weston's all week.

Wednesday morning I gave up, gathered what was important from my space, and moved into his.

"You look good in a room this size," Donovan said when he came in to check on me that evening.

I looked up from the stacks of strategy reports in front of me and blinked several times. I'd darkened the glass walls of the office so that the other staff members wouldn't distract me, but it had the downside of closing me off to the world. My phone had died hours ago. I glanced at the window behind me and realized for the first time that it was dark. Nighttime dark.

"I guess I lost track of time." I stretched my legs out in front of me and flexed a foot. I'd long ago slipped off my shoes.

Donovan sat in the chair across from me and rested his ankle on the opposite knee. "You've been doing that a lot this week."

It wasn't exactly accusatory, but I had the sense that he was trying to tell me something.

"I'm sorry I haven't had any time for you. I had no idea this would be so hard. I didn't think Weston did anything."

"Weston *doesn't* do anything. This is the best his job has ever been done. The rest of us are never going to let you leave." He smiled, and I knew he wasn't saying it just to be kind. "And don't worry about me. I'm taking you away this weekend."

I cocked my head, intrigued with this new information. "Oh really?" I had planned on working all weekend. There was no other way to get through everything I needed to without doing so, even though I'd worked until almost ten every night so far this week.

"You can't work every second of your life and still expect to do a good job, Sabrina. Trust me, I know. You have to have a little downtime."

I folded my arms under my breasts. "And you have so much downtime. Tell me Mr. Kincaid, what hobbies do you have? What occupies your weekends besides work?"

"You."

Okay. He won.

"And I will allow you to have time to work this weekend as well, as long as you occupy part of your weekend with me."

The only reason I didn't say anything right away was because I was too busy melting inside. "You make it really hard for a girl to argue."

"That's the whole point." His brow wrinkled as if he were thinking. "I have to admit, it's a whole lot easier just telling you to go places. Though it was more fun devising ways to get you where I wanted you to be."

"Asking me. You *ask* me to go places. You don't tell me."

"Yeah. That's what I do." He smirked, and I couldn't decide if he was indulging me or if I was indulging him, but when I thought about it, I didn't really want to find out.

"So where is it that you want me to be this weekend?" I asked, gathering the papers in front of me into organized piles for the morning. I'd worked long enough today. My brain was mush at this point. "Do I get to know? Or is it a surprise?"

He considered before answering. "My parents' country house in Washington, Connecticut. They will be there as well. I apologize for that. My mother hates the city in the winter, and she pretty much stays in Washington from the weekend after Thanksgiving until New Year's. But it's a big house, and my father is just as much of a workaholic as we are, so we won't have to spend very much time with them."

I couldn't stop smiling. "You're taking me to meet your parents?"

He raised a brow. "Did you hear anything else I said?"

"Not really." I was practically giddy. Schoolgirl giddy. "Meeting the guy's parents, Donovan... That's a big deal. I'm really kind of flustered right now."

His eyes grew warm and soft like melted cookies. "You're a

big deal to me," he said quietly, and the air left my lungs. With more energy, he went on. "I'm serious, though. My parents are cold and formal. Don't expect much from them. They will engage with you transactionally."

I thought it wasn't a good idea quite yet to remind him that *he'd* engaged with me transactionally as well. "Then why their country house? We could go someplace else."

"Because it's beautiful, even in the winter. *Especially* in the winter. I want to share it with you."

Almost as an afterthought, he said, "And I want them to meet you. Even though they don't deserve to know you."

Silently, I ran my hand flat along the surface I had just cleared on the desk, overwhelmed by the things he'd just said. When I found my voice again, I agreed. "I'd like to go there. Please. I'd like to meet them."

"We're driving out at four sharp on Friday. Have everything you need here and ready by then. We'll take a driver so we can even work on the ride up. I can help you with anything you're behind on. I should have all my operations projections in place before we leave."

"All that sounds really fucking fantastic."

He was staring at me, hard and deep, the way he did when he was unearthing me, bringing what was buried inside me to the surface.

Also the way he looked at me when he was scheming. When he wanted to test my boundaries. When he wanted to play.

I was afraid to ask. "What?"

"Take off your panties."

"What?" I'd heard him, I just didn't know if he was teasing or not.

"It's after nine. You and I are the last people here. Take off your panties."

What was I thinking? He was never just teasing.

"Why?" I wasn't disagreeing. But I wanted to know.

"I'm going to fuck you on Weston's desk."

Oh God.

Now I *needed* to take off my panties because they were drenched. Why did that turn me on so fucking much? Because it was someone else's property? Because it was my boss's desk? Because I could sense the primitive alpha reasoning behind Donovan's desire to do it?

"There are probably cameras," I said, scanning the most likely spots for their location.

"I *know* there are cameras. They are visual only. Weston will be able to see everything we do if he decides to look through the security footage. Don't tell me that doesn't turn you on, because we both know it does."

Yep. That sure did.

My breath shuddered as I drew it in. The reality was Weston would have no reason to look at the footage. I'd been there for three months and we'd never looked at security footage. In all my years at Now, Inc. we'd never once looked at the cameras. They were always there, "just in case." "Just in case" never happened.

But. There was always the possibility that Weston *could*.

I was already going to do it. I was already slipping on my shoes, standing up, coming around the desk to Donovan.

"What about you? Are you into this because the voyeurism turns you on as well, or because you want to show Weston I'm yours?" I pulled the skirt of my dress up so that my panties were visible and turned, as if making a show of it for the cameras. Then I tugged them down my legs seductively, maneuvered them over my heels and handed them to Donovan.

His expression said he was pleased with my performance, if not also a bit surprised. He took the panties I offered him, sniffed them, and tucked them in his front suit pocket. "Both," he answered. "Definitely both."

He pulled me to him and kissed me, sucking on my tongue, before swiftly turning me around and bending me over the desk. The skirt I was wearing was full and easy to gather. Donovan pulled it up around my waist so that my pussy and backside were on display.

I felt vulnerable and exposed—so very exposed—knowing that there were cameras in the room. Knowing that Weston could see any of this one day. Even certain that he would never watch, I wasn't sure I would do this if it was anybody *but* Weston. He had seen me naked before. He wasn't seeing anything new.

But what about Donovan? How did he feel about exposing me to another man? Was he not bothered by the idea that Weston, specifically, might see me?

I was both tormented and turned on by that strange juxtaposition of ideas—Donovan wanting to keep me to himself and also owning me so completely that it was his prerogative if he wanted to show me off.

It turned out he had his own conflicting desires.

He removed his jacket, undid the cufflinks at his wrists, and put them in his pocket. After he pushed up the sleeves of his shirt, he glided his palm along my ass. "All of this, Sabrina, belongs to me," he said, definitively. "No one gets to touch your ass but me." He moved his fingers to my pussy and dipped inside. "No one gets to touch your pussy but me. No one gets to see any of this but me."

I moaned as he stroked in and out of my hole. He hadn't even touched my clit, but I was so aroused, I didn't need it.

"Do you understand? This, right now, in front of these cameras, is on my terms. And it's the last time Weston has a chance of ever seeing you like this. Tell me you understand, Sabrina."

"I understand." Two words and they were so hard to get out while he was massaging that spot inside me.

But I understood. I got it. Donovan was claiming me, and I had absolutely zero problem with it.

Suddenly, his hand was gone. Then it was back, landing on my behind with a crisp smack.

I jumped with a yelp but Donovan was already smoothing away the ache.

"That was for teasing me, Sabrina. For flirting with Weston in front of me that night at the restaurant."

Uh, what?

He spanked me again, this time on my other cheek, harder. I whimpered as he chased the pain with a circular massage of his palm. "This is for dancing with him at his wedding when you should've been in my arms."

He was punishing me. Punishing me for being with Weston.

Fuck. That was hot.

I pressed my thighs together as though that could ease the buzz between them, as though it could stop the liquid dripping from my cunt.

Another smack and my orgasm was already building. "That was for accepting the job when he offered it to you, when I worked so hard to provide you with a nice career in Los Ange-les." His tone was more strained, more ragged with each new strike.

The next hit came closer in spacing, with barely enough time to achieve relief from the last. "This is for the doe eyes you gave him every day for half a semester at Harvard. And this one is for thinking even for one minute that he could ever give you anything you needed."

That blow was the worst, the pain bringing tears to my eyes, but it wasn't any worse than hearing the pain in Dono-van's voice, pain he'd carried for years. Pain I'd never known about, that he'd never truly blamed me for, and if I could in this small way feel it for him, then I would take a hundred more blows.

But that wasn't what he had in mind for me.

"And this," he said as I heard his belt being worked open, his zipper being drawn down. "This is for spending a weekend in his bed. You were never his to give him what you let him take."

I reached across the desk and held onto the opposite edge, attempting to prepare for Donovan's thrust.

Still, he caught me off guard, slamming into me with such force that it felt like he was hitting the very end of me, like he'd found every single part of me there was to know, every last secret, every last hidden sin, and had driven it out of me with his entry.

He didn't let up, pounding into me with quick, frenzied, punishing strokes, and I knew he was chasing his own demons, and that this fuck was maybe more for him than any other time I'd spread my legs.

But this was for me too, as everything he did was for me.

And any last worry I had about Sun Le Chen was fucked into a bad memory. There was no way that he could need me this much, be this hurt by my relationship with Weston, and be carrying a torch for someone else. It just wasn't possible. He'd said to me once that if I could see inside him that I would know that there was no one else.

Well, I couldn't see inside him, but I could *feel*. He was making me feel everything he felt, and it was raw and jagged and dirty and hard.

But it was love, and it was rich, and he lavished me with it.

His speed and tempo were erratic. His balls slapped against my clit. That, plus the erotic scenario sent me toward climax, despite the lack of manual stimulation. Donovan still came before I did, rutting into me as he released, even after he was completely empty, as if he needed to be sure that every drop had been spilled inside me. And when it was, he lifted me so that my back was against his chest, then reached around and massaged my clit. Just a little nudge was all it took before I was spiraling into a sea of bright lights and warmth and pleasure.

I was still spinning when Donovan turned me around to face him and kissed me sweetly, luxuriously, for much longer than I would have expected considering that we weren't in our own space. It were as though I were his oxygen, and he'd been flying a bit too high, or diving much too deep, and he needed me to catch his breath, to fill his lungs, to make him right again.

Finally he broke away. "I don't want to stop touching you," he said, straightening my clothing.

I kissed him again. And again, because I didn't want to stop touching him either. But I hadn't brought any clothes with me to stay the night at his house, and I had to be to work too early in the morning with too much to do the next day to risk not getting a good night's sleep.

But it didn't mean he couldn't come to my place.

"You could—" I started to say.

"I'm coming to your place," he said at the same time.

"Good." I had a feeling it was the only way we were getting out of here tonight. I pulled myself away and went to the closet to get my coat and purse while he straightened out his sleeves and put on his jacket.

"Ready?" I asked, standing at the doorway.

"Just one thing first." He went to one of the shelves where Weston kept his comic books displayed, and picked one up. "I wanted to borrow his first edition of The Walking Dead," he explained on the way out.

I was too tired to make anything of it at the time, even though it was immediately strange—Donovan reading comic books? But it wasn't until I was drifting off to sleep in his arms much later that night that I realized:

When Weston found his possession missing, he was going to watch the security tapes.

SIXTEEN

Washington, Connecticut was two hours outside the city. We left on Friday afternoon shortly before four o'clock so that I could stop by my house and pick up my weekend bag before hitting the road. I hadn't wanted to take it to the office with me. Even if most of the staff knew that I was dating Donovan, they didn't need to know what we were doing with our free time. I certainly didn't want to feed their imagination.

We took the Tesla, which was equipped with an all-wheel drive system that made the car exceptional in all weather, according to Donovan. Apparently he was quite proud of his cars and extremely willing to boast about them when prodded, a rather fascinating fact to learn about him. Since he'd brought his driver along, we were both passengers, and the two of us knocked out a bunch of the work that had lingered from the week on the ride up, so by the time we turned down the tree-lined lane, white from snow, I felt relaxed and ready for some social engagement.

The car came to a stop at the end of the long driveway in front of a sprawling two-level mansion. It was gorgeous from the outside, a well-kept home with sweeping vistas over hundreds of acres of preserved land. It was private and hard to get to, a real getaway location, and much too big for a family of three—two, now that Donovan was grown.

"Only your parents live here?" I asked, stepping out of the car.

He nodded with an embarrassed sigh. "And only part-time, at that."

"Wow. There's certainly a lot of room." We hadn't made it inside yet, but I was guessing it was probably ten thousand square feet. I'd grown up in a house that was barely twelve hundred square feet.

"My parents like to have the option to keep as much distance between themselves as possible. You'll see. Let's get out of the cold."

He led me to the door, which opened before we had the chance to knock, and there stood a tall, middle-aged gentleman dressed in slacks and a sweater, too young to be Donovan's father.

"Mr. Kincaid," he said in greeting, eyes cast down. "Welcome back to the Pinnacle House. And welcome to your guest."

"This is Sabrina Lind," Donovan said in introduction as he helped me remove my coat. "I apologize; I don't remember your name."

"No apologies, sir. It's Edward. I can take that for you." He took my coat and hung it in a nearby closet, then returned to take Donovan's.

The driver entered behind us to drop off our luggage. "Where shall I park the car?"

"The third garage is empty," Edward said. "I'll meet you there in a moment to open it for you. Your mother suggested I put you in the upstairs master, Mr. Kincaid, is that still fine with you?"

"That will be perfect."

"I'll bring your things directly if you'd like to go up and wash for dinner. Your mother wishes I remind you it will be served at six thirty precisely."

I watched the exchange between the two men. Donovan was always guarded and stoic, but I found it interesting how reserved the butler—or whatever his title might be—was. He was the person designated to greet us. He'd been hospitable, technically, but nothing about his words or actions had felt warm or welcoming.

Maybe that's how servants were supposed to act; what did I know? I'd never been around any before.

"Yes, dinner at six thirty precisely," Donovan said with a bit of annoyance. "Heaven forbid my mother's schedule vary even a minute from her routine."

"Is that a message you'd like me to give her, sir?" There was a bit of a challenge in those words from Edward, despite his formality, as though he were loyal to his employer, which I suppose he should be.

"No," Donovan laughed gruffly. "No message. We'll be there." He shifted his attention to me. "Sabrina, I'd love to give you a tour but we can't right now. We have just enough time to change if you'd like. Shall we?"

He offered his hand, and I took it. The entryway opened into a large free space with plush rugs covering the wooden floor and fancy brocade couches in front of the fireplace. The far wall showcased a giant window that overlooked the land below. It was too dark outside and there were too many lights inside to fully capture the view, but I had a feeling it was going to be breathtaking.

To our left, a grand staircase wound upward. Donovan led me to this, and once we'd reached the top, he steered me down the hallway to a room at the end of the house with double doors. These opened into a grand master suite with a large four- poster bed, a fireplace with a fire already burning in it, a sitting area with a desk, and an en suite. A set of glass doors opened up to a private balcony. I peeked outside. The snow had started falling softly though, and I couldn't see very far in the dark.

Donovan came up behind me and put his arms around my waist. "It will be beautiful in the morning, especially as the sun comes up. Trust me. But right now we have fifteen minutes before dinner. Will you be ready?"

I turned to make a comment about not having my bag yet, but a knock on the door said that Edward was just outside. He came in and placed my luggage on a bench at the foot of the bed, and set Donovan's bag on the floor next to it.

Immediately, I opened up my suitcase and started digging inside for something to wear. I hadn't actually planned on changing for dinner, but now I felt obligated. Thank goodness I'd thrown in an extra couple of outfits so I would be prepared for any spontaneous occasion.

Except even with all the choices, I had no idea what to choose. I was already in an A-line business skirt and jacket. Was I supposed to dress up or down?

"I don't know what to wear," I said, frantically throwing a

couple of items over the bottom of the bed to better view my options.

Donovan came back from the closet where he'd hung up his suit jacket. "The Ann Taylor," he said, "with the black. I'm going to wear slacks."

I grabbed the skirt—a feminine floral pattern—my makeup bag, and the sweater in question, turned to him and gave him a quick peck on the lips. "Thank you."

Then I ran to the bathroom to change.

I came out ten minutes later wearing the new outfit, my mascara and lip gloss freshened.

Donovan was waiting at the door, as though he had just been about to knock. He had changed too, and was now wearing slacks and a burnt red pullover that brought out the green in his eyes.

"You're beautiful." His gaze said he maybe didn't want to go downstairs as much as he had just a minute ago.

"But am I *appropriate*?" I was suddenly nervous, I realized. My throat was dry and my palms were sweaty.

He looked as though he were debating the answer, or at least as if he had something that he wanted to say but wasn't sure if he *should* say it or not.

But before I could get too worked up about it, he said, "You're perfect." He glanced at his watch. "And we've got to go."

I slipped on my pumps and followed him out the door, ignoring the gnawing feeling that he wasn't telling me something, an emotion that was hard to distinguish beneath the fear that I was woefully unprepared.

Downstairs, we crossed through the free area we passed when we walked in, then another living area, into a formal dining room with a beautiful cherry wood dining set and an ornate crystal chandelier above it. French doors led out to a patio, and I could imagine that in summer the room could be opened up that way to hold generous banquets.

But it was still winter. It was dark outside, and the table, which had seats for twelve, was set for four. An attractive gentleman with silver hair and a beard sat at the head. Next to him was a stunning redhead with a long neck and green eyes.

The man stood when we entered, and Edward, whom I hadn't noticed standing at the wall, approached to pull a chair out for me at the place across from the redhead. Donovan sat next to me. His father sat again at the same time he did.

There had yet to be any introductions, yet to be any greetings at all, when the redhead—Donovan's mother—glanced up at the gold filigree clock on the wall and said, "Six thirty on the nose. Hmm."

She was clearly unhappy, though we had made it on time so I was confused as to her demeanor.

"We're here, mother," Donovan said, letting out a breath audible only to me.

"I'm simply so startled that your manners have declined to such a degree. There was a time when six thirty service meant that we were in our seats no later than six twenty. Is punctuality not that important on the other side of the world?" She leaned in toward her husband. "You've been to Japan more than I have. Is that what this is, Raymond?"

Now I understood why Donovan was so anxious to make it down here on time.

Raymond tilted his head from side to side, considering. "I imagine it's more a product of his bachelor status, Susan. They're pretty punctual there in Tokyo."

As he spoke, Edward returned from wherever he'd disappeared to after seating us carrying a bottle of wine, which he poured first into Raymond's glass.

"We are on time," Donovan said, smoothing the napkin in his lap. "We did not make it in any earlier than the designated dinner time, which is a product of traffic and weather, and has no reflection at all on my respect for punctuality. On *our* respect for punctuality," he corrected, including me the second time.

His mother sat straight-backed and silent, and I thought for a moment she might drop it.

But then she said, "You should have left earlier."

"Are you really going to be like this tonight?" Donovan asked at the same time that I said, "It's my fault. I left my luggage at my apartment and we had to make an extra stop."

Susan looked at me for maybe the first time since we'd arrived, her eyes narrowed as though she'd been approached with a puzzle that she couldn't understand.

"Leave them alone, Susan. Arguing will just delay the meal," Raymond said. His wife seemed to want to say more, but as if her husband was the final word, she pressed her lips into a tight line and didn't say another thing on the subject.

Next to me, Donovan took a long swallow of wine. Raymond signaled to Edward to serve salad plates. And I stared intently at the empty dish in front of me, unsure where to look or what to say. Donovan had told me his parents weren't friendly, but I'd expected to at least be acknowledged. I'd expected my boyfriend to point me out if they didn't.

I was jumping the gun.

Because as soon as Donovan set his glass down, he said, "Sabrina, these are my parents. Raymond and Susan." He shot his mother a daring glare. "I am instructing her to address you by your first names, Mother, so don't get your panties in a wad when she doesn't call you Ms. Kincaid like you've trained everyone else in the household."

"That was awfully presumptuous of you, Donovan. I really wish you would've asked." Susan's green eyes flared when she was angry, like her son's, I noticed.

But what a thing to be angry over.

I didn't know if I wanted to laugh or tell her off. What I did know was that we hadn't been in their presence very long, but I was already irritated that my date had allowed me to walk in so unprepared. Couldn't he have given me a heads up? Like, *hey, my mom's a crazy bitch. Ignore everything she says.*

Maybe that's what he'd wanted to say as we were walking out of our room, and given up. Well, I understood that it might be hard to speak ill about your folks, but he really should have tried harder.

"I'm happy to call you Ms. Kincaid, if that's what you prefer," I offered congenially, intending to address her as little as possible.

I could feel Donovan's displeasure with this suggestion.

Susan, however, seemed to like it very much. "Thank you, Sabrina." To her son she said, "She has manners, Donovan, that's key in a woman."

It wasn't like *she* had any to know.

His mother returned her attention to me. "I do appreciate that offer; the gesture says everything about what type of person you are. But my son is right. A first name basis is probably more practical, especially if we are going to be seeing each other from time to time moving forward."

Seriously?

Okay, Donovan couldn't have prepared me for this. No

matter what he'd said, I would not have been able to predict what kind of answer a woman like this would want from me. No wonder he hadn't tried.

I wanted to say something snide in return but her latest comments had been fairly polite, and it was perhaps best not to rock the boat.

"Wonderful, Susan," I said instead, and reached for my wine glass.

Edward had better have another bottle on hand, I thought, because this evening was going to take a lot of alcohol to get through.

"SO SABRINA, will you quit working after the wedding or will you wait until you are pregnant?"

I almost choked on my chicken roulade.

After our initial introduction, the evening had gone better. Early on, it was obvious that Raymond and Susan's only interest where I was concerned was in how well-bred I was. Or how well-bred I *wasn't*, as the case may be.

But poverty had always been my beginning, and that was unchangeable. I was used to the looks I got when people from better means heard about my upbringing. I had gotten it a lot when I had been at Harvard, in fact. And when someone like Donovan showed up with someone like me on his arm, of course his parents would want to know about my education, my current means. They probably were afraid I was after their son's money, and it was only natural to make sure that I had legitimate feelings for him.

I did my best to speak affectionately about him at every

turn possible. When the time came to speak about my job, I made sure I sounded independent and secure, not reliant on Donovan for my position or his paycheck, so the Kincaids wouldn't have to worry that I was attaching myself to him for reasons other than romantic. I had thought I was easing them into our relationship.

Then Raymond completely took me off guard by asking about weddings and babies.

"We're not engaged," I said in unison with Donovan.

I was thankful he'd had the same answer. For a moment I wondered if I'd been brought here under false pretenses.

Though at the same time, I was intrigued by the idea. I almost wished I had time to consider it longer before he'd made it clear those weren't his intentions.

"Not yet, maybe," Raymond said, in between bites of his entrée. He took a swallow from his water goblet. "But why else would Donovan bring you here? He's never introduced a woman to us before."

"I knew you weren't gay," Susan said as though she had discussed it many times in the past.

Donovan blinked, shaking his head almost indiscernibly. "I'm not even acknowledging that comment."

"You've never introduced anyone to your parents before?" I patted my mouth with my napkin, trying to find a safer topic, one that might not have me on such pins and needles.

"They knew Amanda. Who else would I have brought here?"

I supposed no one. He'd told me that he hadn't had feelings for anyone since his fiancée had died so who would he have brought? It wasn't surprising that there hadn't been anyone.

Still, I was reeling from Raymond's comments. Why would

he assume that engagement was inevitable when I'd only just met them?

Was it inevitable?

"You didn't answer the question," Susan prodded. She seemed to have decided to like me, but that wasn't saying a lot. I wasn't even sure she liked Donovan very much.

"What question?" The question about whether I'd quit working or not? Did she seriously expect me to answer that?

Thankfully Donovan intervened. "Sabrina worked harder than a lot of people do to get her degrees and to earn her reputation in the industry. I doubt that she will want to end her career if or when she marries, no matter how well off her husband is. She is very independent and strong-minded, and I'm certain she would enjoy contributing a paycheck almost as much as she enjoys the work itself. Not that it's any of our business what she chooses to do, since as I said, we are not betrothed."

"Right. I like working." I didn't know if I liked his answer, though. There was nothing wrong with it, and we absolutely weren't engaged, but did he have to seem so adamant about it?

Despite his son's argument to the contrary, Raymond seemed not to be the kind of guy who thought anything was out of the realm of his business. "But you will quit when you're pregnant?"

Donovan rushed to answer this as well, but this time I decided to fend for myself. "I don't see why I'd have to."

Not that I was getting pregnant. Not that I was getting married.

Raymond and Susan exchanged anxious glances.

"Oh, but dear, you can't work with a baby," she said patiently. A bit condescendingly, too.

"It's not a woman's role," Raymond agreed.

"Not in polite circles. You can volunteer for the PTA. You can head charities—that's what I do. You can still work, per se, but earning an actual paycheck is..." She searched for the word that she wanted. "Tacky. And it's not a good example for the baby."

I dropped my fork and looked at Donovan incredulously. He had his eyes closed and his jaw was working. It occurred to me that perhaps it was his parents that were the initial cause of the chronic clench of his teeth.

It sure wasn't *his* fault they were who they were.

But somehow, he was who *he* was because of them.

And so, for that reason alone, I didn't want to alienate them, no matter how archaic and idiotic their notions.

So when he began again to defend me and my future choices, I slipped my hand onto his knee under the table, letting him know I had this.

"I'll certainly consider your advice," I told them. "Of course, when the time comes to make those decisions, Donovan and I will have to seriously discuss it together."

I didn't even look to his parents for a reaction. I only looked to him. And though he didn't smile with his lips, his eyes did. Under the table, he laced his fingers through mine, and we held them together like a secret only the two of us knew for the rest of the meal.

AFTER DINNER, Susan went to bed early and Raymond asked Donovan to join him in his study for a cigar. It was clear that I was not invited, possibly because I was not his son, but I had a feeling it was because I was not a man.

It was fine. I was perfectly content to be left on my own. I went upstairs to our suite and spent an hour entering data I'd gathered on the ride up into my computer now that I had Wi-Fi. When I'd finished and Donovan still hadn't come up, I put on some slippers, stole the blanket from the bottom of the bed to wrap around me, and slipped out onto the balcony.

The night was cold and crisp, wetter and thicker than in the city. My breath was visible as I exhaled like I was smoking cigarettes. I leaned against the railing and looked out over the property and the land that stretched out beyond. It had stopped snowing and the moon was out now, and the stars. And without the lights of the city, I could see for miles—an ocean of trees and snow. Here and there a glow came from beneath the canopy, suggesting a residence underneath. But mostly there was nothing but woods. No one.

It was lonely.

As lonely as this house—this behemoth of a house that lodged two people, and perhaps an employee or two.

Donovan had told me he'd spent most of his time growing up in the city, but that his parents preferred the country home because of the space it provided them. And standing outside in the cold, alone, after the most unfriendly dinner of my life, all I could think was—how much space do three people who barely even talk need?

What a lonely way to grow up. What a lonely life Donovan had growing up.

As if summoned by my thoughts, the door behind me opened, and Donovan stepped out onto the balcony. "Two cigars and a glass of whiskey and I still didn't hear all the highlights of his stock picks this quarter." He came up next to me and held his hand out in my direction.

I looked down at his offering. A tumbler of scotch.

I accepted it and threw back a large swallow, enjoying the instant warmth that it provided.

"What are you thinking?" he asked, swirling the liquid in his own matching tumbler.

"That my amazing, loving, supportive, understanding parents both died too young. And yours are still alive. And that it's not fair." I regretted it as soon as I said it. I turned to meet his gaze. "I'm sorry. That was terrible."

"Raymond and Susan are terrible," he said, doubling down on my statement. He took a swallow from his drink and looked out over the distance. "I wish I could have met your parents."

God, I missed them. So much sometimes that my insides felt raw.

And sometimes I barely thought about them. That's how life went.

But wouldn't that have been something, for them to have met Donovan? For Donovan to have met *them*. "I don't know what would've happened if my father hadn't died—what would've happened at Harvard when I returned. But I wouldn't have made it to Harvard at all without the life insurance from my mother's death. So I suppose I can't wish that she'd never died and still have you."

He turned so that his back was to the railing, and he could face me better. "Do you still want me after tonight? After meeting them?" He nodded toward the house, as if it were a stand-in for his parents.

"I do." Maybe even more than I did before.

"You know they aren't me, don't you? I would never ask you

to give up any part of who you are to fulfill some outdated societal role."

I sighed, because he couldn't understand how many times a day I was asked to do just that. How many times a day a woman in a world of men was asked to fulfill some outdated societal role—it was too many times to count, too many to know, too many to solve between the two of us and two tumblers of scotch.

"It could be kind of fun though, if you pretended that you might." I peered over at him and let him imagine the filthy kind of ways we could play 1950s housewife.

"You're such a dirty girl."

"Come on inside and let me prove it."

I put my hand in his and, together, we walked out of the lonely night.

SEVENTEEN

"Damn. That's some yard." I stood with Donovan on the terrace that ran along the length of the back of the house. And I was in awe. It was the highlight of Pinnacle House—the views. No doubt about it.

Our morning had started late. We'd eaten breakfast in bed. Donovan had brought it up on a tray, egg casserole with gourmet coffee and orange juice, and a side of roasted potatoes. He hadn't said it was the reason, but I presumed we stayed in our room in order to miss his parents. Which we did.

After our meal, we dressed for the day. I bundled up in layers with a warm sweater over my T-shirt and jeans, as per Donovan's instructions. Then he gave me the tour.

We started inside, walking from one room to the next, Donovan pointing out the use and function of each. But despite the size of the house, there was nothing very remarkable about it. Most of the rooms were rarely used, but were acted as show-cases instead. The second living room had a Christmas tree that had been professionally ornamented, he'd told me. The guest rooms were all decorated with impersonal taste, as though being staged for a house sale. Even a bed and breakfast had more personality. The master suite on the lower floor was closed off, so I couldn't see if it was more lived in, and Raymond had locked himself away in his study so that room was also off limits.

I did get a glimpse into Susan's life in the country house. Her personal space, as the family called it, was located on the other end of the top floor, as far from the study as possible. She'd gone to spend the day in town at some local antiques fair, so we snuck a peek into her room. It was good sized, large enough to hold a desk and sitting area as well as a bed and dresser. Like the guestrooms, it hadn't been personalized. I did notice a few items lying around that indicated an actual human spent time here—reading glasses on the desk. A glass of water on the nightstand.

"Does she sleep here?" I asked. Even if she didn't sleep with her husband, there were plenty of other rooms in the house available. She didn't have to fit her entire life at Pinnacle House into her office.

Donovan shrugged. "I'm not even sure she really sleeps."

How strange to not even wonder about the people that you live with, to share a roof and a table with walking mysteries.

Though I supposed it had been a long time since he had lived with them for real.

"What about your things?" I asked when we'd gone through the whole house and I'd seen nothing that reminded me of Donovan. "Are the remnants from your childhood stored away somewhere here?"

"Whatever I didn't take with me when I moved out, they threw away."

"Saves on storage, I suppose." Actually, I was wondering why the Kincaids even had a child. Between the lack of warmth and the erasure of his existence here, it was hard to imagine they'd really wanted him in the first place.

"I didn't have anything I wanted to keep. There wasn't anything here that I was attached to. What I like about this house is outside."

And that is how we ended up on the terrace looking out over the endless property beyond.

The land closest to the house was tiered and landscaped. The first level had a pool that had been covered for the season. The next level appeared to be a long stretch of lawn that was now just a bed of snow. A stone wall surrounded it, and beyond were trees and hills and land. Endless, as far as the eye could see.

It was the kind of yard meant to be played in. It was the kind of yard that needed children.

"It's beautiful. Absolutely stunning." I put my gloved hand in his as we walked down the icy staircase to the lawn below. "But what did you do here? Were you one of those little boys who climbed trees? Did you capture bugs and hang them on the bulletin board in your room? Did you swim? Did you have friends around here that you met in secret forts just beyond the property line?" I tried to imagine him. He'd been on the rowing team in college, so sport wasn't completely out of the realm of possibility in his background.

He shook his head dismissively. "There are no neighbors for miles. All that land is protected. No one can ever build on it."

"Then what?"

His lip lifted into a bashful smile. "I snowshoed."

"Snowshoed?" I was taken aback. "Like those flat things that trappers used to walk on?"

"Are you making fun?"

I shook my head. "I'm just surprised. I could never have guessed that. How did you get into snowshoes? I didn't even know that was a thing people still did."

We were at the bottom of the stairs now, treading through the yard, our boots sinking into snow that had drifted two feet deep.

"Well, as you can see, the snow was very wet in Connecticut. Not like that dry powder you have in Colorado. As a kid..." He trailed off, his jaw working as he got caught in his reminiscing. "Let's just say there wasn't much to keep me in the house. Or near it. Out there in those woods it's quiet. You can hear your own thoughts. I discovered early that I could hear myself better out there than I could in that house, silent as the house is.

"But it's not so easy to wander through the snowdrifts. You don't get very far without getting worn out." He laughed as the toe of my boot got stuck and I stumbled into him

"Yes. I see that," I laughed too, clutching onto him.

He wrapped his arms around my waist. "I would go for miles on those snowshoes. No one even noticed I was gone." He gave half a sardonic smile. "As long as I was back for dinner on time."

My chest pinched so tight. Like a fist wrapped around my heart.

He'd had so little nurturing in his life. Almost no one had modeled how to care for someone else. All the ways he'd cared for me, as misguided and inappropriate as they had been, they'd come from something truly organic. Something he'd devised completely on his own. No one had taught him how to love another person—and yet he'd still tried.

I had so little to give in return.

"If I had known you then," I offered what I had, "I like to think I would've met you in those woods."

"And if I had known *you* then, I would've schemed some way to make sure that you did."

I lifted my chin and pressed my mouth to his, hoping the heat of my body could do what the heat of his always did for me. Hoping it could erase the past and create images of a life with a vibrant house filled with warmth and love and never ever any clocks.

"YOU WERE president of your high school's campaign-finance board *and* the political action club?" I asked, reading the information from my phone.

"And the debate club," Donovan said smugly.

"And you were on the chess team. Figures."

After a walk around the property, we came inside to work. Raymond had gone into town to meet his wife for dinner, so it was just Donovan and I who'd sat at the long banquet table at six thirty precisely, eating a delicious meal of veal piccata and cranberry spinach salad.

When we finished, we poured ourselves some after-dinner drinks and headed upstairs. Earlier in the day, I'd received an email from Ferris containing the background report that Donovan had ordered on himself. I'd forgotten to cancel it in the craziness of the week. So now we were seated by the fire,

Donovan in the armchair and me on the floor, while I read highlights from the report out loud.

"I didn't get this for you just so you could make fun of everything, you know," he said when I laughed about his letter in snowshoeing.

"I didn't know you could letter in snowshoe! I didn't know that was a school activity!" I was still laughing.

"It wasn't. I had to get special permission. It was taken to the school committee and there was a judicial hearing." He circled his hand in the air, signaling much to-do. "They voted in my favor."

"It was that important to you, huh?"

He shrugged. "I wanted to see if I could do it."

"Mm hm." I took a swallow from my tumbler to hide my smile. Sounded like him.

I scanned further through the document. "'Businesses identified with ownership by subject.' This is a longer list than I was aware of, Donovan." I'd known he was a wealthy man, wealthier than the investment at the advertising firm, but wow. "'Reach, Inc., Gaston's, King-Kincaid Financial.' You have ownership in your father's firm?"

He nodded. "Weston and I both have stock there."

I went back to the list. "'Ex-Ore.' That's a gas company, right?"

"Yes."

"HtoO is that water foundation... 'Lannister End?'" I looked up questioningly.

"A bed and breakfast in Connecticut. Not far from here. I'll take you some time."

"I'd like that." I scrolled past the rest of the companies he held stock in and found the list of organizations he was associated with. "Did you found all these? 'A Better Day," I read.

He seemed startled. *"That*'s on there?"

"Yeah. What is it?"

"Just a charitable foundation. It's an umbrella for a bunch of other foundations." His brows were furrowed. Then he shook his head. "It's my father's organization, but he must have me listed on some of the entity papers."

"Ah." I'd moved on. "'MARCA?' What's that?"

He swirled his glass and watched the liquid dance around the bottom, as though it were more interesting than his answer. "It's, uh, it's an organization. Against rape. Men against rape culture and abuse." He let that sit, let me absorb the enormity of it.

Then he explained more. "It's geared at education. Teaching youth, especially—about consent, about women's rights."

"And you're the founder?"

"Yes."

"And you did that because of me?" I had a swell of pride and sentimentality. He was trying to be modest. I wasn't going to let him.

"Yes."

I set my phone down and stretched my feet out in front of me. The report hadn't been such a bad idea after all. I'd learned a few interesting things about him. But I'd learned just as many interesting things spending time with him this weekend.

And if I was going to learn more, I'd rather just ask.

"You graduated from Harvard with a Masters in business and stock in your father's financial firm. You already had an interest in finance and politics and ethics. You obviously felt compelled to start organizations that help people. Why did you choose to follow that by opening an advertising firm?"

He rested his elbow on the arm of the chair, his chin in his hand. "Why do *you* think I chose to open an advertising firm, Sabrina?"

"I don't want to sound narcissistic, but based on the pattern of things you've told me so far? I can't help but wonder if you chose it because *I* chose advertising as my emphasis."

"Go on."

Like I had tried to imagine him earlier in the day as a little boy, I tried now to imagine him as the young man he'd been in Cambridge. Intense and haunted. At the time, I thought he'd still been haunted by Amanda.

Now I reframed it, imagined him haunted by me—a woman he believed he shouldn't have, even when I was there in front of him. Even when I was in his arms.

"You chose advertising because that's what I chose," I said, my eyes fixed on my toes. "And you knew the irony of it because you never intended for me to work for you or with you. You just wanted to feel near me. Even when you were half a world away. Am I close?"

"It always felt like I was running away from you and running to you at the same time." His voice was low, the same timbre as the crackle of the fire behind me. "I'd lose myself in women—so many faceless women. Women who would let me treat them in terrible, terrible ways, just so I could forget you. And I never could."

I felt like he must've felt then too—like I wanted to run into what he was saying and run from it at the same time. I didn't want to know about other women. It hurt to hear it. But I wanted to hear how they would never be me.

And I also needed to know, just for my own peace of mind...

"I hate to ask this, but when you say you treated them terribly..." I trailed off, hoping he would fill in the blanks.

He did. "Most of the time I was in Tokyo, I was part of the underground BDSM scene. I never had relationships. Just sex with women who wanted to be dominated, mostly."

Now a new anxiety was building inside me. I sat up straighter. "You are a... Dominant? But we don't. I'm not." I didn't really know how to say what I was trying to say. We did some kinky stuff, but I wasn't about to be collared. "Don't you need that? I'm not a submissive. Not really, am I? Why are you laughing?"

He wasn't laughing so much as chuckling. "You are submissive enough, Sabrina. Trust me. I do need it. But it's not about the sex for me. I get what I need from you in other ways." He meant by taking care of me. By interfering and bossing and scheming to make my life the way he wanted it.

That's how he dominated me. That was what turned him on.

It was simple, and yet I had to process it. Had to let it sink in.

"Does that bother you?" he asked when I'd stayed silent for perhaps longer than he'd expected.

I tilted my head. "I'm just taking it in."

It was stirring something in me—something bigger, that I couldn't quite grasp yet.

Donovan tried to grab at the strings, tried to pull the something bigger into place. "It doesn't mean I'm not into what you need too, Sabrina."

That wasn't it. I wasn't worried about our sex life. He'd

been fully present there. "I think that's been kind of obvious that you're into that."

"I'd hope so."

But that was close to it, sitting right next to the bigger thing. Because all those years that we were apart, I'd held onto Donovan through this kink that I needed. This fantasy that he would do unspeakably filthy things to me. Thinking all the time that I was crazy and sick and wrong. I'd run from those thoughts, and if he'd been in my life, I would've run from him. I *did* run from him when I first saw him again. I ran right into Weston's arms, a place I never belonged.

All the while, he held onto me through this kink that *he* needed, watching me, saving me, taking care of me. He probably thought he was crazy. I knew he thought he was sick and wrong. He tried to run from me. He hoped I'd never find out. He ran across the ocean, to a place he never belonged.

It slammed through me then, like a gale force wind, taking my breath away and taking any doubt that lingered with it.

I looked up at him sitting in the chair gazing down at me. "I love you."

He was still, silent. He blinked in natural time.

"Did you hear me?"

His lips curved up ever so slightly. "I'm just taking it in."

I abandoned my tumbler and crawled into his lap, straddling him. His arms came around my hips. "I love you," I said again.

He searched my eyes, studied my features as though he expected to see doubt etched in my expression.

My doubts were gone, and he had to already know, had to know exactly how I felt about him. He always knew everything about me before I did. Didn't he know this too?

If he didn't, I'd tell him again. As many times as it took.

I put my hand on his cheek, stroked my thumb across the stubble, and bent down to graze my mouth against his. "I love you." A whisper this time.

I sucked his upper lip between mine then let it go. "I. Love. You."

I couldn't tell him again in words for a long time. Because the next time I brushed over him, he snapped into action, and took over. His hand clasped behind my neck and held me tightly in place as his lips ground into mine, and his tongue thoroughly fucked my mouth.

I moaned, rocking my hips along the length of his stiffening erection.

My body ached under the weight of my clothing. Every movement with them on was like wading through a river in armor. My limbs were too heavy. There were too many layers between his skin and mine.

I tugged at his sweater and whimpered; frustrated that it wasn't already off.

He broke from my mouth with a discontented grunt, letting me know he was just as eager as I was. With frantic hands, he pulled my shirt and my sweater off over my head together and tossed them to the floor. Then he leaned down and sucked along the top of my breasts, covering every square inch of flesh with his mouth, as though I were a paint-by-body-part project, and this section of my landscape had been designated to be painted with his lips.

I arched into him as I reached behind me to undo the clasp of my bra. The cups fell down, and he pushed them away so he could take a peaked nipple between his thumb and finger while he flicked the other lightly with his tongue.

"Oh my God, I love you." I was already seeing stars. What this man could do to my breasts...

I had to have more of him. I tugged with more urgency at his sweater, and he got the hint, withdrawing from me just long enough to shed the material keeping his torso from mine. Then finally, I ran the flats of my palms along the dips and planes of his bare chest. He was so hard and solid and warm. I drew his nipple into my mouth and nipped and was rewarded with the pulse of his cock underneath me.

But that wasn't where he wanted my lips.

He gathered my hair behind my neck and pulled sharply, tilting my chin up so that he could reclaim my mouth with his. I pressed into him, rubbing against him like he was a scratching post and I was a kitten with a bad itch.

Soon he stood, lifting me with him, never breaking our kiss. I wrapped my legs around his waist and held on as he carried me to the bed. He laid me down and immediately worked on ridding me of my jeans and panties, then he pushed my thighs apart and buried his head in between.

He sucked me and fingered me, tormenting me to climax twice before he stood to remove his own pants. When he was fully naked, he stood above me and fisted his cock, heavy and thick.

"Say it." I was greedy. He'd told me he loved me more than I'd told him, told me *before* I told him, but now I decided I wanted to hear him say it again too.

I didn't know if he could guess what I wanted. Whatever he said would work. I just wanted him to talk to me. I stretched my hand out toward his hard thigh, unable to reach him. "I want you to say it."

He stroked himself. Up and down. "You are mine, Sabrina." Close enough.

He crawled between my legs, and I spread them farther to make room for him. "Because I love you," he said, dragging the head of his cock down the split of my pussy. "Because I've always loved you."

He punctuated the last line by sliding all the way inside me.

I cried out as his tip touched the deepest part of me. "I'm yours."

He lowered himself over me, holding me closer and tighter than he usually did when he fucked me. "You're mine," he repeated as he moved inside me, establishing his rhythm, steady and brisk.

"And you're mine," I said, breathless.

He slowed ever so slightly, caught by surprise. Then he nodded and picked up his swift pace. "I'm yours." He kissed me. "I'm yours."

We made love like that well into the night, holding each other, kissing, whispering words we'd never said to anyone else. We wrapped ourselves in this chrysalis; this love we'd found that would change us both. This filthy love that had reminded me what it felt like to be cared for. This rich love that taught Donovan for the first time in his life what it could feel like to belong to someone.

EIGHTEEN

"**I** wouldn't move that if I were you," Donovan said as I waved my hand over my last remaining knight. "It's going to leave your queen vulnerable."

Oh, right. I could see it once he'd said that. It was Sunday afternoon, and we were sitting in the living room in front of the Christmas tree—me on the floor, him on the sofa. We'd have to leave in a few hours for the city, but first, at my request, Donovan had brought out a chessboard and was teaching me how to play more than just a basic game. I hadn't ever really attempted it seriously, but I'd thought I was better than I was. Apparently, chess is hard.

I moved my hand toward the nearby bishop, intending to pick it up, but stopped as he exclaimed, "If you touch that you have to move it."

"I want to move it." Didn't I? It was really the only move I had. He'd already captured most of my pawns. The coffee table was littered with dead white pieces, the board covered with strategic black pieces still in play.

"You might *want* to move it," he said, all smug and sexy. "But if you do, I'll have you pinned."

I looked innocently at my wrists. "You'll have me pinned? Is that a threat? Or the prize?"

He narrowed his eyes, which had gone dark with desire. "There is no place for seduction in chess, Sabrina." Despite his words, his gaze scratched down my torso, lingered at my breasts. "After, though. Definitely after."

"Then stop trying to tell me what moves to make. *After* will come a lot faster if you let me make my own mistakes." And there it was. The move I needed to make. I saw it now.

"You said you wanted me to teach you." His cell phone rang as I reached out to slide my rook.

I couldn't help it—I looked for his approval.

"Good girl," he said, looking at the screen on his phone. "It's the Tokyo office. I have to take it."

"Tokyo? What time is it there?" I didn't really expect him to answer.

But he did. "Five o'clock Monday morning." He hit the talk button and brought the phone to his ear. Then his conversation transformed into Japanese as he took his call, and I melted.

God it was hot when he talked in a foreign language.

He was hot no matter what he did. I was so completely smitten with him. So head over heels. So totally in love.

Without seeming to miss a beat in his call, he reached over the board and took the rook I'd just moved with his knight.

Fucker.

He could look that sexy, speak Japanese, and beat me at chess all at the same time. He'd better be planning to keep me.

Because more and more, I wasn't sure how I could live without him. Wasn't sure how I ever had.

The nature of the phone call seemed to intensify, requiring more of Donovan's attention. He stood to pace as he talked. I made another move on the board—probably a stupid move. I couldn't tell without his discerning commentary. I spent a few minutes after that trying to imagine the next moves, the way he said good chess players did. He'd move this. I'd move that. All the way to the end of the game. But I didn't have that kind of vision. I couldn't sit with it that long. And I wasn't good at guessing what he would do.

I never had been.

I looked up at him, one hand buried in his slacks pocket as he stood, muscles tense, in front of the window. He would need me later to distract him from the dilemma happening on the other side of the world. I would soothe him with my mouth, with my pussy. Let him find release inside me in whatever way he needed.

Right now, I couldn't help him.

I stood up and stretched, and headed down the hall to find the closest bathroom. When I came out, I could still hear Donovan on the phone so I wandered towards the opposite end of the house, studying the artwork that I hadn't really looked at during our tour.

"It's you, Sabrina. I thought I heard you kids out here."

I turned around to find Raymond had stepped out of his study.

"Just me. Donovan's on the phone. Work. Of course." I peeked around him as discreetly as possible. The study was the one room I hadn't seen, and I was curious by nature.

Raymond's brows lifted. "That works out perfectly, actually. I've been meaning to talk to you. Alone. Won't you step into my office?"

Goosebumps ran down my arms despite the sweater I was wearing. Nothing good could come from a conversation that Raymond Kincaid wanted to have with me alone.

But as I said, I was curious by nature.

"Sure thing."

I stepped into the study with my back straight and my head held high. Whatever happened in here, I reminded myself, Donovan was not Raymond Kincaid. Raymond could say what he wanted. It meant nothing about my relationship with his son.

The office was impressive, but not my style. The walls and furniture were all completely done in mahogany with leather accents. His desk was oversized and ornate, gold filigree lined the scrollwork on the edges and the legs. The shelves over-flowed with books that looked old and as if they'd never been cracked open. Showpieces. Probably a lot of first editions and out-of-print collector's pieces. There was a faint smell of cigars and cologne—a scent Donovan would never have worn. Too strong. Too musky. All of it was very masculine and rich. Boast-ful. Arrogant.

I was such a judger.

No. I wasn't judging. I was preparing.

"Have a seat. Please." Raymond gestured to the chair in front of his desk rather than the intimate seating area by the fireplace. It was a move that established authority. One that put me in my place.

Next, he'd pull out his checkbook, wave it around.

I could see his moves. Maybe I wasn't so bad at chess after all.

I took a seat, crossed my legs. But I wasn't vulnerable. He didn't have me pinned like he might've thought.

"Is this where the rich financial mogul offers the lowly girl from the wrong side of the tracks some exorbitant amount to stop seeing his son?" I said it with a smile so that we could play it off as a joke. If I needed to.

Raymond barely reacted, but he did react. I wouldn't have noticed if I wasn't watching as carefully as I was, but since I was watching him so carefully, I saw the slight jerk of his eyelid, heard the soft catch of his breath as he sat down across from me.

Then he let out a hearty laugh. "Amusing. Amusing." He straightened the calendar pad on the corner of his desk.

Everything on the desk's surface, I noticed now, was straight and tidy. In its place. I wasn't so sure he liked things clean or immaculate though, so much as he liked the look of the lines and right angles. The room was full of both.

"With Donovan just in the other room..." he said, in continued amusement.

Maybe I'd been wrong about his motives. I wouldn't be upset if that were the case.

He looked up suddenly, his brows furrowed, eyes inquisitive. "What would be an exorbitant amount? Half a million? A full million?"

My stomach sank. Even knowing this was where it had been leading, I'd hoped I was wrong. Not so much for my sake, but for Donovan's. He knew his parents were terrible, but wouldn't it be nice to find out that they weren't?

I didn't answer Raymond. I couldn't. It was too degrading.

"A full million could go a long way," he prodded. "Could

pay for all of your sister's students loans. Get her set up real nice after she graduates."

He'd checked into me.

Well, I didn't have to ask where Donovan had gotten his stalking genes. I gritted my teeth and nodded as I inhaled slowly, reminding myself it wasn't cool to punch out a seventy-year-old man. If I even could—he seemed to be in pretty good shape for his age.

The shittiest part of it all? That he thought his son's happiness was only worth that much. I'd been around their kind of money long enough to know how fast a million dollars ran out. I'd felt Donovan's love long enough to know it ran deeper than money could buy.

I laughed now. It was all I could do if I wasn't going to beat him up. "I think by definition, exorbitant means there isn't an amount you could name."

Raymond studied me carefully. I could see he was forming the next bid, wondering if two million would do it. Or three. Even despite what I'd said.

Whatever he saw in my face eventually brought him to the conclusion that I was telling the truth. "I wondered as much," he said.

It felt powerful. Like I had check.

I wanted checkmate. "And even if there were an amount, you would be hard-pressed to convince your son to let me go."

Raymond nodded knowingly. "That's not surprising. Donovan likes to marry for love. Susan and I—we get along, don't get me wrong. But we both understood the reason the practice of marriage was invented. It's a social arrangement. It shouldn't be based on emotion or tied to sentimentality. It's meant to protect her assets and mine, and those of our heirs.

You can understand why I would therefore be concerned about you. You would be the mother of our grandchildren. While I would prefer a more suitable wife for him, we certainly cannot dictate whom he spends his life with. It didn't hurt to try."

"Wait—that's it?" I was reeling, disoriented like a fish pulled fresh from water. I couldn't keep up my own reactions to his revelations. First, that he and his wife had a loveless relationship—which I could've guessed—but for him to admit it was something else entirely. Then, to hear his outdated stance on marriage, and finally to arrive at the conclusion: 'oh well' he'd tried?

And Donovan and I weren't even engaged!

"I'll certainly recommend that Donovan choose otherwise if he asks. But he won't. A decade ago, I'd have told him there is nothing wrong with having a marriage for propriety and a mistress on the side. Prince Charles did it. Now even *he* is married to his mistress." He might as well have said, 'what is the world coming to?' The subtext was evident.

"Yeah, no. I could not stand to be a mistress." This was the oddest conversation to be having with my boyfriend's father. "And Donovan wouldn't stand for that either," I added with certainty. "And we are not –" *engaged.*

I stood up and rubbed my sweaty palms along my leggings. I didn't want to talk about this anymore with him. After this weekend, I actually could begin to see a future with Donovan. Long reaching winters, and summers, and chess games, and children.

But those were conversations to have with him. Not his father. Not because it was best for the future of the family name.

"You're welcome to leave anytime," Raymond said, rising to his feet. "I've said my piece."

And I'd said mine. I nodded, unwilling to say thank you for whatever this had been.

As I turned to go, my eye was caught by a series of plaques on the wall by the door. They were honorary plaques that had been given over several years to an organization I recognized—A Brighter Day. I stepped closer to examine one.

"This is from the president," I said in awe.

Raymond came up behind me. "Ah, yes. We are very proud of what we've done with A Brighter Day. Donovan has been very involved since high school."

"You must be. What kind of organization is it exactly?" I was only interested because Donovan's name had been attached to it. And obviously the organization was a big fucking deal. Plus, the man really needed to brag more, assert his authority.

"It's a series of foundations," Raymond explained. "They address a variety of different issues, each one tailored to a specific need. There is one that helps children prone to asthma that live or go to school in areas near freeways, which studies have shown can increase asthma attacks. Another provides free education to coal miners who are searching for another line of work."

So Raymond wasn't completely terrible after all. No one ever really was, I was learning.

"Another provides scholarships to kids with exceptional IQs, particularly those who have graduated early, and are seeking help to bridge the gap to Ivy League schools since those universities don't generally provide full rides. Another—"

The hair on the back of my neck stood up. "That one," I interrupted. "What's the name of the scholarship foundation?"

I already knew the answer. I could already see this move. It was a move I should've seen so long ago.

"The MADAR Foundation."

NINETEEN

The words were still throbbing in my ears, still pulsing in my veins, still vibrating in my body when a different voice piped in from behind me.

"I can explain."

I shifted to see Donovan at the door, panic clearly written all over his expression.

"Sabrina. Come with me, I'll tell you everything." His hand reached out, beckoning, his voice pleading. His eyes pierced through me, but I couldn't see him the way I had previously. He seemed blank to me, or my eyes were too glazed. If there had been a piece of art there, I'd no longer see it.

Raymond clapped his hands suddenly. "That's why I know your name!" he exclaimed. "You were one of the scholarship girls. I'm not very good with names, especially out of context, but I should have put that together sooner."

Me too, Raymond. I should have put it together sooner, too.

Though now he wasn't so sure. He squinted, trying to

recall. "That *was* you, wasn't it? What happened? You dropped out of school."

"Let's talk about this on—"

I put my finger up to hush Donovan. He'd had his chance to talk. He'd had weeks, months, *years* to tell me the truth.

I turned instead to Raymond. "My father had a heart attack. And I missed the end of the semester to go home to watch him die." My throat was tight as the rage from all those years ago returned like bile. "My scholarship was pulled because I missed finals, and when I appealed..."

I turned my focus on the younger Kincaid; there was venom in my stare. Just like before when my past had been reformed in my mind when Donovan had shown where he had been the puppet master behind the scenes, it was being re-created again now. The anger and hostility I had felt for a decade had been toward some vague corporate charitable foundation. Now there was a face to hate.

But which one?

I spun back toward Raymond. "Who decided?" I was desperate for the answer. Desperate for the answer to be different than the one I knew it was. "Who decided to deny my appeal? Did you even read over my case or was the decision all in Donovan's hands?" My elbows were tight at my sides, my hands in fists, and I was shaking. Shaking from rage that made my breathing shudder.

Raymond lifted one brow and turned his stare toward his son, understanding lighting his gaze. "You already tried to give her up," he said pointing a finger in Donovan's direction. "That's why you didn't want her back at Harvard." It was clear he was just putting pieces together himself.

He hadn't been part of this.

It had all been Donovan.

And I'd been such a fool.

I needed some space to breathe. Needed to be away from the two pairs of eyes staring me down, watching my every reaction. I wanted off their chessboard. I brushed past Donovan, running from the room, no destination in mind except to get away.

He was right behind me, on my heels, as he always was.

"Don't listen to my father. Let's talk about this. Let me explain. It was better if you weren't there, Sabrina."

We were in the middle of the house when I whirled around to face him. "Better for *who*? For *you*?"

"For *you*. Always for you." His voice was thick with agony.

But his misery couldn't dare to compare with mine. His was a lie. A boldfaced lie.

"Better for me because I wouldn't ever have to face your family? Because you'd never have to bring home a scholarship girl to meet your folks? Because you thought I'd be ashamed to stand in the presence of the almighty Raymond Kincaid?" I'd believed him when he'd said he wanted me away from him because he was afraid he would love me too much.

Stupid, stupid me.

He wasn't afraid of loving me too much. He was afraid his parents would hate me too much.

"No, it's not true. What he said is not true. He's guessing. He thinks I give a shit about their opinion, and I don't. I never cared about that."

I rocked back and forth on the balls of my feet. I wanted to believe him. It could be so easy to let him take care of this—of me—like always.

Down the hall, Raymond stepped out of his study to watch

us, and I knew I had to ignore "easy." He was a visual reminder that he'd had Donovan first. I couldn't dispute that he was at Donovan's roots any more than I could dispute that my parents, and Audrey, were at mine.

I shook my head. "I'm finding it hard to believe you right now."

Before he could argue again, I turned away and ran upstairs to the room we'd been sharing and slammed the doors behind me.

He followed. I knew he would.

"What about trust?" he said, bursting through the doors. "You said we should trust each other."

I bent to pull the cord of my charger from the wall by the bed, then dropped it into my purse along with my cell phone. "Well, that was stupid. I was stupid to believe that someone like you could ever learn anything about trust."

"Don't say that. I've shown you parts of me that no one else has ever seen." He stood at the foot of the bed, his fist anchored on his hip as if that was the only way to keep it from reaching out to me.

"You mean I saw you vulnerable?" I spat. "So fucking sad. I'm sure it doesn't even compare to the parts that you saw of me."

"I was only ever trying to protect you."

"Bullshit. I am tired of the fucking bullshit. Just tell me the goddamn truth!"

"This is the truth," he yelled.

I tilted my chin up defiantly. "Okay. If it's all true, why didn't you tell me that day in the office? Why didn't you tell me when I asked you if there was 'anything else?' Why didn't you confess this when we decided no more secrets? What about that?"

His lids shut halfway, as though the things I said were too heavy and hard to bear. When he opened them again fully, they were glossy and deep green.

"Because I knew this would hurt you," he said softly. "And I was done hurting you. I didn't want to hurt you anymore."

"You didn't want to hurt me. Of course." My tone was thick with sarcasm. "Let me guess—you 'didn't want to hurt me' is the reason you snapped away my scholarship too. Just like the reason you didn't want a relationship with me. *You didn't want to hurt me.* It's the reason you always run. The reason you always fucking end up hurting me."

"It's not that simple." His body was tense with how complicated it was.

"It never is," I laughed sardonically, spotting a stray earring I'd left on the nightstand. I grabbed it and stuck it in my purse.

Donovan took two steps towards me but didn't go farther when I put my hand up in protest.

"If you had been with me, I would have destroyed you," he said emphatically. More emphatically than he would have if he were closer. "Look how close I came to destroying you while you were at school. Look what I did to you with my jealousy over Weston. With your grades. I couldn't have you at Harvard. You were better off away from me."

And there it was, spelled out. Finally. His reasoning. His confession. His truth. No better than the excuses Raymond gave.

"Do you have any idea how nearly you destroyed me by taking that away from me?" My voice was as unsteady as my hands. School had been the only thing I thought I had left to live for after my father's death, besides Audrey. "Harvard was supposed to have been our way out. It was going to be the future for my sister and me. And you took it away because you couldn't handle yourself around me?"

His shoulders sagged with the weight of this truth. "I took care of you. I tried to make it up."

I blinked back tears, but it was useless. They were coming anyway. Angry and hot. "Did you ever even really love me? Or was the decade that followed just a way to assuage your guilt?"

"How can you even ask that?" Deep in his throat, his voice broke. "I love you, Sabrina. All this time, I have loved you."

I bit my lip and tugged my purse up on my shoulder, hugging my arms around myself. "I don't think you know what love is."

With tears streaming down my face, I strolled past him out the doors. His mother had come out of her room at the other end of the hall, but she didn't try to talk to me. Just watched. A family of watchers and stalkers—none of them knew how to connect with people. None of them knew how to love.

I'd feel sad for them all if I wasn't so busy feeling sad for myself.

I trotted back down the stairs. My luggage was already by the door, waiting for our trip back home. I waited in the foyer for Donovan to arrive, because of course he would.

And he did.

"You're wrong," he said, as he walked toward me. "I might not love you in the pretty traditional way that you're looking for, like some *hero*, like Weston might. But I do love you. Everything I did—everything I *do*—is because I love you."

I ached for him.

Every limb, every joint, every cell ached with the pain of

his words. Because I loved the way he loved me. I preferred the way he loved me a million times to the way a man like Weston could—or *any other man* could even dare to try.

But I couldn't heal his hurt.

Because I hurt too much right then too. I hurt with my own pain, pain that he had inflicted with his lies and deceit and betrayal. Maybe he wasn't lying about why he sent me away, why he took away my scholarship. But at the very least he had lied by keeping the secret since we decided to be together.

He should have told me.

I couldn't say whether I would've forgiven him or not.

But he should have fucking told me.

"I'm going to call a cab," I said, not looking at him directly. "I can't be in a car with you."

"Don't be ridiculous."

I spoke right on top of him. "I'm not being ridiculous. I don't want to be in a car with you for two hours. I can't stand to look at you. I can't stand to hear you breathe. I can't be near you."

His nostrils flared. He opened his mouth, his expression saying he was about to argue more.

But then I added, "I'm too hurt." And if he couldn't see how wounded I was, how absolutely heartbroken, then he was blind.

He looked at me a moment, and his shoulders sagged. "Fine. John can take you. I'll take one of my father's cars."

Good. It was what I had wanted.

And not what I wanted too. Part of me wished he'd have put his foot down and said he was coming with me. Wished he would prove to me the truth he wanted me to know. Everything hurt and I wanted it to stop. I wanted to bury my face in his sweater and sob. I wanted him to make it better like he always did in his crazy Donovan ways.

How ironic that I still wanted that? That the cause of my pain and the source of my balm could be one and the same?

But we were done talking. No more words were exchanged, none with meaning anyway. There could be no comfort. There could be no balm. He didn't try very hard, and I couldn't let him give it to me.

I refused his help in putting on my coat. I turned away from him as I waited for the car to pull up. But while John put my bag in the trunk, I snuck a peek in Donovan's direction and caught his eye accidentally.

Immediately, I turned my head away, but he'd already seen me.

He took that look as an invitation, and rushed to get my door.

"This isn't over, Sabrina," he said holding it open for me. "You can take whatever time you need to be angry with me. We can fight. We can be silent. But you and I are not over. I think we can agree that I've already proven myself a patient man."

I pursed my lips together, unwilling to give him anything— not a scowl, not a pout. Definitely not hope. I climbed into the back seat and refused to watch out the window as he became a tiny figure in the distance.

DONOVAN'S DRIVER WAS A PROFESSIONAL. He was trained not to react to what happened in the backseat of the car, whether it was sex or a woman crying her eyes out all the way from Washington, Connecticut to Hell's Kitchen.

I was thankful for that. It gave me the quiet I needed to think. To mourn.

Maybe mourn was dramatic. But was it?

I wasn't a teenager involved in my first real relationship. I didn't assume that the first fight equaled the end. I was mature enough to understand that even the most aggrieved wrongdoings could be forgiven. That even the most horrendous betrayals could be overcome.

But this thing with Donovan was so complicated and multifaceted. It wasn't just about whether or not I could forgive him. It was also about whether or not we could move on from this. Whether there was a decent enough foundation.

And one thing I did know about relationships was that people never changed. How could I ask him to be a different person? Someone who understood how to really love someone else. Someone who could truly put my needs and wants before his own self-defeating behavior. Was it even possible?

I couldn't think about any of it right now. I couldn't even think about talking to him. I was in too much pain. Too heartbroken. And too angry.

I got to my apartment building around eight thirty that night, exhausted and worn down. John offered to help with my bag, but I insisted I'd take it myself. It wasn't heavy and I didn't want to deal with a hassle.

I was alone on the elevator, and when I got off, the hall was quiet except for a deliveryman standing at my neighbor's closed door. His ski hat was pulled low, his head bent and hidden by the white paper sack filled with something that smelled like curry. I trudged past him to my door with my suitcase and fished in my purse for my keys.

I must've been too distracted by my thoughts, by the avalanche of emotions that had buried me, because I didn't notice the deliveryman slip up behind me as I slid the key into the lock.

I didn't notice him until his hand was on my hip and the knife was at my throat and his mouth was at my ear.

"Hello again, Sabrina," Theo Sheridan said. "Did you miss me?"

TWENTY

I didn't scream. Because of the knife at my throat. But I made a shuddering noise as I inhaled, as close to a wail as I dared without risking my life, and the blade trembled against my skin, my heart pounding underneath it.

I might've thought this was a dream, that I'd fallen asleep on the ride home and this was yet another one of the frequent nightmares I'd had over the years about Theodore Sheridan coming after me. I'd had so many.

As real as those had felt in the moment, when I woke with sweat pouring from my skin, my heart pounding against my rib cage, the hair raised on the back of my neck, I could see now how very different reality was from the nightmare. I could see how it really felt to have a predator at your back, threatening, in control. I *remembered* now. Remembered how much more terrible the real thing was.

"Careful," Theo warned, pressing the metal against my

jugular. "You won't make another sound now, will you." It wasn't a question. It was a command. It was a directive.

"No." But that was a sound, so I shook my head carefully, quickly, both erasing the word uttered and acknowledging that I would do as he said. The feel of the blade against my neck as I made the movement was nearly paralyzing. But I couldn't let it be. I had to do what he said.

Because if I didn't...

I couldn't think about what would happen if I didn't do what he wanted. I couldn't think about what would happen period.

"Good girl." Those familiar words, a phrase I loved to hear from Donovan, now made my stomach turn, and I had to fight not to throw up. He eased the knife away. "Now put the key back in the lock and let us in."

Sound rushed in my ears like I was in a wind tunnel. The hallway felt like it was closing in around me. Like soon there wouldn't even be enough room to take a full breath. I knew if I went into that apartment with him, alone, my chances of walking away unharmed decreased exponentially.

Yet there wasn't a single alternative action I could think to take. A dozen self-defense classes over a decade and I was stumped. Any move I made, he'd have that knife on me. He'd cut me where it hurt.

I had no chance. No choice.

I nodded and lifted my trembling hand back to the lock. Though I intended to keep silent, a long whimpering sound came from my mouth as I tried to align the key. What was he doing here? Why was he out of jail? I sent up a quick furtive prayer to whoever would listen that someone would walk down the hall and discover us. Maybe if I took my time...

The metal of the blade scraped my skin again and I jolted.

"Hurry it up, Sabrina," he warned. "I'm telling you right now, I'm not putting up with any games from you."

I hurried, got the key in the lock, turned it, heard it click. I moved my hand to the knob and opened the door.

I didn't move until Theo nudged me with his knee. I couldn't bring myself to enter my dungeon so willingly. That's what it would be now. A place I couldn't escape. A place that was no longer safe.

I choked back a sob as I started across the threshold.

"Take your suitcase," he said when I'd made to leave it in the hall. "Grab the delivery bag, too."

He moved away from me so that I could grab the items and I wondered if this was my chance to escape, but I couldn't think fast enough. He was too big. And I was too scared.

And now he had me at another disadvantage—when I walked into the apartment, my hands were full. My purse was on one shoulder, my hand clasped the suitcase handle, and the other arm held the delivery bag. I stood frozen, unmoving, waiting for his next order.

Theo shut the door behind me and locked it, not bothering with the deadbolt. The sound the lock made was a simple click, but in my ears, it clanged like the closing of a cell. He flipped on a couple of lights, then scanned the interior of my apartment, looking at *my* things. At my *life*. At pieces of me he had no right to look at.

How had this happened? How had he gotten past my doorman?

The overwhelming scent of curry coming from the bag I held gave a clue. "Is this how you got in here?" I asked.

"Yeah." He was visibly proud of himself. "I hung around

until someone else was walking in. Then slipped in with them. No one shuts the door on food delivery."

He'd planned this. It wasn't just a whim. He'd carefully planned this.

Theo took the bag from my arms and laid it on the ground. "Drop the suitcase. Where's your phone?"

I blinked. The question was easy, thinking was not. "My purse. It's in my purse." My phone was in my purse! I was so close to a way of communication. It felt like I was handcuffed, having it so near and not being able to use it.

"Hand it over." He held his palm out, waiting.

Slowly, I dragged the strap from my shoulder and looked inside. I was still shaking, but I made more of the production, going slower than I needed to. If I could find it, if I could call Donovan with a swipe of my thumb...

"What's taking so long?" He was too smart. He pointed the knife at me like a gun.

I stayed focused on my goal, peering into my bag, doing my best to ignore the weapon aimed at me. "I have a lot of stuff in here. I'm looking." I already had it in my grasp. Just couldn't get it unlocked.

"Give it to me." He yanked the purse from me and the phone dropped into the belly of the bag. He found it easily and swiped at the screen. "What's the code?"

I hung my head, defeated. My defeat was in losing the phone, not in surrendering the code to get into it. I didn't really have anything in there that I was afraid of Theo finding. What I feared was already standing right in front of me. "1123."

He punched the numbers in and smiled when he got access. "Sit on the couch," he said without looking at me, distracted by the contents of my cell.

I shuffled to do his bidding, but was this my chance while he was distracted? I looked around the room for an opportunity, for something that could be used as a weapon against his knife. The lamp next to the couch—was it too heavy? The fire poker—was it too far?

A rustling of paper caught my attention. Theo had reached into the delivery bag and pulled out a bottle of beer. He snapped off the bottle top and took a swig as he came around the couch.

The beer was in one hand, my phone in his other. Then where was the knife?

I quickly searched down his body, my eyes landing on the sheath fastened at his hip.

"Don't even think about it, Bri." He caught me looking. "I'm a fast draw. And I'm not too bad at improvising, either."

His expression said he wouldn't mind if I tested him. I had a feeling he enjoyed the idea of improvising. I was sure I wouldn't.

So I wouldn't cause trouble right now. Not until I was sure it was trouble I could get away with, or at least trouble that had a chance.

"When did you get out of jail?" I didn't want to talk to him, but just like the delivery question, I wanted to know. I needed to know how all of the things that had been set up to keep me safe had failed. It was a less terrible form of torture than imagining the things he was about to do to me, and anytime I stopped thinking about the *how's*, my mind immediately went to the *what's next's*.

"So you knew about that? I wondered." He paced a couple steps in front of me. "Was that your idea? Sending me away in the first place."

He said it casually, but the subtext was undeniably filled with vengeance.

Oh shit.

Was that why he was here? Revenge?

"I didn't know anything about that until just recently. I promise." I sounded desperate for him to believe me. I *was* desperate.

I pulled my coat tighter around me. It was warm in the apartment, and I didn't need it, but it was a barrier between him and me. Small, but I'd take any barrier I could get.

"Doesn't really matter." He shrugged. "See, I know it was Kincaid who put me in a jail cell."

"No. It was you. You put yourself in that jail cell when you raped that woman." I regretted the words as soon as I said them, true as they were. It wasn't a good idea to provoke him.

Yet, here he was provoked. He slid my phone into his back pocket, and stared at me hard with greedy eyes. "What's with the coat? Hiding something?"

"Just..." *myself.* "Cold."

"I don't like it. Take it off. Make yourself comfortable. We're going to be together a while." He set his beer bottle on the coffee table.

I trembled so much it was hard to slip the buttons through the holes as I removed my coat like he'd asked. I kept my focus on my task, but I knew he watched me the whole time. I could feel the weight of his disgusting, captivated gaze. When it was off and bunched up around me where I sat, I felt naked, even though I was still completely dressed in my leggings and the thin nylon sweater I'd been wearing all day. I suddenly wished I'd worn something heavier. Something not so light. Something that didn't show my form or the line of my breasts. Something much more difficult to remove.

I forced myself to look at him, and my vulnerable feelings only intensified. His expression, though still dark, was now also terrifyingly excited.

"Much better." His smile was gleeful as he pulled out his knife and came around the coffee table to bend down in front of me.

I cowered back involuntarily.

He grabbed my sweater and fisted the material in his hand. Then pressed the knife down at the V of my neckline.

There was nowhere to go, but I tried, I really tried to press myself into that couch, to make myself smaller as he cut down the center of my sweater with his knife. To make myself not exist. To make myself nothing because if I was nothing I couldn't feel this or know this or ever remember what it was like to feel a madman breathing over me, sawing through my clothing with the blade. It was a really sharp blade I discovered. He nicked me a couple of times with the tip.

Because he wasn't careful.

Because he didn't care.

Because he wanted me to know just how sharp the blade was.

When the entire front of my sweater hung open, he leaned back to look at his work. "I think I'd like it better if you didn't have the bra." He looked at me expectantly, as if waiting for me to do something.

I was already trying to be someplace else. Where did I want to be? Anywhere was better than here. But if I could find the perfect place, I could lose myself completely, and not be here at all.

After I didn't move, he said, "Are you going to take it off, or am I?"

I shook myself from the daze. He wanted me to do something. Something gross and terrible and I couldn't do it, but I couldn't let him do it more. "Just take off the bra?" I asked.

"Stop procrastinating. Take it off or I will."

I reached behind my back and somehow managed to undo the clasp. Then I slid the straps down one sleeve of my sweater and pulled the whole thing out of the other sleeve.

Theo bent forward toward me, and I shrunk away.

"Stay fucking still." He flashed the knife, and now I had to do his bidding. My face crumpled, but I didn't move this time when he leaned in and arranged my clothing, pulling the sweater open wide enough that the inside curves of my breasts could be seen.

I felt disgusting. Like trash. Used, and he hadn't even used me yet.

Yet.

I sat silent for him, but inside I was screaming.

He sat back on the coffee table, and studied me appraisingly. His eyes darkened. "That's really nice."

I tried to imagine what he liked most about what he saw. The damaged clothing that proved non-consent? The blood trickling down my skin? The hint of flesh that he would soon take as he willed?

I had to lose myself. Where could I go? I could be in the cold, in the snowdrifts of Washington, Connecticut, holding onto Donovan, letting him kiss me warm.

"I would've gotten off," Theo said, turning back to the earlier conversation. "I had the better lawyers. That woman couldn't afford shit for lawyers. And that's what really matters in these cases."

Jesus, he was such a sick fuck.

I wanted to ignore him, and I tried, tried to live in Donovan's arms, in the cold, in the snow. But I could still hear Theo's voice penetrating my fantasy.

"Then Donovan Kincaid shows up with his million-dollar law team and suddenly the trial goes an entirely different direction. That is not how that should've gone down. What the fuck was with that? Why did Donovan care about *me*? It didn't make any sense." He was angry and animated.

He paused to pull on his beer bottle before going on. "So I've been in jail. And I've had time to think about it. You have a lot of time to think in there. I thought about you—about that night outside The Keep clear back at Harvard. I have to admit I couldn't remember your name for a while. I wasn't sure that you were the connection, even with that history."

He set the bottle down, and leaned forward again, his elbows on his thighs. "But then two things happened." With one hand he held up a single finger. "First, I was told I was getting early parole at the end of the week." He held up a second finger. "Second, the day after I came home, my brother said he'd been at a wedding with Donovan, and his girlfriend was some chick named Sabrina Lind."

I'd been scared about how he'd violate my body since the minute he'd shown up in the hallway. Now I was terrified that wasn't all he had in mind.

"Yeah," Theo said registering my fear with a new gleam in his eye. "All the pieces fell together for me." He stretched forward and set one finger at the base of my throat, right where my pulse was. My heart was pounding, and now he could feel it. He could actually feel my fear.

I didn't move.

I didn't breathe.

I tried to will my heart not to beat.

After a few seconds, he trailed his finger downward, between my breasts where sweat had gathered, through the blood that stained my skin. "Kincaid put me in jail as some sort of revenge for you. Which is bullshit." His volume increased sharply on the word bullshit, making me jump.

He sat back again and brought his finger to his mouth to suck on. Calmer, he said, "I never even got to fuck you. There was no reason for revenge."

I was shaking again, or shaking *more*; I'd never really stopped.

How could I get out of this? How could I possibly get out of this?

"You don't want to do anything to me. You just got out of jail. You don't want to go back." Jesus, I was begging. Did begging even work with predators? I couldn't remember what I'd read over the years.

"Why not? Did you know I have to register as a sex offender for the rest of my life? No one's going to give me a job on Wall Street. I'll never get to work with money with a prison history. I really don't have much to look forward to, Sabrina, besides this." His eyes narrowed into slits as he hissed, "Nothing's fucking taking it away from me."

He had nothing to lose. That made him more dangerous now than he'd been a decade ago.

I sucked my lower lip under my teeth, and tried not to cry.

He retrieved my phone from his pocket. "What was the code again?"

I told him, and he entered it into the screen.

"This wasn't me though," I said, trying to find a way to reason with him. "I wasn't the one who stopped you that night, even. And I had nothing to do with Donovan getting involved in your case." It was all true, but I felt like the most terrible person in the world to pretend I hadn't wanted Donovan to save me. To pretend I wasn't proud of the actions he'd taken against Theodore.

But this was about survival. Whatever I needed to do to get out of this. Whatever I needed to say, I'd say it.

"That doesn't really matter, like I said. This is about what will hurt Kincaid." He glanced at me. "I'm pretty sure hurting you is going to hurt him more than anything else I could do to him. Plus, this is going to be pretty damn fun for me. I haven't been able to play in a long, long time."

He slipped my phone back into his pocket. "You and Kincaid don't text much, huh? Was sure a sweet shot of your pussy you sent him, though. Makes me nice and hard." He rubbed a hand over his erection.

Bile crept into the back of my throat. I swallowed it down.

I'd only sent one picture in all the time I'd been with Donovan. The picture with his initials drawn on my skin in an intimate region. It was probably the only naughty picture on my phone. Of course that's what Theo would find.

I started rocking back and forth now, hugging myself. And the whimper I'd been trying to hold down returned.

"What are you going to do to me?" I knew already. He'd basically already said. But I didn't know the details, and maybe if I knew them, maybe if I heard him say the words, I could better prepare myself for what was coming.

Who was I fooling? There was nothing that would prepare me for this. Tears streamed down my face.

Theo cocked his head. "I haven't decided yet."

"Really?" I could hear the stupid waver of hope in my voice.

He laughed, a big hearty laugh. "Oh, I'm going to fuck you. I just haven't decided how I'm going to like it most."

I pressed my thighs together instinctively.

And then, when I saw how much my fear and panic turned him on, I jumped and ran, darting for my bedroom. It was automatic. Spontaneous. I didn't think; I just did. It wasn't like the bedroom was any safer. It was simply... away.

I didn't make it very far before he grabbed me. Wrapping his arms around my waist, he lifted me off the ground in a horrible parody of the scene with Donovan at Weston's wedding. I kicked and screamed, which earned me his hand on my throat. My scream transformed into a choked gurgle.

"I told you to shut the fuck up." He dumped me face down on the couch, and held me with one hand at my neck, while the other pinned one of my arms at the small of my back.

I managed to turn my face so I could breathe, so I could see the room. He had knocked over the beer bottle when he bolted after me. It lay only a couple of feet from me now, the remains spilled but unbroken. I watched it roll towards the fireplace and wondered if that would be my focal point while this asshole raped me.

And I was mad at myself now, too. By running, I'd made it more fun for Theo. He might've waited a while before deciding he was ready.

Not that waiting would've mattered. He would've raped me eventually, and this time I didn't have Donovan watching from above.

Or did I?

A new flame of hope kindled inside me. *There are cameras in my bedroom.* I didn't know if they were in the main part of my apartment. I'd made Donovan promise not to watch me on them anymore. But I'd learned tonight that he'd broken promises before—and wouldn't he be more likely to want to watch me when it was the only way he had access to me? When we were fighting, and I wasn't answering his calls?

If I could get Theo to the bedroom, maybe I would have a chance. It was a small chance, but a chance.

"I'm sorry," I said, trying my best to feign obedience. I gave him my other trembling hand voluntarily to demonstrate how sorry I was. "I was just thinking you might like it better in the bedroom."

"I like it better when you don't do any thinking," Theo responded gruffly.

Right. I knew that.

"I meant," oh God, oh God, it was so hard not to sob as I said it, "I thought you'd like it better if you had to chase me."

He had moved his hand from my throat so he could hold my wrists while he undid his jeans. At least, I was guessing that's what he was doing from the sound of the belt and the zipper—I couldn't see him from this position. But at my words, he stilled.

"Sabrina," he said, a note of awe in his tone. "If we play chase, you're likely going to get hurt."

As if I wasn't going to get hurt anyway.

"I'm not advocating against it. I'm just telling you how the game works." He pressed against me, and even though I still had my leggings on, I could feel he was bare. His naked penis rubbed up and down along the crevice of my ass. He felt thick and gross.

I started crying harder. He was going to put that inside me. I didn't even know *where* he was going to put it inside me. He could put it in so many places. He was going to hurt me. He was going to violate me.

And I had to fight.

He let go of my hands, to maneuver my pants, and with everything I had I pushed up off the sofa, shoving him backward and off of me.

He was slightly surprised, but he knew I was his captive. And he enjoyed the chase. So he was more amused than upset.

Like before, I made a beeline for the bedroom. If I could just get in there, if Donovan could see us, he would call the cops or the doorman—someone who could get here immediately. I believed it. I had to believe it.

But Theo jumped in front of me, cutting off my pathway to the door.

Fuck, fuck, fuck.

I pivoted and ran in the other direction. Acting as much on instinct as anything else, I bent down as I ran past the fireplace, grabbing the beer bottle that had rolled over there, then circled around the sofa with the item behind my back. Suddenly, I could see his moves in my head. Theo would double back and head me off. I had him pinned, and he didn't know it.

He did exactly as I'd guessed. He doubled back.

And when I came face-to-face with him, I pulled the bottle

from behind my back and swung with all my might, hitting him across the face.

Check.

He stumbled backwards, cursing incomprehensibly.

Just then my front door burst open and Donovan stood there. "Get the fuck away from her, Sheridan," he shouted.

Checkmate.

TWENTY-ONE

"Donovan!" I cried. Dropping the beer bottle, I rushed for him.

I could feel a tug on the back of my sweater, but I didn't give into and I made it safely into Donovan's arms. When I did, I turned back and saw Theo was wielding his knife again. If he'd managed to grab me—if I'd given into that tug—the blade would be in my throat by now, and it wouldn't matter that Donovan was here.

I'd been aware of the danger I was in all night, but now that it was nearly over, it consumed me. I burst into sobs and buried my face in Donovan's chest. He held me tight against his side, angling me so that I was away from my predator.

"Let me out the door," Theo said, as if he had room to bargain now, "and we can forget all of this, Kincaid."

"You're not fucking walking out this door. You're lucky I'm letting you live right now." I'd never heard Donovan so riled.

"I don't think you're in the position to bargain. I'm the one with the weapon." He waved it around a few times, proving he knew how to use the blade. "Let me go. We can forget your mistakes. Forget everything you've done to me."

"Done to you? That's a laugh. But you're right. I've made two mistakes. Not persuading Sabrina to prosecute you the first time and deciding that jail was good enough for you the second time."

Theo grinned, as though Donovan's "mistakes" were his war trophies. "I guess I'll have to go through you. The only question is whether or not I take Sabrina with me when I do."

I started to scream.

Just then, a voice from behind us shouted, "Drop the weapon!"

I peered around Donovan and found a handful of police officers at the door, guns pointing at Theo. He had no chance, and he knew it. He dropped his knife and fell to his knees, immediately placing his hands behind his head. The officers ran to attend to him. Though he'd surrendered, Theo struggled and spat in the face of an officer as another one placed him in handcuffs.

"Careful, boys," one of the officers said after reading his rights. "He's trying to provoke us so he can sue the department." He addressed Theo directly. "We know your type, and it ain't gonna work. My men don't play your games. We're the good guys here."

It was satisfying to see Theo deflated, though I personally wouldn't have minded seeing him roughed up a bit.

Actually, I didn't want to look at him at all.

I turned away from Theo and the police and into Donovan who was waiting for me when I did.

He tilted my chin up and searched my face. "Are you all

right? Tell me you're all right. Tell me I got here in time."

I didn't know how to answer. I wasn't all right, and I was. I would never be all right again, yet he hadn't gotten to me like he had before. Maybe the question was wrong. Maybe the answer wasn't important.

"He didn't hurt me," I managed, a compromise on a thousand different levels.

Donovan was inspecting me anyway. His face went white when he reached the bare skin of my torso. "There's blood..."

I looked down at my wounds. I'd barely felt them; I'd been too afraid of the real damage that could be done with the blade. "They're scratches," I assured him. "They don't hurt."

"Where did he touch you?" The question sounded almost caught in the back of his throat, forced out by mere will.

"He didn't. I'm fine." I was obviously not fine. Tears kept streaming down my face and I kept shaking even though I felt feverish.

Donovan scraped my cheek with his knuckles, gathering my tears, and then looked at me as if it were a challenge to tell him yet again that I was fine.

I crumpled. "I was so scared. I thought he was going to..." I couldn't even say what I thought he was going to do. "I tried to get him into the bedroom because I knew there were cameras there. I thought maybe if you were watching, you would see us and you'd get help."

He caressed my jaw, his other arm pinned firmly around my waist. "There are cameras everywhere. When you didn't lock the deadbolt..." He took a deep breath as if recalling what he'd imagined, as if it had been the worst. And then when he'd looked, he'd actually been *faced* with the worst.

"It's tied into the security system," he explained after a

minute. "It sends me a message. You *always* slide that bolt when you're home." The pain in his expression was unbearable. "Forgive me. I worried."

It was almost laughable. He was apologizing because his overprotective obsessing had saved me from sexual assault and possibly saved my life? How could he be sorry for that? I was fucking out of my mind with gratitude. I was hysterical with relief.

And then I remembered how I'd left him last.

It was a gut punch in slow motion. I could feel every part of the blow. The renewed awareness that we were in a fight. That he'd betrayed me. That years ago he'd stolen my dream in order to make his life more comfortable. That what he'd ministered as love for a decade had merely been retribution for what he'd taken from me.

I felt like a stone sinking slowly through the mud. My mind was sludge. I'd been in danger and all I wanted was Donovan, all I thought about was him. I'd turned to thoughts of him for safety, and he'd been the one to save me in the end. If he didn't really love me, would he have looked at those screens? If he didn't really love me would he have even cared about that years-long retribution at all?

I wasn't sure.

But he was here, holding me when I wanted him to hold me. That seemed bigger than anything else happening between us at the moment, and to be honest, if being here when I needed him wasn't the very definition of love, I didn't know what was.

"Thank you," I hiccupped. "For worrying."

We stared at each other, our eyes locked. He swiped at my tears again with his thumb. I grabbed his hand and brought it back to my face, pressing my cheek into his palm. I was never not going to love him, I realized. No matter what happened between us from here on out—I was never not going to love him.

And maybe I could survive that. With him at my side.

Perhaps he felt the weight of the moment too. The lines at his eyes pulled down and the creases by his mouth tightened. "Sabrina, I—"

He was cut off by the bustling of the officers escorting Theo out of the apartment. I refused to look as he was taken out. I kept my face buried in Donovan's shoulder until he was gone, concentrating only on the feel of Donovan's hand as it rubbed smooth concentric circles over my back.

Once the perpetrator had left, all the attention shifted to me. An officer came over to speak to me about what had happened, along with a paramedic, to determine that I was indeed unharmed. Donovan was taken a few steps away to be interviewed as well, and while I wanted to hear him, to listen only to him, my attention was mainly on the questions being asked of me—Does it hurt here? Have you had a tetanus shot?

I didn't miss hearing the policeman though, when he asked Donovan about the cameras, and when he did, I stopped listening to the people talking to me and focused only on that.

"I'm not clear on why you have surveillance on Ms. Lind in the first place," the officer said.

"I own the building," Donovan said, clearly trying to dance around the answer.

"It's consensual," I called from where I sat on the couch being treated. Both Donovan and the officer turned toward me. "It's complicated and private," I went on, "but all that should matter to you is that it's consensual. And it is."

I caught the exchange of glances between the officer and his partner that clearly said they thought we were into some kinky shit—which, I supposed, we were. Under her breath, the paramedic whispered, "Hot."

"Damn straight," I said with a smile. I snuck another glance at Donovan and my smile settled into something more somber when I found him already watching me. I really did love this about him too. I really did love all of the parts of him. I really did accept all of it as *us*.

I would forgive him for what he'd done all those years ago. There would be scar tissue, but we'd work through it. Because this thing we had, whatever it was, it was stronger.

Then why did I still feel like there was such a chasm between us?

Probably because there were so many people in the room, and still so many loose ends to tie up before they left. I was worked up and fragile. A million people kept asking what I needed. What I needed was to be alone with Donovan. He was the only one who could fix this restlessness inside me.

It took hours, literal hours, to go through everything with the police, but finally sometime after midnight they had everything they needed and were ready to go.

"Are you going to be okay staying here tonight?" one of the officers asked before he left.

I hadn't thought about it before then. I looked at the room, testing how badly it might haunt me later. I couldn't deny that my stomach tied up in knots just thinking of being alone in my living room, sitting on my couch. Would I have to move? That was silly. Or it wasn't. I didn't want to decide tonight.

I turned to Donovan, seeking guidance.

"I can take you to my place. Or a hotel." He was gentle and

concerned. "Or I can stay here with you. I can sleep in the guest room or on the couch."

My brow rose at the suggestion that he wouldn't sleep with me. Did he really think I was still angry with him after all of this? Or maybe he was being respectful of how I'd feel after a near rape. I'd fix that when we were alone.

"Would you stay here?" It felt weird to ask him outright, even when he'd just offered.

"Of course."

I told the policeman I'd be okay, and after they left, Donovan watched while I triple checked the deadbolt.

Then they were gone, and my apartment was empty of everyone but us and my ghosts. Donovan leaned against the back of the couch and studied me intently. "What do you need? A drink? Something to eat? Would you like a change of clothes?"

I tightened the belt of the robe I was wearing. The officers had taken the damaged sweater as evidence, and Donovan had thoughtfully brought my robe from the bathroom when they had.

I didn't want any of the things he'd mentioned though. I didn't know what I wanted, exactly. I felt restless still, and irritated that he didn't know what I needed. He *always* knew what I needed.

And why was he so far from me? Physically. Emotionally. Why was he so distant?

"You're blaming yourself," I said, suddenly. It was a guess. A blind shot in the dark and it might be so far off that he'd laugh, but that would be better than this weird tension.

But he didn't laugh.

And he didn't say anything, and he didn't move closer. He just stood there.

I'd hit the nail on the head.

I sighed, walking toward him. "You can't blame yourself for this," I said gently. "I'm okay. I didn't get hurt."

"You could have."

"And I didn't because you got here in time."

"I wouldn't have *had* to get here in time if I had handled him differently."

I was face to face with him, my hands curled up in fists at my side so that I wouldn't be tempted to touch him before he was ready to be touched. I wasn't going to coddle him.

I also wasn't going to let him play the martyr. "How differently could you have handled him? *Not* sent him to jail? He *belonged* in jail! That was a good thing you did when you helped Liz Stein send him away. Think of all the other women you saved from him."

"There were other ways I could have gotten rid of him." He was dark and dangerous as he held my eyes. His stare, piercing and void, let me know he meant murder.

I slapped him. Because that was dumb. Because I didn't want him to be a murderer. Because I was wound up with energy and adrenaline and anger—at him and Theo and everyone—and I needed to hit someone.

Then, with my palm still burning, I wrapped my hand around his neck, dug my nails into his skin, and kissed him.

His mouth responded, but I was the one driving the kiss, raging and greedy. I bit his tongue and clawed at his skin. I pressed my body against him, writhing like a feral cat.

Despite his responsiveness, it wasn't long before he put his hands on my hips and pushed me away.

My rage flamed higher, and I slapped him again. And again. He grabbed my wrist the third time so I beat at his chest with my other fist, fighting him much like I did that day he took my virginity in his office.

He seized this wrist too, circled them both with his large palms and stared sternly into my face.

"Is this what you need?" He twisted my arms behind my back and pulled me against him where I could feel he was hard. My heart rate spiked, my mouth watered. "Is it?"

Yes, I screamed silently. Didn't I always? I needed Donovan to erase everything that had happened earlier. I needed him to re-create it with his face and his body and his mouth and his words, so that when the nightmares came—which they would because they always did—I would have better memories to replace them with.

That was how we did it. That was how he saved me from this darkness. Every time.

I didn't need to tell him, though. He'd already gotten into character. His eyes had clouded and now he was hungrily studying the bare skin at the neckline of my robe.

"Where did he touch you?"

I swallowed back a sudden surge of shame and tugged my arm where he had my hands bound. He got the hint and brought one around between us so I could show rather than tell. Guiding our hands to his mouth, I put one of his fingers and one of mine between his lips. He sucked on them, getting them nice and wet.

"Undo my robe," I told him.

He tugged the knot free then I laced my hand back in his and brought his wet finger to my chest. Together, we traced the path that Theo had drawn along my torso.

I watched Donovan's eyes as he drew along my skin, saw the weight of his lids as he fought to keep them open, as though it was unbearable knowing that Theo had seen this part of me, had touched me like this.

"And the blood?" It was almost a whisper.

"He nicked me when he cut my sweater open." But I didn't want sympathy. I didn't want that pitying look in his eyes. It wasn't what I needed right now. "Believe me, I'd rather have had the knife than his slimy-ass fingers."

Donovan's jaw twitched, his expression hardening. He wrenched my arm behind my back again, and spun me so that I was backed up against the couch. He needed this too. I could feel it in the way he kicked my legs apart, making room for himself between my thighs. I could feel it in the steel of his erection pressed up against my belly.

"Where else did he touch you?" he asked with a growl. He let go of my hands and pushed tighter against me so they were trapped between my ass and the couch. "Here?"

He opened my robe more and groped my breast, squeezing it until I whimpered.

I shook my head.

He lowered his touch past the waistband of my pants and reached inside my panties to finger my hole. I was tight and mostly dry, but I grew wet immediately. "Did he fucking dare to touch you here?"

"No." My knees buckled from the sudden wave of pleasure. "No," I said more forcefully, twisting my hips to push away his hand because that was the game, but also because the sensation was already too much. "He didn't touch me anywhere else."

"Good. Because you aren't his to touch."

Warmth shot through my body, electric pulses ran down to

my pussy like lights along a runway triggered by his possessive words. Roughly, he pulled my robe from my shoulders, down my arms, and flipped me around so that I was facing the sofa. He gathered the silk material at my wrists and twisted it until my hands were trapped inside the bundle.

Then he pulled my leggings and panties down together. I struggled as he did, instinctively, because that was also the game. His knuckles knocked against me and into me as he maneuvered my clothes down my legs. There would be marks tomorrow — marks I could focus on instead of the ones that Theo had left. I'd wear them like badges. I hoped they were dark.

I struggled more to make sure they were.

I'd never taken off my boots and Donovan didn't now, so my pants stayed chained around my ankles. With one hand pressing on my restrained wrists at my lower back, he used his other hand to work on getting his cock out. I could hear the zip of his slacks, the familiar rustle of his clothing as he fought for freedom.

I wanted to watch, but I didn't look back. The angle was too awkward. Instead, I closed my eyes and pictured him undoing his slacks, tugging down his boxer briefs just far enough to release his erection, then fisting his hot throbbing cock before notching his firm crown at my pussy and shoving inside.

My eyes flew open, and I screamed at the delicious invasion. He'd gone in to the hilt then pulled out right away to the tip, not giving me any time to adjust or stretch. He plowed in again at full force. It was uncomfortable and painful, and incredibly amazing all at once. There was anger in his thrusts. There was cruelty. As though he were mad at me for what had happened tonight. As though he were taking his anger at Theo out on me, and this, *this* was what I needed. This scouring. This primal fucking. This savage violation. This exorcism. It declared me as his, and his alone. It left absolutely no room for anyone else to possess me.

There was also pleasure. He always made sure that I felt the beauty in our filthiness, and this time was no different. He wrapped his arm around my hip and massaged my clit in progressively aggressive strokes, the approach so deliberate and contrary to the frenetic tempo of his fucking.

I was mindless, able to only concentrate on the space between this thrust and the next. I focused on what was ahead of me. The fireplace, the place I'd stared at while Theo had me pinned on the couch earlier in the night.

Then a sudden flashback burst into my head, like lightning, striking me just as forcefully. I was sitting—my sweater open, my skin exposed—and Theo's hand was at my throat, pressing into my pulse point.

"My neck," I said breathlessly. "Put your hand on my neck."

And the thing about Donovan? The thing that made him fit me so perfectly? Was that a demand like that from me never made him ask *why*. He just did it and he understood without an explanation.

He circled his palm around my thin neck and squeezed, ever so lightly.

Though it wasn't exactly the same way Theo had touched me, the pressure was similar, and it was just the push I needed to fall over the edge. I lost myself, spinning in a rush of euphoria and joy. I gasped, lifting my chin up as I went rigid, a flower turning up into the sun after a devastating rain.

I felt good. Unbelievably good. So good and wanted and

loved, and after the shitty way that Theo had made me feel, I was desperate to hold onto it for as long as possible.

Too soon, it was over. My vision cleared and my muscles relaxed. The dizziness was fading, and I realized I was now empty—literally empty. Donovan hadn't released and was no longer inside of me.

I bolted upright and found him standing to the side, already tucked away.

"Uh-uh," I said, trying to twist my way out of the makeshift shackles. "I know what you're doing and I'm not letting you do it."

"Really. What is it I'm doing then?"

The robe dropped to the floor and I hurriedly pulled up my pants so that I wouldn't trip on them as I walked over to him. "You're still trying to play the martyr," I said as I drew near to him. "But it's coming off as playing the asshole." I reached for his zipper.

He shoved my hand away. "I could have gotten you killed!"

I jumped at his sudden volume, but was undeterred. His passion only made me more resolved to show him this wasn't his fault. That I didn't blame him.

"You're right—I could have died." I backed him up against the wall by the kitchen. "But I didn't. You saved me. And we're in this together." I had his zipper down and his cock in my hand now. It was still stone hard and wet from being inside me.

Damn, he made my legs tremble every time I touched him.

And I needed him to feel good and release as desperately as I had needed it for myself. I pumped him with my fist and wrapped my other hand around his neck to bring his mouth down to mine.

He resisted at first, but I refused to give up. Because I

couldn't have if I'd wanted to. His taste was the best drug, his lips so firm and familiar, it was like going to church. I suckled on him, savored him as I stroked him, molded his mouth until it became pliable against mine.

And then he was desperate too—lifting me up, carrying me to the kitchen table. He shoved a chair aside so he could set me down and it toppled to the floor. With my ankles wrapped around his waist, I hoisted my hips so he could pull my pants down enough to get inside me. He rocked against me, gently but eagerly, searching for my entrance, and when he slid in, we sighed in unified relief.

"I fucking love you so much," I whispered against his lips. "My dark warrior."

He kissed me brutally, then pressed his forehead against mine. "I'm so weak when it comes to you." He cupped his hands around my chin. "So fucking weak. You make me lose my head. I make bad decisions around you, Sabrina." Then his mouth was too busy kissing me to say anything else.

I relished everything he said, every second, every glorious sensation as he rode me harder and faster to his release. I tried to memorize all of it. Tried to take it all in, because while this was the closest to heaven I'd ever been, the knot in my stomach wouldn't go away. Because I could see the board. I could see his next play, and I prayed to God I was being paranoid, that he wasn't already distancing himself. That fucking me against the table wasn't his way of saying goodbye.

When he came, he let out a long guttural groan. He looked into my eyes and clutched onto me, his fingers dug into my skin so deeply it was like he'd never let me go.

But he did.

He picked me up off the table, set me on the floor, and

helped me readjust my clothing. The tenderness wasn't gone, but he was reserved, as if we'd just shared an elevator and not our hearts.

"Don't do this." I reached for him, but he stepped back.

To his credit, he didn't deny it. He looked me dead in the eye when he made his move.

"I don't deserve you," he said plainly. Matter of fact. Like the simple slide of a bishop along the diagonal spaces of a chessboard, knocking out the pawn at the end.

My throat suddenly felt tight, and I couldn't swallow past whatever was stuck there. "And that's going to be your excuse?"

"It's not an excuse. It's—"

I cut him off. "It's bullshit!" He jerked at my exclamation, but didn't defend himself. "And what? You'll go back to hiring private detectives to follow me around everywhere? Watching from a distance? 'Loving' me from afar?" I'd have to move now. It would be bad enough working with him. Living in his building with his cameras on me knowing I'd never get to see into his life again—that would kill me.

What was I thinking? Being without him at all would kill me.

"It's better for you this way, Sabrina." There was no energy behind this breakup. That's how pathetic it was. He'd just decided that it was the right thing to do, the virtuous and noble thing, and even though he didn't *want* to give me up, he was going to do it because this was one thing he knew how to commit to.

Donovan Kincaid knew how to run away.

Well, fuck him.

"Fuck you." I crossed my hands over my chest, hiding myself, as if I could un-bare what I'd bared to him. As if I could cover myself up when he'd already seen all of me. "You don't deserve me? You're right. You don't. Maybe you don't know how to love someone, and it's not your fault that you didn't learn before. But you're a grown up, and you're old enough to start trying. Your parents are hard; I'll admit that. But I don't see you even trying to love them. And now you're not trying to love me. And I deserve someone who will try."

I was crying now, tears fully streaming down my face, but despite the display, I felt a burst of strength. "Love doesn't have to be perfect or traditional, Donovan. I can put up with a lot of mistakes, and the way I'm loved doesn't have to look like the way anyone has ever loved me before. It doesn't have to look like the way anyone has ever loved anyone else in the world. And that will be enough as long as someone tries."

I wiped my cheeks with the butt of my palm. "But running away every time there's a problem isn't trying. And peering in on my life and nudging now and then like you would on the paddles of a pinball machine isn't trying either. Which is a real shame, because I really did try with you. I really did fall in love with you."

"Sabrina..." He trailed off, and I waited for him to say more but more never came.

He didn't even know how to try to console me.

I swallowed another threatening sob. "I'm going to bed. Stay if you need to, but I'm going to be just fine if you go."

I didn't look at him again. I swept back to the sofa and picked up my robe, determined to leave as little of myself with him as possible. And then I headed straight to my bedroom, shut the door behind me, and immediately sank to the floor, my back pressed against the wood, and silently sobbed while pretending I hadn't just told the biggest lie of my life.

TWENTY-TWO

I knew my apartment was empty when I woke up the next morning. In my mind, he'd left during the night. I was sure of it before I opened my eyes. But my heart held hope that he'd stayed, and so the first thing I did after I found my living room empty was to check the guestroom to see if the bed had been slept in. I stared at the pillows. Had they been rearranged? The comforter certainly looked unruffled.

He'd really left.

Not just politely given me my space. And the only way he would've really left, after the horrors of last night, was if he was really *gone*.

I would grieve this more when I let myself feel it. Right now, I was numb.

I shuffled into the bathroom and faced myself in the mirror. I'd slept in, but my reflection's puffy face and eyes indicated I needed at least another two hours of sleep. I called my secretary and told her I would be in later in the day then asked her to transfer me to Weston's assistant since I was still filling in for him.

"Mr. Kincaid said not to expect you at all," Roxie said when I informed her of my plans for the day.

I pricked at his name, like it was a thorn I'd stumbled upon unexpectedly. And then I hated myself when I looked for the rose attached. "Really? What did he say?"

"That you had a rough night. You sick?"

I deflated. I didn't know what I was expecting. That he would've left some clue that he was still thinking about me with an administrative assistant at our company? Of course not. He was simply thinking of the business. And himself. Explaining my absence beforehand so that no one would come looking to ask him later if I didn't show up.

"Yeah. I'm not feeling too hot." It wasn't a lie.

I took three Advil and laid back down, barely resisting the urge to give the middle finger to the empty space of my bedroom, in case he was watching.

Honestly, I was afraid he wasn't.

Mostly I was afraid he never would again.

"I DIDN'T EXPECT to see you in the office today," Nathan Sinclair said, leaning back in his red modern high-back swivel chair, his hands laced behind his head.

I sat down on the white faux leather chair opposite him. Nate's workspace was the most artistic of the men, fitting for the creative director of the agency. He did have a desk, but it was a standing desk and he never conducted meetings across it. If he wanted to have a conversation with someone, he would most likely have him or her seated where we were now.

I rarely came to this corner of the floor, but since I was coming into work nearly three hours late, I figured I should check in with one of my superiors, and I was not voluntarily going to Donovan.

"I live to exceed expectations. What can I say?" It was my attempt to be cute, but without any "cute" behind it, the attempt failed miserably.

"You sure you want to be here? You don't have to stay."

"I'm sure." I pulled my hair over my shoulder and tugged at the end, letting my answer sit to be sure I was sure. Luckily Nate was good with silence.

I'd napped fitfully. While I'd slept dream-free the night before, my morning rest had been filled with nightmares of a faceless man standing behind me, his hand on my throat. I'd awoken wanting Donovan with an intensity that I couldn't begin to examine. Not just because he'd always been my go-to balm for these situations, but also because I hadn't begun to truly imagine that we were over. It hadn't settled in the deepest parts of me, the parts of me that seemed to need him most.

"If you're trying to prove something to him, I think he already knows."

I pulled my gaze from the silver and blue metal floor sculpture that I'd been absentmindedly staring at.

"What did Donovan tell you?" I was surprised he'd said anything. Donovan never talked to the guys about his personal life, it seemed. And Nate rarely butted in, though I had a feeling he was aware of much more than he let on.

He dropped his arms and looked out the window instead of at me. "Not a lot, but enough. I hope it doesn't embarrass you.

He told me there was an assault attempt. That the man's in custody. That you had a frightening encounter."

That hadn't been what I'd been expecting either.

Why I thought Donovan might've talked about *us* instead of my near rape, I had no idea.

"It was pretty terrible. But, horrible as this is to say, it's not my first rodeo." I already knew from experience that what had happened with Theo would take a long time to deal with. I didn't know how long it would take to deal with what happened with Donovan.

I wasn't sure it was possible to fully recover from either.

It was a terrible thing to say though, to Nate. Most people had a hard time knowing what to say in times like this. I didn't need to make it harder for him.

"Does that make this time better or worse?" He surprised me by appearing truly interested in my response.

I didn't have to think about it. "It just makes this time the next time."

He nodded without judgment, without opinion. As though he understood that there were things that happened in the world and some of them were fine and some of them were not fine, and living was what happened in between.

"Last time I *did* stay home all day," I admitted, remembering how I'd stayed in bed for two whole days after Theo's first assault. "And this time I wanted to try out the distraction of work."

"Work is good for getting your mind off... a lot of things." His pause was loaded with baggage, and for the first time since I'd entered his office, I thought to look beyond my own burdens and notice someone else's. Nate had circles under his own eyes and worry lines in his forehead. He had something on his mind too.

"Why, Nate Sinclair. You sound like a man who has a woman under his skin." It was strange how discovering someone else's romantic woes could suddenly lighten your own.

He rubbed his hand over his face. "Is that why I can never really get her out of my mind? Because she's under my skin?"

I totally knew how he felt.

"For me, he's in my veins." I didn't need to say his name for us to know who *he* was. "So it doesn't matter what I'm thinking about, because he's still coursing through my blood. Even when he thinks he's walked away."

Nate stretched his legs out in front of him and crossed his arms over his chest. He understood me. Better than he should, maybe. "I thought you and Donovan were making it work together."

"I thought so too."

"Well, aren't we a sad mopey pair?"

I narrowed my eyes. With Nate's David Beckham looks and his broody artist personality, I had a feeling he was a chick magnet. No one complained about men like him being mopey.

Women in my position, on the other hand, were supposed to be strong and steel. Bitches.

I was feeling bitchy, but not strong. Not steel. "I imagine I'm pretty impossible to be around right now."

"I don't know. You seem like good company to me."

I laughed, which was nice. It felt good to laugh. "You're a fellow moper, though. I don't think you are a good judge of company right now."

"Perhaps not." He drew his legs in and sat forward. "But I'll tell you what—I haven't given up. And neither have you."

My burst of humor was short-lived. I was somber again. I wasn't sure what *he* had to not give up on, but I knew about myself. "Actually, I think maybe I have this time."

"Nope," he insisted. "Want to know how I know?"

"Sure." I was humoring him.

"You came into work today."

I THOUGHT about what Nate said for the rest of the day. Maybe he was talking broader than I'd thought. Maybe he didn't mean I hadn't given up on Donovan. Maybe he meant I hadn't given up on life, and that's why I got out of bed and faced the world.

But even if that wasn't what he meant, he'd put the thought in my mind that he was talking about Donovan. And then I wondered if that was really why I'd forced myself to come in. Because I wanted to see him. Or be near him. Or just feel his presence. And every time someone came to my door, every time there was motion outside the glass, I sat up, hopeful.

But Donovan never came down the hall. He never called or passed by, and eventually I darkened the glass so I could focus on my tasks instead of wondering whether or not my ex-boyfriend meant it when he said it was over.

By the end of the day, I'd given up on him altogether.

It was quiet, and employees left me alone until Roxie came in and said goodbye at five. She made me promise not to stay too late, and I vowed that I would finish what I was working on and then close down for the night. She'd been my only interruption all afternoon, so when there was another knock right after on the doorframe, I expected she'd forgotten something.

But when I looked up, it was *him.*

I wasn't prepared.

I was never prepared, and seeing him at my door—at *Weston's* door—asking for entrance, something so out of charac-ter, was like seeing him for the first time after a decade all over again. It felt like he was trying to prove we couldn't possibly have a personal relationship, one that would allow him to make assumptions or just walk in. Jesus, he couldn't even allow himself to be my boss. Couldn't exert authority over me. He had to knock like we had nothing between us.

Yet we had *something.*

The mere sight of him sparked a chain reaction of the things he did to the inside of me—the stomach drop, the heart race, the butterflies. *Ah, the butterflies.* Those reactions were strong and sudden and dramatic—the kind of intense reactions expected after being apart from someone you love for several years, and not several hours.

Did I not spark anything similar in him?

"Can I come in?" he asked, and if he were a vampire I still would've said yes knowingly.

But I couldn't look directly at him as he walked past me to stare out the windows. Not until he was behind me, facing away, could I look. He had his hands in his pockets and his stance was wide. He wore my favorite three-piece bespoke gray suit. It fit him like he'd been sewn into it. The fantasies I'd had with him wearing that suit. With him taking off that suit...

Would I ever stop being turned on by this man?

Would it ever stop hurting to be near him?

"I meant it when I said you look good in this office," he said his back still to me. "I can go back to Tokyo and you could have mine. Operations isn't your thing, I know. Weston isn't attached to marketing, though. You could shuffle duties between you."

My heart had already been broken. Now he was just stomping on the pieces.

I wouldn't cry. I refused. "Is that what you're planning to do?" Somehow I managed to sound ambivalent.

He turned to look directly at me. "No. I'm not."

And now I didn't know what to feel. Was he playing games? And if he was, why on earth was I surprised? He'd always been good at that, slinging me back and forth and back and forth.

I opened my mouth to scream or yell or tell him to stop once and for all, goddammit. Tell him to go to fucking Tokyo at this point. I'd hurt less without him here to yank me around.

But he cut me off before I even started, his own anger more impossible to contain than mine. "Do you know why I waited to come out and help you that first night?"

"At The Keep?"

"Yes. Then."

He'd taken his time before rescuing me from Theo. Long enough to notice what was happening and then fully lace up his boots. I'd always figured he couldn't decide if he really wanted to get involved. Theo, nasty as he was, still had a better pedigree than I did. He was the "right" kind of person, and Donovan had no loyalty to me. I had always understood Donovan's hesitation.

Now he was suggesting there was more reason than that?

I shook my head.

"Because you were the one who was supposed to save *me*." He let that settle on me like a heavy chain around my neck. "Don't you get it? I was never good enough for you. All the days

I spent in that classroom with you, you never saw me, and I just knew that if you did, you'd be able to fix everything that was wrong inside me. But you never looked up.

"And then there you were outside my door. Then outside my window. And it was *you* who needed someone. You who needed help, and I knew that once I played that role for you, there would be no turning back. You would never see me any other way, so I waited before coming down there. Waited for someone else to help you. Waited until it was almost too late."

He paused, making sure I understood exactly how he'd struggled.

And I did. Somehow, I did.

"You saw me then," he went on. "But it wasn't how I'd wanted to be seen. I wasn't a hero. I didn't want to be your demon, but that was more accurate. The way you looked at me after that night—like you didn't know if you wanted me to fuck you or forget you—I didn't know what to do with that. What could I do with that?"

His voice was harsh and raw and his words impassioned, and I had no answer for him. Nothing to give him for this burden he'd been carrying for so long, nothing to offer in exchange for this weight that he was finally laying in front of me except to listen.

He crossed in front of the desk, his hands still safely in his pockets. "So I tried to be your hero, Sabrina. I tried to give you everything you needed. Tried to take care of you. I wanted to keep you from everyone I thought would do you harm, and that included *me*. Because I knew I could hurt you. I wanted to, even. You can't imagine the contradiction of wanting to hurt you and wanting to save you at the same time. Rescuing you from the frying pan meant throwing you into the fire. From

Theo to me. But I was never supposed to save you, Sabrina. It's your name that means 'savior.' *You* were supposed to save *me*."

He suddenly became clear, like the signal from a radio station when the interference was removed. I could see him, and he was in focus and I understood him and I understood everything that had happened between us. He'd been so alone and desperate after Amanda's death, and he'd found me. And all I'd seen was the sun. All I'd seen was Weston, while Donovan had waited for me to find him in the dark. Waited for me to save him.

And, man, did I know what that was like, because when I finally saw Donovan, I thought he was the one who could save *me*.

And then he did.

And wasn't that what people did for each other?

I had a feeling Donovan's intent with his confession was to make me see how impossible everything was between us. But it did just the opposite.

"I guess I thought we could save each other," I told him.

His eyes widened, like he hadn't been expecting that. Like I'd caught him off-guard, which was hard to do with him.

He chuckled even—he was so surprised. "You always were smarter than me."

I would have made a big deal about his compliment because he rarely gave me credit for my brains, but I didn't give a flying fuck about what he thought about my IQ at the moment.

I *did* care about what it meant that he'd said it, and I sat up, wary. Hopeful.

"I don't want to love you from afar, Sabrina." He stood in front of me, naked, vulnerable, and I was already lost to him.

"I've done that already, and it's not enough anymore. And I've fucked up. But no one else can love you like I can up close. No one."

Of all the things he'd ever offered me, it was the first time he'd only offered himself. It was the only thing I'd ever wanted from him, really.

"I know," I said, and my voice caught.

"You do?"

"Of course I do." I pushed aside my laptop and climbed across the desk because it was the fastest way to him. "Who else is going to love me like you do?" I rubbed the palm of my hand across the scruff of his cheek, and he closed his eyes, sighing into my touch. "This isn't how everyone wants to be loved. But it's how I want to be loved. I love the way you love me."

He opened his eyes and brushed a strand of hair out of my face before planting his hand on the side of my neck. "The way I love you brought a rapist into your house," he said, with both worry and apology.

"And the way you love me brought you there to save me in time. Both last night and ten years ago."

His mouth opened slightly, and I brought my thumb up to trace along his lower lip, silencing whatever regret he meant to share next.

"We can't look back and say 'what if this happened' or 'what if this didn't'," I said. "We've both lived long enough to know that sometimes the good is anchored to the bad, and if we changed a single detail, who knows if we'd be here now? I want to be here. Now."

"I tossed and turned on the sofa last night." *So he* had *stayed.* I should have known he wouldn't leave me alone.

"Knowing you were just in the other room, wishing I knew how to say exactly that."

"You don't have to *know*. That was my point. You just have to *try*." My knees were going numb from kneeling on the hardwood of the desk, but I didn't care.

"This is me trying." He brushed his knuckles across my cheekbone, and when he did, his fingers were trembling. "I'm going to fuck it up sometimes."

"Just fuck it up *with* me, not on your own anymore." But I didn't want to talk about failures, because we were always going to fail. That was a given. And maybe—together—we wouldn't fail sometimes too.

"I can do that." His mouth hovered over mine, but he had yet to kiss me.

"I love you so much I don't know how to keep it all inside of me."

"Even though I'm controlling and interfering and frequently cross boundaries?" His lips grazed mine, and I wondered how he'd ever managed not to light me on fire with his kisses before this. I was kerosene. I was waiting to be destroyed.

"Do you even know the *meaning* of the word boundaries?" I teased.

The smile he gave seemed almost like a shrug. "You're moving in with me. I decided already." He wrapped his arm around my ass and pulled me tighter against his body. "I can't stand thinking about you in another building after last night. I need you close to me, where I can keep you safe." Finally, he kissed me, likely trying to stifle any objection I might have.

I didn't actually have any objections. Mostly because I was still stunned by the declaration in the first place.

I pushed off him gently. "Are you...serious?"

"Completely. Except that wasn't exactly the whole truth." He paused, watching for my reaction. "I want you with me to keep you safe, yes, but also because I want you in every part of my world. I want it to be *our* world."

"I always wanted to be in your world," I said, nodding. I was saying yes.

"Sabrina, you *are* my world." He studied my face, his hazel eyes warmer than I'd ever seen them.

He kissed me again, tender and brief, but it was powerful in its simplicity, like the single square a pawn moved when it finished its journey across the board and was crowned queen.

"Come on. Let's get out of here before I'm tempted to give Weston another show." He lifted me off the desk and set me on the floor. "The movers should be at my place with your things soon anyway."

"Movers? At your place?" I smoothed my skirt as I sorted out his words in my dizzy love-struck head.

Wait.

I froze, comprehension settling in. "Did you already have movers packing up my apartment?"

He looked mildly guilty. "Is there a wrong answer here?"

I'd just told him I would accept him and how he did things. But surely he hadn't moved me in with him without my permission. Had he?

Wasn't I kind of hoping that he had?

"The only wrong answer is an untrue one," I said honestly.

"Then, yes. I've had movers packing since shortly after you left to come to work. I didn't tell you until now in case you were planning to argue about it. I thought it was better the office was empty for that so we could have proper makeup sex when you

were done." He gave me his best devilish grin, and if it wasn't a
purposeful test, it was a test all the same.

And it wasn't even hard to pass. Because I was only a little
bit irritated, and even that was only because I thought I
should be.

Mostly I was happy. Completely, overwhelmingly happy.

"You were that sure you were going to win me over?" I
asked, teasing him. I reached behind me to shut my laptop, and
turned back to where he was waiting.

"If I didn't, I was going to kidnap you."

Damn, he'd make a sexy kidnapper. There would be ropes
and blindfolds. I could imagine all the ways he'd violate me...

"Can we pretend that's what happened?"

"You're such a dirty girl." His tone was filled with mischief.
He reached his hand out toward me.

"And you're such a filthy man." I put my hand in his, and it
fit, exactly. "I guess we're perfect together."

EPILOGUE

NINE MONTHS LATER

S he's tight as my finger pushes inside her. Tight and hot and soaking wet.

"Donovan," she scolds, pressing her thighs together, as if that will keep me out. Her cheeks flush and beneath the thin cotton of her sundress, her nipples turn into hard beads. She glances up at our driver in the front seat, but I think she'd rather find he's looking than that he's not.

Her pink tongue flicks along her bottom lip and her lids have fluttered closed as I rub against the wall of her pussy.

Fuck, I want to suck on that tongue. Then I want to wrench her hands behind her back and shove her to her knees in front of me and make her use that tongue on my cock.

"How am I supposed to finish looking over Tom's report when you distract me like this?" Her hands are shaking as they continue to try to hold the tablet up.

"Do you want me to stop?" I *should* stop. We only have ten minutes or so before we'll arrive at Pinnacle House, which is not nearly enough time to satiate either of our needs. I shouldn't have even started this. But I'm antsy. Eager. And it's always hard to keep my hands off her.

"No!" She grows more coy. "I mean, your hand is already down there." She spreads her thighs, making room for me to explore, sighing as I do.

"Put down the iPad," I coax, nibbling along her jawline. "We're on vacation now. Tom has things covered at the office."

She mumbles something that I assume is acquiescence since she drops the tablet and succumbs to my ministrations.

It's different to love her like this.

Near her. In her space.

It's not harder, but it's not easier. It's different.

I can no longer move pieces on a board without feeling the consequence of their shift. Before, I could send her to LA. I could give her a new job. I could deliver her an opportunity. And then I could sit back in my chair with a cigar and a drink and feel good about the decisions I had made. For her.

There was no living in those moments with her. I was an emperor who ruled her, and though I was pleased when she yielded, though it fulfilled me, my love for her wasn't directly attached to her.

But now, there are times she sits next to me, and I can feel her breathe. Or when she's trying to work out a problem, she gets moody and short and her words are brusque and I feel the brunt of her agitation. I never felt those details when I loved her from afar. Then when she figures out her solution, her glow is nuclear. She could solve a small country's energy crisis with that fucking smile.

These are all details I never got to know before. They are precious. The touch of her hair, the smell of her, the feel of her skin. How her body feels when it bucks against mine. The sounds she makes when she laughs, when she cries, when she's mad. When she comes. Her heartbeat as it drums against my fingers when I run them along her neck. The weight of her in my arms. The taste of her mouth, of her cunt. The way she's sometimes fragile and sometimes strong and sometimes both at once.

She rarely surprises me. I learned her in that decade, like a man studying for the final exam that comes before a dream job. She is my dream, and now I'm living. *With* her.

Which is somehow a whole hell of a lot better than living *for* her, and that was pretty incredible already.

I manage to bring her to climax just as we turn down the driveway of my parents' country house. Good. She's relaxed. Soft and affectionate. I adore her like this. She always seems so pure and vulnerable when she's just come, and it makes me want to treat her very, very badly. I want to fuck her in fifty filthy ways.

I'm uncomfortably hard thinking about it.

But it will have to wait.

We've visited my parents a few times in the nine months since our first visit together here. She was right when she said I'd never tried with them. Nothing can make up for the relationship we had when I was growing up, but I'm an adult now. I can accept responsibility for my part going forward. I can't say that we've grown close, but we're definitely closer. We talk about mundane things—business, the weather. Scientific advancements. Safe topics. My mother, it turns out, is very fond of Italy, and enjoys talking to Sabrina about her heritage. It's not much. But it's a start.

They are roots that Sabrina and I have begun to plant. It's

exciting. Different. Not what I ever imagined for us, but I'm only looking forward now.

Especially after today.

Today.

I can't believe it's happening.

I'm suddenly nervous as the car stops in front of the house. My knee bounces with wound-up energy, and Sabrina notices.

"Make a beeline for the bedroom, and I'll take care of you," she whispers as we climb out of the car, thinking my agitation is due to my raging hard-on.

"Let's go into the front room," I say, trying to remain vague so I don't give any of my plans away.

"Oooh. This sounds exciting." The blush in her cheeks says she's thinking I have something dirty in mind.

She's going to be surprised. Pleasantly surprised, I hope.

She walks into the house ahead of me, greeting Edward as she enters, then strolls into the front room. I don't have to wait for her to notice the crowd outside. The windows are large and the backyard is the main focal point. They're impossible to miss as they mill about drinking champagne and punch, and talking in the late summer afternoon sun.

"Is there a party going on?" she asks innocently. She scans the scene more closely as I walk up tentatively behind her, and I can feel it when she realizes. Her breath catches audibly. It's obvious. The chairs are set up in rows facing an archway decorated in flowers. All our friends are in the yard—Weston and Elizabeth, Nathan and his girlfriend, Trish. Some employees from work have been invited. Roxie is here with Frank and Tom Burns has brought his wife. Dylan flew in from London, but, since he's such a Scrooge about love, and because he can't stop sneaking glances at Audrey, I gather she's the real reason he's here.

And if nothing else gives it away, it's her presence that must. Sabrina's sister wouldn't be here if this was anything else.

My girl—the love of my life—turns to me, visibly trembling. "Donovan...?" Even her voice is shaking.

I've already pulled the ring out of my pocket where it's been burning against my hip the whole ride up. "I'm not asking you," I say, stepping toward her. "That's not how we do things."

Her eyes are tearing up despite the smile that won't budge from her gorgeous lips. "That's okay. I have a safe word."

She does. And that's why I knew I could do this—could pull off a surprise wedding without ever having talked about marriage and know it wasn't a huge mistake.

Still, I'll give her the chance to call this off. "Are you going to use it?"

I hold my breath even as I begin to slip the platinum diamond ring on her finger. I'm not wrong about thinking she wants this—I know I'm not—but I've been wrong before.

"No," she says softly, and I can tell she's too choked up to say anything else.

"Most men want to hear the word 'yes' when they're slipping a ring on a woman's finger." I slide the band past her knuckle and into place, and then bring her hand up my mouth to kiss her palm.

A tear falls down her cheek. "Thank God you aren't most men."

"Thank fucking God." I pull her to me and kiss the hell out of her. There's a hair technician and a makeup artist waiting upstairs for her as well as several wedding dresses for her to choose from. Audrey will come in to help her sister get ready.

Weston brought a tux for me and I'll need to change as well. Our guests haven't been waiting long, but they'll grow antsy soon, so we need to get hustling.

But not right now.

Right now, I'm kissing her. I'm holding her. I'm loving her. These aren't moments to be rushed. These are the moments I want to live in.

The Dirty Universe continues with Kincaid.

Past and present weave together in Donovan's point of view for the next chapter in Donovan and Sabrina's life.

Get Kincaid!

Did you love Dirty Filthy Rich Love? Enjoy reading it again in ebook or audio!

THE DIRTY UNIVERSE CONTINUES...

The epic final trilogy in the Dirty Universe is coming soon!

Are you ready for Wild Rebel?

We were supposed to run away after high school.
When she didn't show up at our meeting place, I gathered my courage and went after her.
It was a mistake.
I left bloodied and bruised.
My heart didn't fare half as well.

I had no choice but to walk away.

Years passed. A decade. More.
I traveled, settled halfway around the world, made myself a name and enough money that I didn't have to look back.

But I never got over her.

And when my memories got the best of me, I went looking. Put all my effort behind the search.

Even the best of the best private eyes couldn't find the woman I'd deeply loved.

Then, out of the blue, she calls.

And, what she asks for, the favor that she wants?

I never thought I'd be willing to take a life.

But the truth is, and always has been: I'd do anything for her.

Don't miss Wild Rebel!

And don't miss my other dirty men:

Dirty Duet - Donovan Kincaid
Dirty Filthy Rich Boys - Read for FREE
Dirty Filthy Rich Men
Dirty Filthy Rich Love

Dirty Games Duet - Weston King
Dirty Sexy Bastard - FREE
Dirty Sexy Player
Dirty Sexy Games

Dirty Filthy Fix - Nate Sinclair

Dirty Sweet Duet - Dylan Locke
Sweet Liar
Sweet Fate

ALSO BY LAURELIN PAIGE

Visit my website for a more detailed reading order.

The Dirty Universe

Dirty Filthy Rich Boys - READ FREE

Dirty Duet (Donovan Kincaid)

Dirty Filthy Rich Men | Dirty Filthy Rich Love

Kincaid (coming 2022)

Dirty Games Duet (Weston King)

Dirty Sexy Player| Dirty Sexy Games

Dirty Sweet Duet (Dylan Locke)

Sweet Liar | Sweet Fate

(Nate Sinclair) Dirty Filthy Fix (a spinoff novella)

Dirty Wild Trilogy (Cade Warren)

Wild Rebel | Wild War | Wild Heart

Man in Charge Duet

Man in Charge

Man in Love

Man for Me (a spinoff novella)

Dating Season

Spring Fling | Summer Rebound | Fall Hard

Winter Bloom | Spring Fever | Summer Lovin

Also written with Kayti McGee under the name Laurelin McGee

Miss Match | Love Struck | MisTaken | Holiday for Hire

Written with Sierra Simone

Porn Star | Hot Cop

AUTHOR'S NOTE AND ACKNOWLEDGMENTS

Donovan Kincaid and Sabrina are characters that gnawed at me and fought to have their story told in ways that no other characters have before. I think I would have gone crazy with their pestering if I hadn't gotten the chance to sit down and write this, and I absolutely wouldn't have been able to work on this book without the help and input and support of so many people. I'll try to name them here the best I can.

First and foremost, I have to acknowledge Billy Wilder and Samuel A. Taylor for writing the play *Sabrina Fair* and then gush over Audrey Hepburn and Humphrey Bogart for starring in my favorite romantic classic movie, *Sabrina*. This story was the inspiration for *Dirty Filthy Rich Men*. I hope I didn't dishonor it with my own twisted version of events.

To Sierra Simone for rolling and fussing and going through the death process with me on a daily basis. It probably doesn't get any better. But, hey! It probably doesn't get any worse! At least there's Donovan. Thank you for loving him enough to make me want to keep writing him.

To Roxie Madar for being an absolute candle in a dark time. And for loving D and telling me what I did "wrong" with no hesitation. Maybe we should be looking in New Zealand instead of Australia...

To Liz Berry for always knowing just what to say and how

to say it, and for telling me to write that epilogue. It was the right choice. Thank you, my friend.

To Kayti McGee—Donovan came in the way of Screwmates, and for that I will always feel guilt. But I love you so much for understanding and knowing what I needed to be doing instead. You carried our baby well to the end. I'm proud of you, Mama.

To Melanie Harlow for reading early and saying all those nice things that made me feel so special and amazing. Pretty girl attention always feels good, but Melanie Harlow attention is indescribable. You make me warm and gooey inside, you cold-hearted bitch.

To Ashley for being my keeper and my jouster and my friend. I'll likely always tell you that you're wrong. Thankfully you've realized that isn't a deal breaker, and, besides, you're getting really good at convincing me otherwise.

To Rebecca Friedman for everything you are. You're my soulmate, and I love you pretty damn hard. To Flavia Viotti and Meire Dias for promoting and pimping and supporting and loving my books. And for just being the best people on Earth.

To Jenn Watson for having a great ass. I meant for having great ideas. (And a great ass.) Also to Social Butterfly PR. What a wonderful company. I'm so glad to be a part of it!

To Candi Kane and Melissa Gaston for keeping me from falling apart. You are both incredible, talented, insightful women and I'm so lucky to know you and work with you. Thank you so much for being part of my team.

To Lauren Blakely, Christine Reiss and Kristy Bromberg for talking me off ledges and teaching me how to do my job all the time. I'm useless without you gals. And for the friendship. It means so much in this crazy world we've found ourselves in.

To ShopTalkers and FYW and FUNK and WRAHM and Order and all the women and authors who engage and share and teach me on a daily basis. I appreciate you more than you could know.

To the members of the Sky Launch—I love you ladies so much! You thrill me and excite me with your enthusiasm. Please keep sharing your love for books and romance. I enjoy watching you—especially the men you post.

To all the bloggers and readers who read and share and review and message—I wouldn't have a job if it weren't for you. Thank you. Everyday, everyday, thank you.

To my most favorite people—my husband, Tom, and my three littles (who aren't so little anymore). We're a messy bunch, but we fit together, and I'm glad I have you. We'll get through. I promise.

To my God who sees what I don't see and knows what I don't know and gives me every breath I breathe. Help me remember that you're only always as far away as air.

ABOUT LAURELIN PAIGE

With millions of books sold, Laurelin Paige is the NY Times, Wall Street Journal, and USA Today Bestselling Author of the Fixed Trilogy. She's a sucker for a good romance and gets giddy anytime there's kissing, much to the embarrassment of her three daughters. Her husband doesn't seem to complain, however. When she isn't reading or writing sexy stories, she's probably singing, watching shows like Killing Eve, Letterkenny, and Discovery of Witches, or dreaming of Michael Fassbender. She's also a proud member of Mensa International though she doesn't do anything with the organization except use it as material for her bio.

www.laurelinpaige.com
laurelinpaigeauthor@gmail.com

Made in the USA
Middletown, DE
28 December 2024

68186962R00402